BOOKS BY RICHARD RAYNER

Los Angeles Without a Map
The Elephant
The Blue Suit
Murder Book

MURDER BOOK

RICHARD RAYNER

HarperPaperbacks
A Division of HarperCollinsPublishers

HarperPaperbacks
A Division of HarperCollins*Publishers*
10 East 53rd Street, New York, N.Y. 10022-5299

This is a work of fiction. The characters, incidents, and
dialogues are products of the author's imagination and are not
to be construed as real. Any resemblance to actual events or
persons, living or dead, is entirely coincidental.

A hardcover edition of this book was published in 1997 by
Houghton Mifflin Company.

ISBN 0-06-109737-3

HarperCollins®, ☷®, and HarperPaperbacks™ are trademarks of
HarperCollins Publishers, Inc.

Cover photograph © 1999 by Photo Disc.

First HarperPaperbacks printing: April 1999

Printed in the United States of America

Visit HarperPaperbacks on the World Wide Web at
http://www.harpercollins.com

❖ 10 9 8 7 6 5 4 3 2 1

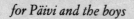

for Päivi and the boys

With an host of furious fancies
Whereof I am commander
With a burning spear
And a horse of air
To the wilderness I wander;
By a knight of ghosts and shadows
I summoned am to tourney
Ten leagues beyond
The wide world's end—
Methinks it is no journey

—TOM O' BEDLAM'S SONG, ANON.

MY NAME IS BILLY MCGRATH. I'M FORTY YEARS OLD, a little under six feet, and find myself in my office late on this sulfurous Los Angeles night, talking to a tape recorder out of both sides of my mouth. I'm half American, half English—offspring of two nations, two languages, and two different ways of seeing the world. I was conceived in Arizona, born on the sixth floor of Santa Monica Hospital, but made my first confession in England, where I learned to shoot among dry stone walls old as Julius Caesar and studied philosophy three years at the university of a northern town dominated by a soot-blackened cathedral on a hill, medieval reminder of man's lofty aspiration and worldly impermanence.

It was a scholarship that brought me back to America, to study postgrad at UCLA, though the Ph.D. was already out of the picture by the time I met my wife, from whom I'm now divorced, at Marty McFly's sports bar off Interstate 5 in Burbank with a Jack Daniel's in my hand only three days before she saved my life. We have a kid, a girl, Lucy, and we used to live together in a two-story house that was painted muddy brown on one of those walk streets in Venice where you can't park a car.

After I moved out, my wife had the house remodeled and it's now a pretty blue. I'm a cop, though it's a while since I had anything to do with law and order.

Hanging from the ceiling in my office is a redwood sign that says HOMICIDE and has on it a little picture of a smoking gun, a 9 mm, lest I forget. Spinning in my chair, I see the locked filing cabinets that surround my desk on three sides. These cabinets, very different from the wrecked metal models elsewhere in the building, are custom made from pine by a carpenter in Mar Vista, a guy who also makes coffins, as it happens, and, perceiving an appropriate symmetry, offers the Department a rate.

The cabinets gleam and shine; there are eight of them, each six feet high by three feet wide, each containing seven shelves, and each shelf in turn supporting thirty two-inch blue plastic binders, the murder books, the records of every homicide investigation in the precinct. Some have a red dot on the spine—unsolved, still in progress. Those with the yellow dots we've closed: arrived at perpetrator and motive, teased out the causes of obvious or sometimes seemingly random events, brought order if not meaning to bloody chaos. Seven of the cabinets are completely filled. Only the one immediately at my back has any space left in it at all—two empty shelves. At my feet there's an open box containing a stack of handsome new binders, ready to go, but it's behind me that I reach, for one book in particular.

Before opening it, I want to mention that my very first homicide wasn't here, in Venice, but down in South LA, Sixty-fifty and Vernon, a nice-looking wood frame house next to a host of similars and every one of them had bars on every window. Two victims. First was a black guy, the back of his head taken away by a cross-nosed bullet. Second was his white girlfriend; she'd been shot in the face, and both her arms had been hacked off. The shovel that was used for the job was on the floor amidst a butcher's mess of blood and bone. One skinny white arm lay next to it, and we never did find the other or figure out that particular detail, though the really bad thing was the little girl, a child of mixed blood, two years old and fine, at least not physically hurt. She'd been strapped in her highchair with her mouth taped shut so she couldn't scream while she saw the death of her mother and father.

I was just a rookie, a raw recruit, a *boot,* a uniform at the door trying not to get his feet in the mess, but when I went home that night the soles of my boots were clogged with blood and a dried grayish matter I realized must be brain. I sat at the kitchen table to clean them off and asked myself how such things could happen. I wondered at what point an act became evil. How bad and premeditated did it have to be? I swore that I'd keep in contact with that little girl every six months or so to make sure that she was OK. I made good on the promise until she was a six-year-old with pigtails who still refused to talk, but then for no good reason I can remember I missed an appointment, then another and another, until at last I felt embarrassed to go back.

I don't want to make too much of this, though I think the story, along with my lack of the proper equipment of roots, my missing of that cathedral on a hill, does have a bearing on all that happened. I grew too used to seeing evil done. You begin by trying to make a difference and end by doing it yourself, though even that sounds like casting around. At forty I had twenty years' English and twenty American, which might be to say that I had nothing.

2

I COULDN'T SAY HOW BIG THAT CROWD WAS ON SANTA Clara Avenue, there was so much rain and so many glistening umbrellas, and people kept jumping, moving, and shuffling in the storm, but I did see that most of the faces were the same, with identical expressions of eager, drenched excitement, all keen to see the show. I saw a black street kid with his head shaved, maybe ten years old, gangstered down in a dripping white T-shirt and baggy, sodden jeans with the crotch almost at his ankles.

"Hey, kid. What's your name?"

"Nelson." Grinning, he turned to show his buddies that he wasn't afraid. Rain flicked from his eyebrows and caught me under the chin.

"What's happenin', Nelson? Tell me what's up, man."

"Some lady got killed."

"Just one?" I grinned back at him, but Nelson wasn't sure whether I was joking or not. Before he could decide and start acting tough, I'd moved on and was making myself imagine that there was no crowd, that there were none of those thirty or more uniformed guys, milling and looking busy, that I was on my own, trying to figure this out. I tried to sweep away all the clutter and noise, to put my mind in a silent place, as if I were about to step into the woods after dark, and every little thing from now on—each falling leaf or twig that snapped—would have to be recorded and remembered if ever I were to find my way out again.

The house was better than I'd expect in the Oakwood neighborhood of Venice, with a pair of plump white sofas, a new and expensive carpet, and pale, freshly painted walls. Up above the fireplace was a Jesus in an ebony frame, and beneath it, to the left, on a round glass coffee table, seven or eight family portraits. There was an expensive stereo and five VCRs all hooked up together for copies, and there were lots of CDs, hundreds, maybe even a couple of thousand. Someone in the house was crazy for music. There was a powerful smell that didn't fit—strawberries.

In the kitchen I saw a black woman lying face up, with her head pointing south. She was about fifty and dressed in white—white jogging suit, white socks, expensive white sneakers. Her ankles were tied with white nylon cord, and from the way she was lying bumped up around the waist, I guessed her hands were tied behind her back as well. There were spots above the right trouser knee of the jogging suit, blood specks, like tadpoles with the tails pointing up.

The suit had been yanked open, ripped, and there were burns on her neck and chest. I counted seven, almost like brands on an animal, still bloody and sore, each the size of a red-hot dime. Could be they'd been made with the angry end of a cigar or cigarette. She'd been shot in the left eye, and blood had dribbled from the nostrils. Her open right eye gazed at the ceiling. The other, the wrecked one, was a mess of red and black, turned inside out like a crushed snail. A thick gray ooze of brain escaped at the corner.

The back door was locked and bolted. On the counter next to the water cooler was a clean spoon and a plastic honey bear lying flat on its belly; two or three drops had leaked out, and the ants, fled inside from the rain, were starting to gather.

The doors to the cupboard under the sink were open. A folded report card sat like a little white tent over the shell casing where it had fallen, beneath the U-bend. Sitting in the sink itself was a black garbage bag, also folded, as if it had come right out of a box. This was odd, since there was a full roll of them up on a spinner by the back door.

I put that little detail away.

Sitting next to, and almost concealed by, the garbage bag, were the strawberries, two untouched trays and a third with just a couple taken. I turned to a uniform standing at the door who told me the victim's name.

Mae Richards.

Maybe some basehead had broken in and got carried away—unlikely, since there was no sign of forced entry or struggle.

Maybe she'd been surprised by a knock at the door, and had opened to invite in some random scum bag posing as a salesman or the guy from the gas company. It happens.

Maybe this was done by someone she knew, to whom she owed a debt or with whom she'd been in love. Very possible. In my work, motives tend to be simple and strong: anger, fear, or love turned sour; and money, of course, always money.

Some cases are dramatic from the start and muscle right into the TV news. Others, the sleepy ones, seemingly more commonplace, merit only a few lines in the local rag, but each, on closer examination, is a story, a melodrama within a mystery. People understand this; hence the fascination, mingled with the fear that they themselves could be killed, and the giddy, almost reassuring, suspicion that they too are capable of murder. Hey, I'll blow your head off, mother*fucker:* these days the almost instinctive response to affront or rage or boredom, an answer like installing cable, but with more lasting if unanticipated personal consequences, and not only for the murderee.

From the distance came a church bell's weary clang. This didn't seem such a special one. I was trying to figure out why there was such a crowd outside when Cataresco and Diamond came in, the duty detectives, Cataresco first, ducking beneath the yellow tape, and then Diamond, who lifted it so he could walk straight under. Cataresco unzipped her leather jacket and met me with a smile. Blond, slender, with a talk-show host's nimble alertness, she had a gift for getting into the minds of suspects. Diamond was squat and square-shouldered, powerful looking, a spiritual Dillinger who exuded boredom like the smell of dry-cleaning fluid. He wore a striped tie and a stiff sports jacket that hung slackly from his shoulders, as if suspended from an iron bar lashed across his upper back, and he thrust a hard paunch in front of him like swag. "Hey hey hey," he said, popping a cigarette in his mouth without bothering to light it. "And to think last night I was almost like a human being. There I was, at home, Johnnie Walker in hand, Pavarotti on the CD. Of course this was while I was with your wife," he said. "Must be a surprise to you that she's an opera fan, huh?"

Cataresco rolled her eyes. One of the homicide section's more tedious routines was the pretense that we spent the weekends trying to score with each other's wives, a gag that had no real sting anymore, unless made by Cataresco.

"Knew she liked the opera," I said. "Didn't know she was so fond of you."

At forty-five, Diamond had more years on the job than I did, though I was the one who made head of the section, six weeks previously. The money in our line of work wasn't great; thus our struggles for power and status were intense, though everyone pretended otherwise, with the willed, taut nonchalance cops bring even to the world's most obvious wrongs.

Sniffing, Diamond took the cigarette from his mouth and slid it back with its comrades. "Yeah, well, anyways," he said, hitching up his pants to reveal a holstered Marine Corps Colt, a cannon. "That was yesterday I was with your wife."

Twin gouts of blood had hardened to a mustache beneath Mae Richards's nostrils. Her sneakered right foot turned in at an angle, as if the bone had snapped. Ants were on the march now up her neck and cheek. Soon they'd gather around the blood and meat of her eye and march back again, bearing their treasure. In my experience dead people never look like they're sleeping. They look like they've been shocked out of their lives, and dropped, dumped bones suddenly no more connected than a bag of parts.

Drew Diamond went on. "And today here I am, back hanging with the brothers in Oakwood. You missed the party."

"A gangster shows up, tries to break through the line," said Cataresco.

"Not just any gangster," said Diamond.

"Ricky Lee Richards," said Cataresco.

Diamond did the thing with his pants again, pleased by the effect of the name.

"*That* Ricky Lee Richards?" I asked.

"The very same."

"The Prince of Darkness?"

"The gang banging piece of scum."

Ricky Lee Richards was street-famous, already almost a legend. He'd entered the drug trade with only $200, supplying rock houses across Los Angeles, before in time becoming a chief cocaine wholesaler, the funnel through which the drug arrived from Colombia and Mexico and flowed into the United States. He was easily the biggest-time dope dealer to come out of Venice, yet he didn't flaunt himself with gold and sports cars like some of the high rollers. He was known as the ten-million-dollar man. There were rumors that he was so rich now he was trying to get out of the business, but no one really knew. The guy was a mystery.

"Seems that the victim was Ricky Lee's mother," said Cataresco.

"Yeah," said Diamond. "Musta put a dent in his day. Now he's under arrest for assaulting a police officer."

Cataresco said that Richards had arrived on his own, not surrounded by his crew, and had asked if he could come in; when they'd said no, going by the book, he'd gone crazy, hitting one patrol guy in the stomach and butting another in the face before they could cuff him. "That was when the crowed started showing up, and the press, boo-boo-*boo.*"

"Anyone from the DEA show up yet, or the Bureau?" There were so many good guys chasing drugs, all cranky about their acronyms and antsy for their budgets, all playing games with each other, all much too concerned with the size of their dicks, basically, that it was a miracle any big time dealer ever got busted The smart ones mostly didn't, and Ricky Lee was smart, but there were a lot of people trying to find out what was going on in his life. "What about ATF, CRASH?"

"Not yet," said Cataresco.

"Does he know she's dead?"

"I don't think so."

Cataresco filled me in on what else they'd got. "Victim's name Mae Richards, age forty-five, place of birth yeah yeah yeah you can read my report later. The body was found by a neighbor, one Louise Szell. She stopped by to ask if the victim would be going to church tonight. Evidently they usually walked together. She phoned in her report at three-thirty-one. No one heard a gunshot, no one heard or saw any signs of a struggle or anything untoward or unusual. Louise Szell said that someone did leave the house, about two-thirty, a guy, white, not young. Maybe fifty, fifty-five. He drove away in some fancy boat, a Cadillac or a Lincoln, dark color, maybe gray or blue."

"Plate?"

"She remembered three letters. GSG."

Diamond chipped in, "Gigli, Siepi, Gobbi."

"Mafia guys?"

"Singers."

Drew won that round. I turned to Cataresco, "She reliable, this Louise . . ."

"Szell."

"Right."

"The neighborhood busybody. Yeah, I'd say she's reliable."

"That's something." I went back to Diamond. "There's a folded garbage bag in the sink."

"I saw that," he said. "Maybe our shooter brought it with. Or somebody with our shooter."

"Messages on the machine?"

"None, or wiped."

Diamond had opened the fridge for a peek. "I'm hungry," he said to no one in particular. He picked a strawberry from the box on the counter. "I hate strawberries," he said. He ate one anyway.

This was the job, so much of it routine, an attempt to keep boredom at bay while assembling a picture of the past in terms of time and inches, like crawling on your hands and knees, trying to put back together a mosaic out of ancient pieces, tiny, millions of them, a near-infinity of details that must be re-created, and sometimes you never do find out which are the bits of gold, the ones that make the pattern.

Diamond and Cataresco would be there most of the rest of the night. They'd map the precise position of the corpse. They'd measure the dimensions of the kitchen and how far away from the body the spent cartridge had been found. They'd supervise the taking of prints and photos, and they'd go on gathering information about the victim. They'd watch while the coroner arrived and, to determine the time of death, slid a pointed thermometer into the victim's liver. It would make a popping noise, like bubble wrap.

Every murder cop goes about with a parasite in the heart. It's handy, this little worm. It eats up the feelings before they have time to reach the brain. In the end, though, there's the question: which will survive, the parasite or the man?

"I'd better go see Ricky Lee."

"Go right ahead and be sympathetic," said Diamond. "But before you do, take a look at this." He slipped on a pair of surgical gloves and, squatting by the side of the body, pushed his hand under and heaved it up gently.

Mac Richards's hands were tied behind her back. The killer had sliced off the last joints, where the prints were. The ends of her fingers were stumps clogged with gore and bits of splintered bone.

Diamond said, "Not too much blood. My guess is she was tortured and killed somewhere, then dumped back here."

I wondered why the perpetrator had bothered to cut off her fingertips, usually done, along with smashing the teeth, to prevent an easy ID of the body—but pointless if the killer was going to leave the victim lying on her own kitchen floor. Perhaps she'd put up a fight after all, and the killer was on the ball enough to know the coroner would cut her fingernails to look for blood and skin tissue.

"What about the shell under the sink?"

"What about it?" said Diamond with a shrug.

"Any ideas?"

"Nope."

"Nope?"

"Gee, Billy, don't start."

"I'm sorry, excuse me, but I seem to see a dead body here. I don't know about you, Drew, but I'm out to *get* the murderers."

He was about to say something, but I held up my hand. I said, "Call me old-fashioned. Thieves I can live with. White-collar fraud, blue-collar rip-offs—be my guest. But let's think about rapists and child abusers. Let's think about *murderers*. It's unreasonable, of course, but it seems a good idea if maybe, *maybe,* guys like you and me step in and take a hand. What do you think, Drew?"

"Very funny, Billy," he said, straightening his neck, squirming in his too-neat clothes.

"I'm not joking. Maybe the shell's not from the same weapon. Maybe it's a decoy. Maybe the perp was simple or wired or nuts. But someone really did this lady wrong, and I'm going to find him. Or her."

On the way out I paused, attention caught by a framed photograph on top of a bookcase in the dining area, apart from the other family snaps. It showed Ricky Lee with one arm around the woman whose body was on the kitchen floor; in the other hand he held a tennis racquet. I slipped the photo out of its frame, into my pocket, and told Cataresco to remind Diamond about the garbage bag.

"He won't forget."

"Remind him anyway."

"Don't you think you should go a little easy on him?"

"Something about Drew makes me crazy. Maybe it's those fancy clothes he's started wearing. I don't know, but I'll tell you what—he's a loser."

"Come on, Billy, the guy's been having a tough time. And you're riding him hard."

"Fun, isn't it?"

I started to push my way through the crowd and past the reporters into the rain. The boy Nelson was there by my car, dripping and on his own. "Hey, mister. Can I see your Beretta?" he said, as if asking for a quarter or candy.

Making a gun of my thumb and forefinger, I aimed it at him, and said, "Pow!"

3

IN THE CAR, GLANCING AT MY WATCH, I FIGURED I COULD just make it, so instead of going back to the precinct, I drove through the rain to Ellen's house, that's to say my wife's house, my ex-wife's house, which once belonged to us both, and had been rebuilt, cherished by the two of us together. It was less than a mile away, where, California Avenue having been crossed, Oakwood abruptly turned into a desirable Venice neighborhood.

I was leaving my work for a little while, but this was no big issue; on the one hand there was a crime scene, a body that wasn't going anyplace, and on the other, family obligation. A practiced observer of the various discrete portions of my life, I was accustomed to such sliding and juggling. I figured I'd let Ricky Lee stew for a while—it might even do him good. I didn't realize this was going to be the most important investigation of my life or that along the way it would turn into something else, or rather, just that—an investigation of my life—and that even this seemingly insignificant choice would later seem fateful. For now, Mae Richards was only another body bag in Ghost Town, and I was worried more about my wife's, my *ex*-wife's, reaction should I fail to show up for the Sunday visit.

Ellen was pretty frank about what was required. For some years now she'd been saying, "I want you to be a good father to Lucy, Billy, and not just for her sake." This meant devotion, taken as read; it also meant money, of which I had little, and showing up on time for my visits, somehow never a problem, even with the case load. In this one area I was strangely reliable.

Lucy, eleven now, was outside and ready. On this wet gloomy day sheets of rain fell in front of the stoop, but she redeemed the weather, waving, then splashing toward me, rushing, in sneakers, jeans, and a hooded bright yellow slicker like the sun. She had a way of walking, a stooping slouch, with long strides, as if, head down, she were contemplating the entire universe and all its mysteries. She was like her mother, fearless, though where Ellen's face was proud and strong, decided, Lucy's was still open, radiant, and vulnerable. She didn't want life to come and court her. She rushed toward it, as she did toward the car that Sunday, with elbows flailing.

"Hey, Luce, how ya doing? Look, I got you this." Opening the glove compartment, I took out the pencil set I'd got from an art supply store up in Westwood. She wanted to be an artist and seemed to have the gift, a puzzle both to her mother and myself, since Ellen's leaning was toward music and my only known talent that of wedding corpse to suspect.

Her green eyes slid down, then up again; she quickly smiled and I knew I'd got the wrong thing. The one she'd wanted came in a sandalwood box with brass fittings and cost more than $250. "They said these were the best, really."

"They're cool, Dad. They're great."

I reached out fingers to comb away drops of rain from her forehead. I'd let her down again.

When I looked at my watch, she said, "What happened this afternoon? Was there a murder? Shouldn't you go?"

"It's OK. There's a guy, he can wait."

"The suspect?"

"I doubt it, but not a good guy."

I'd always tried to encourage in her the idea that my work was real, mundane, not like TV and the movies, though of course sometimes it couldn't help seeming that way. "Lucy mythologizes you," Ellen once said. "She thinks you're some sort of a hero." Then Ellen had smiled, adding, not without wistful regret, "For those of us who've lived too long with the reality, this can be a royal pain in the butt."

Thus: my ex-wife, who, after I'd failed her, dumped me because I was bringing her down. That sounds too bitter; if resentment and anger were remaining, and they were, they were in me. Love's best habit is trust, and I'd been unfaithful. The blame for everything that happened lay at my door.

"How's your mom? She found herself a new boyfriend yet?"

Lucy shrugged and looked out the window at the rain. "Dad, you know you're not supposed to ask me that."

"What happened to the last guy? He of the stutter and the Rolls-Royce."

"Dad!" Laughing, tickled, she tried and failed to keep a straight face. "That was ages ago. She only saw him once."

"I should think so. His toupee was an open book."

"He looked like a cauliflower," she said.

"With a million-dollar bank account, no? Your mom's doing OK. She *is* OK."

All this was cheap, no doubt, beneath me, but I couldn't say I felt bad. Lucy and I had ceased to be just ordinary company to each other. Each meeting came freighted with an expectation I had to unload as quickly as possible; otherwise I felt challenged and overawed by my own little girl. Lucy was a normal enough kid, a tomboy, not too fond of school, happy most of the time, but with her senses overly tuned to whatever atmosphere prevailed between her mother and me. Our lightning rod, she wished the weather would always be clement; it rarely was.

"Thanks, Dad, these *are* the best," she said, and as she leaned over to kiss my cheek, I was, if only for that moment, a fallen angel returned to paradise.

When we reached Draker Street the party was already in full swing. A young guy took our coats in the entrance and stuffed them into a rack beside a host of sodden others. Beyond that, in the gallery itself, everything was warm and dry, the overhead lighting was soft, and individual spotlights picked out each picture on the white walls. Waiters wafted nimbly through the crowd with laden trays. While Lucy went off to inspect the art, I positioned myself in the center of the room, where a fountain, set among palm fronds, blocks of grainy green marble, and orchids flown from Hawaii that morning, tinkled forth its message of wasted money.

The crowd was young and beautiful. What else is there to say? It was a typical Westside bunch. Some wore clunky boots and brightly colored flannel work shirts with small gold rings puncturing their eyebrows, their lips, their noses, and doubtless other bodily areas. They all looked about nineteen. The slightly older set, the ones who were making serious money already, wore cashmere and silk and grumbled about the weather spoiling their Doc Martens or their loafers by J. P. Tod. The oldest of these wouldn't admit to being twenty-seven. And the only guy actually older than me was my friend Ted Softly, who owned and ran the gallery.

In his sixties, short, and supporting a stout paunch, Ted was dressed in outrageous tweed. His white hair was clipped short and he kept stroking it as if it were a teddy bear. Sweating, his forehead covered with enormous beads of perspiration, he smiled in a friendly way and raised his glass toward me from the far end of the room, then laid his hands on the shoulder of an exotic-looking beauty from Japan. He was one of those guys who always seemed to be running, waving in a crowd, or honking from his car, a white convertible he'd bought from a homeboy, even though the engine was clapped out, because the homeboy's father had died. That was Ted: a tender, funny fellow. When sober, he had good ideas, a sense of style; he was reliable; but then he was sober only fifty percent of the time. He'd been a banker, a good one, and now, dealing in art, he used all his knowledge of art while displaying an unbankerly lack of cynicism. He supported artists whose talent was greater than their fashionable potential, and threw splashy parties, like this, where the pop of champagne corks was barely muted by the trill of Pavarotti. Somehow he made a go of it all, and was quite unlike anyone on the Venice art scene.

Ted brought the young Japanese woman over with him. White-skinned, black-haired, she wore a short black dress and stood with aplomb on platform soles of maximum thickness. This wasn't, to the best of my knowledge, his regular girlfriend, though I'd been drunk the two times we'd met. "I don't know if I believe in God," he said to the woman on his arm, whose name was Holly. His voice was soft and quick, and he laughed a lot, like someone wooing a lover, his intention no doubt. Ted was a terrible ham and liar, but he had great charm. I liked and trusted him. He said, "Yet there's a power that cares for goodness, right? Surely somewhere justice counts? Look at this guy—he cares. This is a great, a unique cop."

He was drunk already. I said, "Cut it out, Ted."

"No, listen, this is how Billy and I know each other, right. It was about ten years ago. Empty Westside apartment. Bill gets the call, goes in, there's a body that's been hacked into . . . how many pieces?"

I said to Holly, "This man doesn't know me. Besides, he's just hoping to impress you. He's inflamed with lust to the marrow of his bones."

"Six hundred, right. Six fucking hundred." He sprayed me with spit as he said that, booming the words so loud that people turned to stare. His reply to them was a grin and a sudden stiff-armed wave, more desperate than assured. I'd seen him wired and wild but never quite like this before. He went on, telling the story of the most vicious crime, the most horrible I'd ever seen, and I'd seen some bad ones. The unidentified corpse had been cut into more than six hundred pieces—in fact, it was 658. I sat in the crypt at the morgue with a doctor and an investigator from the coroner's office while we sorted each of those body parts into tiny chocolate boxes and guessed where they belonged. The process, which became an obsession, went on for months, until we were able to establish that the corpse was young, male, Asian, maybe ten years old. We were able to reconstruct his neck, where there were bruises and lesions to suggest that he'd been strangled. This led me on a search for known sex offenders, both state and federal. Eventually, months later, more than a year after the crime, I found my guy, a Pakistani who'd fled back to Pakistan. The victim had been his son. He'd strangled his own blood, then strung him up in a shower and cut him into little pieces.

"It's how Billy and I got to know each other," said Ted. "The Pakistani guy used to come in here with his kid, that same kid. He stood right where we're standing now, and talked about his collection of Robert Longo. The guy really had the eye. It was totally fucking unbelievable."

"What happened then?" Holly said to me. She was fascinated now, by this story she'd rather not have heard. People were either frightened of me or else saw me as a turn, cocktail theater, a little too heavy for the entrée. It's why cops tend to seek out other cops and stand with faces of defiant stone, brooding behind the barrier of being misunderstood.

"I went to Pakistan and brought the guy back."

"Did he want to come?"

"Not very much."

Ted threw his head back, roared, and grabbed a glass from a passing tray. The champagne flowed from glass to throat without the courtesy of stopping in his mouth. I wondered what was up—some problem with the gallery? No doubt Ted's frenzied art world dealings brought him all sorts of hassle. Or was it Holly, who, faced with this crazy man, looked past him toward me without a smile. "Tell me," she said, head tilted to one side. "Don't change the subject. How did you make him come back?"

"Yeah, Billy," said Ted, and covered his mouth to stop a belch. "How'd you do that? I don't think I ever heard this part."

"Trust me, you don't want to hear about it."

"Shock us," said Ted. "We can take it. Whatever happened, it happened in Pakistan, right? Which of course completely excuses your behavior. No rules in Pakistan. No morality."

"There's that everywhere, Ted. Morality's not a movable feast."

"Oh, shut up and tell the fucking story. Amuse and amaze us."

"OK," I said, and shrugged. I told them that I'd asked the guards to leave me alone with the man in his cell. I had a metal case with me, which I opened, and from which I took fifty small white individual chocolate boxes, laying them carefully on his bed, on his table, on the window ledge in front of the black iron bars so that in the slanting light they threw shadows the shapes of coffins. "I told him, which was true, that each box contained a piece of his son, and that if I came back in an hour and he hadn't eaten them, he could either confess or I'd bring him fifty more, and we'd go on doing it until he'd eaten all six hundred and fifty-eight, because I had the rest back at the hotel, and if at the end of them he still hadn't confessed, then I'd shoot him in the head."

Ted tried to smile, but it wasn't really a smile. Holly, a tougher proposition, looked at me with a light in her eye. She said, "You're joking."

"Yes. I don't think I'd have shot him in the head. But he coughed before it came to that."

"Coughed?"

"Confessed."

"Jesus, Billy, that's a horrible story," said Ted.

"He was the horrible guy, not me."

Holly was looking at me strangely. "You're a passionate soul."

"It's been a while since anyone's accused me of that,"

I said, looking around to find Lucy. She was off in one corner, beneath an oil painting of a lighthouse, a big piece, about twelve feet by four.

"Is that your little girl?" said Holly. She still had a goofy look in her eyes, as if at any moment she was about to ask me what my inner voice was saying. "She's so full of light. She seems just to breathe it in."

"Watch her too long and she'll break your heart. She might of course break your head first. She has a temper."

Seeing how autonomous Lucy was, knowing how much her own person she'd been, right from birth, almost as if she were my parent, watching over me, rather than the other way around, I was reminded for the hundredth time that she could live without me, a thought that brought both grief and comfort. During the first years of her life there'd been those among our friends who'd seen nothing of me in her. Later, they all agreed, reluctantly, that she'd taken qualities from me as well. I'd taught her persistence, a way of laughing at the world, and, maybe most important, I'd taught her that she deserved to be admired. Like me, she was assured, angry, moody, cautious. At least I used to be that way once—cautious.

"Excuse me," I said to Ted and Holly, and went over to join her. "So, Luce, tell me what you see."

"The big light's reaching out. The sea's so wild, but the light will guide you across it. It's scary, a little, but wonderful, like watching lightning from inside the house on a stormy night."

When Ellen and I were in the middle of the break-up, Lucy had watched *E.T.* over and over, sitting with her face inches from the screen, believing that she herself was the extraterrestrial and that Ellen and I weren't in fact her mother and father; her real family would be arriving soon to take her home in a spaceship.

"You watch any football today?"

"Dallas got their butts kicked."

"Great."

She and I shared an affection for linemen whose brief glories came when they struggled from the trenches to squash six-million-dollar quarterbacks in the dirt. She turned back to the picture, saying quietly, "Dad, are you going to stop seeing me?"

I blinked, knowing where this came from but shocked, and with no easy reply at hand. The words escaped in a nervous blurt. "Jeez, Luce, you want another Coke or something?"

"I mean, it's OK if you won't be able to see me."

"What kind of a thing is that to say? I'll always come to see you, wherever you are; you know that."

"I wondered, that's all," she said, very serious, and I was left with a mixture of oppression and anxiety, sadness. Kids know much more than we think; they pick up on atmospheres better than anything else. I remembered it from my own childhood. "You want that Coke?"

From behind came a hubbub, sharp voices, a scuffle, and I turned to see Ted, no longer looking faded or rumpled, though still very drunk. His face was red and his jaws were clenched so tight that a nerve jumped on his cheek. I suddenly noticed how pale and startling his deep-set eyes were; they stood out huge as portholes. He gripped a revolver, two-fisted.

Someone screamed. Others, slower to realize, started laughing and hastened to stuff their mouths with food before they too backed off, leaving Ted in the center of the room by the fountain with Holly and a young Japanese guy who stood at her side. Dressed in black, head shaven, maybe a boyfriend, he was, together with Ted's sweating, booze-driven rage, the immediate cause of the argument. Ted's voice was shrill and tense. "You don't think I invited you here for this, do you? But I'll do it if you make me. I swear I will."

I didn't know if Ted was serious. I didn't even know if the gun was loaded, though I knew he was drunk enough to pull the trigger. I said in a whisper to Lucy, "We're leaving. Come on." I grabbed her coat and walked with her out to the car, where I said, "Stay here, sweetheart; don't move. Promise? This will only take a minute. Draw me something while I'm gone."

Back inside, working my way through, I bumped and shoved against those coming the other way. Some had stayed, retreating to the sides of the gallery, or even throwing themselves flat on the floor, from which vantage points they watched Ted, still in the now empty center of the gallery, still holding the gun in Holly's face, and still talking. The shaven-headed Japanese boy was nowhere to be seen.

The smart thing here was for me to call for back-up. Failing that, I knew I should stand at a distance, gently collect Ted's attention, and talk him down from this nonsense. Instead, I watched my feet march across the floor, placing me between him and the girl, the gun inches away from my face. "Boy, I must really be flailing here," I said. "This isn't what I learned in tactics school at all. Ted—I'm afraid you're going to have to shoot me." My voice sounded calm, staring down the barrel of that .357, another piece of grotesque and gleaming machinery. "Give me the weapon. Come on, Ted, before you do something you regret."

He gazed at me with sweat on his forehead and no interest in his roaming eyes. This was something else I'd learned: a guy was more likely to shoot if he was refusing to make eye contact, or else negligently making too much. Ted came into the latter category. He said in a strained and too-patient voice, "Billy, will you please get the fuck out of the way?"

I was wondering if I dare take the chance and try to knock the thing out of his hand. I was thinking, this gun doesn't look like it's ever been used, but then most guns don't; they never look worn, they don't have a visible history like other objects. Human life never shows in them; only their ability to take it away.

Someone dropped a glass. The Japanese kid bulled past, dragging Holly with him, and Ted swung the revolver out of my face toward her again. I jumped to keep in the line of fire.

"Billy, oh, Billy," he said, pressing the barrel straight into my forehead. I felt the metal leave its print. "It's not you I want to shoot."

I leaned forward into the barrel until it pressed so deep, Ted himself had to take a step back. "You know what? You're going to have to. So go ahead and do it. Fuck me up, and yourself. Or else put the gun down, and we'll do the cha-cha-cha. Because that's what I'm thinking. I tell you, Ted, as a dance this is a fucking joke."

Blinking, sweating, baffled, Ted ceased all movement. I thought, "Shit, I'm insane, this guy's out of control." Off to my right I heard the fountain as it went on wasting its money.

"Do it, Ted. Pull the trigger. It'll make you think you're a man. You won't be."

For a second his eyes went all wrong, flicking this way and that. There was a moment when I thought he was going to do it, when my own eyes felt like the only still points in the moving-up-and-down of the rest of me. Everything was quiet before he lowered the revolver, letting it dangle and bang against his knee, and burst into tears. "She left me, man. Suzie left me."

I took the gun from his unresisting hand and checked the chamber: six bullets in any language. Suzie was the name of his girlfriend, I remembered. She was a nurse, in pediatrics, working out of UCLA. I'd seen them at the beach, tossing a football. My lips blew little raspberry pops of relief. Someone laughed, very loud, and I couldn't help joining in. "So that's what this was about?"

The waiters were back at work already with their trays. Tears rolling down his cheeks, his pale brown myopic eyes moist and sad, Ted said, "But it's Holly I'm in love with. I love you, Holly. I mean it, babe, I do."

"Suzie's left you and you're devastated but it's Holly you really love? This sounds a little strange to me."

"Oh, *man!*" he said. "You don't get it, do you? It's Van Gogh! It's Renoir painting with the brush between his teeth because the arthritis in his fingers has got so bad!"

Shrugging, waving his hands, eyes crazily ablaze, Ted was talking all of a sudden like a picture he'd taken down from the wall. He was an actor who believed in very little, especially himself, and when he felt passion he needed to convey it with heartfelt magic. "It's Mozart ripping out the last chords of the Jupiter Symphony when he's freezing to death in Vienna!"

"I've eaten strudel, but I have to disappoint you— I've never been to Vienna."

"We've got to walk toward the light, Billy. What else is there?"

My exhausted eyes drooped. I listened while Holly, in tears herself now, stretched up on those enormous heels and touched his face, telling him, "Shush, shush." This was what the whole show had been, a lovers' spat, a childish cry for attention with a firearm capable of decapitation or cutting a man in half. On the way out to join Lucy, I shook the bullets from the chamber into my pocket and, having dumped the gun in the trash, turned to say, like the proper English copper I wasn't, "Evening, all."

Schopenhauer offers metaphysical consolation to the man driven by confused or puzzled will. He offers the solace of a heartfelt and intense longing for death, for total unconsciousness, for complete nonbeing and the vanishing of dreams. He was German: what can I tell you?

I had done more than duty required, knowing that Ted was more likely *not* to pull the trigger. He wasn't that kind of a nut case. All the same, he'd been drunk, and those were real bullets. The unfunny thing was that part of me had itched for him to go ahead, had longed for that final flash. It wasn't, in those days, an unusual feeling. Sometimes I'd sit alone in my apartment or in a restaurant, and hours went by while the devils of guilt and loss of self-esteem perched on my shoulder, whispering country-and-Western songs and thoughts of self-removal. Suicide would be like walking into a room bathed in cold blue moonlight. The mess and hulla-balloo would be over, a prospect by which I was tempted every day, but then I'd whip myself up again into action, to work, to eat, catching, only while with Lucy or some-times with Ellen, blurred glimpses of a former happi-ness. I'm not saying that any of these were unique or unusual feelings, only that they were too powerful to live with for long. I moved between sweet but shapeless hope, the perhaps foolish faith that life could be better, and moods of oceanic desolation. There were, if you like, two Billy McGraths. The suffering Billy was a ship packed with dynamite waiting to go up and therefore down, while the worldly Billy—witty and shrewd, smart and sometimes even wise, capable of footing it neatly on the dance floor of homicide—hoped that the passion and frenzy of work might make everything better, but no longer quite believed that it would.

I walked to the car wondering how it was that, though I loved my daughter more than anything in the world, I still couldn't make myself care whether I lived or died.

4

THE INTERVIEW ROOM WAS SMALL, A DISPIRITING BOX without windows. There was a battered steel desk with broken backed swivel chairs on either side. The walls were pale brown, with no decoration, and the floor, which had once been painted the same color, was now scuffed and scratched. In this room a sixteen-year-old had confessed to me how she'd shot her father. Drunk, he'd made the mistake of falling asleep in front of the TV, having sodomized her the previous night. I'd shown a mother photographs of her homosexual son, beaten to death with a frying pan; his body wasn't found until five days later, by which time maggots had got to his face, and his scrotal sack was swollen the size of a football. Here I'd told a hundred, maybe a hundred and fifty people about the death of a loved one. As a situation it was no longer quite real for me but one of those moments when I felt the awful unreality of the real.

I glanced at the snapshot I'd picked up in Mae Richards's house. Technically, this was a no-no, against all the rules that said never to monkey with a crime scene; legally, it was a misdemeanor. I wasn't even sure what had made me take it. In the picture Ricky Lee had a full, soft, grinning face. He'd probably been about six-teen at the time. Thinking about the tennis racquet, I remembered reading somewhere that he'd been a star athlete at Venice High.

My own mother had died in a hospital ward in the north of England, the room so hot the paint had blistered on the walls, her shivering body eaten so thin it scarcely left an impression on the mattress. She'd died sorry to miss the performance of *The Mikado* that was coming up in next year's amateur theatricals. She'd been afraid, though I was the one who'd gripped her hand tight: don't go.

Maybe there's no such thing as an easy death. My mother's had been slow, a terrible disintegration of the sort we all fear, though most people's special modern dread is reserved for sudden death, by which we don't mean unlingering death—that would be OK—but violent death, in the street, or on the freeway, a quickening of fear and then . . . what? Extinction? For a few seconds, from out of nowhere, at a stupid art gallery party, I'd heard the engine turning. I didn't feel shaky. I felt like I'd been watching TV too long. My nerves were lasered.

A uniformed patrolman brought in Ricky Lee with his hands cuffed behind him. Tall, skinny, aloof, his face much gaunter now, Ricky Lee wore a black suit and a trim goatee beard. His dark eyes popped out and his dark hair, falling thick on either side of a middle part, was cut off at the top of the ear—a warrior's helmet of dreadlocks. Thick blood oozed around his nose and mouth, staining the brilliance of his teeth. I wondered if Mae Richards had thought of him as she died. His eyes met mine without greeting or any noticeable change of expression. He glanced down at the floor, and when he raised his head he let his eyes hit me this time with a murderous, searing rage. "Where's my mother?"

The beefy patrolman was a Cuban, a tortilla cowboy who'd once played ball in the minor leagues and carried at his hip not the Department automatic, but a Smith & Wesson special issue six shooter in a quick-draw holster. I said, "You the guy who made the arrest?"

"Yes, sir," he said carefully, talking Pentel pencil language, the one they write the reports in and rub out and change later. The Department used more erasers than the entire LA Unified School District. "The suspect rushed at me and my partner, sir, and we were compelled to restrain him."

"Very good." I glanced at the name on his badge. "Officer Campes. I'll take the report now. Thanks. You may leave us."

When he'd gone I took the report and ripped it in two, then in four, then in eight, and scattered the pieces on the floor. I said to Ricky Lee, "You and I both know this is bullshit. Your lawyer'll show up any minute and he'll serve you out of here faster than Archimedes jumping out of the bath."

"I'm supposed to be impressed?" His voice was neither high nor low.

"No, you're not supposed to be impressed." I'd read in a book about a doctor out in the Midwest who healed people with the smell of herbs and flowers. She cured senility with laurel leaves, asthma with geraniums. For high blood pressure, rosemary was best. It was mostly in the people's minds, of course, and therefore she had to be very careful about the way she presented each of them with their different flower. She had to gain their trust, almost as if she were trying to seduce them. Interviews are like that. You have to hand over the flower, just so—sometimes gently, or the other way. "You're free to go," I said. "But before you do you should probably take this with you." I held out the snapshot I'd taken from the house. "I took it. I *stole* it. I'm sorry. I shouldn't have done that."

He glanced at the photo, then into my eyes, but it was his that changed. "What's happened to her? What's happened to her, man?"

"There's no easy way to say this. Your mother's dead. She was murdered."

He staggered, about to fall, but when I reached out to grab him, he pushed me away and drew himself up again. "Get your fucking hands off me. Fuckin' asshole. Fuckin' *cop.*"

Ricky Lee's rap sheet was pretty much what I'd expected: burglary, burglary, assault with a deadly weapon, possession of . . . possession of . . . possession of . . . Most of these convictions had occurred before he was twenty, and he was now twenty-seven. Until tonight there'd been only one arrest in seven years; extraordinary, given that so many acronyms were intent on taking him down. Ricky Lee was the real thing, no doubt about it, a live proper gangster. There was a story that once, after a drug deal turned bad, the two colleagues who'd double-crossed him were tied, blindfolded, and bundled into the back of a closed truck, where Ricky Lee himself had shut their mouths with duct tape. The truck had been driven down to San Diego, and all the while Ricky Lee was in the passenger seat, reading out poetry and passages from the Bible. The word was that Ricky Lee liked to read. He'd only learned when he was in jail in his late teens, and now he was making up for lost time. The men must have known, during the two-hour drive, that they were certain to die. They were taken to an abandoned motel, where Ricky Lee shot them in the head. The bodies were found stacked in the bathtub. No one had been able to prove this, but no one doubted it either. It became a story everyone in the Department heard at one time or another, a part of Ricky Lee's legend, along with the usual Robin-Hood-of-the-ghetto bullshit.

He'd become famous following that one recent arrest, when he was put on trial for the attempted murder of a federal officer. This was after a rush-hour shoot-out on the Santa Monica Freeway. He'd escaped by getting out of his car, jumping over the meridian, and somehow weaving his way through the traffic. The pursuing ATF agent, busy capping off rounds from his machine pistol, was swiped by a Mexican in a 1962 Chevy flatbed and wound up in Cedars-Sinai with both legs broken and early retirement on full pay.

The ATF guys claimed that Ricky Lee had fired a shot at them, initiating the shoot-out, and that he'd fled, leaving behind a kilo of coke in the trunk of his car. The trial was a fiasco. Ricky Lee's attorneys established first that it was the federal agents who'd fired *all* the shots, and after that it was only logical to conclude that the coke had been a plant. Ricky Lee walked; he skated; he made fools of them all.

I had no feelings about any of this one way or the other. There'd be media heat on the case because of his involvement, which would mean pressure from within the Department to come up with a perpetrator quickly. If I did, I'd give myself some help toward the next promotion; if I didn't, I'd lay the blame on other factors, whether human or not. Homicide was a career and not a moral problem. For me it hadn't always been such, but then, as my father once said, "Age doesn't bring wisdom, but it sure makes you more tired. You can't go on beating your head against the world." I didn't feel the full extent to which I'd become an outsider; nor did I sense the beginnings of a long journey to the inside, free fall.

"Here's some of the precinct's special poison yolk. The comedians among us call it coffee," I said, setting down two plastic cups, at which he didn't even glance.

Ricky Lee's watchfulness was impressive, frightening, but he registered only the important details: my face, the Sony tape recorder I took from a drawer in the table, the door, which was still open behind him. "Suppose you tell me about it, when you're ready. I'm going to use this, OK?" I held up a cassette tape and flipped it into the Sony. "Let's talk about your mother. Easy stuff. When was the last time you saw her?"

He wasn't about to cave so easily. His hands were steady in front of him on the table.

"Maybe you killed her yourself."

He kicked back the chair and stood, raising his fist and baring his teeth. "I'll kill *you,* motherfucker."

"Hey, good! You have feelings."

"Fuck you, asshole," he said, but wiping blood from his hand on the table.

"She didn't get shot by magic, Ricky Lee. It happened. One billiard ball hit another and somehow it led to her death. Are you going to help me or not?"

He sat back down in the chair, his eyes challenging mine with the same defiant stare.

"When did you last see her?"

His eyes didn't budge. "Three days."

"Where?"

"At her house."

"Did you see her often?"

"Once, maybe twice a month. We kept in touch.

She'd never take money from me, or nothing like that."

"What did you talk about?"

"Shit, man, I don't remember." His eyes went dead as the moon. "She was always wanting me to go to church. We listened to some music. She loved to hear music."

Ellen loved music. "Moody food," she called it. Her brain fumed with that, while my own still sometimes steamed for our lost love.

I said, "What music?"

"Old stuff, her stuff. Jazz, soul."

At first he was unable to accept even that the murder had happened, that the power of its prevention had eluded him; now he was starting to think about the perpetrator. Later, grief would bring him all the way back around the track.

"Someone do this to get at you?"

"Any fool on the street know better than to pull some shit like this," he said, and as his eyes fired up again, there was the bright flash of something in the upper right corner of his mouth. At first I thought it was gold set in a tooth; it was a diamond.

"Who killed her?"

The dreadlocks danced on his head. "I don't know, man, but when I find out, that fool is a dead fool."

I was calm, sipping my coffee. "You ain't gonna pull any of that revenge shit, because if you do I'll bust you, Ricky Lee. You'll go down just like I shot you in the head. But you know what? That ain't gonna happen. You're gonna help solve this case. And you're gonna start by telling me as much as you can about your mother. Who she was. Who her friends were. Where she worked, if she worked. Cop shit. Then I'm gonna go get the bad guy. That's the way it works."

Some statements are meant to soothe, some to echo, others to entice. This one was a confrontation, and he rounded on me, lashing out, yet not quite relaxing the tight control of his anger. "You're a cop. You ain't interested in who killed my mother. Making yourself look good, that's all you fuckin' care about. I spit on you, cop. Your fuckin' clearance rate, that's what worries you, keepin' your ship nice and clean so you look good for your superiors. You know nuthin' 'bout where I live. You know nuthin' 'bout justice or the way I feel. How could you? Fuckin' uniform."

I said, "You finished yet?"

For a moment he fought the impulse to jump across the desk and try to kill me then and there. I said, "Where's your father?"

"Don't know. Ain't never seen him."

"Never?"

"He took off after I was born."

"Did she talk about him?"

"He didn't have nuthin' to do with this."

"That's for me to find out. Did she talk about him?"

He sighed, giving way a little. "Yeah, she talked about him. He was some kind of a musician, living up in San Francisco last I heard."

"Address or number?"

He shook his head. This was Jack the Bear, getting nowhere.

"Any brothers or sisters?"

"I had a brother. He died. He was shot." His bulging eyes stared straight into mine. "That was to do with me."

"When?"

"Seven years ago."

"What happened?"

"Two cholos from Culver City took him out. Was me

they was looking for. Now those two cholos are long gone. Missing in action."

Poor Mae Richards: husband fled, one son murdered, the other a dope dealer; she must have been a remarkable woman to have come through such catastrophe and chaos, all that *life,* and then only to end butchered, dead on her own kitchen floor. Some cases are simple. Others take you on journeys you never forget. Connections spark, doors open. There are unexpected tunnels and detours. Drew Diamond talked about the termite holes of cause and effect. A case might take you into not just one other world, but several. You might find all the rules altered. You might sink there like a stone.

"You know she'd never take nothing from me. Nothing. She went to clean houses rather than take my money. I could've looked after her, man. She didn't need to live in that house no more."

"Where did she work?"

"What?" His eyes shot out again, weapons.

"You mentioned that she cleaned houses. Where did she do that? Any names and addresses?"

He shook his head. "Nope."

I leaned back in my chair. On the table between us the tape was still running in the Sony. "I know how you feel."

His look wasn't watchful now, or even contemptuous. He wanted to burn me down.

"I know you don't believe that and I don't really care whether you do or not," I said. "But you have to do better."

"Why the fuck should I?"

"I need more. Think, Ricky Lee. Help me help you."

His shoulders quivered a little beneath the discreetly

expensive black cloth of his jacket. My own was from Loehmann's, year-end sale. He said, "Was it quick?"

I thought about the burn marks on Mae Richards's chest, about the fact that she'd been tied. "It was quick."

"You lyin'?"

"No, I'm not lying."

He absent-mindedly put his hand to his mouth and then to his forehead, leaving a smear of blood. "You're a murder cop, right?"

"Head of the homicide section."

He said something strange. "You a good man?"

This wasn't a matter I sat around discussing with Diamond, Cataresco, and the others in the squad room. Mostly we talked about where and what to eat. "I try."

"Yeah, I reckon you do. And you'll catch who did this?"

"Usually happens."

"If you do, *when* you do," he said, "I'll give you five hundred thousand dollars."

The tape went on hissing through the spools in the Sony.

"Five hundred thousand. That's how much this means to me. A half a million dollars. Don't arrest the fuck. Just give him to me. Deal?"

For a moment I was lost in my thoughts, staring at the dull brown wall. Maybe I even felt a little afraid as well as insulted. I threw my cup of coffee in his face. He didn't react as scalding black liquid splashed his cheeks and doused his beard.

I wanted to take him by the throat. I waited slowly while I counted to five and called out for the Cuban, Campes.

"I don't need any further motivation to do my job. Have you got that, you arrogant shit?"

"I'm talking about my mother, man." Slowly he mopped at the coffee on his face with a blood-stained tissue. "My *mother.*"

"I know that, and that's why I won't bust your face *and* your ass for trying to bribe a police officer."

Campes was at the door, fingering his Smith & Wesson.

"Take Mr. Richards home."

I'd confused Campes now. Despite his build, the would-be gunslinging air, he had the puzzled expression of a small dog done down by the world, a Pekinese, say, paddling in its own urine. He said, "Excuse me, sir, but my report. The arrest."

"There are no charges. Take Mr. Richards wherever he wants to go. And then you can come back and pick up your report." I nodded down at the scattered pieces. "It's right here."

The precinct house was packed tight with smells: coffee, sweat, stale food, spilled soda, disinfectant—all cooked to a fug by the heaters. I walked back to the detectives' squad room, where the homicide section was located in a corner behind a dry wall section that stretched two-thirds to the ceiling, and positioned myself in my chair in front of the cabinets smelling sweetly of varnish. Often at the end of the day, I'd sit for an hour with the paper, clearing my head. In the early days I'd had the idea that if I sat here and did that, I could rid myself of all thoughts of death or violence; they'd be sent away into the murder books that surrounded me, stored there for the night, brain patterns invisibly imprinted, and I wouldn't have to come back for them until the next morning. Now I did so merely from habit, hoping for the sign that would tell me it was time to go home, to *leave*—I didn't really have a home anymore. And wherever I was, I wasn't sleeping much. I napped for an hour at night and caught, sometimes, another hour in the car during the day. My eyes were pots simmering at twice the temperature of the rest of my body.

On that night I was hot, tired, and my head was so tense it seemed to sprout from my shoulders through a neck of steel angry at its rusting decline. I'd been dumb, letting Ricky Lee get to me. He was a gangster, someone who, because he risked everything, saw himself absolved from ordinary codes and demands. He believed he was whole, because he was brave and rich, because he'd made a run of big scores. He believed that death was meaningful because he'd lost his gangster friends. His mother was supposed to be outside the game, a nonparticipant, and when something happened to her, he knew only one way to respond: he'd offered me money. He probably didn't even know he'd shown me disrespect, and now he'd even got me thinking in his language: they killed each other over that thing, the other currency of their world, *respect*. I didn't want or need Ricky Lee's respect.

I took a new binder from the box, stuck a red dot on the spine, and began the murder book on Mae Richards. I wrote in her name. I wrote in the date and the area of occurrence. Under the section marked ASSIGNED DETECTIVES, I paused and out of instinct looked up. I had a sense of someone or something moving behind me, in the corridor that led to the interview room, a quieter and swifter motion than cops employ when stomping around on their own territory; then it was gone.

There's no section you go to in a bookstore called "How to Solve a Murder." Each Department in the country has evolved its own technique. New York does it different from Chicago does it different from Denver and LA. Each section within each Department adds special twists and refinements, whatever works. My new job was to oversee all the cases within the precinct, to make sure things were running smooth, to keep up the clearance rate, our batting average, and only help out with particulars if needed, like tonight, interviewing Ricky Lee while Cataresco and Diamond were busy at the crime scene. There was nothing that said I couldn't take on a case myself. I was, after all, the boss, but such a move was unusual. I had three other detectives under my command, though, in the normal run of things, Diamond and Cataresco would be assigned the book, since they'd been at the original scene. It didn't always work that way but nearly always. Nonetheless, I hesitated.

The beefy Cuban was back, swaggering in the doorway of the squad room. I said, without quite knowing why, "Did you see someone out there?" He shook his head, puzzled, and then I was struck by something else. He'd been gone only ten minutes or so. "What are you doing here anyway?"

"He went to the front of the station to call a cab. He said he wanted to take a cab."

"Listen, Officer Campes. I quite expressly told you . . ."

"Sir, with all respect, he didn't want . . ."

"I don't care what he said he wants or doesn't want. Get back out there and give him a ride."

"He said the smell of pig was making him sick, sir."

"*What?*"

"He said that the smell of rotten pork was in the air."

I heard myself say something like "That little asshole." I grabbed the aluminum baton from the belt of the puzzled Campes and stormed through the duty room toward the front of the station. "The little prick,

I'll kill him," I said. I went over to the soda machine, whacked it with the baton, and kicked it as well for good measure. A faulty strip light fizzed, crackling. My eyes scanned beneath the photographs of officers killed in the line of duty that looked down at me from the wall, fifteen guys, three of them friends. There was no sign of Ricky Lee.

A voice came from behind me, saying, "Detective McGrath?"

About thirty, with blond hair cropped shortish, she wore a black cashmere blazer, black silk blouse buttoned to the neck, and blue jeans. A raincoat that looked expensive and might have been a Burberry was folded behind her on the bench. Ward Jenssen wasn't, with her slightly asymmetrical face, her lopsided cheekbones and too full mouth, a conventional beauty, but it was the eyes that got you. Their presumed honesty and gentleness had made her career. Not only was she holding a tape recorder, but now, as her companion stepped from the station entrance, where presumably he'd been filming the entire scene with the inconspicuous equipment he toted on his shoulder, I saw that she'd brought along a cameraman, a guy with a dripping combat jacket over an Aerosmith T-shirt and his name, ZED, stenciled on the outside of his chest pocket.

"Hello, Ward. I'd heard that you were working TV these days. Congratulations." I turned to the cameraman. "You can't film in here. You need a permit. As Miss Jenssen knows and I'm sure you do too." I turned for support to the front desk, but it was empty. No duty sergeant. Great.

I'd met Ward years ago, down in South Los Angeles, when she was a beginning reporter for the *Times*'s Metro section, sent to cover a multiple homicide where one group of gangbangers had walked into a place and killed nine others. The inside of that room had looked like lasagne. It was inevitable that we'd run into each other again sooner or later. "How's it going with you? Climbing toward the top of the mountain? What's the view like?"

She said, "I was wondering if I could ask you a few questions."

"No comment."

"Come on, Billy. You don't even know the questions."

"No comment."

"Is Ricky Lee Richards under arrest at this time?"

"No, he is not, and no further comment."

"Was he under arrest earlier tonight?"

As she pushed the tape recorder closer toward my mouth, I had a sudden vision of my own machine, sitting where I'd left it, on the table in the interview room. The tape of my conversation with Ricky Lee was still inside; no need to panic, and I didn't, but I needed that tape.

"Look, Ward, I'm not trying to snow you or put you off, but there's something I've got to take care of." I pointed beyond the deserted front desk into the heart of the precinct house. "If you tell Zed here to turn off the camera so we can talk like civilized people, I'll come back in a few minutes and answer some of your questions."

"As charming as I remember," she said, smiling with her head a little on one side.

"You must be thinking of some other guy."

At her signal Zed eased down the trim camera, and then she herself turned off her tape recorder, unzipped her leather bag, and stowed it inside. She zipped her bag up again. She said, "How's it all gonna go in court tomorrow? Big day, huh?"

"You know me. No shortage of big days."

"I'll see you in a minute then."

"You bet."

I walked to the interview room, knocking shoulders as I went with a guy hurrying out from the squad room in the other direction. I didn't see the face. His presence was dark and bullish, and he strode away, waving his hand in apology and farewell. I assumed he must be with drugs or vice. They came and went at all hours. Thinking nothing of it, I pocketed the forgotten tape, locked the Mae Richards murder book in the varnished cabinet, and chugged out into the precinct parking lot. Right at that moment, talking to Ward Jenssen again was the last thing I needed.

5

THERE WERE TWO CARS I DROVE, THE DEPARTMENT'S unmarked Chevy and my own, a six-year-old Porsche 911, which was a bright fiery orange, had an eccentric shift, and which I'd bought mostly because, back at the beginning of the sixties, when my parents were still together, my father had driven an original Speedster in just that color. I remember his making me drive it in circles around the empty parking lot at Dodger Stadium, terrifying at first, but then I began to scream and laugh as we bumped along and I peeked up through the arms of the steering wheel at the sun-dazzled shield. I would have been five years old at the time, maybe six, and it was only a little while later that my mother left him for good and I took a plane with her to England, where she remarried. My father meanwhile quit his job with the Department and set off on his own travels. He went here and there, to Arizona, New Mexico, all the way up to Montana, but he never did exactly make a journey. From time to time snapshots would arrive, showing him at the wheel of, or leaning up against, his latest ride—a Mustang, an AC Cobra, a pretty pink Cadillac. No one ever knew where the money came from, and only when I was in my teens did it occur to me to ask who was taking the pictures—his latest ride, presumably. That sounds bitter, but I couldn't forget or quite forgive the brilliance of that orange Speedster, and when people who'd known him told me—as they often did—how strikingly my own appearance resembled his, I was filled with shame and even anger. His memory was something I tried not to dwell on, though when Lucy was born I promised myself that I was going to do it different, that I wouldn't mess this up the way he had. I messed it up anyway.

My Porsche, I'd discovered, leaked in the rain. I drove it that night nonetheless, descending deserted boulevards I knew by heart, Culver and then Centinela, before making a left and heading down to the ocean on Washington, with a puddle slowly expanding beside me in the empty well in front of the passenger seat. By then it was after two in the morning, and the rain was still refusing to give up. It had been going on all day, pretty much all week. Great rivers ran in the gutters. Rain smashed against the windshield and drummed up a million tiny detonations on the hood. The center of Lincoln was a rink. In front of me a Cadillac skated slowly sideways and came gently to rest against a signpost. The top of the post buckled forward, a guy tipping his hat.

I started thinking about Ricky Lee Richards. After all, it was possible that even if I did find his mother's murderer, did my job, and delivered him into the big top of the justice system, the murderer would still walk away. The top didn't always spin right. I'd seen it happen. What if I were to find the guy, give him to Ricky Lee, and take the money? Really make sure that it was *the* guy, then let Ricky Lee's savage justice take over? It would probably be more efficient, certainly more sure, and I'd save the city the cost of staging a trial it might not win. It didn't really seem like an option, even though I needed the money. And I *did* need the money, but I also had a code, and the path it provided, though crude, was at least certain. Do the job and try to keep your head above the hullabaloo.

I waited until the driver had untangled his Cadillac from the post, waved, and then got on the car phone to order pizza, one pepperoni, one pepperoni with mushroom, and one four cheese with extra cheese in case I changed my mind. I hadn't eaten since lunch and I still wasn't hungry. I figured both that I needed to be tempted and that I had time enough before the delivery boy arrived to swing by Ralph's for a quart of milk and a bottle of Jack Daniels, so I made the detour, negotiated the flood in the parking lot, and was sidetracked by a pair of young German tourists stalking the brilliance of the liquor aisle. The guy had a big beery face and bright eyes behind shiny and expensive steel-framed specs. The girl was skinny and goosebumped in cowboy boots and shorts. Jet-lagged, settled not so snugly at the Jolly Roger Motel, they couldn't believe the weather. Wasn't the sun always supposed to shine in Southern California? They were rock and rollers, they said; they needed to buy drugs and I looked like the kind of a guy who might know someone.

That's a thing about police work. It shows you the most heinous human shit, and then comes at you with outright human farce. I didn't even try not to laugh. I exploded in their faces. "Yeah, I know some guys, but it's because I'm a cop," I said, and watched their eyes go panic stations. I took mercy. "Look, I'm not going to bust you or do anything except tell you that, at this hour, in this neighborhood, if you try to buy drugs you'll get fucked or worse. I'm just a guy, OK? Be safe. Go to Universal Studios. Try to meet Steven Spielberg. Enjoy the city."

I'd seen tourists who'd got themselves killed in just this way. On a gurney down at the county coroner's they still looked young and alive, in their new Gap jeans and with the laces in their sneakers the way they'd tied them that morning; then there was the bullet hole, the wound from the knife. It made me wonder about human stupidity or optimism. They assumed they could handle a dangerous situation without knowing the rules. Sometimes they were right, they could; but they always invited the chance of wrong day, wrong guy, and ending up in block capitals on the first page of a murder book. When I first came on the job it amazed me, some people's unceasing quest to get themselves killed. Then a part of me came to see the modern world as a hospital—most citizens unwell. So the hucksters step forward to put us together with drugs, with therapy, with sundry other glues or slogans, but they can never quite smooth away our feeling that, at heart, a human being is self-destructive, that in the heart's innermost recesses there's a secret urge just to be done with it.

I lived by the ocean, in an apartment I'd bought too quickly for too much money, part of a new complex at the marina that looked as though it'd been built to house a bunch of voyeurs or robots. The complex consisted of four crescent-shaped buildings in white concrete. Grouped together, facing each other, they formed a broken circle. From any apartment, when the weather was fine, you could spy on a hundred others. Consequently, about half of the residents kept their drapes drawn tight while the rest of us tried not to look, and tried to ignore the music, the coughs, the flushes and gurglings, all evidence of human activity, as well as the weird echoes and emanations that came from within the buildings themselves.

At one time, during the boom years of the 1980s, the marina had threatened to be a new Westwood or Montana Avenue. Bronzed yuppies had invested at the top of the market, bringing with them their Jeeps, their weights, and the hissing cappuccino machines, which were another contribution to the concrete symphony. Now, following the crash, the neighborhood hadn't exactly gone on a downward slide, but it was poised. From the front I saw the ocean, the boats that sailed on it, and the purple and pearly skies that rose like shells from the horizon at Sunset. The view from my bathroom, however, at the back, was of swamp left undrained, ill omened real estate, above which a floodlit sign showed a smiling young couple with the hopeful message: BRIGHT HARBOR DEVELOPMENTS—THE FUTURE IS YOURS.

An aging Toyota, a car of the type Drew Diamond referred to as a Border Brothers Cadillac, was in the building forecourt with a Domino's Pizza bucket upended on its aerial like a tawdry lantern. Outside my apartment, way up on eleventh, the delivery boy pounded at my door. Seeing me, he grinned with relief. He'd been thinking no delivery, no tip, or maybe even that he'd have to pay for all those pizzas himself. He was a little Latino kid in a rustling nylon tracksuit that dripped all over the carpet. I told him to come in and he stood leaking there too, so I gave him a towel to dry off a little.

I had a living room, a walk-through kitchen, which I rarely used, and two bedrooms, the second for when Lucy slept over. After a year or so, when it began to be apparent that her mother and I weren't about to rush back into each other's arms, she'd started to make her own room cozy. As for the rest of the place, the carpets were clean, the plants watered, the twin black-and-white sofas arranged at a perfect right angle, and I might have moved in yesterday. I'd been there ever since Ellen and I split, though the only evidence of this passage of time was the slow filling of a stripped pine bookcase. I bought four or five new books each month, mostly philosophy or fiction, and underlined in pencil any passages I thought pertinent, a help in life. I'd bought the bookcase unfinished, and, since I'd never got around to painting it, the shelves were starting to warp. The meaning of those passages I'd marked never seemed so urgent or true when I went back to them a second time; indeed, I was beginning to doubt the consolations of philosophy in general. A cripple goes by wheeled by his buddy in a supermarket trolley or a little girl is murdered by a charmer who blows air kisses to the jury. After that, I'm supposed to read Bertrand Russell?

I said to the delivery guy, "How d'you dig LA?"

His face lit up and he said, "Oh, man, I love it," and I could see that he did. This, for him, was still the land of opportunity. He was young enough to be able to enjoy the weight that the struggle to survive made against his heart. Actually he looked young enough to be still living with his mother, but if he did, it was most likely in a one-bedroom apartment in Mar Vista or the Culver City projects with his own wife or girlfriend and children. The Latinos were the only ones who still believed in family through thick or thin, and they worked, they were America's new blood; you didn't see these guys holding out Burger King cups on Santa Monica Boulevard. "Hey, bro," I said. "How about you take two of these pizzas?

Just remember me when you're mayor, OK?"

A little puzzled, bobbing nervously on black suede trainers that oozed, he said thanks, tucked the pizzas into an insulated delivery bag of red plastic, jammed his baseball cap over his eyes, and moved into the night with a squelching saunter, leaving me with a brief and absurd feeling of elation, as if I could win myself a little piece of redemption by making successful connection with the sprawl of the city beyond the window, with at least some of the millions who came here, urged by ambition and drawn by its irresistible magnetic dream.

I checked my messages: only one, from my grandfather, asking me to call. He was sick, that old guy, but he was tough. He'd discharged himself from a VA hospital six months previously, saying he wanted to die at home, a process—I was happy to say—that looked like occurring no time soon. He lived surrounded by medals and weaponry in an aluminum-sided bungalow in Culver City. Heaven help the homeboy who tried to rob the place.

I opened my mail, a depressing train of bills and final notices, until I was derailed by a letter from Ellen's attorney about the sale of the house on Nowita Place, detailing the division of this last asset of the marital spoils.

I think it was Voltaire who said that nothing in a marriage is ever settled. Marriage is never a completed state, he said, so even after the divorce I'd clung to the fact that the house was still in both our names. Now this last knot was about to be untied, or not even that—cut. She'd found a buyer. I'd known, telling myself this could all fall through. Now my signature was required on a piece of paper, and then our house would be gone, and so would she.

I splashed more whiskey into the glass. Ellen's big

plan about Seattle: for months now I'd been trying to tell myself that everything was all right, that I'd still be able to check in every day and see Lucy whenever I liked, that everything was the same as it had always been, at least since the separation—but Ellen was moving on. Agreeing with her that the two of them should go was like an appointment I'd made way in advance and had never quite expected to have to keep. Now I was kicking against the day immediately at hand. I called her.

"Billy," she said, with quickly restrained exasperation. She was patient, a little sad, too used to this. "It's three in the morning. Don't you have to be in court in a few hours' time?"

"I'm tired, I want out, I want us to get back together."

"Oh, Billy." She sighed. "No, you don't. And you know we won't."

"I don't know that and I certainly don't accept it."

"Billy, we've been over it a million times."

"A gangster just offered me half a million if I'd find who killed his mother."

"Take it. Leave the Department."

"You don't mean that."

"Why are you telling me this? I don't need to hear these things anymore."

"I'm astonished you said that. I've never taken money from anybody."

"I can't discuss this now." She sounded tired. "I know you'll never take money from anybody."

"So what do you want to talk about?"

"I don't want to talk about anything. It's the middle of the night. I feel like Bert being tormented by Ernie in *Sesame Street.* What I really want is to go to sleep."

"How's Lucy?"

Asking about Lucy, knowing that Ellen would have to answer—this was another of my unfair moves, and she sighed, reluctant commitment to the conversation's continuance. "She was upset when you brought her back. She ran straight to her room. Something about Ted and a gun? I couldn't get to the bottom of it. I was going to ask you tomorrow."

"It wasn't anything. Ted was being a fool. He was drunk. He produced this gun out of somewhere and started threatening a girl. I sent Lucy to the car."

"What happened then?"

"Ted put the gun down."

She was silent for a moment. "You're not telling me everything."

Basically, Ellen always knew the score. She was the measure of my soul, tough to fool. I changed the subject, saying, "There was a murder today."

"How many times do you think I've heard that? Or, 'Ellen, I was at a crime scene.' Or, 'Ellen, Drew Diamond went off like a loose cannon again.' Or, 'Ellen, there's been a triple down in the southland and they need an extra guy.' You soak it up. You're a sponge. This job hasn't just taken you over. You're *infected* by it."

I was always almost glad when I goaded her to anger; it made me feel less guilty. "Let it all out, Ellen. Tell me what a shit I am."

There was a silence on the other end of the line while I walked with my glass to the window and pressed my forehead against the coolness of the pane. Outside, the storm was loud as ever, so violent it spread a kind of silence around itself. I was surprised when a smudge of light loomed up out of it, a glow, shapeless at first, but soon defining itself as a triangle, a sail, I realized, getting bigger and brighter as the boat beneath it tacked toward the marina. I wondered who'd be out sailing on a night like this.

An invisible car sluiced and swished on Admiralty Way below. She'd gathered herself. She said, "This is an amazing thing you're doing for me, Billy, and I really appreciate it. I'm grateful, truly. I need air. I need to get out of this city so bad. It's a fresh start for me."

"I'm not so sure. I think now I *want* to stand in the way. I want to make myself as huge an obstruction as possible."

"No, you don't. Try and get some sleep, Billy, OK? Night."

I'd been a rookie when we met. She was younger than I but she'd already had two years on the job by the time I joined the Department, having been detained by the bookish education of which she was now in pursuit—hence Seattle, where she'd been offered a teaching job while completing her doctorate in criminology. At Marty McFly's the first time, I asked if she liked Wittgenstein, and she said she couldn't stand that German beer. She had red hair and clear green eyes, the best eyes and the hardest head in all of LA County; she was tall, with big bones; she had a wonderful, mysterious face. Women adored her, men feared her, and for the same reason— she fascinated them. In those days she usually knew what I'd do before I did it. Nothing much had changed. She was a giggler. She had a blazing honesty that could make other people uncomfortable. She looked at me, her green eyes smoldered, and though she laughed at herself, knowing what she was doing, I still went up in flames, all in all a beautiful, if slightly giddy and drunken, beginning. She was someone I could talk to right from the first moment. A part of me flew across the room and became hers as soon as I saw her. Three nights later we were together on a routine call, domestic violence, in an apartment building in what wasn't even one of the worst sections of Oakwood. A guy came sauntering down the steps, smiling, cool as you like. It all happened so fast. I didn't even see him reach behind his back, and suddenly there was a six-inch blade in his hand. I went for my gun, but the holster was stiff and new—too slow; the guy was going to stab me. Then Ellen came up on my side, shot him in the shoulder, and the knife flew away as if in an unseen hand. She'd been my training officer that night, and the whole caper was over in a flash, five, maybe six seconds.

Her father was a Woodland Hills building contractor, and her mother ran a little diner on Ventura Boulevard. I wasn't the sort of man they expected her to fall for. Back then I was driven, edgy, and half foreign to boot, while I in turn regarded them as a pair of hayseeds, first opinions that failed to modify themselves down the years during which Lucy was born, started to grow, and both our careers prospered.

Ellen made detective and worked Internal Affairs, a route I was to follow, and then she helped start up one of the antidrug programs for schools, which turned out great, a big success. She only went back into uniform when we separated, and it's my belief that otherwise she'd never have done that. A sergeant by then, she was leading a team in pursuit of a suspect when she fell through the skylight on an abandoned sweatshop on Olympic. The suspect, naked for some reason nobody ever explained, streaked with blood, came at her, capping off rounds like crazy. Hit, flat out on a bed of broken glass, she shot and killed him. Afterward, the surgeons found a bullet in her hip and a nine-inch shard of glass puncturing her kidney through to her spine. She was paralyzed from the waist down.

Sipping at my whiskey, slowly now, I listened. A door banged and a man said, *What the fuck.* One of my neighbors, drunk, most likely the guy at the end of the corridor who tended bar in Santa Monica. I thought of the tape in my pocket, the conversation with Ricky Lee now snug and safe at my hip, and wondered, idly, if there was some way I could make Ellen take the money. I knew she'd never go for it; besides, it really wasn't an option. I'd do my best to make sure that the system did work, keep myself aloof, above that sort of damage. I'd managed it thus far. My peers regarded me as a straight arrow that would never plummet. I was the guy Internal Affairs came to if there was a problem, and they trusted nobody; they were mean, nasty people.

Ripping open the cassette, grabbing a pair of scissors, I sliced the tape into strips that immediately curled up into little springs. I opened the window and threw out the whole bunch. One of them stuck, briefly clinging, a smudge on the glass; then it too was gone, whipped away into the storm's heavy rumble.

6

NEXT DAY I GOT UP EARLY, BUT CATARESCO WAS ALREADY at the precinct house ahead of me. It was damp and cold, still raining, and I felt niggly, because I'd thought I'd better dress for court and my best suit was an expensive thin wool summer thing, but I'd put it on anyway and my skin itched against a white shirt with too much starch from the cleaner. I didn't feel right. Cataresco's quick glance took in the suit and I said, "What?"

She said, "Nothing. I wonder why you're in such a lousy mood this morning."

"Yeah, I wonder."

In front of her at one of the long tables she had the opened murder book of Mario Angel Martinez, a Latino gangster who'd made the mistake of presuming to poach on the drug turf of Ricky Lee Richards. We'd found him about two weeks before, sitting up straight in a stolen Ford. He'd been shot in the back of the head three times with a 9 mm and was wearing his face like a bib.

Cataresco, different when she was by herself, could be shy and awkward; she was sure she still sometimes spoke with the stammer that had worried her as a child, though I'd never heard it. She'd grown up back East, in

Brooklyn, where her father owned an Italian bakery. There was a younger sister she believed prettier and more talented. I'd like to have seen the sister.

She sipped at her decaf. "Let's think about Mario Martinez. Nineteen years old, a Culver City gang member. We got a good idea that one of Ricky Lee's homeboys made the hit, which means the word on the street must be they did it for sure. A week later someone takes out Ricky Lee's mother." She tossed off the rest of her coffee. "You gotta wonder."

Maybe Cataresco was right, but the obvious solution felt like too much. "Kill the mother of Ricky Lee Richards and you're not talking tit for tat. You're talking extermination. And those burn marks. Burn marks on the body of a forty-five-year-old woman. Does that feel like a gang thing to you? I've got the strongest feeling that this was to do with her, not him."

"So what's Ricky Lee's next move?"

"The word'll go out. He'll let the street know how well he'll reward a favor. Maybe he'll even try and call a truce. One thing for sure is that we've gotta find the perp before he does. We do everything we usually do and make sure we get seen doing it. The brass will squat on me because for sure all the press and TV will be swarming all over them. We solve this quick. Go back and talk to the neighbors again. Find her friends. Try and find her husband, or her ex or whatever the hell he is, Ricky Lee's father. Why did someone slice off her finger ends?"

"What was it you told me? Murderers do dumb things."

I'd once caught a perp driving around in a victim's car, with her credit cards and driver's license in his wallet, and a Gideon Bible with her name in the front open on the passenger seat beside him, and this was five days after the murder, as if he'd done the deed and slipped into a trance. "Talk to your guy at DMV and get some luck with that partial plate."

"GSG? The three tenors?"

Drew Diamond was there now, constrained on all sides by a pinstripe suit of almost funereal sobriety. "I don't want to make an issue of this," he said in a huffy way. "But Tito Gobbi was a baritone. At his best in villainous roles. Like Scarpia in *Tosca*. Scarpia's the head of the Italian police, and he's in love with this singer, Tosca. So he snatches her boyfriend, and he's got the guy holed up in a cell, torturing him so that Tosca can hear the screams while he's trying to get inside her panties. Man, he's one nasty perpetrator."

"Drew," I said. "This is clearly something of importance to you, so I'm very glad you *are* making an issue of it. So he was an evil dude, this baritone, Toto Gobbi?"

"*Tito,*" said Drew.

"Didn't I say that? Now if we could return to the trivial matter of the homicide at hand."

All of a sudden my anger came spitting up. In that moment I hated him, his attitude of feigned dry-cleaner boredom, his opinions, his way of going about our work. He'd had his jeweled, enchanted moments, brave acts, beautiful women, important cases cracked and won—though not recently. These days his soul sang in the pistons of his restored Jaguar XKE while his 1982 Detective of the Year Badge from the Elks Lodge on Pico Boulevard still contrived to assure him that he was the glue holding Los Angeles together.

I said, "Listen. What I've decided is that I'm going to work the Mae Richards case with Cataresco."

There was a silence. Cataresco shook her head at Drew, as if to say this was the first she'd heard about it, and then looked at me and rolled her eyes. I meanwhile stared at Diamond to see how this would go. Not well; his eyes were vacant and a little dazed, momentarily uncomprehending. Cops live by the book, love the rules and regs, and all at once I'd offended the accepted order. I couldn't have shocked him more if I'd pulled a gun; indeed, I'm sure Drew would have preferred that. He said, "For Chrissakes, Billy," and swept his hands through his hair, trying to calm himself. "I've had a rough time recently and I was looking forward to getting back in the saddle."

I glanced at my watch. "C'mon, Drew. We'd better go. We're due in court at ten. I won't ride with you. I'll take my own car. Is that a problem?"

Denise Corcoran was white, twenty-five, gorgeous, and she'd been found on the floor of her living room, shot twice in the face with her own pistol, a pretty little over-and-up Derringer with a pearl handle and a silver-plated barrel. From the start there was something that worried me about the crime scene, and though I never quite put my finger on what, this unease still nagged, a light that flickered and guttered.

The house had been ransacked: cushions ripped, chairs turned over, TVs and glassware broken, paintings slashed, a once beautiful interior reduced to a nervous breakdown. Our first assumption was that she must have interrupted a burglar, but soon we began to find evidence to the contrary. Nothing seemed to have been taken: no cash, no jewelry, none of the undamaged art. There was no sign of forced entry. Her husband Charlie Corcoran's fingerprints were all over the murder weapon, and his alibi proved to have more holes in it than one of Madonna's string vests. Corcoran had dated

Madonna, once upon a time, before he met Denise in Las Vegas, where she was a blackjack dealer and he was in town for a shindig organized by motion picture distributors.

The district attorney had been reluctant to take the case, because it was another dubious-looking celebrity murder; and Corcoran himself, as time went on, put up a more and more plausible front. He was great on the stand: modest, forthright, shattered by this tragedy. He was an actor, but he didn't come off like one in this, the best, least self-conscious performance of his life, while other witnesses confirmed on his behalf that Denise had been no piece of cake. In the months before her death she'd been weeping, breaking down, crying. She drank; she took drugs; she had an impossible temper.

The problem here was that I believed I *knew* Charlie Corcoran had killed his wife. He'd told me so himself, outside his house on Mulholland Drive, minutes after Drew Diamond had asked him if he'd mind coming in to answer a few questions. He'd been in a state of shock. He'd blurted out, "I lost my head, man. I killed her." His head had ducked down into his hands. "Did you see her face? One of her eyes was still open. Oh, God, what have I done?" No tape recorder had been running, and Diamond hadn't even read him his rights yet. The confession had not been admissible. Truth was, we'd been surprised, not to mention dazzled, taking down a movie star. That hadn't been a phony blood-spattered Picasso up on the wall of his house, which was a contemporary masterpiece by Rem Koolhaas. By the time we'd charged him and got him into the interview room, his lawyers had joined the party.

They peppered us with experts. They conducted weekend seminars to judge each of the jury's nuanced sways. They roughed up Drew Diamond's reputation with stories that worked in my favor, when, early in the trial, it came down to him and me for the promotion. They pointed out that Corcoran's prints had every right to be all over the Derringer, since it was registered in his name, after all, and he'd used it for target practice at the Beverly Hills Shooting Club the previous night, before negligently forgetting to clean it and bringing it home. Much emphasis was placed on this last word, *home,* where, the defense pointed out, with heavy irony, a ghastly crime had been committed, the perpetrator of which was still allowed to roam free by the city's esteemed Police Department.

It was another of LA's shows, though not as big as many, because from about halfway through the trial pretty much everyone was guessing at Corcoran's acquittal. The media lost interest in him and even the disorderly mental state of his murdered wife, turning instead toward us, the Department. Only Drew, so bulldoggish and straight-ahead, kept his nose down, sniffing at the idea of a conviction. The job, with all its strictures and prejudice, had shaped him out of clay with its own hands. He knew no other existence. Police work was his life, yet he seemed to have lost the knack, and it was his testimony that finally decided the course of the case.

Drew couldn't cut it on the stand. In court he'd been dry-mouthed and twitching inside those fine clothes. His concentrated brooding face made it appear he was trying far too hard. He *was* trying far too hard. Drew didn't understand that sometimes you have to be an actor, a liar even, to be a good witness. Corcoran's lawyers made a fool out of him, this one-time Department high-flyer who laughed inappropriately at his own jokes, muddled his syntax under pressure, and clipped his words as if sealing them in a coffin. He thought the system should believe him and have done with it; simple as that. He didn't understand that people tend not to trust police officers these days; or, rather, he understood the fact but inarticulately raged against it. He *died* up there.

I remembered the first time I met him. It was about ten years ago, some months after Lucy was born. Ellen and I had found a sitter for the afternoon and gone to a party at Drew's house. He was living up in Glendale with his then wife. This was soon after I made detective, and Drew was, I guess, something of a role model. Even though we'd never crossed tracks, I'd certainly heard enough about him. He was the arrogant homicide star back then, always with a cigarette in one hand, often with a glass in the other. To Ellen and me, convinced that nothing could ever break us, it was obvious that day that Drew was about to explode as a husband. He and his wife were at each other's throat; mildly drunk, he was rude to everyone else. He spent most of the afternoon teaching his little girl how to hit the curve ball, a phenomenon she'd encountered to her recent distress in junior league softball. With her he was gentle and patient. It's funny; you can think someone a total asshole until you see him with his kids, and then you realize, hey, this guy might be all right.

We didn't work together at that time, though we saw each other pretty regularly for a drink or two, trading stories. When his marriage ended, he seemed blank and numb, but with a suppressed anger waiting to be turned on. Then he was out of my life for years, working East LA, working too hard, messing up his instincts, and by the time he came back to the Westside, to Ocean precinct, he seemed exhausted, as if suffering reaction and remorse, though nonetheless still expecting the promotion I got. He was, after all, the more experienced man.

I'd asked him after the promotion, "What keeps you at it, Drew? Why do you still bother? You've put in your twenty. You don't seem interested anymore. You could quit, take your pension."

"I'm keeping my eyes open," he'd said, glancing at the sleeve of his blazer. "Maybe I'll have an astonishing second act in my life."

Charlie Corcoran was in his late fifties and had survived as a star in Hollywood for more than three decades, staying power he was reputed to take with him into the bedroom, where his prowess was legend and where he'd seemingly met with them all, from Fonda to Pfeiffer, from Seberg to Silverstone. Watching him, I thought I'd measured the true nature of his charm. He didn't calculatedly seduce, but desired seductively, making each individual he looked at—whether man or woman—feel that he or she was, for that instant, the most important person in the world. He let you know how well he understood the rough-and-tumble of ambition, the tender comedy of imperfect human wanting. This is all far from a joke, his eyes said, but if by any chance it were one, I know the joke would be on me. He had the gift of seeming modesty. He had a still boyish charm.

The court room was packed. There were the larger than life personalities, the TV anchors, waving and smiling at each other. There were the high-profile print reporters, sharp in Armani, who added to their corrosive reputations during the course of the trial. There were the hardcore crazies, who waited outside each day on the off chance that they'd win the lottery for the leftover seats. There were the court reporters beneath the judge's bench and the lawyers on either side of Corcoran himself, who gave off a carefully humbled air of confidence, with graying hair that was cut short and stood up in porcupine quills. His suit was dark blue, his shirt plain and white as the innocence that his blue eyes and even his spiky hair contrived to make hover around him like a halo.

It was over in minutes. The judge came in, a balding distinguished black guy who gathered his robes about him as he sat, swished and banged his gavel with self-conscious theatricality, and asked the foreman of the jury if a verdict had been reached in the matter of the State of California versus Charles Emerson Corcoran. The foreman—a woman actually, in her late forties, with red-framed glasses and no less susceptible to Corcoran's strange magnetism than anyone else in that courtroom—said yes, nervously fingering a piece of pink legal-size paper she'd folded in two.

At university I'd read philosophy, not for its logical niceties, its fancy footwork and arguments, not for its frequent visions of very smart angels dancing on the heads of extremely intellectual pins, but for the sense it sometimes gave of another mind grappling with what it means to be human, with the problems of living well and fairly. I turned to the study of law and jurisprudence with the same idea. For the rule of law, for the enforcement of common order and justice, for a restatement of the principles of the Republic and why the United States had divorced itself from Britain in the first place—for all these, America seemed to cry aloud. And though I'd no intention then of becoming a cop, when in time I did I still believed I could make a difference. I was passionate, naïve, and young, a man all bright and quivering, primed for fifteen years of the streets and disenchantment.

Justice is a commodity, I now knew, and this was the Los Angeles County Superior Court, which gave to monied might the means abundantly to confuse, confound, and humiliate the right. It was a disaster I was used to living with. In this court the poor got screwed, while the rich broke all the rules, duly expecting, and being granted, the sorts of privileges and exemptions that in England are given to the kings, queens, dukes— the aristocracy.

In the eyes of my colleagues and most people in Los Angeles I was an admired, even a celebrated, man. I solved big cases and got my picture on TV. I'd twice won the Department's highest decoration for bravery, the first time for stepping out onto a bridge high above San Pedro to pull back a jumper, and then for saving a couple of kids from a burning apartment building. I had a certain fame myself, which, to be honest, I liked, though I tried never to let it interfere with the work. There was a mystique about homicide, something beyond the hours and the dead bodies. We crossed the border to touch finality. The most bizarre, terrifying murders could and did happen every day. True, mostly they happened to certain people, those whose unlucky birthright is crime, the chance of victimhood, though every now and then homicide would reach out to remind us of how it too cherished democracy, and those of us whose job was to deal with it would be reminded in turn how democracy reserved special favors for wealth. This was the way of the world, the system of which I was a part; justice was just only part of the time, a tough reality against which you'd break your foot kicking.

All this I knew to be true, watching Corcoran as he glanced at the neat, square nails of his right hand. And yet, in that hushed moment of waiting, I suddenly found myself willing a guilty verdict, *needing* a guilty verdict, and I realized that it wasn't Drew Diamond who'd been rousing my anger that morning. It was Corcoran, and not just because he'd done this shit and most likely I was going to have to eat it.

"Not guilty," said the woman in the red glasses, her voice with a smile in it while thirty camera shutters clicked as one, while Corcoran's eyes didn't budge from his own lucky hands, while people all around me gasped, then cheered, and the judge called loudly for *"order, order,"* even as lawyers swooned around, clapping Corcoran on the back.

I rubbed my eyes, stunned, so obviously deflated that the woman next to me, one of the lottery winners, said, "Hey, detective, are you gonna faint?"

Outside, in the corridor, I pushed through the crowd of reporters into the corridor, fleeing down the stairs, hearing my heels clatter a couple of flights down the stairwell before I struck back into the main body of the building and splashed water in my face from a drinking fountain. I didn't quite know where or who I was. My heart was going fast and my skin prickled. A woman went by, rolling her cleaning cart with its wafting stench of ammonia and filthy water.

Corcoran had been a movie star, an American aristocrat, for so long that he thought he needn't concern himself with matters of honor, trust, and fidelity. Given the chance to be completely corrupt, he grabbed it. He'd had affairs, and his life hadn't been messed up. He'd killed his own wife, and gone free. Apparently for him it was a cleaner way of dealing with things than divorce. Throughout the trial, even in his performance of grief, he made clear to the jury, the audience, that he was the one who had suffered, who'd been oppressed; it was always Denise who was doing things to him. Taking drugs. Trashing the house. Sleeping around. He never for one second showed feelings of guilt about how both their lives had ended up, whereas in my case I felt as though I'd fired the bullet that smashed Ellen's hip, as if I personally had picked up a shard of glass and severed the nerves in her spine. I didn't understand how he could absolve himself in this way. I thought it evil, this ether of wealth in which he lived, high above morality and its tedious demands. He raised in me not revolutionary feelings, but, as Rousseau said, the smoldering hatred of a peasant. He made me feel cheap about myself and my own best qualities.

I walked down the remaining six or seven flights toward the lobby of the building, where outside, beyond security and the sliding glass doors, I saw the waiting hullaballoo: the TV and radio crews, the crowds and well-wishers waving placards that said, WE LOVE YOU CHARLIE. I wasn't planning to join them. I was going to head down into the basement parking lot and out that way, when Ward Jenssen appeared from around the side of the elevators, with her cameraman, Zed, trotting alongside her. She was wearing jeans again, with cowboy boots, and a tweed jacket today that had hairs on it, with a dinky little leather vest beneath. It was the same microphone she held toward my face, asking how I felt about the verdict.

"Great. Justice took its course. How do *you* feel as a woman watching a guy get away with something like this?"

"But he wasn't guilty. The jury found him not guilty."

"Do you believe that?"

"Are you engaged in some sort of vendetta against Charlie Corcoran?"

"Why would you think so?"

I wanted to tell her that this wasn't fair, that the guy had killed his wife and here she was coming after me; but I knew fair didn't come into it. Zed's grin told me how greedily the camera was gobbling this up.

"You don't like Mr. Corcoran, do you? Maybe you were thinking about a little payback—by trying to frame him, take him down?"

"This is absurd," I said, hurrying past them both, down the stairs toward the parking lot, where it was chill and the ground was slippery, dangerous with oil-slicked puddles. I looked for Drew, wanting to tell him that we were both on the same side, that I'd been astonished by the dizzy vehemence with which I'd willed Corcoran to be convicted. Between cops there was supposed to be brotherhood.

"Hey, Drew. Thanks for waiting."

The dim neon lights crackled and made an angry fizz. Drew was sitting on his own in his Jag, arms spread wide across the bench seat in the back. His eyes were wide. "Fuck you, you two-faced prick. Fuck you, Billy."

7

THE NEW COUNTY CORONER'S OFFICE WAS A LOW REC-
tangle in beige concrete. On the edge of East Los
Angeles, snug beneath a curve of the Golden State Freeway, as architecture the building was neither tasteful nor
the reverse; it was anonymous as a factory, across the
parking lot from the old building, a rather more impressive structure in birdshit-spattered red brick that had
been badly damaged in an earthquake in the 1970s, and
a thrift shop in whose doorway a drenched cat was taking shelter and where, if you desired, you could buy the
unclaimed clothes that dead people had come in wearing; of course they'd been washed and fumigated. Round
the back there were deserted picnic tables with rain
bouncing off the top of them.

Randy Juster met me at the door to his office and
took me down in the elevator to the basement. Following a busy weekend, bodies lay beneath blue and pink
sheets in the docking area, lined up and ready to be
weighed. Bodies were in the report room, waiting for
their toe tags. The door to the crypt opened to reveal
each steel shelf filled, a hundred or more bodies swad-
dled in thick, clear plastic. Some bodies were white and

doll-like. Others were bloated, flesh squeezed against the wrapping, and some were already decayed and dehydrated. It all depended on how long after death they'd been found. A brown toe stuck out from one package, like a rotten stump waiting to be broken off. An orderly came by and shut the crypt door, leaving in the corridor a cold smell of decay barely contained.

This was Randy's kingdom, and he strode through it like Patton visiting the countryside. Graying, a guy of about my age, he was the coroner's chief investigator, responsible for determining who all these people were and how they had died. He treated everybody alike, both the dead and the living, as though they were highly contagious. He had a huge, round, pockmarked face that drooped at the cheeks as if the air had been let out, and I'd never seen him when he wasn't smiling. He'd said to me once, "You think you know about death? I guess you think you do, being a murder cop. And I guess that in your career you'll handle two hundred cases, three hundred tops. I see more death than that in a week, every week." Upstairs, in his office, he had a vast library on the subject. He liked to keep himself up to speed.

We were in the changing room when he said, "So what's up? Who was this lady anyway? I mean, I know her name. Mae Richards. But there's a guy from the FBI here and one from the DEA. She's got herself an audience."

"Her son's a big time dope dealer."

"He's here, too."

I paused while loosening my tie. "Ricky Lee?"

"Yeah, that's his name."

"You let him in?"

"Hey, Billy, how many times you been to one of these? A hundred, a hundred and fifty. But it always lives with you, right? You think I'd let a son watch his own mother get sliced and diced? Give me credit for not being an asshole the size of Hollywood."

After that Randy went on for a while, riding his hobby horse, muttering about how even though the soul had left the temple the body still had to be treated with as much dignity as was feasible while the job was getting done. There was something about the guys who worked here. They spent their days cooped up with bodies, weighing bodies, photographing bodies, cutting them up or scraping skin from beneath their fingernails. No wonder they were a little kooky. I'd seen Randy once with a mad Peter Lorre look pumping a tray of shriveled fingers full of a chemical brew of his own devising so that they'd swell up again, become supple and pliant, and prints could be taken. Sometimes months went by before the formula achieved its effect—depended on the state of the finger. While doing this portion of his job, he sat in a former broom closet surrounded by severed digits in jars.

Randy mopped at his forehead with a tissue and slipped his fingers into surgical gloves. He put on a green cotton surgical suit and helped me into one. He picked out a mask, handing it to me as if it were a bridal bouquet, and we passed into a secured area leading to the autopsy suites.

The naked body of Mae Richards, clean and slightly blue, was laid out on a table. The dewed flesh seemed already less than human. The sleeve of Randy's green paper suit went straight and crackled as he reached forward to touch a scar above the hairline on her forehead. "That's old," he said. He peered into the ruined jelly of her eye before introducing me to the three others who were already there—the doctor and the guys from the DEA and the FBI, indistinguishable in their protective gear. I'd no right to be smiling. With our big surgical boots and masks with conelike filters on either side, this was probably the closest any of us had ever come to being mistaken for a rocket scientist.

The doctor, impatient at having been kept waiting, was all brisk purpose. "Whatta we got here? Head shot, mmm, mmm. I assume I'm checking for the ordinary? I see your perpetrator didn't leave us any fingernails to clip. Inconsiderate; clever. Look at these burn marks." With a scalpel he scraped skin into a jar from one of the burns on Mae Richards's breast. "Hey, I'll get my money down on Havana. Any of you been in Cuba?" He pronounced this *Hoooba,* not expecting a reply. "Check it out. You can vacation there now, and the fishing's excellent. Just excellent."

He got his little buzz saw going and did the Y-cut, popping out the chest plate. He cut from the vagina to the anus, turned the corpse on its side, and cut out the anus itself while the guys from the DEA and the FBI traded looks beneath the masks. Randy Juster meanwhile watched with feigned nonchalance. He didn't show anything at all.

The doctor perked up. "Well, *here* we are. Contusions, trauma, evidence of blood and other fluids. I'll have this sent up to the lab. This should help you some, you ever find yourself a suspect."

Randy said, "There's no way I'm going to let any guy see this happen to his own mother, I don't care who he is. I sent the kid upstairs to wait in the souvenir store."

He wasn't joking. There really was such a store, upstairs by the elevators. It sold books, key rings, license plates, and jackets or T-shirts in black with white fallen-body outlines printed on them; but Ricky Lee was gone from there by the time the autopsy was completed and I'd changed back into my suit. I found him in the lobby, in front of the LA city district councilmen up there on the wall. Dressed in black, he didn't move when he saw me. He wasn't a big man, but there was a sense of threat about him. All his life, and at that moment all his rage, came shooting through his eyes, so forceful you'd think the rest of his body would have been shocked into movement by their power, yet he stood quite still.

He said, "I have to see her."

I thought of what he'd witness in the autopsy suite: body parts being sorted into different bags, a scene from the charnel house. I said, "Not like that."

"It's my right, man. I'm her son."

"I know, but that's not your mother anymore down there."

"I want to see her so I'll know what to do to the human being who took her life away."

"I thought we agreed you weren't going to pull any of that revenge shit."

"We agreed *nothing,* cop." He wheeled away, as if the anger in his eyes had at last burned his body into movement. He stood with his back to me at the window. There was a brief pause in the rain. Clouds sailed quickly by, wrestling with their cargoes. A wind nipped from the north, clattering the lobby doors. "I had you checked out, Detective McGrath. Seems that you used to work Internal Affairs, busting the bad cops. Word on the street is that you're some kind of a magician at this murder stuff. You wave your wand and cases get solved, like you're some kinda Merlin 'n can do magic 'n shit."

I was supposed to feel stroked.

"Word is, you're a cool motherfucker, and you once wasted a dude."

I said, "That's not quite fair or accurate. Did you? Ever waste a dude?"

His bitter laugh rang in my ears. "Shit, that's *good.*

'Did you?' I like that." He raised his hand, and from a ramp beneath the spattered old building, a black four-wheel drive, a Toyota Land Cruiser, flashed its headlights and came sailing up into the parking lot like a statement: I'm efficient, low key, I don't need to flash around in no BMW or sky-blue Cadillac. There was a woman in the back, a blonde, but it was a guy, one of Ricky Lee's crew, also dressed in black, who got out of the driver's seat, while another black Toyota made a U-turn outside the thrift shop and, having pulled up, disgorged three more bodyguards, impressive and imposing feats of nature who planted themselves on the sidewalk like redwoods—Ricky Lee's show of force.

Now I was supposed to feel small.

"These are the rules. One of my guys will call you each morning with a new number and you can check in if you need to. I can't have cops calling me whenever they get the urge; hear what I'm saying?"

I smiled at his assumption of who was calling the shots. I wondered if he'd give me the shtick about how white cops had let a white guy get away with murder, but he didn't; he said not a word about the Corcoran case. He knew Los Angeles was out of joint and didn't worry about trying to set it right. Maybe he *expected* criminals to be rewarded, so long as they knew how to work the system. Ricky Lee tried very much to come on like a movie star himself, with class, no longer needing to strive, but still restless and mercurial, edgy, almost overly conscious of the qualities that had made him who he was. No fool, a ghetto star who no longer lived in the ghetto, he needed the bodyguards in case rival gangsters tried a kidnap. There were probably Uzis stashed beneath the seats in those Land Cruisers, weapons for which he'd have obtained permits.

He said, "This is how it was between my mother and

me. I lied to you last night. I didn't see her much at all. She wouldn't let me. She wouldn't let me help her or see her. Everything changed for her after my brother died. She was a good woman, she was in pain, and I know everything would have come right between us in the end."

Wanting to keep this going, I said, "My mother died about twenty years ago. It was cancer; back in England."

"You spent time in England? Hey, my girlfriend, she's always talking 'bout going to Paris. See the fashion shows 'n all that shit."

In the distance there was the rumble of heavy thunder. "Paris is in France."

"Shit, I know that; you think I'm a dumb nigger?" The back door of the first Toyota was opened by one of the redwoods, and Ricky Lee's girlfriend got out, a blond model type, one long black-sheathed leg languidly coming after the other. "Sugar," he called, waving, and I briefly glimpsed the diamond in his dental work again before the smile was wiped from his face and he got down to business. "That other thing I spoke of last night? Stands. I'm not insulting you, man, I'm serious. Five hundred thousand. Like I said, I *need.*"

This time, before I could respond, the elevator doors opened and out stepped the guy from the FBI and the one from the DEA. The former wore a black slicker and a black baseball cap above whose sides the bony cartilages of his ears stuck out like flags; the latter sported cowboy boots, a snakeskin belt, and flowing blond hair like George Custer. The serious law-and-order merchants looked like a pair of clowns.

Ricky Lee took them in at a glance. "Feds? Tell them they can't have me," he said without a smile, and I watched as he walked outside to hug his girlfriend. The two of them got into the first of the black Toyotas; then both cars headed in convoy out of the parking lot before merging with the traffic on Mission Avenue and speeding toward the freeway.

The DEA guy came up to my side with his fingers tucked inside that snakeskin belt, saying, "Nobody even really knows if that guy's dealing drugs anymore. He's more secretive than the CIA and he's spread his cash around. Real estate. Corner stores. Stocks and bonds. Several boats." He hitched up his pants. "But I'll tell you something. That guy's not gonna go on getting away with what he's been getting away with."

"I'm not sure I quite understand that."

"You think he killed his own mother?"

He'd scarcely be offering me a fortune if he'd killed her, not unless he was a lot more twisted and tortured than I thought. "Hey, that's quite a notion," I said. "Excuse me."

From a phone in the lobby I dialed the office. Various business cards had been stuck to a bulletin board above the receiver. There was one from Forest Lawn, quite a few from other funeral homes, and one I'd never seen before: "Crime Scene: Steam 'n Clean." Cataresco answered and this time the subject of Corcoran did come up. "That guy should be exterminated," she said.

"Maybe he'll have a thrombosis signing the first of his no doubt various three-million-dollar book deals."

"I'm praying," she said, while I thought, Five hundred thousand dollars; that's also a shitload of money. I wasn't really aware of being tempted. I was just wondering, idly, off-handedly, not even seriously, what I'd do with it. Five. Hundred. Thousand. Dollars.

Cataresco was saying that Mae Richards had at one time been a singer. "This was from one of the neighbors who just called me back. Mae also paid her bills on time and worked hard. Turns out she wasn't exactly a cleaner herself but ran a small cleaning business, organizing work for eight or nine other women."

"What kind of a singer? When was this?"

"Don't know yet."

"My mother used to sing."

"You never mentioned that. Do you *have* a mother, Billy? I thought you were created by the Department with a murder book in your hand."

"Used to. She always blamed my father for the fact that when they split her career was about to happen. Divorce denied her a glamorous Los Angeles screen career, and she had to retreat to England. Most likely it was bullshit."

Maybe it was, but that was my mother's story. Something was always denying her something. She saw no romance in her failure. The damage to her pride made her spit and lash out, and yet, oddly enough, it wasn't my father who'd made me dream of and long to return to America. It was my mother, together with my grandfather. She didn't talk about the place or her experiences there very often, but when she did, it was with a bitter glow, remembering a promise broken, fulfillment almost attained and then denied. I don't think she ever wanted to have children. She talked about America the way Drew Diamond did about the sixties; you knew it could never have been quite that good, but your curiosity was aroused. America continued always as a part of her story, her myth.

My grandfather told me of the grit, the reality, first in terse and funny letters, and later when he came to see us in England. He and my mother always got along. He called her Princess. He himself was Duke, though the suggestion was anything but aristocratic. To witness this duke in an English seaside boarding house was to watch a man uncomprehendingly at war with an alien horse. He held cucumber sandwiches as though they were Venus fly traps, possibly deadly and not for nourishment. He never spoke to me about his work in those days. This was soon after he'd retired, decked out with every medal and merit badge the Department had to offer; and at that time, even more so than now, the Department went in for status decorations in a big way. He and I would sit in front of a small TV set and wait for the BBC to bless us with a Western. He took my plastic soldiers, built a model on a low table with sand from the beach scattered beneath it, and illustrated for me just how it had gone down at the OK Corral. "You don't wanna be a cop, Billy," he said. "Get some education. Remember what the job did to your father." I didn't know then what the job had done to my father. I inferred something bad.

"Maybe we should discuss this over a drink, your mother, your family," said Cataresco. Down the other end of the line I heard her eating, avocado and alfalfa sprout sandwich, I guessed, her usual office snack. She never went out for lunch. The first time I met her I'd known she was ambitious. This was up in the Hollywood Hills, at the Academy. I'd been requalifying for shooting. She sat at my table in the cafeteria for coffee, just a rookie, having decided to become a cop after taking a degree in business administration. She asked how long I thought it would be before she made captain. These days the smart people in the Department viewed it not as an instrument of justice, but as an unwieldy and manipulable corporation, a series of rungs up the promotional ladder to a decent salary or transfer. Behind the wheel of a car, she drove smoothly but fast. Drew was out of date, she was the new model, and I was in between, the crossroads man.

"A drink, right," I said, wondering about "Crime

Scene: Steam 'n Clean." Maybe they went in and laun
dered your home after murder was done there. Some
job; but if there was an angle to be found, someone in
Los Angeles would find it. Across the lobby the guys
from the FBI and the DEA were exchanging business
cards. "You know anything about Steam 'n Clean?"

Her voice was exasperated. "Billy, what are you talking about?"

"Listen, I've been thinking about the details that don't
fit. The strawberries. I don't know why, but I've got a feeling she didn't buy them herself. The shell casing—I think
it was put there because someone wanted us to find it.
And the garbage bag. Did anyone check on that?"

"You gave the job to Drew, remember? Before you
fired him from the case."

"So I did. But let's find out where that thing came
from. There's usually a batch number somewhere. I'll
see you at the office later, OK?"

Having hung up, I saw the conversation between the
two federal agents flicker and die, as if they'd been talking about me, most likely asking each other whether I
could be trusted, comparing notes on what they'd heard,
wondering how I could be used to get to Ricky Lee. This
time the FBI guy spoke, the one with the baseball cap
and the hard pink ears. "I heard about the job you did
on the Farber case. Outstanding! Out*stand*ing! Farber
was a swift and evil perpetrator."

"A stone killer," said the one who fancied himself
like George Custer. "I heard you got him right between
the eyes."

"I was shooting to miss." I told them to be in touch if
I could help in any way, and crossed the lobby to pass
through the glass doors into the sparkle and deluge of
the rain.

8

VENICE, OR SO I UNDERSTAND, THE OTHER VENICE, Venice, Italy, is a city of museums, of picturesque gondolas, of splendid palaces somewhat in decay, and canals that, come summer, turn to soupy swill. My Venice was likewise a city of contrasts. Millionaire actors rubbed shoulders with gangsters. Flophouse motels butted up next to fancy gyms and stores where you couldn't even buy a T-shirt for $95. Parrots and palm trees were nature's aerial accompaniment to baseheads, dope dealers, hookers (known as strawberries, as in pick what you like), and other, more earthly essentials of urban life. The streets at either end of the local high school were barricaded off to discourage drive-bys. Restaurants opened and shut again within weeks, only to give birth to others on the exact same location. The beach, by day the blond capital of the known universe, was transformed at night into a battleground of the lost. My Venice was small, brilliant, spacy, and mean.

I lived and worked by the beach and I loved it. This was my place, where homeboys paraded their pit bulls alongside the tourists, the tarot readers, the scam artists, and the panhandlers hustling a dollar for the next ham-

burger. Drew Diamond accused me of being too kind to
these people. "What's it with you and the dude in the
liquor store? You ain't turning into one of those touchy-
feely guys, are you, Billy?" I didn't bother telling him
that compassion was a tool like any other.

The house where I'd lived with Ellen and Lucy had
been bought at the top of the 1980s market with the help
of a loan from Ellen's father. Later, when his business
was failing, we'd taken out a hefty mortgage to pay him
back, and that was the big beginning of our money trouble. Part of Ellen's thinking for the move to Seattle was
that at least she'd be able to escape with some of the capital we'd sunk into the place, our lovely white elephant,
which to me these days now belonged on a continent
apart, even though I'd helped build the porch and had
hung the wind chimes above the rocker with the faded
and now drenched cherry-red cushions.

I walked up the ramps to find the doors open and the
TV on without the sound, as if Ellen were expecting
someone. Channel 5 was showing *King Kong,* the remake
with Jessica Lange, the part where Kong staggered lost
through the streets of New York. Kong was scratching
his head as Ellen's quick voice came from the kitchen.
"You want a cup of coffee?"

"Please, that'd be great."

There was a pause before she said, "Oh, Billy, is that
you?"

I picked up a book from the coffee table, a fat new
biography of Mozart. "Who else were you expecting?"

"I'll be with you in a minute," she said.

I'd loved living in this house. The rooms were light
and high, a lofty dream of peace. Now, every time I came
back, there was a change. Books and flowers seemed to
be breeding, filling the tables and the shelves on either

side of the fireplace. A great red-and-yellow paper bird hung from the ceiling, swaying this way and that in the currents from the central heating. The old curtains were gone, replaced by ones with green and white stripes, which, in the rain, gave the room a pleasant underwater ripple. There was a table with a computer on it in the corner where my reading chair had been. I came here to be restored and replenished; it was home still, but it wasn't *my* home. I felt pangs of regret for those times in the past when I should have been here, with my family, and instead had been out there, on the streets, on Broadway, or at Sixth and Alvarado, or down in the Southland, obsessing about some guy with a gun or a knife in case he did it again and destroyed another family. There was the irony: I'd helped others but had been unable to save myself. I'd had a great wife, a great life, a beautiful daughter, and I'd blown it. It weighed, this sense of having failed.

Marriage is improvised. It's quicksilver; it rolls this way and that, needing to keep moving, needing to feel inspired. I knew, because I'd watched the treasure spill through my fingers.

Ellen said I romanticized the memory of our marriage, as Lucy romanticized me. Ellen herself romanticized only Marlon Brando. She admired Brando unreasonably. Before the shooting she'd pad through the house barefoot or, if the dog was shedding fleas, in a pair of thunderous clogs, mumbling lines from *The Godfather* or *Apocalypse Now.* She'd sprawl in a chair, legs dangling, and then leap up, waving her finger to make a point. All that energy was still there, inside. She'd always taken the world seriously, granted it due weight, so she wasn't surprised when it turned around and clobbered her. She put on a pair of gloves and hit back. Before the shooting, she'd been strong and tireless, and I suppose that since then I'd tended not to see her as a real person with real faults. She had poise and imagination, but she could be childish—can't we all? She had a cool front that said she was totally in control of her life; she wasn't. My guilt had put her on a pedestal, which she hated. She wept and raged sometimes against the uselessness of her legs.

With her, my unsure self kept popping up like a stain. "Billy Zero," I introduced myself to her new friends, and she knew that truth glimmered in the joke, as well as an inappropriate self-pity. I was nothing without her; at least, I was having to search for what I could be. "Face it, man," Ted had told me, in his cups again but for once on the money. "Without her, you're fucked."

She was where I turned when I was losing my bearings and didn't even know it.

I said, "Where's that cup of coffee?"

She came to me, wheeling her chair from the kitchen with one hand and balancing my coffee in the other. She wore black leggings beneath a loose-fitting smock of purple and gold; her feet were bare, because she couldn't feel the cold, though the toenails were carefully polished. She stopped the chair, cleared a space between a pile of books and a flower vase on the dining room table, set down the cup, and offered her soft mouth for me to kiss. She was quick, observant, energetic. She was beautiful still, though gray had mingled with the younger chestnut. Shit, I thought, I have nothing to offer this woman.

I surprised myself, saying, "I'll quit the job. Move with you guys to Seattle."

She seemed not to hear, or else she was weighing this, trying to take it in. She said, "I heard about the verdict. I'm sorry. You must be furious."

"It was predictable."

"Which doesn't make it any better."

"No, I guess not. I half hoped there'd be a riot—you know, a spontaneous outburst, anger, *something*. The guy would know what an asshole the world thinks he is. But people seemed pleased."

"Corcoran's got charm as well as money. He's brilliant, capable, funny. In their book Denise got lucky, made an ambitious marriage, and getting smacked was all a part of it."

"You're angry."

"I guess I am. How does it make you feel?"

"Right now? Exhausted, ready to quit." In recent months, as it became certain that we'd lose the case, I'd reminded myself that people in shock sometimes confessed to murders they hadn't committed, as if they needed to release a different guilt they felt, maybe about having let the victim down, not having done enough. "Maybe he didn't do it, after all."

"You were there, Billy. You were the one. Tell me whether he did it or not."

From outside came the brief rumble of rap as a homeboy's car cruised by, and I thought of something else I loved about this house. It was beautiful, but close to the boundary. You couldn't hide here and forget what the city was like. You saw the dangerous edge of things. Most cops I knew didn't live in the city anymore. They bought tract houses in Simi Valley or drove an hour or more at the end of their shift to retreat behind the walls of security estates in the Inland Empire. I suppose I resented that. Venice was difficult, dangerous, and certainly a mixed place to raise a child, but still a great place to live. I shook my head. "I can't believe you're leaving."

She turned in the direction of the CD player and put

on something big and romantic. "How do you like this music? Lucy's gift for my birthday last week, which by the way you forgot."

I'd forgotten? How could I have done that? "Last Wednesday. Jesus. I was helping a homicide guy from West Covina."

"It's OK; it's OK. I've heard the story often enough."

"*Shit.* Oh, Ellen, I'm sorry."

"I don't want your sorrow, Billy. I'm your ex-wife. Not your *crippled* ex-wife." Her slim strong hands were shaking a little. "I don't understand what you want from me anymore."

There was a pause, her eyes not leaving mine, and then she glanced away, toward the fireplace.

"Hey, a sandwich would be good," I said, and she looked at me again, her eyes crinkled and lit up with a smile.

"You're such an idiot."

"Don't rub it in. Come on. Let's have a hot date in the kitchen."

Once upon a time, back in the fairy tale days, we'd sat together in these rooms, listened to music, and planned the future. Ellen had written questions on index cards and quizzed me about the next promotion exam. I always thought I was the driven one, the homicide star, the half-English guy who was nonetheless on top of the need to get to the point quickly, comfortable on the streets, soothing the victims, and easing the ride for the management jockeys. Early on, even before the Pakistani who killed his son, I'd had a couple of good cases, easy cases, really, not much detective work involved, but high profile: I busted a terrorist who slit the throat of a secretary in the Federal Building on Wilshire a couple of months prior to the '84 Olympics, and then I talked down the serial killer who started taking potshots from the roof of a motel. I remembered being up there, baking in the heat, hot Santa Ana winds scorching my scalp and making my dazzled eyes water. That was in San Pedro, too. I didn't care much for San Pedro.

There seemed to be good reasons for the presumption that my career was the more important, and those reasons had been part of the implied bargain between us, a flaw in the marriage. "We were apart when I was hurt," she'd once said. "Doesn't that tell you something?"

In the kitchen after Ellen's accident we'd torn out all the previous fittings and replaced them with counters at waist height and cupboards below so that everything was in reach of her wheelchair. Guys I'd never even met before had collected money from all of the city's eighteen divisions and come around to help. They'd hired an architect, a studious-looking young German, who'd said where to put in the ramps and had rethought the place and redesigned the bathroom. They'd put in a security system and an intercom that connected with the neighbors. I'd always been a loner within the Department, but, looking at Ellen and seeing the work they did and the help they gave, I had the same dangerous and sentimental feeling that so many of them shared, namely, that because being a cop was the greatest and the shittiest and most thankless job in the world, no one else could understand us. I started feeling guilty and anxious, and soon I was never not feeling that way, even when the immediate cause was something else.

"You want mustard or mayonnaise?"

"Both. Plenty of each."

"How bad was the rain when you came in?"

"Still pretty bad."

"I've got to try to get to the store later."

"I can pick up some stuff if you like."

"No, really, it's OK." She smiled. "Thanks, though."

Through the kitchen window I watched steam rise from the asphalt tiles on the garage, against which Lucy's bike leaned, covered with a tarp; on the washing line an old denim shirt hung limp and heavy. From here at night I used to watch the moon rising among and then above the palms.

We kept going over the same ground, and I could never quite admit to having lost the battle. I lost all balance in her company, there was so much there still tearing at me. It was like the job: aging and bad luck had fucked up what was a noble thing. But that was too easy; in the case of my marriage there was also the matter of my bad choices.

She said, "Ted called. He said he wanted to apologize, not to me, but to you. I don't get it. Why was he calling here? Did you tell him you'd be swinging by today?"

I couldn't say it was because Ted held to the notion that Ellen and Lucy and I would one day live together again. "Ted's confused."

"He was always confused. Just what did happen last night?"

"Like I said, nothing. How was Lucy this morning?"

"She's fine. Yesterday she asked if it would be OK if she became an astronaut. Then she said she had a crush on a boy at school and should she be thinking of sleeping with him?"

"Christ, she's eleven years old."

"I thanked her for sharing this with me, and told her it was really way too early for all that."

Ellen spread butter on the bread, then mustard and

mayonnaise; she built layers of ham, cheese, tomato, and lettuce, one on top of the other, and pressed down gently on the two slices before cutting them in half with one firm, confident stroke.

"If you're going because of the money, don't. I'll find the money, OK?"

"Billy the optimist."

"Billy the hope-deserted," I said. "I only feel good at work. Think how bad things must be."

"You always felt good at work," she said, holding on to her calm. "I'm not going because of the money. I've got a job, remember?"

"And you couldn't get one here?"

"Maybe. I don't want to. I want the one I've been offered up there."

She turned in her wheelchair, touched hair out of her eyes. "I can't discuss this now. I've got an appointment in half an hour."

"With Megan?"

Ellen, resolutely unflaky in all other matters, went to see a psychic, or rather consulted one, for these days psychics had gone straight. No longer were they middle-aged hippies living in ramshackle bungalows near the exits to freeways. Megan had another of those degrees in business administration and read the runes by phone or fax. She talked about closure, completion, journeys, and all the rest of that New Age paraphernalia, while of course continuing in vague terms to see success, a new job, the possibility of a life lived according to love.

"No, with someone else."

As she moved her hand to close the fridge door, I saw that she was wearing a bracelet, a silver thing inlaid with linked silver-and-turquoise dolphins. I remembered a warm spring afternoon in the bedroom right above our heads when, home from work early, she'd walked toward me naked except for gold earrings and a gold chain around her ankle. She'd always loved jewelry. It made her feel wanton, she said once. I think I'd made some stupid joke about Chinese food.

"What?" she said.

"Nothing."

"You were looking at me weird."

If I hadn't been unfaithful a couple of times when I was working down in South Bureau, Ellen and I might never have split, and if we hadn't she might never have fallen through that skylight on Olympic. All this was spilled milk, I knew, and no use sobbing, but I'd cheated; I'd married a quality person, messed around, and lost her.

"That's new?" I said.

"What?" she said, touching her wrist.

"There, the bracelet."

"Oh, this. Yeah, it's new. You'd better go now. I've got to get ready."

It was only then that I put it together. "You're seeing someone."

She nodded, sighing, before her eyes met mine full on. "Yes, I'm seeing someone."

"You're having an affair?"

"Affairs only happen to married people. We're not married anymore, remember?"

The computer where my reading chair had been, the freedom bird on the ceiling: this wasn't a casual thing. "Is it serious?"

"You have no right to ask."

"Of course I do."

"Yes, maybe. It's serious."

"Who's the guy?"

"Someone I like."

Jealousy made the furious sprint from my liver to my brain. "No kidding? I'm not questioning your taste. I know you've got Lucy to think of and will be smart in this area."

"I've learned, you mean?"

Touché, I thought, a hit, and the blade was unbuttoned; I was bleeding. "I guess you have. Who is he?"

"I'm not going to let you interrogate me."

"He's on his way over now? In the middle of the day. He's not even a working guy?"

"Oh, sure, that's right, I've picked a member of the idle rich. Frankly, Billy, it's none of your damned business. A guy's made the time to come and take me for lunch. It could be Mickey Mouse, and you'd have to like it."

"I'd have no problem with Mickey."

"Here's yours." She handed me a plate with the sandwich tightly wrapped in tinfoil.

"This is it? I have to go now?"

She was looking toward the living room. "I think you'd better watch this."

On TV King Kong had been gunned down by the U.S. Air Force and Channel 5 had the news. Ellen hit the sound.

First of all there was the headline item, a restatement of the trial verdict and a review of Corcoran's career. There was footage of the guy, grinning and sheepish, at the Oscar ceremony, as if saying to the world: "What, all this for little old me?" There were shots of various beautiful and famous women holding his arm as if it were everything, and there was a reminder of how he'd looked on the night of his arrest, with his dark suit rumpled and his eyes shut down.

The reporter herself popped up next, with her tweed jacket and black leather vest. It was Ward Jenssen. Her hair seemed even shorter than I remembered from just a couple of hours before, but then it was very possible she'd had it styled during the interim. "And now yet more clouds loom on the horizon for this once prestigious Police Department." There was film of the crowd in front of Mae Richards's house, a picture of Ricky Lee, one of me with my hand in front of my face, and then Ward Jenssen was back, retelling the more romantic aspects of Ricky Lee's career, laying it on thick that he'd given thousands of dollars toward the building of a sports center in an abandoned movie theater down in South Central. They showed a clip from a movie in which he'd had a small part, and that was news to me. Then there was the sound of my bleating, "No comment, no comment," and "Will you turn this thing off?" After that, Ward Jenssen wore a wolfish grin and said I was being handed this week's award as the most obstructive and rude member of a famously obstructive and rude department—of which more in a moment, she said. Then it was back to Charlie Corcoran, squinting, with a match between his teeth in a gangster role he'd played.

"I guess they figure they had to let him go because he's been famous for more than fifteen minutes," Ellen said. "You sounded like an asshole."

"Thanks."

"No problem." She was looking, not at me, but still at the screen, as she said, "She's even more attractive these days."

Now it was my turn to play dumb.

"Who?"

"Ward Jenssen."

"Oh, her. I thought you thought she was a snake."

"No, you were the snake, Billy."

It was Ward I'd slept with while I was working down in South LA. It had only happened a couple of times, but Ellen had come by the precinct house when Ward was there, and she sensed the shock of electricity that passed between us. After that there'd been no retreat into denial, and this had happened when Ellen and I were going through stormy weather: not having enough money, not fucking often enough, not getting enough sleep, arguing about when and whether to have another child. I'd wanted the second youngster.

Ward was back on screen now, about to come in with her big punch. I should have seen it coming after what happened back at the courthouse. She said, "McGrath's father was also a detective. He resigned from the Department in disgrace some thirty-five years ago, following a case that involved none other than Charlie Corcoran."

"Oh, shit," said Ellen. "I don't believe this. They never quit, these people . . ."

Ward told how a young woman, an actress, had got drunk and drowned off Malibu in November 1961. A lone, mysterious witness walking his dog said he'd seen Charlie Corcoran in the water with her, though Corcoran, then at the beginning of his career, denied it, and several other witnesses stepped up to say they'd been with him in Santa Barbara, where he'd been attending a charity function. No charges were brought, and my father, one of the investigating detectives, left the Department in disgrace three months later. Corcoran, meanwhile— incredibly handsome—had risen above the scandal to success, sustaining a glittering career through his thirties, forties, on into late middle age.

Of course I'd known the story: it was the beginning

of my father's inexorable downward slide, though Ward said nothing of that, nor of certain other interesting details. For instance: my father had received a sworn and signed statement from that mysterious dog walker on the beach, while the Santa Barbara witnesses, all of them, had been on the payroll of Corcoran's press agent.

Ellen said, "But you told his lawyers all about this, didn't you?"

"Sure I did, because their investigators would have dug up the story anyway." Its one real bearing on the Denise Corcoran case was the obligation I'd felt to slip aside from the wheel and allow Drew to drive the investigation. "And now they're having their fun."

Her distress was genuine. "It isn't fair, Billy. It isn't right."

"I know it. Everything's out of whack."

I was on screen again myself, denying that I'd tried to frame Corcoran. I looked angry and defensive, saying, "This is absurd," and then it was Charlie himself, smiling, with "No comment, no comment, no comment," and one of Charlie's million-dollar lawyers, maybe even the one who'd slipped Ward all this, looking into the camera with a thoughtful pause before: "We didn't bring up any of this before, because we didn't want the trial to turn into a personal issue, and because of Detective McGrath's great reputation. Now that it's come out in the open—well, I'm not saying the guy is *necessarily* a bad apple. I'm saying this revelation may throw some interesting light on why the city has harassed an innocent man and thrown away millions of dollars on a futile case they could never have won. Sons, sadly, do turn into their fathers."

Storm clouds heaved and shouldered in the Sepulveda Pass. The unmarked Chevrolet followed a surge of water down the throat of a curving exit ramp choked with rain, and I stepped on the gas, reckless up San Vicente, then north toward Sunset, the hills beyond, and the gates of the house whose address I was apt to remember. A camera eye inspected me as I announced myself through the rain to the buzzing intercom. Almost to my surprise, the gate opened and I drove up the gravel drive to where four Cadillacs, five BMWs, three Rolls-Royces, and a pair of twin red Ferraris were huddled together out of the rain under a carport in the parking area. Corcoran was having a party.

The house was spare, beautiful, an idyll, its huge windows commanding a view of the city all the way down to Long Beach. Standing by the pool at the back, I remembered, you seemed to float above the entire San Fernando Valley. Either way you were up above the world. Charlie also had a ranch in Utah and a Manhattan triplex overlooking Central Park. He kept a suite at one of the big hotels in Beverly Hills and Triumph motorcycles, each with the same lock, in airport parking garages at twelve of the country's major cities. Sometimes he disappeared for days on end, apparently to ride his bike from St. Louis to Chicago or from Denver all the way to New Orleans, to hit the road and hear the engine sing.

Maybe I'd misheard when I was out here the night of the murder. Maybe my ear had been only too greedy for what it thought Charlie said, for what it wanted Charlie to have said: *"I lost my head, man. I killed her."* We can hallucinate, we may be wrong about the exact nature of something we touch, but no sense is as vulnerable as hearing; then again, I'd felt so sure: this guy is guilty as sin, guilty as me.

All through the trial I never thought that I might be interested in vengeance. I tried to behave honestly and honorably, admitting the connection between him and my father, making a tactical withdrawal from the daily detail of the case. Now all my certainties slid away in the swirl and extravagant hammer of the storm.

I was thinking about my beginnings, about how I was made in the back of that Porsche Speedster, my mother primed with schoonerfuls of Scotch whiskey. She said many times she wasn't sure where I got my temper, Johnnie Walker Red or Black. I was thinking about Ellen and her new boyfriend. I felt under attack. I felt crazy and enraged. It was as if Charlie and his people with their power were trying to annihilate me.

I didn't know what I was going to say. I thought maybe I wouldn't have to say anything at all, not about the trial, not about my father. I thought maybe I'd let my mere presence ruffle his feathers. I thought maybe I'd hit him, hurt him, or worse. I was thinking a lot of things.

I was met at the door by the bodyguard, six-foot-five and wiry-haired, an agile hulk who looked me over with no great affection before lifting a fat cigar, rolling his lips around the butt, and luxuriating in what was less a puff than an insult. "Detective," he said. His name was Ari Van Duzer; I'd have thought twice about picking a fight with him even had I not known that he'd been trained by the Mossad. "Don't you think you've bothered him enough?"

"Not nearly."

"I can't let you in. You know that. I'm gonna have to ask you to leave, unless, of course, you have a warrant. Do you have a warrant?"

His voice was calm while the smile leaked out of his eyes and we stood facing each other, him with the cigar still between his teeth, in the wide open space of the white entrance hall.

Ellen had told me not to do anything stupid. Ward was only doing her job. What did I expect? Reporters sought intimacy so that they could betray you. I'd told her it wasn't Ward I was blaming.

There was a sculpture alone on a table in the center of the hall: twelve inches high, a girl, upright, holding a bowl; it was simple, beautiful; it looked ancient. I picked it up, felt its history and beauty in my palm. I tossed it by its feet and caught it by its head. "How much would you say this is worth?"

"A lot more than you've got," said the bodyguard, starting toward me, then backing off. He thought I might really break it. He was right.

"You don't say?" The statue, by its feet again, by its head: the neck was surprisingly strong. "They built things to last back then, didn't they? Not like the cheap crap you get these days." I pantomimed dropping the statue, then juggled with it. "Whoa!"

A door opened to my left, and Charlie Corcoran himself came in, hair still wet as if he'd come in from the rain or, more likely, just stepped out of the shower. Perhaps a woman had been waiting for him back here, a first romp around the mattress after six months in jail, though there were rumors that he'd been taken care of there, too; perhaps he'd told himself he could wash it all away. He was wearing a white T-shirt and black sweats, with no shoes.

For a moment he looked at me in silence while he massaged the top of his scalp with a towel. "McGrath, isn't it?"

Corcoran's voice was one of his great assets. Its studied use was low and hesitant, giving him a diffidence, as well as a charm, that belied his chiseled, still almost beautiful features. He was tall for a movie star, about six-three, and in company he tended to lean forward, an apologetic seeking of intimacy, all part of the act. In front of his own mirrors he was probably a peacock, though his habits of solitude hadn't been easy to imagine even before I was sure that he'd murdered his wife.

"I see you're admiring my statue. It's Babylonian. Fifth century. That's B.C."

"Really?" I did the head and feet thing again. "My wife's got one just like it from Pier One. Tell me how it feels; tell me how it feels to be you."

"You still think I killed her, don't you?"

"I know you killed her."

"How can I tell you how it feels to be me if you misunderstand this most basic of facts?"

"You shot her, Charlie. Pow. How can you live with yourself?"

"Very easily: because I'm innocent."

One of his friends appeared at the door. "Charlie, everything OK? Want me to call the cops?" I recognized the attorney from the courtroom and, more recently, the TV. "Oh," he said. "How wonderful. This *is* the cops."

I tossed the celebrity lawyer the statue and he caught it, but not like Socrates neatly pouching a troublesome toss from Plato. There was a certain amount of agonized uncertainty, even, I'd say, juggling.

"It's over, Corcoran. Your career's over."

He pretended not to hear, and instead continued to rub his hair with the towel. "Are you sure you won't stay for champagne?"

At that moment I thought that getting away with murder was perhaps a less difficult problem than not murdering. I tried to hit where I could, screaming inside because I knew I couldn't touch the guy. "You're rich, clever, and lucky, and you're still finished. You'll never come back from this."

"We'll see," said Corcoran. "Meanwhile, why don't you do your job?"

"I am doing my job."

"No, you're not. Your job is to catch the butcher who killed my wife, but you're too lazy and arrogant and probably too incompetent to do it."

"I'll fucking nail you, Corcoran."

"You'll *nail me.* You'll *fucking* get me? Where are we now? In the schoolyard?" With his towel still in hand, he turned to his bodyguard. He moved slowly, like a man who takes care of his heart. "Ari, deal with this, please."

I'd barely moved myself before a fist drove the air from my body and I was dumped out in the rain.

9

LARRY MURAKAMI ALMOST ALWAYS KEPT THE DOOR TO his office open. He liked to eavesdrop on whatever was happening in the rest of the squad room, so I knew something was in the air when his secretary shut it behind me without a smile. Larry himself was rocking in his black leather chair, feet up on an open desk drawer, and bouncing a Ping-Pong ball against the wall. He didn't bother to turn in my direction. "Just had a chat with the mayor," he said, and the ball returned to his hand with a cruel slap. "Who in turn has been the happy recipient of communications from Charlie Corcoran's attorney and Mr. Corcoran himself, threatening a five-million-dollar suit against the city for harassment. You can imagine that the mayor was delighted."

Larry Murakami was chief of detectives and, to be honest, not much of a detective. He was cool and reserved, neither truthful nor trustworthy, a small man with dark eyes that missed very little. I liked him. He used the word "incent" as a verb. Larry had been my great ally in attaining the promotion over Drew. He kept a TV in his office to follow the news and, if he didn't get home in time, to be sure not to miss the latest episode of *Jeopardy.*

He was devoted to *Jeopardy* because he generally knew more answers than the contestants. Politics was his game, though he also patrolled the aisles of discount warehouses in search of designer suits with the labels torn out, or, during the sales, Fred Segal, with his two teenage daughters in tow. Three years running he'd won the award for Best-Dressed Detective of the Year. Even though I appreciated that the Department, strange and labyrinthine, liked to mark out its employees in unusual ways, I'd thought Drew Diamond must be kidding when he told me about this, though the proof was there, x3, in black ebonized frames up on the wall against which Larry was playing Ping-Pong without the paddle.

"This is stupid, Billy; this isn't you." Larry wasn't brilliant, but what he had he used well. He ate cheese, not meat. He drank Pellegrino and shared a dentist with Robert Redford. From the outside, my career looked the more glamorous; in reality, I was at the dark end of a murder tunnel while he cruised an open road toward a bigger paycheck and professional advancement. His hand went up once more, Indian style, and closed around the returning blur of white. "It wasn't even your case, not really. It was Drew's. Drew's screw-up, not yours."

"Right. And now I'm being accused of trying of frame the guy so his story'll look even better on the cover of *People* next week."

"See this?" he said, holding up the Ping-Pong ball and turning to me now for the first time since the conversation began, his square hopeful face so clean and waxy it resembled the varnished inside of a tuna. His thick black hair meanwhile swept back from his forehead with a pompadoured flourish.

"It's a Ping-Pong ball, Larry."

"It's plastic wrapped around air. It's structure. Take

away either one, take away the plastic or the air, and whaddya got?"

"Two disappointed guys holding paddles? Come on, Larry, what is this bullshit?"

"No structure. And without structure, *nothing.* And you know something else. I envy you, Billy—no, don't smile, it's true—because you have a talent, a gift. You can be great at what you do. There are guys in the Department who get copies of your murder books and study them like works of art. Now you've lost your home and family and you're finally beginning to realize you won't get them back and it's killing you."

"Gee, Lar, thanks."

"The only structure left? This." He tossed me the Ping-Pong ball. "Your work. Without this you will fly apart and die."

I turned the ball between my fingers. "This is a bunch of bull, Larry. You want me to be nice so I'll carry on making you look good and one day you'll be able to run for Congress."

"As for Charlie Corcoran, you're just gonna have to swallow. He'll get his in another life."

"Oh, really? You get that on the channel from Mila Repa, or maybe it was the Buddha himself?"

"Money won it. Fame won it. You did the best you could, and if Drew Diamond or the DA's office screwed up, then it's not your kangaroo. I hate murder. It makes me shiver. Maybe I'm afraid of being murdered myself. What do you think?"

"I think your head's like the inside of this Ping-Pong ball, Larry."

"Murder transforms everything."

"Right," I said. "Because afterward you're dead."

"*Right.* Your case is closed, just as the Corcoran case

is closed. On to the next. It's brutal, but what else can we do?" He made a pretense of glancing at a file on his desk. "The mother of Ricky Lee Richards, what was her name?"

"Mae."

"Get a clearance, and I don't mean next month. And let's keep the media off our backs, OK? That reporter, isn't she supposed to like you? You once gave each other minor flesh wounds, right? Work it, Billy. Be your best." He threw me a shrug and a sheepish grin and made a big deal of looking at his watch, a triangular piece whose black face kept perfect time stretched between the two halves of a luscious alligator strap. Moral faith being so hard to find and so very little in evidence, Larry championed certitude wherever he could find it, all the better if it belonged in a fashion catalogue and could be attached to some part of his anatomy. "Make me look good. I need to hold my head high at Barneys. OK, Billy?"

The Stardust was on Brooks, bad Venice, secret Venice. You could drive by and see only an abandoned motel, boarded up, with its eyes blind, but inside, beyond the crumbling white stucco and the drenched squares of plywood stamping out the windows, there was a world all unto itself. I parked the Chevy at the curb and locked it. Around here they'd steal even a cop car. With a raincoat over my head, feet swiping sideways, I ran down the puddled pathway, up the steps, heaved open the door, and stepped at once into darkness, a stew of putrid heat. The stench of shit, urine, and sweetly rotting garbage made me gag even though I'd known it was coming. This was the lobby, or what remained of it, into which no light ever penetrated because the low ceiling was left intact and a mountain of festering trash now filled almost the entire area. A path went around one side and you had to know about it; otherwise you'd never find your way in. A neat security system, in its own way, though not of the type preferred in Bel-Air. I stamped my feet to the accompaniment of rats.

The open courtyard, piled high as it was with more feces, soiled toilet paper, trash, concrete rubble, twisted steel girders, and old mattresses that steamed in the rain, came as a relief after that. I looked up and saw the sky, even if it was pissing on me.

This black hole had been pretty nice, ten years back, but it went out of business in a section of the neighborhood where it made no sense for anyone to take it over or even smash it down and recycle the empty lot. The rooms were on two levels, with stairs at each corner leading up to a perilous concrete walkway. Graffiti had been sprayed on every door and each remaining wall, or scorched with a blow gun.

At any one time there were fifty, maybe sixty people living here. Some drifted in for just a night or two, on the run, or with no place else to go. Others made it their permanent home. You didn't want to think how far they'd fallen or how beaten and banged up their souls must be. Some gathered strength and got the money together to move on. Others never did. They lived here, for years sometimes, until one day they suddenly gave up and then, after they were found (it might be a long while after), the doors of a red-and-white Fire Department vehicle closed behind them and they were whisked away to become part of Randy Juster's early morning tour.

Halfway along the first-floor corridor a door flew open and a woman's pale and angry face changed when she saw me. "Cop," she said, blank. "What a fucking honor." She was dressed in jeans and an enormous white T-shirt that slopped below her knees with the rain already flogging at it. Behind her on the floor I glimpsed a boom box and a red plastic thigh boot with a five-inch heel, part of her nighttime uniform, I guessed. With folded arms and puffy eyes she gave me the *nada, nada, I know nada.*

This was one of those situations I'd given up trying to make Drew Diamond understand. As a cop not needing a pinch, I could only gain by treating this woman with whatever suave Byronic grace I could muster. By the time I'd smiled, asked her name, and suggested that she might want to step back inside her room out of the wet, she wasn't exactly greeting me like a long lost brother, but her eyes had surrendered their position of sullen hostility. She even managed a smile and didn't slam the door in my face. It wasn't going easy on her; it was putting money in the bank for next time, another part of the game, but my way of playing.

I'd joined the Department soon after my father died, though not because he himself had been a cop. I was idealistic. I wanted to help. I remember sitting with the little girl I used to visit, the one who'd been struck dumb by the sight of her parents being killed. I'd taken her a teddy bear and a book by Dr. Seuss. She'd turned them between her fingers with an expression of intent absorption, processing them into her world, and my fantasy had been naïve, predictable: I thought that if I could stop something like this happening even once, if I could just save one, then being a police officer would be worthwhile. And I did save people, I did do good, when possible; but for every time that happened there were a score of missed opportunities and fuzzy situations, not because of me or even the job necessarily, but because of the way it was out there: tough, with too much compromise and too many degrees of gray. I saw pain, humiliation, and crushed innocence. I saw a lot of death, and yet on that afternoon, running away from my meeting with the Latina whore, running in the rain down the crumbling concrete of the upper corridor of the Stardust Motel, I felt an energy, a buzz, an adrenaline surge. I was actually grateful to Corcoran. He'd shown me I could still be appalled. My heart throbbed like a boat on the water.

Jack Brewster sat on the bed in his underwear. He was black, balding, skinny-legged, with small, dull brown eyes like buttons. He'd lived in this room for three years, working hard to give it a feel of comfort. There was a striped beach chair beside the bed, a chest of drawers rescued from a Dumpster, and a paraffin heater giving off its reeky fumes. Snapshots were pinned to a piece of cardboard, and he had a typewriter on which I guessed he pecked out letters to Social Security. Drapes of white muslin hung from the torn-out walls. The rain that came through the ceiling was caught by three strategically placed white tubs, which had once contained paint or glue and now kept up a drum beat of falling water. He looked at me and in no hurry started to pull on a pair of pants. "You know what Socrates said?"

"What did Socrates say?"

"I dunno. I forget. Wise words. No doubt helpful in this situation." His cough was unhealthy, a dog barking in a bucket of oil. "You know what Shane said before he died? I mean, you know what the *actor* Alan Ladd said before he died?"

"What did Alan Ladd say?"

"Some bitch asked him what he'd change in his life if he had the chance. He said, 'Everything.' I like that, man. *Everything.* You just makin' the acquaintance of Ruthie Pump, or you here to ask me for help?"

"Ruthie Pump?"

"The skinny whore you was being so unexpectedly nice to down the way."

"Oh, right."

"She's not such a bad kid. We take a walk together sometimes. No, not that kind of a walk. You've got an evil mind, detective. We stroll out together for a hamburger. Tommy's Original Famous. Her treat."

Twice a day Jack Brewster queued for meals at the Salvation Army down in Santa Monica, excursions during which he always waited for a bus with a black driver, a brother, so that he could travel for free. The rest of the time he rolled his supermarket cart past the variety of Venice, the bad alleys, the soup lines, the Mexicans waiting for work outside paint stores and auto repair shops, then past the hip restaurants, artists' studios and $500,000-loft conversions, proof of another Los Angeles. He didn't mind. He was by no means the city's poorest, and he accepted his lot. Jack Brewster knew the neighborhood. He heard things. He was steady and unflappable. He had two nephews, one in prison; I knew because I'd put him there after he'd got himself involved in a robbery.

"What do you know about Mae Richards?"

He took a breath. "She was murdered."

"You heard that?"

"Her son's homeboys are turning over every rock trying to find out who did it. Creating a lot of tension. Making people *very* unhappy." He made a face of combined pain and bemusement, tied a piece of string around his pants for a belt, and sat down on the bed again. "They say that anyone who ever did that boy a disservice, however small, lived to regret it in the end. He never forgets, never forgives. Vengeance is mine, I will repay, saith the Lord." With a rag he rubbed the bald spot at the front of his head. With the same cloth he set about wiping off his sneakers, a pair of white Nikes, and pulled them on, no socks. "I think he's like you, Detective McGrath. Someone I'd much rather have nothing to do with."

Brewster, who was younger than he looked, was a little afraid of me, though I regarded him almost as a friend.

"What about Mae?"

"Nice lady."

"How do you know?"

"Gave me her bottles and cans, slipped me a dollar every now and then. I saw her at church, I mean outside the church, I never go in myself. She worked, she was active in the neighborhood, she played the piano sometimes at the community center. Everybody liked her."

"Obviously not everybody. C'mon, Jack, give me something. I need something, like you once needed something from me." Brewster's nephew and a buddy of his had held up a Korean grocery store; the buddy had shot one of the owners in the face with a 9 mm. For a while the two of them were looking at murder, which was why I worked the case, but the woman was a tough old bird and she pulled through. The store security video had been running all the while the caper went down, and on it was Brewster's nephew, pleading with his buddy not to pull the trigger. I'd put in a word with the district attorney. With the kid up for parole in six months, Brewster owed me a favor.

"Heard about Charlie Corcoran," he said. "How that make you feel, detective?"

"Pissed off."

The rain went on filling the tubs with its steady patter while I strolled over to where Jack Brewster had the typewriter. There was a sheet rolled in. What he was typing wasn't to Social Security after all. It was something about his father, who'd lived in Mexico. I read: "I began to understand how different he was from anyone else I knew. He was interested only in making money. He was interested in making money *to keep,* very hard for a black man in America."

He cut me off. "Hey, don't you be looking at that. It's private."

"You writing a book here, or some kind of a story? Is that it?"

"None of your fucking business."

I held up my hands. "You're right, you're right. It's none of my business. Don't get all angry now." He was buttoning up his shirt. "You lived with your father in Mexico? That's interesting. When was that?"

He gazed up at me, embarrassed. I said, "You know, my father, he had the same problem. I guess he worked hard all his life but he could never get ahead of the game. He'd put away a few grand, maybe, but a bookie would always come along with the name of a horse for him to lose it on."

"He was a gambler, your father?"

"He was a cop, for a while."

"A cop like you?"

"No, not a cop like me." I didn't know for sure what sort of cop my father had been, but I was sure of that. I told myself he'd been a good cop. Maybe he'd have stuck at it, given the chance. "Look, Jack, you don't want to hear my autobiography and I don't especially want to read yours." I remembered Ellen's sandwich, wrapped in tinfoil and untouched in my pocket. "Here. My wife made this."

"You gotta wife?"

"Sure."

"She must be a tolerant lady." Pleased with himself, he spread open the tinfoil on his knees.

"She's a tolerant lady. We're divorced."

He was still laughing when he picked up half of the sandwich and tore off a bite. Chewing, he came to a decision. "A white guy came to Mae's house sometimes. Respectable-looking older dude. I don't think he came so they could talk about the civil rights movement or a recent biography of Martin Luther King."

"She owed him money?"

"I thought you were the detective."

"He came when—at night, or during the day?"

"Would vary. He had a way of walking—arrogant, you know, as if he thought he was somebody."

"You ever speak to him?"

"Once. I was there on the street when he pulled up in his big boat, so I hit on him for the price of a cup of coffee. He handed me a dollar bill without even looking at me. 'There you are, my man,' he said. He had kinduvva stiff accent, a little like yours."

"He was English?"

"Hell, I don't know. I never asked him. *You* ain't English?"

"Half and half. Neither fish, foul, nor good red herring."

"*Herring.* Fuck, I hate that shit."

"This guy who might have been English, you don't know his name?"

"No, detective, that I don't. He was rich, though, count on that. He smelled of money."

"And you say you saw him how many times?"

"Hey, I wasn't counting. More than a few."

"He was always on his own, this guy?"

"Why you ask that?"

"Just a question."

He answered carefully. "Yeah, far as I can remember, he was on his own."

I was trying to think around the edges of this woman's life. "What's the word on how she and her son got along?"

"She didn't like what he was messed up with, but what was she going to do about it? Blood is blood."

"And what about you, Jack? You ever meet Ricky Lee?"

"Never," he said, "and never cared to. I *hear* enough about him."

I remembered what Cataresco had told me over the phone. "She was a musician, right?"

"Right."

"She was a singer?"

"Right."

"You ever hear her?"

"Now why would I have done that, detective?"

"I'm just asking. Give me a break, OK? You holding out on me, Jack? You know that wouldn't be a wise thing to do."

He chose his words carefully now, though with a slight mockery. "Yessir, I do know that, and nossir, I'm not holding out on you. Why would I? I'm telling you all that I know. She lived in the neighborhood, she was admired in the neighborhood, she did good work. At one time she ran a theater group for kids, I believe. Her son became eminent in other ways."

"And her husband?"

"Was there one?"

"Ricky Lee had to have a father."

"I guess he did, but I don't know nothing about that."

"He was some kind of a musician. That's what Ricky Lee said."

"I really wouldn't know," said Jack Brewster, and tore off another bite of sandwich.

10

DANNY WEJAHN WAS THE ONLY ACCOUNTANT I'D EVER been able to sit across a table from without wanting to fall asleep, and the only guy in that line who'd ever looked at me as though I had a right to continued existence. He was a friend of Ted's, which maybe explains it, and he kept a boat in the marina, a trawler-class vessel bought with the booty from his most recent corporate layoff. He had a beard, a burly ease, and at first he gave an impression of lazy nonchalance, as if his day hadn't quite happened yet, nor did he expect it to, but then he'd surprise you with his swift and subtle nose for money or a deal. He didn't talk much—he was more of the watchful type—but occasionally he'd swipe me with a blurred rolling surf of speech, usually about one of his ex-wives, or the single life he bitched about but went on living, and then he'd give me a shy self-mocking grin, as if he hoped I hadn't heard.

We were sitting in a bookstore coffee shop on the Third Street promenade. Danny had secured his boat for the duration of the storm, he said, and taken a room at the Georgian Hotel on the ocean front. He was sipping at a low-fat latte. To compensate, he had a full-fat dark chocolate macadamia nut cookie in the other paw.

"How's life?" I said.

"A riot of mixed feelings."

"Don't I know it."

"Yeah, I caught you on the news. You looked—how shall I say?—well dressed. Otherwise, no comment."

A couple of kids were fooling around at the next table, one holding his thumb and forefinger against the other's head as if it were a gun. "So whatta ya gonna do?" the first kid was saying. "Ya gonna knock the gun away? Ya gonna say, 'Whaddya want?' C'mon, ya ain't got time to think. Whatta ya gonna do?"

"I hear you saw Ted last night, at the gallery."

"He was with some Japanese girl. She was lovely, like the girl before and the one before that. Ted's incapable of contentment. It's probably his most human and therefore his best characteristic."

"He told me what happened. He said for me to tell you he owes you—big time."

The storm was beating against the bookstore windows—not so muffled tom-toms.

Danny said, "You should take out life insurance."

"I've tried. They wouldn't have me."

"Perhaps if you decided to wear a bulletproof vest once in a while."

"They ruin my suits. Besides, I mostly deal with dead people. They tend not to shoot at me. I've long considered this a big advantage of my line of work."

"Be serious, Billy."

"You think I'm not?"

I got myself an espresso and we talked about the money I seemed never to have. I wasn't good with money. Even when I had some, it would find some new inventive way to escape me. I'd never had to break a date because I was lunching with a guy from Merrill Lynch. I said, "This is the bottom line. Ellen's going to Seattle. That appears to be written now. I want to free up some money to help her and Lucy with the move."

"There's nothing to free up."

"What about the retirement plan?"

"We cashed that in so you could make a deal on the apartment."

"Shit, I forgot that. I'll sell the fucking thing."

"It's worth less than what you owe on it."

"What about the Porsche?"

"Don't beat yourself up about this, Billy. Ellen's going to be fine. She's got a new job and a pension from the Department. You should worry about yourself."

"I want them to have whatever there is."

"At the moment that would be an embarrassment. *That's* the bottom line." He fingered the crumbs left by his cookie. "Forgive me for being tactless, but it's the truth, Billy. You're worth pretty much zip dead *or* alive. So why not err on the side of the latter?"

I wanted to ask him if he was sure about all this, if there couldn't be a mistake. I'd thought there'd be at least some available assets. If Ellen was truly set on Seattle, I desperately wanted to help, to prove I could still be useful. I felt embarrassed, ashamed, while Danny gave me a look that was part sympathy, part reproach; and one of the kids at the adjoining table mimed taking a bullet, reeling back and then pitching forward, eyes rolling, as if his head had been relieved of its brains.

It was close to four when I parked the Chevy and ran through the rain to the back door of the precinct house. A couple of patrol guys were standing in the doorway, sneaking guilty cigarettes. Smoking was banned inside these days. In the square, brightly lit squad room only Cataresco sat at the table beneath the wooden gun. She was on the phone with a spoon in a carton of yogurt in front of her.

I picked up my messages but first looked over a fax that had come in, a list of the houses worked by Mae Richards's little cleaning outfit. There were about thirty houses on the list, a lot of phone and legwork. All the houses had letters of the alphabet written in beside them; two or three were marked MR, perhaps places she went to herself or customers with whom she dealt on a personal basis. There were six other sets of initials— Mae's workers. I wondered what kind of boss she'd been. Maybe she'd been killed by an ex-employee with a grudge? That didn't seem to gel with the degree of hatred and sadism involved.

Lucy had called, as well as Randy Juster and Ted, and a detective in Denver who was helping me track down a suspect who'd fled out of state. Cataresco was off the phone now, spooning yogurt into her mouth.

"The reporter called. A couple of minutes ago, before you came in."

"Ward?"

"What is it with her? You insult her mother or something?"

"Not exactly."

Without saying anything, she stirred up the fruit from the bottom of her yogurt and then looked at me in a different way, wanting to see right inside me.

I shrugged, asking myself whether I'd answer Drew Diamond if he asked the same question. I wasn't sure; yet somehow I needed to tell Cataresco, to fan the memory back to life. "We had an affair, and I ended it, badly."

"I never knew that. When was this?"

"Five years ago. You speak to Lucy yourself?"

"No, it was Drew. Five years is an awful long time to stay angry, wouldn't you say?"

I called the number on Nowita Place: engaged. With the phone still in my hand, I looked over at Cataresco. "I've surprised you."

"No, no, yes, a little." Cataresco tapped her teeth with the edge of the plastic spoon. "She must earn a lot of money."

"Most likely, now. She was just starting up when I knew her."

"She obviously still likes you."

"Get outta here," I said, because the idea seemed outrageous at first, but I really didn't know what I meant to Ward or how she might view me. She'd given me a jolt, now as then. She came from Vernon, backlot California, about halfway between Los Angeles and San Francisco on Interstate 5. Her father had worked in a slaughterhouse. She'd talked about him when she wanted to say how much she hated drunks and violence. Originally she studied in San Diego, transferred to UCLA, and then landed at the *LA Times*, the beginning of her progress toward the yearned-for spotlight. I'd met her the first week she was working the crime desk and liked her because she didn't pretend to be cool about what she saw. She was naïve but spirited, editing her emotions for no one.

"Was she the reason why you and Ellen broke up?"

"One of them, though I can't blame her. I was the one who fucked up. I met this woman, she was young, bright, intelligent. Beautiful. I was at a certain point in my marriage. I saw all the other guys doing it. I thought, 'Why shouldn't I?'"

"You know, Billy, you're always amazing me."

"You didn't think I had a sex life?"

"It isn't that." She watched me with an amused and almost ironical look, as if she'd suddenly become my wise and insightful sister. "You've got more guilt than any guy I ever met who wasn't Jewish."

A fax came in from DMV, a list of fifty or so vehicles in the Los Angeles area whose license began with the tonsorial letters GSG; one, a gray 1994 Lincoln sedan, fitted well enough the description of the car seen outside Mae Richards's house the previous afternoon. Its registered owner was Richard Francis, resident of Malaga Bay down in Palos Verdes. Looking back quickly through the papers in front of me, I saw with a quick and light shiver of excitement the same address on the list of those houses worked by Mae Richards's little business; indeed, this address was one of those with MR autographed against it.

Strange connections run across Los Angeles like a fault line, and down the years I'd learned neither to trust nor mistrust coincidence. I was neutral toward its neat offering. I trod gently in the forest with a guide; that's to say there were rules about how to proceed, and if the path sometimes looked almost too broad and easy, it was precisely because, sometimes, it was.

Over and over during an investigation chance would turn into a larger design, randomness would become connectedness and even inevitability. I'd worked so many. Homicides in West Los Angeles, in downtown Los Angeles, in East Los Angeles; homicides by the score in South Los Angeles; homicides at the airport, homicides on boats, in restaurants, in cars, in trucks, and on the pier at Venice Beach; homicides where the body was decomposed beyond recognition and those where the body was still breathing when I arrived. Homicide by gunshot, by stabbing, by strangulation, by beating, by suffocation, by poison; homicide by golf club and by boiling kitchen fat. People were always finding new ways to kill each other. Wherever I drove, wherever I looked, there'd been a homicide. Back in the early days I used to cast around for a meaning to this sequence of witnessed death, and then I realized that I was the connection myself, that I was scurrying through an infinite murder map. I kept waiting to get something back. I thought that if I traveled long and hard enough, there'd be an answer; there wasn't, only the next case. My life was linked by murders the way other people's are by the freeways, and though I closed the books in the end they never left me.

The journey down to Palos Verdes, beyond Manhattan Beach and Hermosa and Redondo, was one of twenty miles and, usually, thirty minutes or so, but from the start I made bad time in the rain. At LAX the noise of the jets was drowned out as they emerged from the mist and cloud, lumbering toward the runways' safe refuge with water silently pluming from their wings. Where Coast Highway turned inland toward Long Beach I headed on straight as the road started to loop and rise, past churches, prosperous-looking strip malls, and street lamps that had come on and were bright and swollen through the streaming rain.

I scooted those twenty miles in a mere two hours. All the time I was trying to call Nowita Place and kept getting the busy signal, until at last Lucy picked up. "Hey, it's Daddy. So what have you been doing today?"

She told me about her day at school, all the struggles and conspiracies. She said, "Do you still have the badge?"

"My police badge?"

"No, the one on your forehead, from when you came out of the party last night, right between your eyes."

Now I got it. Ted had held the gun so hard against my forehead, it had left a mark. "It's gone now. It must have been an allergy or something."

"I was afraid you were changing."

"Where'd you get that weird idea?"

"I'm frightened, Daddy. You'll become a different person and won't like me anymore. Because I'm going to Seattle with Mom."

"Do you want to go?"

The question was unfair. She said, "I don't know, I guess. I don't think so."

"Is your mother there?"

"Yes."

"May I speak to her, please?"

It was a while before Ellen came on. I could hear music in the background, something fizzy on the piano by Bach. My fingers gripped tight the steering wheel as I shifted the portable against my cheek. At the next corner a red Freightliner lumbered toward me, shuddering across the fraught sea of Coast Highway.

"Billy?" said Ellen.

"You can't take her away."

"Don't do this, Billy."

The Freightliner went by too close, a scarlet blast.

"It's all settled," she said.

"Nothing is settled. You're not gone yet. You've not moved yet. I love my daughter."

"Oh, Billy," she said, sad now. "I know you do, and she loves you. I shouldn't have to remind you that you agreed to all this. And it's not going to disappear, the love between the two of you. She'll always love you.

She'll always be your daughter. She's proud of that, and so am I."

It was already getting dark. The car had passed low into a canyon surrounded by forests of cypress and eucalyptus. Above me to the left, I saw other people's homes, or rather their porch lights, hanging in the mist and rain like gauzy orange lanterns. At last I said, "You really piss me off sometimes," but by then the line had broken down. I heard only crackle and static.

I thought about Epictetus: "Do not desire that everything happen as you wish, but desire that everything happen as in fact it does happen, and you will be free." That was all very well. I knew the conventional wisdom. I'd read the books, but I also remembered when Lucy was still inside Ellen, lodged in her womb's luxurious hotel, and I'd gazed into the gray screen of the ultrasound and seen the four chambers of my yet-to-be-born daughter's heart, four black holes whose movement shifted and glanced like magic with each steady, predictable pulse of the muscle surrounding them. Wisdom is what we glean, if we're lucky, with our minds from the twisted root of the past—so that our hearts can ignore it and proceed at once in the opposite direction. I was angry, trying not to think about how afraid I was, not of anything out there in the world, but of what was happening in my family and in me.

I didn't have any trouble finding the house, a big two-story place, white, with green shutters; it sailed atop the hill like a ship. From up here, even in this weather, the waves seemed to proceed to the shore in well-cut and ordered lines, like an engraving.

The hallway was wide and open, soaring all the way up the full height of the house. A broad wooden staircase stood back to the right. There was art on the walls, bright stuff in oils, big canvases, and the entire length of the landing was given over to plate glass, beating back the rain's assault. The wood floors gleamed with a sand-colored varnish. On the other side of the hall from the staircase there was an open doorway, and through it I saw five or six suitcases, all black, as if someone was getting ready to leave.

I was trespassing. I'd gone in without a warrant and through the unlocked front door without even knocking. I'd crossed a line—even a lousy defense attorney could make a meal of this if I ever needed to take this guy to court.

In the living room I stood dripping like my pizza boy among the posed sofas and armchairs, the Turkish rugs, the furniture around which lingered the aromas of lemon and wax. There were more modern pictures on the walls, and through French windows I glimpsed blurred gray statuary and the wide, darkening sweep of a lawn. Logs were piled unlit in the white marble fireplace. There was no clutter. Five or six art books were imprisoned between marble horse-head bookends on a table of glass and polished steel.

A man came in, sixtyish, tall and straight-backed, with a luxuriant mane of silver hair. A lumpy pink forehead hung over deep-sunken eyes like chips of dark green glass. He was a drinker, and nonetheless a still smart lizard turned out in black polo neck, baggy black wool pants, and slinky loafers wrapped around black silk socks. A long gold chain with a clunky medallion was swinging from his neck. "You must be the driver," he said with one of those clipped English voices that seem to come at the end of a very long nose. "I didn't hear you."

Five minutes later we were heading down the driveway on our way to the airport. By then Richard Francis had slipped a long green raincoat over those fancy black duds, rubber overshoes on top of the alligator loafers, and I'd gotten myself soaked again loading his bags into the trunk.

"This isn't much of a car, is it?" he said, settling himself. In the mirror I watched him pick at the crinkling sleeve of the raincoat with fussy fingers. "The last driver had a hat."

"I only got the top of my head."

He didn't laugh. "At least you're in good time. I'm on the shuttle to Las Vegas at six. That's always assuming planes are still in the air. Quite a storm."

Even in the approaching darkness the air was so suffused with moisture that it provided its own shimmer and glow. It seemed alive. Lights twinkled yellow and red from the Redondo Beach refinery. Its twin stacks belched out smoke to thicken the dark banks of fog and cloud. As we passed the Tattle-Tale Lounge, the Coco Bakery, a store called Colored Tile, Chic 'n' Burger, it seemed that new buildings were rising above the old, and a new city was taking shape.

"Business trip?"

"A conference."

"What kind of business?"

"I'm a doctor, an obstetrician."

"Pulling out babies?"

"More than five thousand at the last count."

"Hey, doc! And I bet you can remember every one."

I brought the car slowly to a halt at the curb. Red lights glimmered in the wet as if the throat of every streetlight in the city had been cut. I turned to him and said, "Tell me about Mae Richards."

He was blank. "What?"

"Mae Richards."

The sharp look was back again. "Who are you?"

"A detective." I unhooked the badge from my belt and held it out toward the back seat. "Billy McGrath. I'm head of the homicide section at Ocean precinct."

It was as if I'd slapped him in the face. He came out of his shock and panicked, flapping at the door and its locks with hands he could no longer control. "Stop the car. I want to get out."

I pointed out that the car was stopped already, paused in a spectacular storm on PCH. We weren't going anywhere.

"This is disgraceful. It's outrageous."

He was blustering, but I couldn't disagree. Even Drew Diamond would be surprised, and he'd come into the Department at a time when it was still acceptable to give a citizen a couple of slaps by way of saying hello. "Talk to me. Mae Richards."

"I don't know anyone of that name."

The quick lie took me by surprise, and he saw. He subsided back into the seat. He wanted to make a run for it. Sweat stood out in little pricks against his temples. He knew he had to say something.

"Oh, my God. What happened?"

"You tell me."

His head was moving this way and that. I'd put him on the spot. "She was murdered yesterday afternoon. Someone shot her in the eye. Melon shot, meaning the bullet entered the brain and didn't leave."

"Don't be absurd. That's ridiculous. You're lying," he said, and sat quite still, eyes blinking. "I don't understand, please." He ducked down and when he looked up he'd scratched a couple of new marks on the tender, irritated skin of his forehead. "I'm confused. You're not really a detective. This is all some horrible joke, isn't it?"

I handed him my portable, then scribbled a number on a scratch pad and tore off the page. "Call this number. They'll confirm my ID."

The portable didn't work, however, so I swung the Chevy around and aimed it at a diner on the other side of the highway. He scurried inside to use the phone while I kept the hard-working wipers on, so I had a murky view. Not that I suspected anymore he'd make a run for it. He was discomposed, but enough on top of things now to know that would be the dumb move.

Maybe Francis is my suspect, I thought, but then I knew it was too early to tell. I'd wait and watch. I'd be careful. Even if he wasn't my guy, he might be armed. I didn't try to read his thoughts. I'd long ago realized both the futility of that and its danger. On the one hand, you were likely as not to make a mistake; on the other, to enter into the mind of a murderer was to walk into a burning house. Murderers were on the whole ordinary enough individuals who found themselves in desperate situations. Afterward, more often than not, they were destroyed by the knowledge of what they'd done. It lived inside them like a grub. I once had a guy walk into the precinct house and confess to a crime he'd committed twenty years before. It was a strange story. He'd strangled his brother and buried him up in the hills. Later he'd bought the lot and built a house on it, because he couldn't live with the thought that someone else might do the same and perhaps find the body. In time he came to be so certain that one day he'd return to the house to find his brother alive and well, waiting, that he couldn't bring himself to leave it. He kept himself locked up, until the day he forced himself to visit me. "He's there," he said. "When you go in he'll jump you like a bandit. Watch out."

There were those, on the other hand, like Ricky Lee, who could live with the knowledge of what they'd done, not because they necessarily enjoyed it, but because it was an accepted part of their fallen and maybe predetermined world, dog-eat-dog; they told themselves it was the hardcore life, *business*. There were those who enjoyed it. And there were those like Corcoran who never expected to know about the terrible, intense moments of life but who found that—what? That with the help of enough luck and lawyers they could live inside the burning house. I hoped Corcoran carried the scars, or the worm that would live and grow inside. I wondered. It all came down to how easily he could be in a room by himself. Lots of the time he'd be on the phone. He'd be in an airplane or with his driver in the car. He'd spend fifteen minutes picking out fonts for his business cards. There'd be lunch, dinner. Women. There'd be the times when he was shooting a movie and he'd step into another world altogether. He'd show up late and unannounced at the house of a friend, and it would be all right, because, after all, he *was* Charlie. But there'd have to be times when he was alone. He'd read, but the book would bore him. The news would be too depressing. He couldn't bring himself to watch films on video, or sit by himself in his private movie theater. What then, when the only guest is your wavering self-esteem?

Francis got back into the car with a rush of air and the fresh smell of the rain. The skin on his face had lost some of its anxious raw redness. His expression was straightforward and calm. "My dear man," he said, letting me know how eager he was to straighten all this out. "You gave me a hell of a shock. And I gather from your lieutenant . . ." He pronounced this the English way: lef-tenant. "I gather from him . . ."

"From Larry?"

"Yes. Nice-sounding fellow with a Japanese name."

"Murakami."

"Exactly. I gather from him that your behavior tonight has not been exactly according to procedure."

"Really? I just bet that made him mangle a couple of Ping-Pong balls." I brandished the one I had in my pocket. "You play? American *ping,* English *pong?*"

Francis was serious. "He was confused, as I am myself, but he confirmed your identity. Said in fact you were his top man and of course I should help you in whatever way I can."

"What about your flight?"

"Canceled, old boy. Bloody Yanks. Sorry."

He'd got out of the car frightened and angry, almost shattered, but had returned with smiling movie-doctor smoothness, with all the cool confidence he presumably carried into the delivery room. His crinkly smile was supposed to be winning, and indeed it was, but I still made a note to check on whether that flight had really been canceled. I also wondered who else he might have spoken to, apart from Murakami.

11

THE LATINA MAID BROUGHT IN A TRAY, AND I WATCHED Francis watching her while she poured tea into green cups the size of soup bowls and passed us cookies laid in a circle on a plate. When she was gone, closing the door behind her like the least emphatic of denials, he stood, handed me a cup, and put a flaming spill under the logs in the white marble fireplace. He waited with foot poised on the guard rail until the fire lighters caught and the logs began to spit and crackle. His voice was calm, matter-of-fact. "I met Mae Richards—oh, nearly thirty years ago. I delivered both her children, first the boy who was killed, Henry, then Ricky Lee. At the time I didn't know very much about her. She was a patient, that's all; hard to think of her in any other way. I saw her from time to time, professionally, and it was about then that her career as a singer began to get going."

"Tell me more about that."

"She made two records, wrote a lot of her own songs. She was awfully good. Her husband had been a trumpet player. They'd started out in the music business together. She got on a faster track."

"Where'd he go?"

"He was out of the picture by the time Mae and I were involved. She never cared to speak of him."

"Involved?"

"Mae and I were lovers. I can see you're surprised. Really, she was very talented. I wish you could have heard her then."

"How did that happen? The lovers part."

"It was at Henry's funeral. I'm sure you've seen many corpses, detective, but to stand over the body of a being you brought into the world—that's a terrible thing. It isn't supposed to happen. That was an awful time for Mae, of course. She had a breakdown, afterward. At the time she was impassive as stone. I knew she'd have to crack."

His cup trembled in its saucer as he set it down. With shaking hand he brushed back his hair and was silent for a minute or more, staring into the now exuberantly flaming fire.

"I don't know if I can talk about this." He sniffed, embarrassed, and lowered his face into his hands. The chain hanging from his neck was gold, as I'd thought, but with a stone, a diamond, set in the middle. "At the moment I can't even remember what she looked like. Isn't that awful?" He raised his head again, but with the eyes screwed shut. "There. Got her."

In a spirit of resigned sadness, interrupting himself to sip at his tea or catch some hope from the fire, he told me about their affair. "My memory, it's in patches. It's because I still work so hard. I loved her. You've no idea how much. I'd have married her if I could, but she wouldn't have me. Turned me down not once but several times over the years. We became comfortable with each other. Things never got stagnant, perhaps because as the years went by we agreed to see each other only a couple of times a month. We were always going somewhere. During the time that I knew her I was married to two other women without ever experiencing the passion I felt for her. I'm sorry if that sounds decadent."

"When did you see her last?"

"A month ago, Las Vegas again. We slipped away for a weekend, took in a couple of shows."

"You didn't see her yesterday?"

In the fire a log fizzed suddenly. "I tried to, but then you know that already, don't you?"

"Why would you think that?"

He was urbane again. "Someone must have seen my car. Otherwise I can't think what led you here. Mae and I were always very careful, very secretive."

"Why?"

"Again—that was her idea. She said it was more thrilling that way. No doubt she had her reasons. Perhaps she was ashamed of me, the boring white boyfriend."

"You didn't see her yesterday?"

"She wasn't at home."

I didn't have the impression that he was lying, but I tried to stay neutral about it. I looked at the art he had on the walls, abstract arrangements of colors rather than images; originals, probably. The books trapped on the shiny table between the horses' heads were about Picasso, Jackson Pollock, Miró. I needed Ted here to tell me whether Francis had invested his money wisely. Most likely he was worth several million dollars. If he'd killed Mae Richards it hadn't been for her money.

"Did you have a fight recently? A disagreement of any kind?"

"Absolutely not."

"What time were you there yesterday?"

"Two, two-thirty; I can't be any more precise than that."

"And then?"

"I drove back here. No, that's not quite right. We stopped off at the marina to check my boat for storm damage. It was secure."

"We?"

"Didn't I say? I was with an employee, a former student of mine who helps run my affairs."

"No, sir, you didn't say. His name?"

"Radek Gatti." He spelled it out. "R-A-D-E-K G-A-T-T-I. I'll give you the number."

"He was with you all yesterday afternoon?"

He stood up and went to lean against the fireplace again. In the glow from the logs his eyes were deep red pockets, tear-invaded. "How did she die? Who killed her? It was a chance thing, wasn't it? It must have been a chance thing. Quite random." He stared at me with his head on one side and cracked his knuckles. "I did love her," he said, his voice trembling. "I did love her. I d-do love her."

I didn't feel like going home, so I drove on farther up Palos Verdes mountain, thinking I'd cut back into the city on Hawthorne and maybe stop by at the Seventy-seventh Street Division, where I knew one of the night sergeants had been at high school with Ricky Lee Richards. I didn't want to stop working, and I didn't feel tired; these were the longed-for moments, when a case caught me up and swept me along like a surfer.

There'd been a shift in the wind, so as I headed south, rain came in flurries from directly behind me, as if needles and diamonds of water were being tossed over my shoulder at the road ahead, where they spattered or bounced and joined the flood. Through the foul night the Chevy's headlights lit up for a second the sign to the Wayfarer's Chapel. I'd gone past the turn already on the way to Hawthorne and Seventy-seventh when I turned the wheel and headed back into the rain, coming at me now like needles, while the turn and the dark steep lane afterward that led into the chapel parking lot were a fight the wrong way up a waterfall. For a moment the Chevy stalled, and I thought I'd be flushed back down the hill. At last I made it over the obstruction, a fallen log that burst and spun away in splinters from beneath the wheels.

The souvenir booth was shut, but the chapel was open, a building made almost entirely of glass, lit up like a beacon, and quite empty and still inside. Redwoods had been planted close on either side so that it was the growing trees themselves that seemed to form the walls. At the far end, beyond the altar, there was an enormous circular window against which the rain gusted in more pattering flurries. A part of a tree fell and struck the glass with fistfuls and shrubbery and dying wood that glanced soundlessly away.

The first house I remember must have been in Santa Monica, where my mother and father had a bungalow on Eleventh Street between California and Montana. I don't really remember the house at all. I have an impression of a small square lawn, surrounded by palm trees and birds of paradise, where I sat playing on a travel rug. After that, in England, my mother and I lived in drafty small apartments or boarding houses with complex and often direly spelled instructions taped above the toilet. This was when she was still an actress, taking whatever parts she could get. I remember reading *MAD* magazine while having diarrhea, courtesy of a vicious curry from a vindaloo house up the hill from Bradford's Alhambra

Theater. Daubing her cheeks with number three grease-paint, she turned to ask me how my tummy was doing. Her face was such a doomed, tragic mask that I burst into tears. She laughed then, and folded me in her arms, promising that everything would be all right.

We treasure some memories against the despair of living, and certain of mine had happened here, in the Wayfarer's Chapel, where Ellen and I were married on a fine, bright, windy afternoon in May, as fresh and glittering as California was supposed to be. She came almost running down the aisle, not to the wedding march, but to a moment of exhilarating acceleration from a piano concerto she loved by Brahms, feet skipping toward the words in gold that were beaten into the three concrete steps leading to the altar, OUR FATHER WHICH ART IN HEAVEN, and which I now regarded with a sudden depression. Nothing I did made any important difference. I was losing my wife and daughter. I was tired and homicide-haunted. My work, for so long the prop with which I'd hypnotized myself and held the world at arm's length, seemed a sham—bitter, messy, a foolish attempt to re-create and heal the past.

Reflection invited danger. Better and easier to be on top of the surfboard, where the action was, riding without thought to a shore your skill might help you reach, though all at once I found it hard to care who'd killed Mae Richards. Maybe it was Francis, maybe not—he'd put up a good front. I judged him capable of the act, but not of the mutilation that followed.

Rain pressed in on the chapel's sides. My feet made no sound as I left the pew and walked down the aisle toward doors that leaned open quickly in the wind and were then sucked shut again. Above my head the ceiling panels were like soft, fleecy clouds. When I turned again, he was sitting there, a dark bulky figure, one arm draped over the back of a pew. He wasn't old, perhaps in his thirties, yet deep lines had been chiseled into his face, up the sides of his cheeks, down from his unsmiling mouth, and on his forehead, beneath which narrowed eyes squinted at me from either side of a nose like a dagger. His hair was tucked up in a baggy black cap sparkling with raindrops not yet absorbed; otherwise he seemed defiantly ill equipped against the storm, wearing cowboy boots, black jeans, and a filmy black silk shirt that was quite dry and open at the neck. Then I saw the coat folded on the pew beside him. When had he found time to do that? How come I hadn't heard him? The guy must have been more than soft on his feet. "Radek Gatti," he said, standing up and bringing his heels together in mock salute. His teeth were white and stubby, tombstones. His eyes were extraordinary, the palest blue, like chips of frozen sky. I thought he'd come to kill me.

"Hey, baby, don't go for your gun. I'm quite unarmed, I assure you. Guess I'd better explain myself, no, 'cos I stick out like a sore thumb in these surroundings." He spoke English as though unsure whether to caress or strangle it. "I was on my way to see my good friend and patron Richard, Dr. Francis, and I was already calling him on the phone to announce my most imminent arrival when he says that a policeman has been talking to him who also wishes to talk to me and what other event should my eyes witness than an unmarked police Chevrolet pulling out of the gates to his estate. So naturally, having put two and two together to make an equation, I followed you here. No magic. Just this"—and suddenly something black was out of his jacket and in his hand. "Some guy, he once said Los Angeles was thirty-six suburbs in search of a paper cup, or something. Well, now there's a center, baby." He waved the portable like a flag and tucked it back in his pocket. He also had a briefcase with him, a smoothly tooled piece in pigskin and suede polka-dotted by the rain. "This is LA."

"Do you mind if we discuss this outside?"

"I do mind. It's a fucking tropical monsoon out there." His alert gaze ticked off the chapel ceiling, the Cross, and the shadows of a swaying tree framed in the circular glass window behind it. "OK, OK, now I get it. This is a special place for you. Maybe you were married here?" He tucked an errant strand back under the cap, whose peak he scrupulously straightened with the palms of both hands. "I killed her, if you want to know. Yes, I killed her." He brought down his hands and extended them crossed. "Handcuffs?"

"How did you kill her?"

"I shot her, pop! Of *course* I didn't kill her." The hands shot up. "I wouldn't hurt that old lady like a fly. And neither would Richard, the great doctor who loved her with an even greater passion. That's what I'm here to tell you. He's innocent. I was with him all yesterday afternoon."

I took out my notebook. "What's your name?"

"Radek Tadeusz Gatti, born Cracow in Poland, when is none of your damned business."

"Your telephone number and address."

He coughed them up. He lived down in the marina, not far from my crib.

"What time were you at Mae Richards's house yesterday afternoon?"

"OK, so this is an interrogation now. Ricky Lee Richards, he's the one you should be asking. Ask him about the money he kept hidden at Mae's house."

"You know Ricky Lee?"

"Nossir. But I know of him. Doesn't everybody?"

"You never met?"

"No, that's for sure."

"What about Mae? How well did you know her?"

"Not too well, only through Richard, you know. I'd drive them places together sometimes."

"Ever see her by yourself?"

It was like turning the wrong way into the storm again. His look became sharp and attacking. "Sometimes. Sure. What's it to you?"

"How come the two of you went there together yesterday afternoon?"

"Richard doesn't like to drive in the rain." This was offered with a shrug. "He went in by himself to knock at the door. He came back at once, one minute later, sweetheart. He was never out of my sight. She wasn't there."

"And then?"

"We went to the marina to check on the boat. I wanted to check on damage below the water line, so I put on a wetsuit and went for a swim. You like to swim?"

"I love the ocean but I wouldn't want to get involved. What's the name of the boat?"

"*Little Knell;* you know, like the sound the bell makes. Pier Twenty-two."

"K-N-E-L-L?"

"Yessir."

"The water line?"

"Sound."

"How come you think Ricky Lee had a stash at his mother's house?"

"That lady, she looked a good face, but underneath she wasn't honest. She wasn't what she seemed. She was a poisoned vessel."

"Meaning."

"I don't know that I should be telling you this, Richard was so in love with her. He wept for her, real tears. She had secrets."

"Secrets?" I exploded with laughter. "Yeah, well, so did King Tut and JFK, bro, but that's no help to me. Secrets? What do you mean, *secrets?* Let's cut the bullshit. You're obviously itching to cover for your boss and tell me something, so spit it out."

"Good," he said, smiling. "You have temper, I like that. OK, kitty cat, you wish to get down. Here we go, but don't get angry with me, my friend. I'm just the good citizen here."

He popped open the briefcase on the pew and fetched out a black leather portfolio with a zipper on the side. Inside, once he'd opened it, were six photographs. They were all photographs of Mae Richards.

The first had been taken in the living room of the house in Oakwood. She stood in a plain white dress, laughing, while behind her, fuzzy and out of focus, I saw the stereo stack, the VCRs, a fat red candle. The next two showed her at a party, with a glass of wine in her hand, or punch more likely, because there were bits of fruit floating in it; the fourth was a head shot, a profile of her alone against a gray background, while in the fifth and sixth she posed smiling in the driver's seat of a car obviously not hers, a Ferrari. In four of the photos she was with another woman, unremarkable in itself, of course. What was remarkable was the identity of this second woman. She was Charlie Corcoran's murdered wife, Denise Corcoran.

"How come I never seen these before? Where'd you get these?"

"You wouldn't believe."

"Try me."

"In the trash, kitty cat. It's amazing what you find in the trash."

"What are you telling me, Radek? You're the garbage man now?"

"I was waiting for Richard, Dr. Francis, one day outside Mae's house. It was garbage day. There it was, this portfolio, just like I give it to you, poking out the top of the can. Hey, I thought, that's a pretty nice portfolio for someone to be throwing away."

"Ever show these to Francis?"

He shook his head. *"C'est bien simple,"* he said, with a shrug. "It's up to you. Take them or leave them."

12

THE NEXT MORNING I WOKE UP AND MY FIRST AND only thought was that I had to see Lucy. I was fretful, restless, not wanting to go to the office. I needed to hold and hug my daughter. I dressed quickly, strapped on the Beretta, took the elevator down to the parking area, and climbed into the Porsche. Only then did I look at my watch, seeing that it was seven A.M. I'd hardly slept at all. To kill time I thought I'd get some breakfast, read the paper, and catch up with Lucy on her own at school before eight-thirty, before she went into her first class. I ate at a place off Lincoln, where over pancakes and poached eggs I studied the photographs that Radek Gatti had given me and tried to figure out how it was that I'd never seen them before, had never previously heard even a whisper of any relationship between Mae Richards and Denise Corcoran. Murder's a mushroom. You tend to find out everything about that person, though in the case of Denise Corcoran it had been hard. It was as if, aged twenty, she'd roared out of Texas to invent herself anew. Then, after her marriage to Charlie, so much had been written about her, and so numerous were the chat shows on which she'd appeared, that even the legend became crusted over with layers of fiction and hyperbole. All the same—Denise and Mae, the movie star's wife and the gangster's mother? I was surprised.

Ted's office above the Softly Gallery was full of paintings that leaned against the walls, unpacked book boxes, empty bottles, others that were still half full, easels, several computers, a round garden table surrounded by plastic chairs, a camp bed covered with rumpled sheets and a blanket, shirts still in their plastic from the laundry hanging from a wire suspended across the ceiling, and, in one corner, a vague pile of clothes surrounded by shadowy stacks of ancient LPs. There was a big fridge and an expensive stereo system on metal shelving behind a desk. But there was no Ted. The office was empty. Fish blew bubbles from the screen of the one computer that was turned on.

I remember the one time I asked Ellen what it was like when she was shot, when she'd been bleeding in the broken glass, thinking she was about to die. Those seconds had seemed like an eternity, she said, and it had seemed to her during them that she could lead many lives. She said the unbearable thing was the thought: what if I had not to die? What if I could turn this around and live? I'd turn each moment into a century. I'd count every moment and never lose one.

There were the things I'd once thought important or even worth dying for: justice, doing the best work I could, getting the job done. Sometimes, these days, they didn't seem worth the candle. At such moments I thought that if I could make things right with my family, if I could only do that, then everything would fall back into place, the leaves would be on the trees once more, and my disposition would change again from autumn to spring. I'd start the other life, the one without mistakes.

"But you know what the weird thing is?" Ellen had said. "I haven't been able to live like that at all. At first, yes, when I didn't know whether I'd make it, and if I did, whether I'd cope. I lost sight of myself and became a tiger. Then later I got used to things, and life sank into a routine, different, but still a routine, smudgy at the edges."

Uneasy on my own in Ted's bachelor crib, glancing at my watch and seeing that it was at last coming up on time, I left a note stuck to the bubbling mouth of the computer fish, saying I needed his help with something. I wondered if he, or someone he knew, might give me an expert opinion on whether Gatti's photographs could conceivably be forgeries. In my heart I didn't think so, but I wanted to be sure. The photographs worried me, though I didn't quite know why. They sent me running to Lucy, seeking love and the reassurance that I was still a good man.

The Carrefour school was a fancy place on Twenty-sixth Street in Santa Monica. The buildings themselves weren't much to look at, a scattering of pink stucco units set to the side of a gray concrete playground, even though most of the pupils were the sons and daughters of movie and TV stars, directors, agents, and producers, the town's self-appointed aristocracy. That's why I'd sought it out.

There was no lot at Carrefour, only one of its eccentricities, so I had to park on the street. When Ellen was first here she took one look around and said in a sarcastic way that she was amazed they didn't have valet parking, and she soon twigged that whenever I came I drove the Porsche.

Lucy came flying down the corridor with a pack of

other kids. I had my arms spread in welcome before I realized a chase was going on. Spinning, at bay, she faced the others, five of them, I now counted, all boys. What looked like white slugs were trailing in her hair. There were more of these gobs of spit dripping down the back of her denim shirt.

The tallest of the boys, Tom Boggs, had blood streaming from his nose. I'd met his father, a big TV writer, at a PTA meeting. He'd told me a story about walking past a room in one of the studios. There were these six guys inside, around a table, laughing their tails off at their own script. "Hey, Boggs, you motherfucker," one of them had called. "You'd laugh, too, for twenty-five thousand a week." The real joke, Boggs had told me, was that he himself earned fifty.

"Hey, wait up, you guys."

"Dad!" said Lucy, with a look of love and relief. Her face and the front of her shirt were dripping also.

"What's going on here?"

Tom Boggs was nine, a wealthy white kid dressed like a black banger with baseball cap back to front, huge shorts, and a T-shirt five sizes too big. The style was the same as Nelson's, the kid I'd run into outside Mae's house, and the attitude was all from MTV and bad boy basketball stars. Yet six or seven years from now, unlike Nelson, Tom Boggs would be shopping at Fred Segal and most likely still waiting for life's first smack in the head, which I myself, at that moment, felt a rising desire to deliver. His eyes gave me the scornful up-and-down. "Fuck you, cop."

Lucy flew at him with her fists. Before she bloodied his nose any more, I had her scooped up under my arm.

"I'll kill you," she screamed at Tom Boggs.

"C'mon, you kids, cut it out."

"My dad says you're a piece of shit that don't earn nothin'," said Tom Boggs, and the other boys laughed.

"Your dad really say that?" I said. "I guess he must be right."

"And your car's a junker."

"Big time," piped up the boldest of the others, before I was saved by the arrival of the principal, Cervantes, and her assistant, who at once got things under control with a brisk, calm authority that I, the head of the homicide section, seemed in that situation to lack. Cervantes's assistant marched off the boys, while Cervantes herself set about with Kleenex, cleaning up the mess on Lucy's shirt and in her hair.

Cervantes was a slender middle-aged Mexican with a pointy nose, a hawk whose dainty exterior concealed a mind at once supple and capable of tough decisions. Her father had come to Los Angeles because they were going to shoot *his* father in the town square with Pancho Villa. "Those boys," she said, crouching down, rubbing at Lucy's back.

"If you need a weapon," I said.

She glanced up at me.

"I was joking. Well, kind of."

Cervantes had kids of her own who went to a regular elementary school, and I thought now of one of our previous encounters, about a year before, when she'd told me she wasn't sure how well Lucy was fitting in at Carrefour. I also remembered my first interview here when Cervantes had asked me what I could do for the school, if Lucy was admitted. I'd said I wasn't quite sure what she meant. She'd meant $25,000.

I told her I wanted to talk to my daughter alone. With my arms around Lucy's shoulder, I took her into one of the empty classrooms, where she sat in the teacher's chair with her elbows on the desk and her face cupped in her hands while I racked my brain to give her something, some memory of my own childhood, that would make this all right. Beside Lucy's, on the desk, Bobby Kennedy's hopeful face stared out of a frame toward the window and the rain.

"Dad, it's OK," she said. "Creeps, that's all. Tom Boggs spat at me; I punched him out." I didn't know where it came from, Lucy's calm. Every time I saw her it amazed me how Ellen and I had made someone so stubbornly her own person. She was so much herself, I longed to take her up and protect her in my arms. I didn't see how she'd survive another minute. And yet she kept doing it.

"All this stuff about me, about your dad being a cop with no money. Does that happen a lot?"

She shrugged in her tomboyish way. "No, not much, just sometimes."

"Why did he spit at you?"

"Because he's an asshole."

I laughed out loud. "Probably true, but you shouldn't say that."

"You do."

"It doesn't make me right." I was supposed to be a tough guy. There were tears in my eyes as I hugged her close. "I don't want you to tell your mother I said what I'm going to say."

"A secret?"

"Secret. You *are* better. Fuck'em. Fuck *them*. OK?"

She looked at me so seriously my heart ached. "OK, Dad. Fuck *them*."

"I'm driving you home."

"Now?"

"Right now."

"In the Porsche? Cool."

On the way, on Twenty-sixth, at the edge of the 10 Freeway, where shaven-headed homeboys stood surly in the rain outside a shabby stucco apartment building, I turned to her and said, "I hear your mother's got a new boyfriend."

Lucy had her eyes in her lap, fiddling with her pencil box.

"I'm sorry I didn't tell you about him."

I took my hands from the wheel for a moment.

"Hey, no problem. How is the guy anyway? Is he, like, a stud or something?"

This made her laugh. "Dad!"

"No, tell me, I can take it."

"He's kinda dull. He's OK. He's not like you."

"He's nice?"

"I guess."

"You should try and be nice to him. For your mother's sake." I gently shoved her shoulder. "Besides, he'll be out of the picture before you know it. As soon as you get to Seattle, right?"

She didn't seem too sure. Her eyes were fixed on the pencil box again. "I guess."

In the house on Nowita Place I told Ellen I didn't want Lucy at Carrefour anymore, not even for one day. Since the two of them would be gone in a couple of weeks, it didn't make a whole lot of difference anyway, I said. "How long has this been going on?"

Ellen had her wheelchair up by the dining room table. I was sitting opposite. Lucy had gone to her room already and was playing rock music. She said, "A year, off and on. We've dealt with it."

"A year? Jesus." I had my hand against my forehead. "And you didn't tell me?"

"You were always so set on the school."

"Because I wanted the best."

"It's a good school."

The paper bird shifted and crackled its wings on the ceiling, bouncing as if to the music from Lucy's room, Led Zeppelin, the stuff I'd flounced about to when I was in my teens. When my own father left me nothing, not even the Omega watch that had been his father's before him, I'd actually been glad. Here was a clean slate, I'd thought, fit for my determination to do something better for my own kids.

Ellen watched the rain stream down the living room window.

I said, "Do you ever regret we didn't have the second baby?"

"No," she said, not turning toward me, and with a bluntness that first took my breath away and then made me laugh.

"Hey, don't go easy on me, will you?"

"We weren't doing so hot, as I remember."

"It might have changed everything."

"It might have made everything worse. You want a cup of coffee?"

"Thanks, no. We'd have coped. We'd have been together."

"I don't know. I don't think so. Anyway, it's too late now."

"Is it?"

While she stirred her coffee with the stubby end of a pencil, I found the brandy bottle on the kitchen counter, poured myself a shot, downed it.

"Little early in the day, don't you think?"

I was thinking of Tom Boggs and how badly I'd wanted to hit that little rich kid for hurting Lucy.

I said, "Does your childhood seem far away to you?"

"About a million years," Ellen said, smiling now. "We can't protect her from the world."

"We can prepare her for it, though."

"Of course. That's the idea."

The glass shook in my hand as I set it down on the counter. "I was just thinking about what you told me about how you felt when you were shot. Did I ever tell you what a hero you are? I don't know if I'd have your guts in the face of crushing adversity."

Rather than looking at me, Ellen watched the rain's pounding attack at the windows. "You make me out to be better than I am, Billy."

"Despite the new boyfriend. Whoever he may be."

She didn't rise to the bait. She was shaking her head. "Your grandfather called."

"Oh, Christ." I thought of the old man alone in that house up in Culver City, sick, watching football, checking his guns. "I owe him a visit."

"He wants to know that you're OK. He worries about you. So do I."

13

I SPLASHED UP A CONCRETE PATHWAY TOWARD THE PORCH, where a red-and-white awning kept dry a bird feeder and a set of chimes. From the darkened interior came the boom of the TV, a morning talk show. On the other side of the street, outside Mae's house, the yellow tape was down, the uniforms on guard were gone, and instead it was a black youngster who stood in the rain, tracksuit hood all but obscuring his face, one of Ricky Lee's homeboys, most likely.

It was hard to tell whether the woman who came to the door was dressed for night or day. Louise Szell wore fluffy bedroom slippers over her swollen feet and a diaphanous ankle-length garment that was most likely bedwear but could conceivably have been an ancient ballgown. Stuck-on glitter sparkled here and there, a game attempt, like the shoulder-length gray hair that was sprayed and permed. Hard blue eyes stared at me through wire rimmed glasses embedded in a face that tried in vain to announce its cheeks, its mouth, and was instead a tumbling succession of chins. A plastic tube with a stopper in it stuck out of the center of her throat. She must have been in surgery.

We went through a whole routine while she said she'd spoken to the cops already. I spotted the white of a letter through the slit in her mailbox, pulled it out, and handed it to her. The sodden envelope was from GTE.

Her plump fingers tore angrily at the bill. "Mae's dead, ain't she? Don't matter how many questions you ask, you ain't gonna bring her back. You American?"

"Yes, ma'am, I am."

This seemed to appease her. "No Americans live in this city anymore," she said, and led me into a living room notable not just for its darkness, but for the depth of its shag carpet, the several fan heaters, which dried and oppressed the throat, and the huge flat screen TV at the far end, across which characters shimmered like distant sharks in a tank. "*Huffy,*" she shouted, letting GTE's careful calculations flutter to the floor. "HUFFY-MARIE."

A small white dog came scratching in from the kitchen, scampered across the carpet, and jumped up beside her. Behind the sofa were posters of Willis, Schwarzenegger, and Stallone. "My bodyguards," she said primly.

"I was hoping you might be able to tell me about these." Squatting down by the sofa, I opened the portfolio and flicked the photographs slowly in front of her while she examined them without expression or apparent emotion, but never taking her eyes off them either. When I'd finished and had zipped them away again, she let go a colossal sigh, as if someone really had let all the air out of her.

"Ain't no one supposed to know about that."

I didn't say anything. I didn't let my eyes leave her face either.

"Mae had a gift for sympathy, you know. She never

asked how you felt. She could see whether you were up or down from twenty yards away in the street. It was that girl she was trying to protect, not herself."

"Denise Corcoran?"

"*Huffy!*" she barked again at the dog, daring to flee. "Huffy-*Marie.*"

She was already heaving herself in pursuit when I said, "Say, I'm practically dying of thirst. Could I get a drink of water?"—my excuse to follow her past the TV set toward the sink and kitchen counter, where she scattered dry food in a bowl for the dog, pumped me a glass of water, and poured herself a hefty slug of store-brand vodka. An air bubble rumbled up through the cooler, burst, and she downed the vodka with a martyred expression. "Denise Corcoran," she said. "She was quite a gal." She mopped fastidiously at her lips with a piece of kitchen towel. "Well, I guess she paid for it."

I asked gently if I could pour her another vodka. Or should I make some tea? It was the second dose of liquor she plumped for, and duly downed. "In what way, in what way was she quite a gal?"

"You know the story, the one about her and her first sweetheart, before she ever met Charlie."

"Sure," I said. "Everyone does." Back in Texas, as a teenager, Denise Corcoran had married the high school basketball star, one of those guys whose youthful hoop glory was still remembered a decade later, by which time he'd been fired as night manager at the 7-Eleven and was tending bar and picking up whatever little construction work was available in that dirt-poor dustbowl town. He'd been too much the drunk for the military, too proud to claim welfare, and he'd revenged himself on Denise, predictably, by screwing around on her, by beating her, and by raping her so bad one time she had to go to the hospital. She escaped when he was drunk, asleep in the rocking chair with a shotgun over his knees, and rode the Greyhound straight to Las Vegas, a divorce, and, three transforming years later, the arms of Charlie Corcoran—an American dream.

"Horseshit," said Louise Szell. "Every damned word of it. There weren't never no basketball star."

I switched on the electric kettle. Thus far, as it happened, Louise was telling me nothing new. Months deep into the Corcoran case, on the phone to Denise's estranged father in Austin, I'd heard the story of her invented past, the mythology at which she and Charlie had jointly colluded because it sounded sweet for the press. The story hadn't come out during the trial because it was useful to neither side with regard to the outcome. "Do you mind?" I said. "I'd like some tea myself." A weary cockroach strolled indifferently across the counter. "Go on."

"There was a husband, all right, and he was decent, but she ran out on him anyway," and as if to prove the point she took leave herself, back to the living room, where she sat down on the sofa once more and nodded toward a rack of videos beneath the TV. Her glasses gave her a bitter, surprised look. "Got every one of his films on tape."

"Charlie's?"

"Huffy-*Marie*," she shouted, waiting while the dog rushed from the kitchen to jump up beside her.

"Why is no one supposed to know about the photos? Are you scared?"

"Who'd I be scared of?"

"You tell me."

"I ain't scared of anybody." Her fingers tugged at the curls around the dog's neck. "There's another picture I could show, if I wanted." She leaned forward, as if to catch her breath, eyes still with that vacant, almost dazed look.

"Are you in pain, Louise? Does your throat bother you? Here, let me get you some more of that," I said, and lifted the empty glass from her unresisting hand. In the kitchen I poured another shot.

"She used to work down in the little theater with Mae. She was painting scenery; jobs like that. Denise saw herself as an artist, you know."

"I heard that." In a hidden corner of the Corcoran kitchen, far away from Charlie's Picassos and the Warhol drawings, I'd seen a crude but powerful canvas, a female figure in black silhouette against a gray background, the eye drawn at once, as it was supposed to be, to the picture's center—a vagina on fire. Diamond had shuffled around, embarrassed, then shook his head. Are these people fucked, or what?

"What about Charlie himself? Ever meet him, or see him with Mae?"

"What the hell would he be doing in this neighborhood?" In one gulp she emptied the replenished glass. "He didn't want to have nothin' to do with Denise's friends. Nor with his own baby, either."

"He and Denise had a child?"

Ten minutes and two more vodkas later, she told me the story. Denise Corcoran had given birth to a Downs syndrome baby less than a year after her marriage to Charlie, who had wished to abort the pregnancy. Denise had refused, and in turn Charlie had said he wasn't going to have anything to do with the child. Denise went ahead, thinking Charlie wouldn't hold to it, but he proved as good as his word, in this if in nothing else.

Louise handed me the promised picture she'd

brought from the bedroom. It showed Mae and Denise with a pretty little mongoloid boy, perhaps three years old. Louise goggled at me through those thick lenses, evidently assuming she'd communicate the rest the way Rabelais's Panurge had explained philosophy to Thaumast, merely by grimacing with the eyes and lips. She was a tease, as well as a gossip, relishing the power of her story. Eventually I had to say, "Go on."

"Well," she said, putting a pale plump finger to her lips. "He lives with Denise's mother-in-law, the mother of the guy back in Texas. Charlie pays for it all. Pays a pretty penny."

"What's the little boy's name?"

"Andy. Denise's ex, he brought Andy here three, maybe four times, without Charlie knowing."

"Christ. Why didn't Mae come to the police with any of this?"

"She had even less time for the police than me, and that ain't much." She scooped up the dog and, with both hands, hugged it close. "Huffy-Marie, is this man gonna find who killed Auntie Mae? Do you think so? You hope so, don't you, baby? But you surely have your doubts."

Ricky Lee's homie was only a boy, and slight in build, a rasher of bacon buckling in the wind, but he was doing his best to give me the hardcore as I crossed the street. Only as I came closer did I realize that I knew the face. It was the kid I'd seen the other day.

"Hey, Nelson, whassup, cuz?"

He smiled at once, then remembered he wasn't supposed to do that, so it was back again to the tough banging stare.

"Do me a favor and go home, will you, Nelson?"

Maybe Nelson would make it out, or to the top like

Ricky Lee, but the odds were against it. For him, Ricky Lee was like a movie star, a dangerous and impossible ideal. Most likely he'd die trying to be like him; if he was lucky, he'd end up in jail. He didn't have the bank account to protect himself from us or the hurt of the street.

I'd known hardcore ghetto gunslingers, real bad-ass cops from the drug units, who'd get themselves all twisted trying to save a youngster like this. They knew that it was stupid, that the kids were already too deep into the program, but they couldn't stop themselves. They had to believe that, once in a while, they could at least do something, make a difference; otherwise the job was only a matter of filling the juvie tanks and zipping up the body bags.

"I'm going into the house now. Tell Ricky Lee I said to say hello, OK?"

Puzzled, ignoring my stare, Nelson stood his ground, and I found myself once again walking up Mae Richards's garden path. I always liked to go back to the crime scene after a few days. First time around you took all the pictures and wrote everything down, knowing most of that stuff would be redundant; in copspeak, it was for not. But you covered the bases, or else in court they jammed you. On a second visit, however, when the flat feet were gone and the house was empty and you knew a little more about the case, there was time to look for the telling detail.

Homicide—messy, actual—is sometimes plotted and connived at, but often not, and even in those cases where a murder had been premeditated there was often no evidence of that, just reality, random and inconsistent, thousands and thousands of facts to be trapped, to be pinned down in the murder book before any interpretation could be attempted. It sometimes happened that all this clutter got in the way, like doodads and dust in an antique store, and made me miss the treasure. If I were to report every detail in even a single murder book, the deadly dull telling might go on for months. It would be, literally, a trial.

From the detective's point of view, of course, there's always a narrative, always with pretty much the same structure: went there, saw this, spoke with him or her. The *success* of that narrative depends on whether the case is solved; if not, it's a journey to a centerless labyrinth.

Mae's house was dark and cold, with the smell of damp already rising from the foundations through the unwarmed wood frame. The roof had leaked and rain poured from a crossbeam in the living room, down from the roof, streaming *patta-patta-pat* onto an already sodden and plaster-spattered sofa. In the kitchen, where her body had lain, one column of ants marched up the counter, another down, bearing away sweet booty from the strawberries. I'd forgotten about those. When the body's gone, and forensics are through, the mess of the crime scene gets left as it is. At least the weather wasn't hot. Then flies are the problem.

I wondered if she'd owned this place. Probably, since she'd lived here ten years or more; wasn't that what Cataresco had said? I remembered when Ellen and I had bought the place on Nowita, less than a mile away. The feeling was stupendous. This was ours; we could turn away whoever we liked, come and go as we liked, order take-out, and never even get out of bed.

I glanced over her CDs: Ella Fitzgerald, Frank Sinatra, Billie Holiday, Diana Ross, Roberta Flack, Dionne Warwick, Whitney Houston, Charlie Parker, Dizzy

Gillespie, Oscar Peterson—comprehensive collections. There was no question the lady had taste in this area. Her books were a little more eclectic: there were three Bibles, a collection of inspirational poetry, a New Age guide to building a life after forty, a biography of Sidney Poitier, and several cookbooks. She'd gone to church, she'd read, she'd made food, she'd worked. She'd had an affair with a rich doctor down in Palos Verdes. She'd kept herself busy. I wondered about the story Radek Gatti had told me: if Ricky Lee had been stupid enough to keep a stash of money here, that would have been enough for someone to kill her; but then again, there'd been no sign of forced entry, none of the mess of a search, and such a scenario didn't account for the torture.

Outside, a car alarm wailed and whooped. From the window I saw that the kid Nelson was gone, disappeared to report to Ricky Lee, perhaps, or else scared away by the short dark-haired guy who came hustling down the street, face obscured beneath the upturned collar of a long black slicker. Louise Szell stood beneath the awning on her porch with her dog cradled in her arms, indeed like a baby. I could believe that Charlie Corcoran had forced Denise to abandon their child. Vain, arrogant, and, despite his diffident air, impatient of imperfection, he was almost daring in his self-centeredness. During the trial I'd twice seen him rip into one of his attorneys for bungling a minor point of procedure.

I looked at those VCRs stacked one on top of the other, trying to figure out why she needed so many. There were surprisingly few tapes, after all; no Charlie Corcoran collection here. I found a bunch of keys in the dust atop the topmost machine. As a cop I liked keys by instinct. They promised leads, opened doors—a garage, a storage facility, a car with secrets inside, maybe even a safe deposit box.

There were eight keys in all, on a ring with two solid gold charms hanging from it, the comic and tragic masks of drama. One golden face smiled up from my palm while the other regarded me with mouth forlorn. The first time I'd seen a pair like this was around the neck of a dead nineteen-year-old gangster in Culver City, gunned down while waiting for his little girl outside daycare. Comedy and tragedy were big with the bangers. The kid Nelson would know about them. They perceived their lives that way, simple and dramatic, all too likely to turn from one to the other in a moment. It helped them see death not as an event in life, but as an inevitable part of the play. It suited their sense of self-drama.

I turned the little masks over with my finger. Comedy had a diamond embedded in either cheek, and the back of tragedy's broad forehead was inscribed with a message in script so tiny I had to lift it up to my eyes: "To Mom from Ricky Lee. I loved him too and I'll never stop loving you."

He must have given her these on the occasion of his brother's death. What was it he'd said? Those cholos are long gone now, missing in action. I wondered if Ricky Lee had pulled the trigger himself, or maybe he'd used a knife; no, an automatic was the gangster's chosen device for execution, held with the wrist cocked down a little, a slanting style you saw mimicked by movie actors these days—stupid, and of use only if you had the victim on his or her knees less than twelve inches away. No cop or military man would shoot a weapon like that.

Mae Richards had been shot square in the face, straight on, from the mighty distance of three feet. She'd been looking at whoever killed her, as had Denise Corcoran. The killers were both at large, able to breathe, to make love, to laugh.

Comedy and tragedy: turning the two masks so that they faced me again, I felt the rough edge of the gold against my finger. Outside, the car alarm had ceased its wailing. There was only the sound of the rain, drilling at the roof and windows. Inside the kitchen it was dark as night. Comedy and tragedy, stories and plots, thesis and antithesis; it was then that I began to spin some more ideas in my mind. There are two ways of looking at a murder. One is to reconstruct the crime, to worm backward into the past from that moment of violence. The other way is to think that, for the murderer and those connected with him or her, it's not the end of something but the beginning. There are ripples.

Cops see the dirt, the mayhem, the bedlam, yet in a strange way we're protected. We don't have to figure out how to live in the world. Actually, we do, but we're pretty bad at it, because we live in our own discrete world off to the side, a world of danger and sudden excitement, of clear-cut good and evil and a lot of very fuzzy situations, a world so violent and separate it could make you believe not one soul living in the other understood a goddamned thing.

As a murder cop I could slip in and out of many various worlds—indeed, I had to—but was safe only as long as I always returned to my own, the protected world of the precinct and the locker room, the safety of my murder books. Attempt to move into another and I'd be making what Wittgenstein called a category error.

Two murders: Mae Richards and Denise Corcoran.

Two worlds: that of whoever killed Mae, and Charlie's.

Comedy and tragedy: lifting the two masks to my lips, brushing them against my lips to taste the texture of the gold, I had a delicious feeling of spheres coming into inappropriate collision. Excited, even tingling with fright, as if this alteration in my universe were caused by the taking down of a text from the most secret, forbidden part of the library, I could hardly keep still. A page turned in my mind, and I saw what I could do.

Mae Richards had been killed, and Charlie Corcoran had been acquitted of a murder he most assuredly did commit. He'd been in jail at the time of Mae's death, but maybe I could set him up as having been responsible. I was a clever guy, after all. I had medals, learning, and no one would ever suspect me of such a thing. That would be the beauty. Besides, it was such an elegant and neat solution, a story crying out for its own book. I'd sell Corcoran to Ricky Lee. I'd take the money and convince Ricky Lee that Charlie Corcoran was his mother's killer. It was beautiful.

The rain continued to prick at the roof and walls of the house. It was time to go. Without thinking, I slipped the key ring into my pocket as I left the kitchen and walked toward the door across Mae Richards's living room. I closed my fist around comedy and tragedy.

14

BACKGROUND ON DR. RICHARD FRANCIS TURNED UP that he'd been born in Southampton, educated at Oxford, then St. Thomas Hospital in London, and that he'd come to America in the late 1960s, working first in Chicago, then Los Angeles. He was an educated guy. He had almost as many diplomas and degrees as I'd worked homicides, and now, approaching the age of retirement, he was looking to sell his practice. He owned an apartment on Riverside Drive in Manhattan, the Palos Verdes house, two Mercedeses, the Lincoln, and the yacht in the marina, which he didn't sail very often. He ate out, he gambled, though not to excess, and evidently the most interesting and eccentric thing about him was this long-standing love affair with a middle-aged black woman from Oakwood. They'd obviously liked each other very much. There must have been respect as well as passion.

I was at the precinct house. "You've been standing in front of that damned soda machine for five minutes. Like, how hard can it be? I'll choose for you," said Cataresco, binging a button with the fleshy part of her palm, then scooping up the can as it trundled into the tray. "7UP. No caffeine," she said, flipped the top, and handed me the can. "Shit, I think I did my nail."

"Look at it this way. At least you didn't try it with your teeth."

"What's on your mind, Billy?" she said, letting the smile drain from her face as she leaned against the machine. "You're distracted. Am I allowed to say that?"

"Sure," I said, sipping the soda. "I'm worried about stuff. Ellen's moving to Seattle."

"With Lucy?" she said, standing up straight and frowning. "No shit. When?"

"A couple of weeks from now. You remember how when you were a kid, toward the end of a vacation, when time wasn't real anymore? You didn't want it to end. It seemed it couldn't, but you knew it would. You couldn't quite enjoy what you had. You lived in a sort of anticipatory dread. A dream. That's where I'm at."

"You're jiggling."

"Excuse me?"

"With the keys in your pocket. My father does it all the time."

Cataresco was twenty-six; I was forty. "Is that how you see me, Cat? Like your father?"

"Whatever's your fantasy, Billy," she said, sticking her hand on her hip. "Seriously, let me know whatever I can do. I'll work Mae Richards on my own or with one of the other guys. Whatever's best for you. Say the word."

I pretended to put some thought into this. "No, it's good for me to work. Takes my mind off things."

She'd tracked down a tape of a record that Mae Richards had made, and to play it she set up a boom box in the middle of the main table in the homicide section, right beneath the wooden gun. "She was discovered and dropped by Phil Spector," said Cataresco. "That's what my friend in the music trade told me."

"Surprising friends."

"An old flame."

The music started with a soft blur, a rumble of drums, then violins. From the other end of the table Drew Diamond looked up, poised to mock, and indeed the song did turn out to be corny—"Smoke Gets in Your Eyes"—but Mae Richards's voice had an emotion, a freshness, as if she were recalling something long-forgotten, some important initial discovery of childhood. Diamond's square face was shocked. He took a match stick, and slowly, almost wonderingly, popped it in the corner of his mouth. "Her voice gets you," he said.

The autopsy had confirmed that the cause of death was a shot to the head with a .22. The ends of her fingers had been sliced off with a twin-bladed instrument, most likely garden shears, and the burn marks on her chest had been caused by a cigar. A residue of ash was found in each of the wounds. There was sperm in both vagina and anus; she'd been raped before death, as the doctor at the coroner's office had suspected.

"But no scratches or other signs of struggle," said Cataresco. "Maybe she knew the guy. Maybe this was someone with a sexual grudge."

"Maybe," I said. "Maybe it was. You guys eat lunch yet?"

This was something Diamond liked the sound of. He laughed, slapping his hands together, easing his bulk out of the chair, pulling his belt, and straightening that great .45 in its holster. "Where do you think? Friday's or that new chicken place?"

"Koo-Koo-Roo? Or we could do Mexican. Nah, always gives me gas at lunchtime."

Cataresco gave me a bewildered look, shaking her head.

"What's up, Cat, you ain't hungry?"

"I'm wishing you two boys could overcome the need to be hardboiled."

I'd been back to the gallery to see Ted and a friend he'd arranged for me to meet, an expert, a big guy who'd lain on the floor, blinking, because of his bad back, and had pronounced the photographs of Mae and Denise genuine as far as he could tell. I was asking myself if I should call Texas to try to make contact with Denise Corcoran's ex-husband, the first one, to talk to him about Mae. I was wondering what it would take to convince Ricky Lee about Charlie Corcoran. I didn't imagine that if I called him up and said, "Look, the movie star did it," he was going to say, "Hey! Dumb of me not to realize that. I'll smoke that fucker tonight. The dude's *dead.*" I didn't pretend to myself that he'd just make me a gift of the money. He'd need convincing. I had no doubt that I was about to step into the fullest and fiercest kind of spotlight.

Murder books aren't supposed to leave the office, but I went back to the precinct house, lifted the file on Denise Corcoran, its red spinal dot reminding me "unsolved," and drove to a café on the boardwalk. It still hadn't stopped raining, and it was cold, the level of dampness above the ocean about the same as in. From my booth I watched a bum drift past the fogged windows, stumbling this way and that, in no hurry. It seemed worse somehow, in this weather, the plight of those abandoned to the streets.

I sat down and opened the book. I wasn't sure what I expected to find, though I knew what I was looking for: another vein leading from Denise Corcoran to Mae Richards. I flipped through the shots of the crime scene, where her face had been shot away, and studied more closely the pictures when she'd been alive, a young woman, blue eyes humorous and bored, a little on edge; her arms had been strong from lifting weights. I visited again the routine of her days: the gym, the coffee shop, the stores in Brentwood or Beverly Hills, the movies, then a party or a première or dinner. There were copies of her last credit card statements. No doubt Charlie was still receiving mail addressed to her, life's trail winding on beyond death.

One morning, just after we'd got together, Ellen had come down to breakfast to find me in tears, holding a magazine between my fingers. I hadn't ordered the thing. My father had arranged the subscription the week before his death, almost a year earlier. The message with it ran: *To my son, hoping he'll make me a grandfather one day.* I'd been friendly with my father, but hard on him. While he was alive, and while I was intent on pursuing some sort of academic or artistic career, I'd ruthlessly branded him a failure, because that was how he'd appeared to me: washed up, drunk a lot of the time, driving too many miles, and earning so little he was always bumming me for fifty or a hundred.

Outside, beyond the comfort of the windows, the ocean was a frenzy of white ridges and black hollows that plunged and broke themselves against the beach and the stanchions of the Santa Monica pier. Warming my hands on a cup of coffee, I turned the pages of the murder book.

Part of the detective's role is to bring order, not to fix destinies, but to show how they were broken, to tidy up the mess when chaos intrudes. In the case of Denise Corcoran, I'd failed. This wasn't wholly my fault, but I'd been a part of it, and I hated the guy. I wanted the money not for myself, but for Ellen and Lucy. I wanted their respect and love, but I wasn't exactly trying to buy it either. I didn't intend to let them know where this windfall came from. I knew I'd have to work out another plan for that. Even as hate with the one hand plunged me recklessly forward, so love on the other told me to take it easy, be smooth, do this right.

I found my connecting fiber in the sections of the book that dealt with the progress of Denise and Charlie through that last day of her life. It was a small thing, but it caught my eye. During the course of that day Charlie had canceled a guest appearance he'd been scheduled to make at a theater workshop.

From a phone at the back of the café I called Louise Szell and heard her dog yapping in the background. I said, "Louise, this is Detective McGrath. I wanted to ask you about the theater group that Mae was involved with. What was it called exactly?"

"The Powerhouse," she said, wheezing and coughing and turning her head away from the receiver to shout: "*Huffy-Marie!*" Her voice came back, softer but more direct. "It's on Abbot Kinney, junction with Westminster."

"Thanks."

"Y'all any nearer finding who did that terrible thing?"

"Maybe, ma'am," I said. "Maybe. But don't you worry. Someone's going to pay. Say hello for me to the bodyguards."

The Powerhouse was a square, one-story brick building with a green door. Standing outside, though not necessarily on guard, oblivious of the rain, was a ponytailed black guy, dressed in black, gulping greedily at a bottle of mineral water. He didn't look like one of Ricky Lee's boys, but then I couldn't say for sure. He paid no attention as I went into the building, from which issued the sound of an electric guitar, crisply played, chords standing out against the storm's surrounding beat. Inside, it was dark. I stood for a minute or more letting my eyes grow accustomed to the gloom before I discerned the shape of the stage in the middle of a small, dark, empty space. A gantry for lights was suspended by wires from the ceiling, and, to the right, beyond a pile of stacked chairs, there lay the outline of a door.

Before going in I knocked but didn't wait for the answer. The light was on, a single bare bulb, beneath which a black woman sat in a chair with the electric guitar I'd heard. Her hair was short, her crossed legs long and very smooth. I stood by the door of the small room waiting for her to notice me, but she went on playing, striking out chords. There was little other furniture: a desk, a wastebasket, a metal filing cabinet. It was almost like a waiting room. When at last the woman looked up, she wasn't surprised. Certainly she wasn't either angry or afraid. Her skin was the color of rich, milky chocolate; she was a child of obviously mixed blood, with eyes of emerald green, and her deep voice was neutral, as if she spoke to everyone just the same. "Can you wait? There's coffee."

I saw the pot bubbling away and helped myself, watching the woman until she finished playing and was ready for me.

I told her I wanted to talk about Mae Richards.

"You a cop?"

My badge was duly produced, evidence.

"She wasn't really involved with the theater so much these days. Her name still goes out on some of the letters, but it was more of a figurehead thing."

"Why's that?"

"I don't know. It was her decision. She was a busy woman."

"You liked her?"

"Sure." She stared at me without blinking. "I didn't like some of her friends."

"Which ones?"

"The white ones."

She uncrossed her legs and I sipped at the coffee, which did indeed taste like tar. I said, "Denise Corcoran, for instance? Wasn't she supposed to get her husband to come here one time?"

"Mae was so disappointed. We all were. We'd sent out flyers for that event weeks in advance. There could have been a lot of money in it for us. That flake. That fucking uptight arrogant movie asshole. Hey, and as if that weren't enough—he said he'd send a donation, and he never did. I'd like to skin his miserable white ass."

"Really?"

"I shouldn't say that, you being a cop."

"I guess not. Who are they saying killed her?"

She shrugged, pretending disinterest, a strong, sexy, obstinate figure. "I saw her a couple of times with an older white guy. He was obviously nuts about her."

"And Mae?"

"Hard to say. She seemed to be ignoring him, but that was the way she was sometimes, as if she was really the star she'd always wanted to be. Why are you so interested in the time Charlie Corcoran was supposed to come here?"

"I'm not sure," I said. I didn't explain that back then, while investigating Denise's murder, I'd spoken to one of Corcoran's assistants about the cancelation. The assistant was middle-aged, had worked for Charlie for twenty years, and had a weary understanding of all his faults and virtues. In her office, decorated with posters of each of his films, she'd told me he was asked to do about a hundred such appearances every day. One of the reasons he employed her was just to say no. Sometimes, however, Charlie would jump in himself and agree, pretty much on a whim. Invariably he'd get grumpy later and have her cancel, as here. At the time a follow-up visit to the Powerhouse had seemed unnecessary.

The black woman with the guitar was quiet, watchful.

"Do you know Ricky Lee?"

"Don't you?" she said, her voice so neutral, I could read it any way I wanted. Maybe she'd never laid eyes on the guy. Maybe she saw him on a daily basis.

"I thought maybe he'd happily give funds to keep going an organization like this one. Why bother with movie stars?"

"They make better publicity."

"I guess maybe I'll see you at Mae's funeral."

"Maybe."

"What's your name, by the way?"

"You gonna ask me on a date?"

I laughed. "You're tough."

"I've had to be."

"Why's that?"

"Why are you so interested in Charlie Corcoran?"

Back then there'd been no suggestion that Denise herself had been involved in setting up the engagement at the Powerhouse, or that she might have been upset by Charlie's behavior, and there was no suggestion now that he'd met Mae himself or even spoken to her. As far as he was concerned, he'd decided at the last minute against doing something to which he'd agreed in the first place only to hush up his troublesome wife. None of this necessarily implied that Mae had known anything of Denise's murder. Even so, I was intrigued, excited by the proof of some bond between the Corcorans and Mae Richards beyond those puzzling photographs. If this was an ordinary case, the lead would have been interesting but unremarkable, a previously unlooked-for because unnoticed and probably unimportant connection that now had to be chased down. The way I was coming at it, however, gave it the appearance of desired providence, more than a break, a crossing.

She had the guitar laid flat over her thighs now, and was leaning toward me with what might or might not have been a smile. Who knew what or who she was involved with? I'd long since learned to respect the mystery and surprise of character. "I might need to come and talk to you again."

"The door's always open," she said. "Not always to cops. And the name's Renata, since you asked."

THIS TIME AT CHARLIE CORCORAN'S HOUSE A GUY IN HIS twenties, a suited assistant, walked me through to the back, into one of the new additions, a gabled glass-and-concrete structure so long and airy it was almost like a church. This was where Corcoran kept most of his art. No doubt he came often to worship here, to pay respects to his money and his good taste. The assistant touched my elbow and asked if I'd care for a cappuccino. By then I was almost afloat on coffee but figured at least this would be a decent cup. I said sure, not exactly paying attention. I was too dazzled by what was up there on the walls, stuff by Picasso, Warhol, and Rauschenberg that even I recognized, though it was another picture that caught my eye: a ship on its blocks in the shipyard, undergoing refit. The style was broken and fractured, as if the canvas had been slashed to ribbons and then pieced back together through some labor of excruciating love, and the colors were grays, blues, and somber browns, yet the effect was of bustle and hope.

"Charlie's proud of that." The assistant was suddenly standing beside me. "He bought it for ten thousand dollars in 1985. Now its worth more than three quarters of a million dollars. Really." He handed me the steaming cup, precariously balanced on a tiny saucer. "He has a real eye for value."

Rain bit at the well-sealed glass in the gables. Shadows waved and swam, glimmering on the walls between the canvases. Moving my eye from masterpiece to masterpiece, blowing at the steaming surface of my coffee to cool it, I tried to assess the strange heat of the welcome. This time there was no bodyguard, no smirking lawyer on hand, no advisory thump in the belly. The assistant was more than polite. He was fawning. I didn't get it. I looked around for a place to set down the cup, but there was none. The assistant took it for me.

"He's probably got a guy who advises him about this stuff, tells him when and what to buy and sell?"

"Yes, but Charlie usually ends up giving him the tips." He leaned closer to whisper. "He once wrote a really *fabulous* paper on Diego Rivera. He's too modest to like people to know that."

Before the nature of Charlie's unexpected literary excellence could be further elucidated, my eye fell on the man himself, standing alone in a doorway at the far end of the gallery. He looked at the two of us with amused and narrowed eyes, squinting a little, as if he couldn't quite remember who we were, or at least earnestly seeking to convey that impression. He was tanned. He'd been somewhere in the sun and he'd lost a few pounds. In black cotton smock and shapeless black baggy cotton pants he still appeared impeccable, and his movements were looser, more athletic than when I'd last seen him, as if rewarded now with eternal youth as well as the not-guilty verdict. He really was the god that America wanted.

"You were looking at my ship." His diffident voice

was so low, I at once leaned forward. "Distorted vision or beauty, which would you say? There's a question to define a man."

"I like it."

"Bravo." He clapped his hands, once, a gesture that might or might not have been ironic. With Charlie it was hard to tell. Nor was there any sign that he was going to move farther forward. When the assistant started walking over to him, I realized that I was expected to follow. It was a dog thing. Charlie was defining who was the boss of this territory, this situation.

I trailed over toward his waiting hand.

"McGrath. I was thinking you'd send a letter or a fax."

Charlie preferred communications to be addressed to him in writing; that way they were evidence. He himself, on the other hand, dealt in words only orally, for these could always be denied later; but I was wondering why I was supposed to have sent him a letter or fax.

"I'm glad you came. I like that. The personal touch."

Now that the convoy had been assembled, with flagship Charlie in the van, we trailed back to the center of the room, the anonymous assistant dropping behind us and then disappearing. With each step and each shy, boyish grin that he gave me, I felt the full force of Charlie's urge to manipulate.

He said, "Well?"

I met his waiting eyes with a shrug.

"You came here to apologize. Am I right?"

I wondered where he'd got that idea.

"I issued my demand through the mayor. We're good friends. He mentioned that he'd been in touch with your boss. Why else would you be here?"

Now I began to understand. Murakami must have

given some such assurance, then realized he didn't have the nerve to pass on the command to me. He probably thought I'd never go for it. He was right, though now, standing in the midst of Charlie Corcoran's painted millions, I could see the humor in the situation, an amusement not unconnected with the knowledge that I'd shortly be sending this evil rooster to meet the great agent in the sky. I said, "I was out of line, sir. Please accept my apologies."

"You see. That wasn't so hard. Man can get used to anything, if only he reaches an appropriate degree of submission. Jung said that."

"Jung? I'd better check that guy out."

His smile was briefly wide as Wilshire Boulevard; then it was another diffident shrug, and the assistant was back with a red-bound offering in his hands, a movie script. The assistant said in a hushed voice, "This just came over from Mike."

"Good," said Charlie. "What about the other thing?"

The assistant paused. "He says there's a problem with the fee."

Charlie's amusement seemed genuine. "Really?" He turned to me. "They all want such enormous wages. Shocking." The next lines went to the assistant but were also for my benefit. He was like a spider, keeping lots of flies in the corners of his mind. "Tell him this. I'll press the first digit of the number at Warners, and for every ten new pages he delivers, I'll press the next one."

The assistant was gone again, and Charlie tapped the front of the script. "They want me to play the President. What do you think?"

He was the shy and playfully hesitant little lost boy again. Charlie was almost like a miracle, really, a Proust in reverse. It was as if he had no memory, had wiped from his conscience the ignoring of a child, the destruction of an unwanted wife. I wondered where he'd acquired these instincts and capacity for forgetfulness. They made him a natural murderer.

"I think you'd make a great President."

He gazed at me as if no other human being in the world existed, the look of a seducer who nonetheless expected me to do all the wooing. "Really?"

"They'd love you."

He seemed resentful for a moment, as if I'd gone too far, given the hint that I was pissing down the front of his pants. "Hey, it's just my opinion, I could be wrong. I don't know anything about your line of work," I said, and his neutral glance out the window told me that I'd lulled him back into the cozy cul-de-sac of being loved for so long by the *People*-reading millions. He was getting bored with me already. In his mind I'd come and done what I was supposed to do. A few more seconds, and he'd call the assistant to give me the friendly kiss-off.

"There's one more thing, Charlie."

His glance was incurious. I knew I'd have to present this cleverly, as if I were seeing his wife's murder in a very different light now, as if I'd bought his story and was on the case the way he wanted. "What does the Powerhouse Theater mean to you?"

He frowned. "Nothing at all."

Maybe he even believed this himself. "The day of your wife's murder. You were scheduled to make an appearance there. You canceled."

His smile was rueful. "I often do."

"Well, Mae Richards, one of the women who helped run the place, she's been murdered, too."

He took this without a blink. "I'm very sorry to hear that."

"It seems the lady was a friend of your wife's. I was wondering if you'd ever met her."

"No, never. I don't remember the name at all."

"A black woman. Middle-aged. A singer."

He frowned, thinking this through. In business it was his trick to appear straightforward, and this was definitely business. "What are you after, McGrath?"

"I'm trying to find out the truth. This is a lead like any other."

"The person who killed this woman may have had something to do with the murder of my wife?"

"I wouldn't venture to say."

Pursing his lips, reaching for one of the details that was filed away, he said, "I wish I could help. But as I say—I never heard Denise talk about this woman."

"Did you fight about the fact that you weren't going?"

"Certainly not." Composure barely ruffled, he turned to find the assistant once more beside him. "Ah, Robert. Remember the theater group, on the night of . . . Weren't we supposed to send them something?"

"A photograph."

Charlie's head drooped theatrically. "What went wrong?"

A few seconds passed while Robert the assistant, smiling, engaged with the realization that whatever had happened, he was going to have to eat it. He didn't seem to mind. "I messed up. Sorry, Charlie."

Charlie clicked his tongue and shook his head as if he was having to rein in his temper. He sighed, another John Barrymore moment. "Well, that's OK. But I think we should take care of this now, don't you?"

They conferred, Charlie hissed, there was a bustle, and they left the room. I don't know why, but I was enjoying myself. This was hilarious. I moved around the pictures on the wall until I was standing again in front of the crazy ship in its dry dock. In Los Angeles, art was both a status symbol and, possibly, a way to make a lot of quick cash. You could praise yourself for exquisite aesthetic discrimination while socking it away. No wonder there was so much crime in this area. Of course, you had to have capital in the first place, and a sure knowledge of the market.

Robert came back, saying, "Charlie had to take a call. He said specifically to say thanks for coming. Really. He appreciates it."

I took in his demeanor and appearance for the first time. He had tight, curly hair. His face was small and narrow, but his mouth was too big for it, with irregular white teeth. He wore little John Lennon glasses, and his eyes reminded you that the permanent human temptation is the temptation to be mean. He was a nice kid, but he was waiting his turn. He was probably as full of schemes and intrigue as the court of Caligula. When Charlie was out of town he'd lounge around the house, playing "What if?" Maybe he'd take a spin in the boss's swivel chair. I was just speculating. He knew that his job demeaned him, but fifteen years from now he might be the head of a studio with Ivy League graduates of his own to humiliate. Such was *his* gamble.

He had a silver-framed photograph in his hand. "Most of them we have to get printed up. He just doesn't have the time. But Charlie actually signed this himself. Look, it's inscribed."

I was flabbergasted, but I didn't resist when he pressed the thing on me. Handling the frame, turning it to the light of the window, I read: *To my beloved friends and colleagues at the Powerhouse.* I liked that "beloved."

That was *very* Charlie. "This was never sent?"

"No. At the time he hadn't signed it." He went on in an affectionate whisper, "It's a nightmare, trying to get Charlie to do anything, even stuff he's agreed to. Of course there's no one I love and admire more."

"How wonderful." The photo was a good one: Charlie in a dark shirt, glancing down a little, very charismatic and modest. "What exactly am I supposed to do with this?"

"Charlie asks if you can make sure it goes where intended. It's an original by Herb Ritts. It's probably worth five thousand dollars."

I drove away, winding down the canyon, wondering just how I felt about Charlie. I didn't know anyone who was a bigger prick. He was an arrogant asshole, but at least he was a *charming* asshole. He was funny. He was smart. He wore his outrageous good looks easily. When he turned it on, he had a grace that made you feel better about yourself. I remembered a story I'd heard when we were putting together the case against him. It was told to me by a beautiful young Englishwoman who used her aristocratic credentials to get to sleep with famous men. She'd described seeing Charlie walk into a restaurant in New York one time with Mick Jagger. The two of them were laughing, digging themselves, ignoring what they knew full well—that everyone's eyes were upon them. The air was crackling with sex. "These people become stars for a reason," she'd said.

For thirty minutes and more I circled Oakwood in the rain, down California, right on Sixth, left on Broadway, right on Fourth, right on Indiana, right on Seventh, all the way back to California, then Santa Clara. At last I found Jack Brewster. Standing on tiptoe in an alley off

Westminster, he held open the lid of a trash bin with one hand while poking about with a flashlight he held in the other. He didn't have his supermarket cart with him. There was a black nylon bag over his shoulder, but he didn't seem to have anything in it. I watched for a few seconds before he heard the Porsche and my windshield went all scattered diamonds in the turning beam of his flashlight.

I leaned over to open the passenger door and said, "Buy you lunch?" He didn't look excited by the idea, but this was an offer he couldn't refuse. "My treat. Tommy's Original Famous," I said.

He cheered up, remembering something, and smiled as he leaned into the car. He wore a black wool cap, a worn white scarf, and his soaked thrift-shop overcoat was tied with a length of string around the waist. "That friend of mine, that little hooker you met, Ruthie Pump, says she knows someone's soul by the shape of their shadow. She says she can see whether a man is good or evil. Some guys they've got shadows like anvils or hunchbacks or toads. And she says she was scared when she saw you, Detective McGrath, because you had no shadow at all."

"Very funny," I said. "It's raining. Of course I don't have a shadow."

As we drove down California toward Lincoln, he splashed his feet in the puddle beneath the dash and kept the black nylon bag hugged tight to his chest. "You nervous about something, Jack?"

"Nossir," he said. "Just not used to being in a car like this, is all. This is a nice ride."

"You really think so?"

"Sure, who wouldn't think so? This car French?"

"German."

"Yeah, right," he said, nodding vigorously, peeking out the window on my side. "Those guys know how to make machinery."

In Tommy's, at a table by the window, shaking himself dry, he said, "You payin'?"

"No."

"Shit, McGrath. I ain't got no cash."

"Wayne O'Donnell's paying. You know Wayne?"

His eyes kindled with fear, as if I were tricking him into something. "No, sir, I don't believe I do."

"He was sixteen years old, tailback on the football team at Santa Monica High, a kid with a golden future. He was in here one night after a big game, and some little banger from a different neighborhood comes in and wants to prove who's cock-of-the-walk. It started with words, then a shove, then more words. That other kid had a revolver tucked in the back of his jeans. The upshot of all this was that Wayne ended up face down in a quart bucket of chicken nuggets with the back of his head missing and the kid got sent away for life. You and me, we're the only beneficiaries, Jack, because I can come to Tommy's Original Famous and eat their reasonable hamburgers, their notable nuggets, and their truly excellent fries completely for free."

Jack was a little angry with me now. "Don't you ever get sick of it, McGrath? All this shit that you have to wade around in?"

Outside, on Pico, a storm drain was clogged. Puddles merged together so that the entire boulevard was a lake, shimmering, pockmarked by the continuing downpour. A Santa Monica blue bus cruised warily by, fans of water pluming out from its wheels, front and back. On the other side of the street, in a used-car lot, rows of BMWs and Mercedeses were chained down against the flood. I was thinking about Corcoran's poise, his smug assurance, and the negligent way he assumed he could make everything right with a signed photograph. It was breathtaking. He believed the vehicle of his luck to be secure against any storm. Maybe I'd misheard him, misunderstood the shattered daze in his eyes. Perhaps he was innocent after all. But I didn't believe that, just as I didn't believe that he'd been involved in the murder of Mae Richards. Guilty of one, I'd send him the bill for the other, settle the account, and let the rain come down on Charlie.

Jack's cheeseburger arrived. Rending it with strong, bony fingers, he fed in a couple of chunks.

I said, "I didn't bring us here to discuss my character, Jack."

He said, "No shit."

"I'm calling in a favor. A big one."

Wiping grease from his fingers, he lobbed the screwed-up napkin toward the trash. His eyes were shrewd now, but he said nothing as I unzipped the portfolio I'd brought with me and laid out the six photos under his gaze.

A chewed-up portion of burger tumbled a half-spin in his mouth. He said, "That's the movie star's wife, right? With Mae."

"They were friends."

"Get the fuck outta here."

"It's true, Jack. And now I want you to look at something else."

I showed him the photograph in the frame that Charlie Corcoran's assistant had given me just an hour or so before.

"What's this?"

"It's by Herb Ritts."

"Who's he?"

"It's Charlie Corcoran."

Coughing, spluttering, he covered his mouth. "I can see *that*," he said.

"He's the guy behind Mae's murder."

Jack was silent, stroking at his face, trying to ignore my eyes. At last he spoke, "How do you figure?"

"I want you to go to one of Ricky Lee's guys and tell him what you saw."

He exploded, pushing himself back from the table. "Fuck you. I saw *nuthin'*."

"You're not listening to me, Jack. Your memory's playing you false. It's playing tricks on you. Because you saw something in the trash outside Mae's house. When they ask what, you say it was a newspaper, with a story about the trial of that movie star guy, Charlie Corcoran. The picture with the story showed a guy in the background, a big bodyguard with hair cut *en brosse*. That means with hair cut real short, Marine style."

"I know what it means."

"You say you think you saw this guy outside Mae's house on the day of her murder. You say he had something up on his shoulder, a package or something. You say you've told the cops this story but they didn't seem too interested and you thought Ricky Lee Richards might be interested. You wonder if this information is worth, say, a couple of hundred bucks. Obviously you don't say you've had this conversation with me."

"Obviously I won't, 'cos I ain't doing this. I ain't messing with Ricky Lee Richards. You think I'm out of my mind?"

I glanced out the window, where another bus was working its way through the rain, and then I stared Jack in the face. "I hope your nephew is enjoying his time as a guest of the state of California. Because he can forget about his parole. And you'd better think about moving out of the Stardust, about getting away from Venice altogether. Because you walk a thin line with me, Jack, and I'll put out the word that you've been giving me suspects for money."

I packed all the photographs away in the portfolio again. I said, "I don't imagine that will do your reputation on the street a whole world of good. Of course, I could be wrong. What do *you* think?"

"You're bluffin'."

"Please don't try me."

He leaned toward me over his plate, spitting tiny pieces of French fry at my face as he spoke. "Man, I'm ashamed of myself for believing you're different than every other asshole cop I ever met. You're trying to get me killed."

I smiled. "Jack, let's not be melodramatic. Only you and I will know the story's bullshit, and I promise you I'm not telling. Ricky Lee won't know the diff. And even if he did, he'd thank you. Because you're helping me trap the guy who had Mae killed. And it *was* Charlie Corcoran."

"Shit," he said, this street-wise old man, bouncing his knee up and down, squeezing shut his eyes, and shaking his head. "I don't know, man."

"I don't want to be your enemy, Jack. You have to trust me. It's as simple as that." I leaned over, touching his liver-spotted hand.

"People are afraid of this guy, McGrath. He has guys shot. For whispers."

"And there are those who are afraid of me. I won't shoot you, of course, or encourage anyone else so to do. I'll merely spread the word that your well-being has definitely ceased to be of interest to me. It'll almost be like an experiment."

He said nothing, so I smiled.

"You needn't be afraid, Jack. C'mon, shit, I'm your buddy, and don't think I'm made of such dull stuff that Ricky Lee could try something with you and not have me to contend with. OK? I'll look after you. Just tell your story, and be convincing in the telling. Lay it on softly, as though you don't know whether it's important or not."

He looked at me with quick fear and even a little sorrow, as if I'd let him down.

I tried another smile. "You've got to decide where you live, Jack. Are you with me? Or the bad guys."

His expression didn't change. "Oh, I'm with you, detective."

16

THE CHAPEL WAS A SIMPLE A-FRAME. CONCRETE STRUTS rose to a point on either side of a triangular plate glass frontage, with twin glass doors at its center. It had a cuckoo-clock neatness, like a tiny piece of Switzerland planted at the frontier of Seventh and Broadway. Glancing behind me, as I made my way up the steps, I saw the flooded green acre of the Oakwood playground. Two crosses rose high on the church grounds, one dwarfing the other, but each with a loudspeaker at its crux, sending out solemn Bach into the neighborhood. There were cars still jamming into the lot; people were streaming up the steps; and even a couple of TV crews had turned out. I spotted Ward Jenssen but not before she'd spotted me, though she came over on her own this time, beneath a green-and-purple golf umbrella. We stood in the shelter of the porch.

"I wanted to apologize for the other day. That item after the trial came over too harsh. I'm sorry."

"That's OK." I was scanning the crowd for Ricky Lee.

"I don't want to be your enemy, Billy."

"Why not? We have such fun that way." I spotted

Zed the cameraman, sulking by one of the TV vans in a hooded slicker. I raised my hand, waving.

Ward said, "You here by yourself?"

I nodded. I'd told Cataresco there was no need for her to come along and fly the flag as well; she should get on with chasing down other stuff, though of course I had my own reason for not wishing anyone else from the Department to be present.

Ward shivered a little. "I hate covering funerals. They always make me feel like the worst kind of snooper. At least you've got a function here. You're going to find who killed this lady, and every one of these people will thank you, even if they won't be able to bring themselves to say it. Whereas they all know I'm just here for the sick thrill—not that it gives me one."

Mourners came up, jostling one another's umbrellas. I saw Richard Francis, dressed in blue pinstripe, white shirt, black tie, with a raincoat folded over his arm to add to the neat, precise appearance. He came up the steps in a hurry, glancing over at me with a worried nod before disappearing through the open glass doors into the chapel.

"Who's the Cary Grant guy?"

"A doctor. He delivered both Mae's sons."

"This lady was liked, wasn't she? She was a force. She had energy. Look at all these people. There must be, what? A couple hundred?"

"Easily."

"Think you'd get this many?"

"I don't really care."

"Yes, you do. You care very much, Billy. You want to be loved and respected by the people who matter to you."

"Maybe."

"I remember my dad's funeral. Gee, what a day that

was. Five people showed up and one of them was by mistake, a little guy with a Marine Corps pin in his lapel. Or maybe he just came for the food. It shouldn't matter, should it? But it seems to. It must be the thought that it's possible to earn a display of affection like this, actually to deserve it, to know you've moved people in some way. And if you don't, if you haven't, then it's pitiful. Like being a reporter at a funeral."

I'd forgotten what she was like when her defenses were down. She was softer; there was a searching tenderness in the way she looked at the world. She went on, "Other inappropriate things. For a Parisian to have good manners. For an Arab not to be rich. For someone who's been trying to get me fired to bring me fruit in the hospital."

"What exactly are you after, Ward? What do you want from me? I don't get it."

"It's very simple. I want to see you. It would make me happy."

"What *does* make you happy?"

"Oh, I don't know. Let's see now. Sex in the afternoon."

"Twinkling, in this weather?"

"Best of all in the rain, Billy."

A Toyota Land Cruiser swerved around the corner and stopped in the middle of the street, engine running. It was followed by another. Two of Ricky Lee's bodyguards sprang from the first and opened the rear doors on either side of the second. Only Ricky Lee got out. Shaking his head at the bodyguards, he came up the chapel steps on his own. His beard had been trimmed. Black beads of ebony hung down and swayed at the ends of his neatly braided dreadlocks. I briefly tried to catch his eye, but it was no good. Surrounded on the porch by friends, family, well-wishers, he seemed to notice no one. His grief was stubborn and muscular, single-minded. I gathered from his gloom and rage that he'd had no luck with the investigation from his end. In his line of work watchfulness, patience, and timing were all important. He had to know when to back off and when to act, sometimes violently. This, involving his mother, was different. I could sense his puzzlement and frustration. At the same time I knew he was a volcano. Sooner or later he'd go off all over someone. Better pretend that it could never be me.

A little girl ran toward him from inside. "Daddy!"

Ward Jenssen whispered, "I didn't know he had a daughter."

"Me either."

It was something all the files had missed. Not surprising: unless Ricky Lee had pointed out the fact himself during an arrest, no one else was likely to have noticed. He didn't exactly go around advertising the facts of his personal life.

The little girl had her father's big eyes. She was six or seven, a few years younger than Lucy. In a black velvet dress, with shiny black pumps, and black ribbons in her hair, she clung to his hands while he scooped her up into his arms and cradled her against his shoulder like salvation. I wondered why there'd been no picture of her on Mae's table, alongside Ricky Lee with his tennis racquet in happier days. Maybe I'd missed it, but I didn't think so.

A woman's voice came sharply from just behind us, inside the chapel doors. "Angie, come to Mommy now. Angie!"

Something about the voice arrested my attention. Turning, I couldn't see the woman's face in the blur and bustle of the crowd, but then I got her. It was Renata, the woman I'd met at the Powerhouse, dressed all in black, leaning forward with her tall strength to urge her daughter back to her. Even if she wanted to be no part of Ricky Lee's life anymore, she was still the mother of his child. Their exchanged looks were scarcely neutral therefore. She smiled, he didn't, kissing the little girl on the cheek and returning her gently to the ground. She ran back and clutched her mother's legs.

I didn't know what this connection meant, maybe nothing, but I knew now what I'd do with Charlie Corcoran's autographed Herb Ritts original.

Ward said, "Who's the woman?"

"Look, I have to go inside now."

"And I have to stay here. To get you all when you come out." She shrugged. "Work."

"Tell me about it."

"You still mad at me?"

"I never was."

"Don't say that. Otherwise I didn't do my job right. Call me, OK? Or I'll be calling you."

The chapel was packed. These were people who lived with murder. Each time a police chopper was overhead, each time one of their kids was a little late coming home, they'd wonder. So many gangsters died, so many and at such speed, that they were used to funerals. The older among them usually came to bury their children, and the younger to say goodbye to friends and comrades. Since Mae Richards was an exception, respected and older, loved, the outward display of tragedy was much the greater. It was like attending the funeral of a small child who was the unintended victim of a drive-by. This was something that was not supposed to happen. The grief was open and loud.

The coffin was at the front, a shiny brass-handled box laden with flowers. One by one, people walked up to touch it. Some paused to say a prayer or perhaps to caress a memory, while others came straight back, eyes down. It was raining in Oakwood.

Ricky Lee, in a pew at the front, didn't cry. He didn't move. His face had no expression. Once or twice his dreadlocks bobbed, swinging from side to side, as he looked over toward his daughter. The blond girlfriend came in late and slid her legs beside him. She seemed flustered, smiling, and then put on a sad face, getting into character, or maybe this was just her entrance. Ricky Lee's eyes burned at her with a swift, molten fury, and then it was the mask again, stone.

The preacher was a guy I'd seen around the neighborhood. He drove a bronze Cadillac. In his fifties, slim and trim and balding, he had tight gray curls, tufts almost, that flowed down the side of his face into incongruously luxuriant muttonchop whiskers. Driving by the chapel on a Sunday, you'd hear his thunderous voice rolling out.

He took off his glasses, rubbed his eyes, and sighed. He seemed exhausted for a second by having to try to make sense of it all, by having always to explain and offer. "The valley is lurking with darkness. It is lurking with predators," he said. "But Thou art with us, Lord. Thy rod and Thy staff will comfort us. We will dwell in the house of the Lord forever." Loudspeakers buzzed, crackled, then sang into electric life, with Mae Richards's voice this time.

Two women of Mae's own age, weeping, groaning, clung to each other for support. The preacher's voice rang out with tears. He led them now in a throbbing chant of sorrow. "Our Father, which art in Heaven, hallowed be Thy name . . ."

Ricky Lee's lips weren't moving. Our eyes met and

locked above the heads of the congregation. I thought I
knew what was within that tight nut, his mind. He was
thinking: I've got the money, money can buy anything,
and this guy McGrath's good, he's supposed to be the
best. If my guys don't come up with anything and he
does, sure, I'll pay for it; this is important, it's about family, my mother, looking after my own house.

I nodded at Ricky Lee almost gently, as easy as lying,
and after the service gave him a number I'd jotted on a
piece of scrap. It was for a pay phone in a Culver City
restaurant. For a while, after Ellen and I split, I'd been
seeing a woman who worked in costumes over on the
Sony-Columbia lot, and I'd gone there a few times for
lunch. It was Italian, nothing special, one of a hundred
similar places around the city: white cloths, bottles of
Chianti on the tables, distressed yellow paint on the
walls. As an apartment you'd say it was the home of a guy
who hated himself—but it wasn't an apartment.

I got there a little early. I took a table by the window,
ordered a coffee, and watched the rain hammer at an
abandoned art deco movie theater on the other side of
the street. The theater had a ticket booth with gold
wings on the side, like a magic cap that would help you
fly. On the roof there was a spire that vanished upward
into moisture and mist. The waiter appeared at my
elbow with my coffee, and I stirred in low-fat with gentle turns of the spoon. I wasn't even sure that Ricky Lee
would call. I wasn't quite sure that I wanted him to.

I was thinking about the two men I'd killed in my life.
The first had been in messy self-defense, during a
weapons-drawn search early in my career as a cop. A guy
had dropped on top of me from the ceiling with a gun in
his hand. We struggled on the floor, and then I got my
gun close to his body and pulled the trigger twice. The

shudder as the rounds entered his body made me unsure just who'd been shot. I was blinded for a moment by something hot hitting in my face. I tried to get out from under him but I couldn't, and when he went limp, his dead weight pressing down on my chest, the blood didn't stop. A bullet had perforated his lung.

They drove me home without letting me speak to anyone. I was still covered with blood when Ellen opened the door. She said not a word. She led me to the bedroom, undressed me, and stood me under the shower.

The Department's presumption is that if a police officer shoots and kills someone while on duty, it is most likely *in the line of* duty, and therefore subject to investigation, not at first by homicide, but by the Officer Involved Shooting Unit. You cool your heels at home waiting, or getting your story clear in your head. From the outside this seems unjust; sometimes it is. On the other hand the guys in OIS are like Internal Affairs. They're not understanding, forgiving people.

We went through it all, and they made their recommendation to the Police Tribunal. The shooting was judged and found justified, but I was shaken for months. I'd wake, breathless and fighting, in the middle of the night, feeling his weight again, and his life spraying over me in a gush.

What happened the second time, about a year ago, had been raised by DEA and FBI guys down at the coroner's office on the day of the Mae Richards autopsy. The suspect's name was Farber. He'd been arrested in Rampart division, and had been cuffed when the detective knelt down to tighten his shoelaces, giving him the chance to take off. There was a citywide search, because Farber had served time for two homicides already and was suspect in several more. In his mid-twenties, a member of the Mexican mafia, hard-core Salvatora Mara-trucha, he'd been a stone killer since the age of twelve. We got a tip that he was hiding out in an apartment in Palms. Drew Diamond was first through the door, but I was the one who found him, with a Mac 10 machine pistol in his hand, about to climb out the back bedroom window. I shouted at him, "Freeze!" He didn't. I told him to lay down his weapon; he swung it round toward me. I wasn't afraid. I made the shot as if I were a teenager again, nothing more at stake than the future of a Coke can, glittering on top of a moorland wall.

This time I was driven home by an awestruck young patrolman. He kept sneaking glances at me. He couldn't believe he was in the same car with such a hero. I wished I could have slapped that bullshit out of him. I called Ellen from the marina apartment and she asked what I was feeling. "Not much," I said. Did I want to come over? "No, it's OK. Kiss Lucy for me." This time there were no dreams, though it was soon after that my depression began. Farber wasn't the reason, but he was the trigger. With the loss of Ellen and Lucy, with my loss of heart, with the loss of all that was best in me, and the growth of boredom in my work that inevitably followed, I came to feel I had no more right to continued existence than the murderer I'd killed. It was as if I'd lived, loved, lost, and closed the door.

The pay phone was in back by the men's room in a quiet place. When it rang, I calmly put down my cup and signaled to the waiter that I'd take it.

"McGrath," said Ricky Lee. "You wanted to talk?"

The board above the phone was layered with flyers for clubs, apartments for rent, acting classes. A gangster had slashed his tag on the wall in jerky letters that ran up and down the paint: JOKER.

I said, "I guess you've proved your point, Ricky Lee. It seems that every man has his price. But mine's not five hundred thousand. It's a million. One million dollars."

"Fuck you."

"You're asking me to kiss goodbye to twenty years of keeping my head above the hullabaloo. I'm not going to negotiate. I have a name. I know the man who killed your mother. So now it's up to you. One million. Take it or leave it. What do you want to do?"

"I'm gonna kill the motherfucker that killed my mother."

"I take it that you're accepting my proposal?"

There was a pause before he said, "I'll listen to what you got to say."

"Bring the money."

"I'm gonna have to check out your story first."

"No dice, Ricky Lee. I'm on the point of wrapping up my case against this perpetrator. I've got a witness who puts his trigger guy outside your mother's house an hour before the body was found. My murder book is nearly all together, and before I tell you even the first chapter of it, I want to see that money."

His anger emptied the air between us. "It'll be there."

On the way back to Venice I bought a large envelope, put the signed photograph of Charlie Corcoran inside, and slipped this, unaddressed, unsealed, and without a note, through the mailbox at the Powerhouse Theater, figuring that if Jack told one of Ricky Lee's homeboys his story, and the photograph perhaps reached Ricky Lee by this other route, so much the better. I was thinking all this through, planting clues, fixing my story, making my own book.

17

AT THE PRECINCT HOUSE THE PHONES SOUNDED SHRILL. A door slammed so loud it seemed to bounce inside my head. Of course it was possible that Ricky Lee, even though he'd agreed to the one million, would have second thoughts and decide not to go for it. I was prepared for that. I'd just walk from the meeting we'd set for the next day. The important thing was that I'd been given a choice, and now I'd acted on it, made my decision, stepped over a line no one, including myself, thought I'd ever cross. I felt excited, afraid, thrilled with all the electric tingling nerve ends of a kid doing something he shouldn't for the first time.

"Two guys came by to see you," said Cataresco. "A guy from the DEA and another from the FBI. They were like two of the seven dwarves, except one of them was real tall. The other had a ponytail and was so pretty and vain he seemed to think I was about to ask him out for a date. Fat chance. You know what he said to me? This little blond midget said, 'Are you gay, Cataresco? Hey, it's OK if you are. I think it's wonderful that gays and lesbians are encouraged in the Department these days.'"

"What did you say?"

"I said if he wished to indulge himself in every insecure straight guy's fantasy about a strong woman, it was OK with me. I also advised him that he was wearing long hair past his prime. What about you, Billy? Do you think I'm gay?"

"Well, now that you ask. No. Definitely not. It's funny. I don't remember the DEA guy being *that* small. Doesn't the federal government have height requirements?"

We were in the squad room. I was at my desk, hands clasped at the back of my head, the doors of the murder book cabinet locked behind me. Cataresco sat opposite, chewing gum and leaning with her elbows on the far end of the table. Larry Murakami's Ping-Pong ball was where I'd left it, in a cup. I took it out and bounced it on the floor a couple of times.

"So what did those guys want, apart from your favors?"

"They asked a bunch of questions about Ricky Lee."

"And?"

"I told them that as far as we were concerned, we weren't sure that he was involved in any way in his mother's death."

"Good girl. Keep those snoopers out of it."

She stared at me, smiling and folding another stick of gum into her mouth. She was pleased about something, something else.

"What?"

"Guess?"

"I'm no good at guessing."

"I forgot. Intuition's your bag, right. Isn't that supposed to be a woman's trait?"

"I'm in touch with my feminine side, Cataresco. You know that."

"Remember the garbage bag?"

"On the floor at Mae's house, even though there was a spinner full of 'em on the wall. Maybe someone brought their own. I remember."

"Turned out there was a batch number on it. Was sold at a Staples superstore some time between two and three months ago. Guess where?" She held up hands with clear-varnished nails. "OK, OK, I know you don't guess."

"Long Beach."

"Hey, you're *good* at this. That's correct. Long Beach. Which is close to . . ."

"Palos Verdes and the home of Dr. Richard Francis."

"Who also has a clinic at Long Beach Memorial once a week." The ground shivered a little, as if in a fever. "You feel that?"

"Only a little one, a reminder that we're in Los Angeles living on a fault line, lest we ever forget. You were saying about Francis."

"Just that. The garbage bag came from a Staples store on Long Beach Boulevard."

Her look was expectant and hopeful, the way I'd looked myself in college when faced with a teacher I admired. This was why she'd come to work at Ocean. I was the best in the city. I'd teach her to put together murder books so tight and crisp that other tyros would be looking over them in awe for tips in ten years' time.

I said slowly, "The garbage bag is good. I like this garbage bag."

"Look at what we got. He and Mae were lovers. So that's a motive for any one of a number of possible reasons."

"Maybe."

She counted off the points on her slender fingers. "He was at the house the afternoon of the homicide, so that's proximity and opportunity."

"Maybe. And against?"

"You leaned on the guy pretty good and he didn't cough."

"So if he did do it, and I'm not saying I think he did, we're gonna have to get more before I'd feel comfortable going back there or bringing him in to put on some more pressure. He was at the funeral today. He was hurting. I could see that. He probably knew that no one there was exactly overjoyed to see him."

"Would you go, if you'd killed her?"

"Where's Drew?"

"He said he had to go buy a gift."

"A gift? I don't believe it. I thought Christmas went by already."

"What do you think, Billy?"

"About what?"

"About Francis. Is he that cold-blooded?"

I said I wasn't sure. I couldn't tell her that what I was about to do with Ricky Lee and Corcoran, man, *that* was cold-blooded. My own life wasn't at risk. This wasn't a heat-of-the-moment thing, but more along the lines of a prepared hit. It was being done at a distance. Charlie's body wouldn't be lying on top of me like a sack of concrete with blood gushing out. It made matters worse, in a way.

Cataresco stood up from her chair and stretched. She came around to my side of the desk and stared at the Mae Richards murder book, turning a couple of pages, looking for a special sign.

"Tell me what *you* think."

She said, "I think Francis killed her."

"Any defense attorney heard you say that this early in the investigation, you'd never make the case."

"I know I shouldn't jump to conclusions on so little

evidence. But what was it you once said to me? You said it was OK to have hunches, hunches could be fine, as long as you remembered that no one else has to believe them. Therefore they mean you have to gather twice as much evidence. I want to go talk to this guy. Can I?"

I shifted in my seat, rolling the smooth surface of the Ping Pong ball between my fingers. "I don't think that's such a good idea. Not yet."

She ducked her head. "Oh, man, there's something weird about this. I've got such a strange feeling. I just think he did it."

In the Circle Bar after a couple of drinks I glanced up at the TV and thought for a moment about calling Ward Jenssen. The news was on. Her business card was in my wallet, with her home number scribbled on the back; and, dodging past a sullen biker with broken teeth, then a nutty-looking guy with long hair that flew out from under his baseball cap like a pair of wings that had been given an electric shock, I got as far as the phone at the back and had my hand on the hung receiver before deciding instead to go see Ellen and Lucy.

The parking lot was a map of Minnesota, nothing but lakes. Weaving between them, trying to keep my feet dry, I thought about Cataresco. I knew what was going on in her mind. She wasn't going to let this case go. I'd have to duck and dodge to make sure she didn't solve it and get me killed, because if I took one million from Ricky Lee and was then forced by Cataresco to turn up in court with some other perpetrator, he was going to come looking for me with that famously mean temper. I was wondering: even if I knew for sure, for an absolute certainty, that Francis had killed Mae Richards, if I had his freely given confession signed and witnessed in my hand, would I be prepared to hand him over to Ricky Lee? Probably not. I wasn't prepared to have just anyone killed for money.

What I was doing was wrong. I'm not trying to excuse myself. I couldn't even point at Charlie Corcoran's civic worthlessness. He kept thousands in work. Millions more were probably in love with the idea of the guy, and Denise Corcoran had been no angel. When I thought about it, I didn't much like the idea of playing God, handing over Corcoran, and telling Ricky Lee to go ahead and get the job done, like a coach working out the game plan for his top guy: *Now go execute.* Though, of course, for me, that's not what it was all about. There was a sense of planned justice here, the righting of an imbalance, the mending of a terrible wrong; and then there was also the heat and excitement of my personal feelings—my resentment of Charlie, my need for the cash.

I knew that death has ten thousand different doors through which men can make their exits, and here I was, blueprinting one of my own invention, just for Corcoran. Experience told me that such doors sometimes turn out to have trick hinges. They bounce back and catch you in the eye. This was risky; Cataresco and Diamond were no dopes, and I was trying to be smart.

I had my hand on the car door when I turned to see the guy from the bar, eyes wild and rain sparkling in those frizzed-out wings of hair. Drunk, staggering in his boots, he had a knife in his hand, a dull, short blade. "I'm gonna rob ya," he said. "Whaddya say to that? Give me ya money, motherfucker." Then he jerked, a bodily spasm that sent him forward with the knife, but so slowly, so predictably, that I simply stepped out of the way and he almost fell over, stumbling and cursing, carving thin air with the blade.

"I really don't think that's a good idea. First, I'm a cop. Second, I've got this," I said, sweeping back my jacket to reveal the Beretta.

"Oh, shit, man," he said, letting the knife drop to his side, as if this were typical of his life, the unfairness of the world. "Can you believe that?"

"Know what'll happen if you go on like this? Either you'll get killed and I'll see you on a steel tray down at the county morgue, or else you'll kill someone yourself, in which case you'll be mine. I'll *own* you, bro."

"I know it, man," he said, stamping his boot and sending all that hair flying, "I'm so *fucked up*." This came at him as if he'd never thought of it before, with the effect of genuine revelation, prompting a change of course and tactic. "How about you lend me something, then?"

"No, but I'll give you five bucks. How about that?"

He smiled, showing crazy teeth. *"Bandidos desperados."*

"That sounds like really bad Spanish," I said, handing over the bill. "I'm gonna get in out of the rain now, OK?"

I drove away laughing, slapping the wheel of the Porsche and asking myself: how much clearer a warning do you require? What I was doing was precisely the wrong move. As a professional student of homicide I knew what tended to happen to the best, the simplest of plans—they get all fucked up. The guy you try to rob turns out to be a cop. The getaway driver has a fight with his girlfriend and is late. A baseball bat is grabbed, the gun having jammed, and the bat gets used, washed, cleaned, all but for a strand of the perpetrator's hair caught in a crack in the varnish. An unexpected knock from a UPS guy in a hurry, with a special delivery of vitamins for the woman recently deceased in the bedroom, causes the perp to rush about for cash, then for a pen with which to sign, because the UPS guy's has run out, and, in the fumble, what should slip unnoticed to the floor as he extracts two twenty-dollar bills from his wallet but one of his own business cards? Believe me, I've seen it. I've held that card.

The house on Nowita was a beacon, golden light streaming from every window. Running up the muddy path, I heard laughter and Mahler, lushly redolent of the end of it all. I paused at the door, knocked, and heard the laughter die away before walking in.

"Hey, everybody," I called, standing in the doorway and stamping my feet, and then immediately feeling a fool. There were six of them around the candlelit table. I knew all the guests. "Hi, Rachel. Hi, Tom." Rachel was a producer of small independent films, Tom a fancy Venice architect who'd thrown up several as yet uninhabited glass hexagons on Abbot Kinney. The other couple were James and Becky, whose professions I couldn't remember, though I did recall that they had a boy, John, a happy two-year-old with a very big head. The fifth guest was Drew Diamond. He sat opposite Ellen at the head of the table, my one-time perch. He put his glass down quickly, avoiding my eyes, and got to his feet.

"I'd better go," he said, and I suddenly caught a glimpse of a very different Drew, a guy awkward and stumbling, but trying to do the right thing, not because of me, but because of Ellen. "Or do you want me to stay?"

"Stay," said Ellen, holding up her hand, looking at me. "Billy," she said in a resigned way, making herself calm. "Is this urgent?"

My insides were snapping about. "Urgent. I don't know. You tell me. What's going on?"

"Dinner. Isn't that obvious?"

"Really?"

"Can we not get into this now?" she said, looking at the others with an apologetic shrug.

"Oh, but I want to get into this. Right now."

"*Billy,*" she said, pleadingly.

I wanted this to be about her and me, no one else. When Rachel and Tom exchanged looks, I wanted to deafen them with my anger. I felt myself shaking. The thing to do was leave. That was the smart thing; not make a scene. "Excuse me, folks," I said. Ignoring the blaze of Ellen's eyes, I walked past her chair, through the living room, down the darkened corridor, and into Lucy's bedroom, shutting the door and leaning against it so that the back of my head touched where her coat was hanging.

The house's wafer-thin walls made me an uneasy eavesdropper as conversation tried to pick itself up again in the living room. A knife clicked, someone coughed, and that doomy music went on in the background. Drew said it was late and he should be leaving, and Ellen said he mustn't, she wouldn't hear of it.

Drew and Ellen: my anger fizzled into disbelief. How could I have been so blind as to miss something like this? Was he kind? Was he funny? Had I been unable to see so much that was crucial about the guy? Ellen and *Drew?* Was he good in bed? Had they *been* to bed? Oh, God.

A night lamp on the bedside table lit the empty room, brushing with its golden glow all Lucy's drawings, her skateboard, her Brad Pitt posters, the bear with the floppy head that I'd bought the day she was born. Everything felt soft and soothing in here, intimate. There were maps of Africa and Europe on the walls. There was another of those Apple computers on her desk, screen softly aglow and more fish, issuing bubbles. There was a striped cotton rug on the floor that we'd picked up on a day trip to Ensenada. There was a watercolor she herself had painted of the San Gabriel Mountains, mysterious and still snow-capped. There were postcards of favorite art on a bulletin board and stars on the ceiling, recent additions, five-spiked bursts of gold against a backdrop of purple and blue.

It was a room to retreat to, a reflection—I liked to tell myself—of a little girl with a calm and wonderful inner life. I remembered when one of the teachers at Carrefour had asked the kids for an essay on what they expected to do when they grew up. Lucy had written that she expected to exhibit at MOMA, to visit Holland and spend days in all the galleries, to water-ski in Tenerife, to cruise the world on an ocean liner with her brushes, to lie on a beach somewhere hot beneath palm trees and sip coconut milk like Gauguin. My word, the teacher had said, will Daddy be able to pay for all this? Lucy had come home that night with the same question. She'd just wanted to know what the deal was. "It's OK. It's fine if you can't," she'd said. "I'll just have to make it happen up here." And she'd tapped the side of her head.

From the other room I heard chairs scraping, the thump of feet, thanks, and goodbyes. It had taken a little while, but I'd embarrassed them all into leaving. A flush rose up my face. This wasn't any way to behave. Ellen was saying to James and Becky, "If you need Lucy and me to come babysit Wednesday, just give us a shout, OK? We'd love to. And let's do this again before we leave." Drew was the last to go, staying behind after the others and asking Ellen if she was sure she was going to be all right. His tone was affectionate, gentle, unpushy. Ellen said, "It's fine, really. Call me." They kissed.

A few moments later she came in, wheeling her chair

and pushing the door shut, a soft click and then one only slightly louder, a swift sonic combination that, when I was living in this house, putting Lucy to bed myself, or lying in our own on the other side of the hall, waiting for Ellen to come back after having done so, meant family, home.

"You spoiled my party."

"Sorry. Sor-ry."

"Hey, it's OK; there'll be another." Her eyes narrowed and wrinkled at the edges as she smiled. Ellen had the greatest smile, as if she'd been struck in the chest with something happy. This was just a hint of it.

She was doing her best to be calm. I said, "Where's Lucy?"

"Sleeping over. At Dominique's. Remember? The little girl whose parents are French."

"I guess Drew was also planning to sleep over."

"You've no right to ask that."

"I know. But I am asking. Are you fucking him?"

She waited, searching my eyes, before she said, "Yes, I am."

"Well, that's that, then," I said, and flopped on the chair beside Lucy's computer, not exasperated, but drained, exhausted, the life tugged out of me, sucked from me as if by a cruel beak. I didn't want to think about it. A memory came up, of Drew fixing himself a slice of bread at a crime scene, and I was suddenly furious again. "You and Drew? What is this, a joke? The guy has no compassion. He's a loser. Christ, Ellen, the guy likes Pauly Shore."

"You don't know anything about him, Billy. You pushed him out of the way and tried to forget that he'd been your friend. He's not at all like you think. Drew's no loser. And he needs my help."

"So do I." The words came out loud enough that they stunned the air to silence. "I'm in pain."

"We all are."

I stood up, laughing, and leaned my head against the bulletin board, pressing in on all that art. I wondered why it was that I only revealed myself to Ellen, the one person who could be relied on to call my bluff. She'd been the audience for the best and worst of me, the giddy waltzes around the room with Lucy, the smashing of crockery and furniture, the times when a murder brought me to tears. She once said, "I've got your number," and maybe she was right. Sometimes, when we were married, it felt like war, combat to the death, but at least there'd been life in the fight.

"When I came in, and there you all were, I wasn't really seeing any of you. I caught a glimpse of the chaos of my own soul. I could have killed him, Ellen, and you. It scares me, it *terrifies* me, the thought that I could hurt you anymore. Jesus, you know I love you."

Eyes closed, shaking her head, with light burning to gold the chestnut edges of her hair, she said, "You mustn't say that."

"Why not?"

"I care for you, Billy. I have more respect for you and admiration than you know."

"And at some point, maybe not now or in the next couple of weeks, but some time we're going to get back together."

Her voice was soft, but there was no hint of a smile. "Oh, Billy."

"Look, I know that you're going to Seattle and that lately it's seemed unlikely; but we're going to be together, one day, all three of us, right? Isn't it inevitable?"

When Ellen came over, took my hand, and squeezed, a sad pressure intended to comfort, I realized for the first time how hard I'd been holding on to this hidden spark of hope, and how forlorn it was. I was never going to get her back, and while I struggled with this illumination, her hand began to shake in mine. She said, "I'm thirty-seven years old, Billy. I'm a woman on my own. I'm a cripple. I'm never going to walk again on the beach or in Griffith Park. I'm never going to drive a car by myself clear up the coast to Crescent City. I'll never stand again in the redwoods feeling the earth under my feet while the wind whispers through the trees. If I go to a restaurant, I have to have someone help me onto the toilet. Trust me, it's not an attribute most men find attractive. I'll never go to the back of beyond with Drew or you or anyone else, backpacking and fishing, swinging Lucy in my arms. I'm not exactly the world's most energetic lay. I'll never swim out at Point Dume, because I need calmer waters. I need him, Billy. That's the truth."

Her coiled body shook with tears and sobs. "I want this new start so bad, but how in the end do I know I can make it all work out? I can't do this alone," she said. "I'm frightened, Billy."

18

RICKY LEE WASN'T SMILING IN THE ROSE CAFÉ. HE was jumpy and on edge, taking care of necessary if unpleasant business. He looked at me without expression or humor and said, "The men's room. Check it out." Turning to go, crossing past the counter with its hissing coffee machines, I felt his eyes at my back, on fire with the need for revenge.

One of his guys was in there already, a dude in baggy black sweats, staring in the mirror with his right forefinger holding down one reddened eyelid as though there were something wrong with it. Slick, not like one of the regular bodyguards, he turned to me and put on a pair of round-rimmed glasses. He looked more like an accountant than a tree armed with an Uzi, and he threw down a black sports bag from Gold's Gym. Unzipping it, he disclosed a trove of hundred dollar bills, banded together and stacked so thick and high, I couldn't thrust my hand through to the bottom, let alone begin to count. "There's five hundred thousand here. You get this now, when you and Ricky Lee finish talking, *if* he's satisfied. The other half you get when the guy's dead."

"That wasn't the deal."

"It's *our* deal," he said, zipping up the bag, walking out, and leaving me holding my dick, taking a leak while I decided whether or not to make a fuss about this power play. I didn't, afraid I was running out of time. I was concerned that Cataresco had something I didn't know about and would soon close the case behind my back. I was still dazed about Ellen and Drew, anxious about Lucy, and, besides, drying my hands with a paper towel, straightening my suit as if getting ready for an interview, which in a sense I was, I told myself I was on top of everything.

Ricky Lee was waiting when I went back, already seated at one of the high, awkward tables. The Rose was pretty much empty, due to the rain. As well as the accountant guy, who'd taken another table by himself and was unfurling a copy of *Forbes* while the money bag rested securely between his booted feet, Ricky Lee had brought along only one of his regular warriors, his most trusted guy, no doubt, an imposing figure who sat facing away from me near the door, with a leather trenchcoat snuggling up to a neck as wide as most people's backs. The guy was so huge, it was a moment or two before I noticed Ricky Lee's final companion, a chocolate-colored pit bull whose vindictive snout nosed at my trouser leg.

"Yo, Luther," said Ricky Lee. "Don't bite the cop. Not yet."

He fed the dog a torn-off portion of raspberry croissant. This wasn't quite the situation I'd envisaged for my pitch. I said, "Your mother was killed by a man named Charlie Corcoran. You've heard of him, I assume. He was in jail when the murder took place, but it was his guy pulled the trigger."

Though Ricky Lee's hand was still held down at the

dog's lapping tongue, his attention was all mine now. "Bull*shit.*"

"Charlie Corcoran," I said. "He's the guy."

His face was a mask of wild scorn. "You hate the mother-fucker," he said. "I watch TV. You just tryin' to set him up."

Thus far, his reaction was as expected. I said, "Yeah, well, this is an area where you and the district attorney happen to be in complete agreement. It's true that there's no love lost between me and Charlie. It's also true that he had someone rape your mother and then put a bullet in her brain."

He made no sound, but there was a tremor in his hands and a movement in his eyes, as if two continents, one icy calm and one scorching, clashed behind there while he debated whether to reach out and grab my throat.

"I'll do my best for a conviction, but it's most likely for not. The guy's got everyone in the same shape as you, thinking that the cops are haunting him. Well, in one way he's right. I'm his ghost in particular, crazed by the hunt to bring that fucker down. He killed your mother, man, so the question is: What are you going to do? Because my guess is that the DA won't take it to court. If we couldn't convict him of his wife's murder, what chance have we got with your mother, a middle-aged black nobody whose son is a notorious gangster? Excuse me, I'm just stating the facts as the DA will undoubtedly look at them. Of course, he may see an appealing political angle in all this. Don't count on it."

I truly appreciated for the first time how dangerous Ricky Lee was. He had his arm raised, signaling to the soldier at the door. I didn't turn to see what was going on. If, at the end of this, Ricky Lee was unconvinced, he'd probably have me killed. Maybe the guy at the door was getting ready to shoot me in the back even now.

This wasn't fucking around. I was going for broke, determined to bring this off by sheer force of will and cunning, living on my wits as I smiled, saying, "The DA's the kind of guy has his teeth polished a lot, if you understand what I'm saying. He's only interested in dead blacks in Oakwood if they can help his dentistry. Your mother doesn't fit the bill."

I didn't know whether Jack Brewster had yet talked to any of Ricky Lee's people, or if word of that contact had come back to Ricky Lee himself. If both those things had happened, my task would be easier right now; if not, then Ricky Lee would get his corroboration later. It didn't make too much difference, as long as our stories meshed.

No bullet had slammed into me yet. There'd been no sudden or violent motion, though Ricky Lee looked as though he was itching to lash out. His eyes shifted their fire from the guy at the door and locked back into mine.

"I've got a witness who saw Corcoran's bodyguard at your mother's house the day she was killed. He was carrying in something, a package or big bundle of some kind. Now the bodyguard, this is a strong guy, a military guy. He could lift your mother easy."

Ricky Lee relaxed a little. His eyes moved away from my face to the door banging in the wind. "Yeah, I heard something about that bodyguard guy."

Good, I thought; well done, Jack. A good guy, faithful to me.

I said, "This is the way it went down. Denise and Charlie Corcoran had a Downs syndrome baby. He'd wanted her to abort it, but she wouldn't, and he made her hide the boy down in Texas with her former mother-in-law. It's an ugly story, the kind of thing that might have damaged or even destroyed his reputation. But he got the mother-in-law squared away, and he thought Denise would come around in time. But she didn't. She couldn't live with herself. The fact that she'd gone along with this was tearing her apart. All of this was going on around the time she got to know your mother. It was through the theater. Now Mae must have had a big heart, because sometimes Denise's little boy would come to Los Angeles and your mother would let them visit at her house."

Ricky Lee's eyes slid to the six photographs I'd taken from the portfolio. I didn't move my head; I didn't move a muscle.

"Denise wanted to do something for Mae in return, so she arranged for her husband to appear at a fund raiser. It would mean a lot of money. But on the day, Charlie had one of his people call to say he wasn't going to be able to make it. He was a busy guy, a famous guy, he'd gotten confused with his commitments, they were all terribly sorry. Look, there's a picture of your mom and Denise and the little boy, the Downs baby." I laid down the snapshot given me by Louise Szell, and Ricky Lee inclined his head toward it. I figured I should do this as if conducting an interrogation in reverse. I was the one doing all the talking, but I tried to keep my attitude the same: businesslike, calm, carefully not seeming as if I were trying to reel him in or close the deal. "Now, they'd advertised this thing weeks ahead at the theater. It was big for them, and Mae wasn't just about to let it go. So she called Denise. Denise said she and Charlie had been arguing about it. Here, you want to take a look at the phone company records?"

I showed him some of the stuff I'd pulled as a matter

of routine from GTE. There, highlighted in yellow on the first page, was the call from Corcoran's office to the theater on the day of his wife's death. "And this is for your mother. She made a call to one of Corcoran's unlisted numbers. He changes them every couple of months or so. You see?" The number I pointed to was for a dry cleaner's on Montana Avenue, but I thought I could reasonably assume Ricky Lee wasn't going to know that; nor was he likely to be intimate with all, or indeed any, of Charlie's actual numbers.

This was still very dangerous. I was aware every moment of the monolithic guy at the door, scoping out my back while Ricky Lee looked away, nodding to himself, as if to say, *of course, of course.* His eyes came back to me with a sharp swing. "How does all this lead to my mother gettin' killed?"

"Corcoran's people said they'd send a signed photograph or some such bullshit, something worth money she could put up for auction."

"Yeah, that's somethin' else I heard about." From inside his black jacket he took the photograph, the one by Herb Ritts, no longer in its frame but folded in half. He spread it on the table on top of the other stuff.

"Where'd you get this? It wasn't at Mae's house."

He shrugged. "I also heard that you went to see my wife. My ex-wife."

"She tell you that?"

Ricky Lee didn't answer.

"And I never even knew you'd been married. Isn't life full of surprises? I saw your little girl. At the funeral. She's beautiful. You should be proud."

"She's my angel. You got kids, McGrath?"

"One. A little girl also."

"Yeah, that's right. I think I knew that." His voice

was lazy, indifferent, while his alert eyes searched for meaning, first in the photograph of Charlie Corcoran smiling his movie-star smile, and then in my face. His eyes wouldn't let me go. I was their prisoner as they reached forward, probing my guts, reminding me to take nothing for granted. He was a clever guy, mind clear and instincts sharp after all those years of getting away with what he'd been getting away with. It was almost as if he were sniffing at me, just as his dog had been curious about my trouser leg and the flesh beneath. Ricky Lee was getting ready to take a bite.

"You gonna have to explain this to me. So there's a photograph. I still don't see why he'd have to kill my momma."

"That night she went around to the house to pick it up."

His question came back quick. "Corcoran tell you that?"

I was in unprepared territory, no map to guide me. "As a matter of fact, he did." There was no way Ricky Lee could check, but he still wasn't satisfied.

"What else?"

"She saw something she shouldn't have seen. Corcoran didn't tell me that, of course. He told me that she came to the house, got the photograph from his assistant, and left. He was worried that she knew too much, about the existence of the kid, about the murder. That's why he had her killed."

"How you know she saw somethin'?"

"Because she told someone. She was frightened."

"Who she tell?"

"You know I can't let you have that information."

"The same dude who saw the bodyguard?"

I kept my hands and eyes still. Over at the counter

there was a clatter and hiss as a Latina girl made an espresso. I was thinking it was good that Jack Brewster had already told his story. It made me feel safer in implicating him further. "Yeah, I guess I can tell you it was the same guy. He knew your mother. He liked her."

Ricky Lee shifted in his chair, staring out the window. The ice cream store on the other side of the street was bright with candycolored neon. Its reflection bled all over the sidewalk. Maybe some of that lead he had lodged in his compact, wiry body was shifting about, sending electric messages to his heart. A big part of this was that I knew he wanted to believe me. His homies had been out, they'd scoured the streets, and heard no word, sniffed no trace, except that which I'd put there. He was looking for an answer. Right now solving Mae's murder was his fiercest desire.

"I'll be making the arrest next week. Have I got enough to make the case? Well, I dunno, maybe, maybe not. Like I said, the DA wants me to put it aside. I won't. I'm not that kind of guy. So I'll make my move. It gives you some time, but not much, because once I make the pinch, then he's the one that's gone, he's mine. I'm going to bring him down because I know he did it, he killed your mother. Otherwise, he's just going to get away with it again, same deal, except it's a black woman this time, not a white one."

Leaning down, moving slowly, with an athlete's deliberation and grace, he fed his dog another portion of croissant, and when he showed me his angry eyes and bared teeth, it was a hunter's face, a face that had devoured everything in the pond. "Are you fucking with me?"

"Then again," I said, heart racing, speeding, voice level, "maybe you don't want to go against him yourself. This isn't some little Culver City banger. This is a scary, powerful guy. He's a friend of the President. It was an ugly crime, Ricky Lee. They disguised it to make it look like a sex thing."

Light flashed and tigered in his eyes. "Dead," he said, and looked at me as though at something that could not return a look. The pit bull raised its head, flopping out a pink tongue to lick its master's hand. Ricky Lee wiped the drool all over Charlie Corcoran's autographed smirk. "The guy's dead. My girlfriend, she knows about this shit, she says this was taken by some famous guy in New York. Says it's probably worth something. 'Course, it's all beat up now and anyway what I'm gonna do is nail it to that asshole's forehead once I waste him."

They left the bag in the empty second stall of the men's room, still packed with money. I took a cool breath of celebration, walking with the bag to the sink, raising water to my face with a refreshing splash. In the brightly lit mirror my expression was both familiar and new. My skin shone as if freshly minted. I'd told Ricky Lee that on Thursday nights Corcoran ate at Nick's Bar and Grill on Abbot Kinney, an old routine that he'd re-established since his trial, announcing that it was business as usual in the wonderful world of Charlie Corcoran. Ricky Lee had told me he'd let me know when the hit was going to happen. "Hey, hey," I said, turning away from the mirror.

Ricky Lee was gone when I came out, with Luther, nor was there any sign of either the giant of a bodyguard or the slick guy in glasses. From the pay phone, I called the shift sergeant at the precinct to check on my messages. I said I'd stopped off for a coffee at the Rose Café and was leaving now, already starting to cover and muddy my tracks in case any of this came back to haunt me. You never knew. If I was making the high-risk move, and I was, I was determined to do it right.

Outside, the wind blew in quick and sudden gusts. For a moment the rain disappeared and the parking lot lay still and even, gray like a shield, before the rain tore it once more into a thousand twinkling pieces and scattered them. I was soaked even in the time it took me to get to the Porsche. Fumbling with the key, whipping open the door, I pushed the money bag on the driver's seat for a moment and was about to throw it over onto the passenger's side when I saw Drew Diamond sitting there. He had a stiff tweed porkpie hat on his head, an unopened bottle of Johnnie Walker in his hand, and one cavalry twill trouser leg stretched on either side of the puddle in the seat well. He seemed all spruce and nervously expectant, sitting there, his clean-shaven cheeks giving off a hint of lime aftershave.

This is it, I thought; I'm busted already. It's over before it's begun. So much for my career in crime: I was astonished, even angry. "Drew," I said, "how the heck did you know where I was? And how the *fuck* did you get into my car?"

He waved an apologetic hand at the key in the ignition. "Ellen said you always kept a spare taped under the door, driver's side." He didn't seem the cynical Drew of even a few days before, but a guy suddenly astonished by life. "Sorry. Surprised it didn't wash away in the rain."

"I used strong tape, waterproof. It's green."

"Here," he said, and grabbed the bag. "Get in out of the rain." He tried to wedge the bag under the rear window and, when it wouldn't fit, turned it end up and set it on his lap so that I heard the notes shift and rustle inside. "Didn't know you went to the gym."

"Sometimes." I climbed into the driver's seat, pulling the door shut after me. I leaned over across his legs, squashing down on the bag and the money as I opened the glove compartment to fish out a roll of paper towels. I tore off a couple of strips, mopping at my hair and face. "How did it come up between you and Ellen? The thing about the key? Tell me, Drew, I'm interested. Which other of my secrets has she shared?"

"Don't go off on me now, Billy, OK? I feel shitty enough about this already. I believe it came up in San Diego when I got the keys to the rental locked inside the car. She was talking about how smart you are, how thorough, as if I didn't know."

"In San Diego?"

"We took Lucy to the zoo."

"Oh, my God," I said, the towel turning to soggy pulp in my fingers. If Drew was really there to bust me, why wasn't he more smug and cocky about it, and why wasn't the lot teeming with black-and-whites and Internal Affairs? Instead, there was only the rain and a very uneasy Drew, with his unopened bottle. I said, "I've been doing some socializing myself. I just had coffee in there with Ricky Lee Richards."

"No shit," he said.

There was an awkward silence, with no seeming chance of it yielding to an easy exchange.

"You're a tough guy to track down these days. I've been looking for you all day."

"Just how *did* you find me?"

He shifted his butt, balancing the bag between his elbow and the door while he held the Johnnie Walker bottle between his knees and twisted the cap. The car's innards filled with the warm reek of whiskey.

He said, "You wanna snifter?"

"I thought you were trying to quit."

"I'm making an exception."

The sip I took trickled down my throat and warmed my belly. I realized it was OK; he didn't seem to know about the money. "Thanks."

"I'm really sorry about last night, Billy," he said. "I've wanted to tell you for weeks, but Ellen said not to. She wasn't sure. About me, I guess."

A truck snarled by on Electric, tossing up a bouquet of stormy confusion. The Porsche, trapped in its wash, tipped from side to side like a rocking chair. I was hoping that Drew would hurry and get out of the car before he decided to peek in the bag.

"How much you pay for this car?"

"Fifteen."

"Yeah, Ellen said it was a bad deal. Sorry, *sorry.*" He shook his head, as if to say he wasn't used to dealing with situations of such emotional delicacy. "It was a repo, right?"

"I still own the guy for half."

"Insurance?"

"Nine-fifty, way steep."

"You got yourself a leak here, under the glove compartment. I'd put your bag down there, only it's wet."

"Don't worry, go ahead, if you're bored holding it." He did nothing. "How did you and Ellen hook up anyway?"

He took a delicate, almost courtly sip from the whiskey bottle, and turned up his eyes toward rain thundering on the roof. "You ever listen to the radio?"

"Sure, Drew. I listen to the radio."

"To the classical music station?"

"Sometimes," I said, wondering where this was going.

"Yeah. Right. Well." He helped himself to another swig, more hasty, this one seemingly for fortification.

"They advertise, called Perfect Strings. Kinduvva like a meeting place. You go along, and there's refreshments. No alcohol, of course, only wine."

"Right, only wine."

"You snack and you sip a delicate Chardonnay and you listen to classical music." He nodded to himself, dreamy Drew, as his memory went back. "It's up on Pico," he said, as if this explained everything.

"Let me get this straight. You ran into Ellen at a singles club for lovers of the classics? Oh, man, this is hilarious. Oh, man . . ." Starting to laugh, I ended up only with a sigh at the thought of Ellen wheeling her chair into a room where Mozart was playing so that she could talk to strangers.

"She only went there the one time. The whole group was started by that crazy friend of hers."

"Megan?"

"Yeah, the psychic."

"And what about you, Drew? What were you doing there? At Perfect Strings."

He looked out the window for a moment, putting himself back there. He sighed. "It was during the Corcoran trial. Right after I gave testimony. You remember the day that shitbird of a lawyer gave me a lobotomy on the stand? I was at rock bottom. Man, I was down to nothing." He looked up at me sharply, his fleshy, powerful face edged with pain. "You ever think about suicide, Billy?"

"Sometimes."

"I was right there that day. I planned to go home, write a letter to my daughter, get stoned. I was gonna eat the gun. I was just so tired, worn down by the grip and slog of it. Then I heard the ad on the radio." He shook his head. "I thought, what the heck? At least get a chuckle before I go off, right? And there she was. The first person I saw when I walked in the door. Like she'd been put there to save me. She came up to me, brushed the hair out of her eyes, and talked about meeting me years ago."

"You were teaching your daughter to hit the curve ball."

"Yeah, that's what Ellen said." He turned his neck, embarrassed again, and touched an area of skin scraped raw and red from too fervent application of the blade. "I don't really remember the particular occasion. But she was a pretty useful ballplayer, my little girl."

"Where is she now?"

"At college. Up in Santa Cruz. She's gonna go to law school. Can you believe that?" He nodded, proud. "She's a stunner. Beats me how she turned out so well."

"You were pretty good with her, as I recall."

He touched the hat on his head, then nervously scratched at an untidy clump of hair. "So you were seeing Ricky Lee? What was that all about?"

"He's thinking of going to Paris to write a novel."

He slapped the money bag with his spare hand, the one without the bottle in it, to show that he'd got the joke. "He's calling it *The Scumbag Also Rises*. Shit, Billy, we used to be pretty good friends, didn't we?"

I was now getting to be less scared about Drew finding the money than the prospect that he might invite me along on one of his fishing trips.

"What happened?"

"Our careers, the job."

"You screwed me, Billy," he said, not angrily, but with a calm and almost bemused shake of the head.

"You screwed yourself."

"Ain't that the truth?" He sighed, raising the bottle

to his lips but lowering it again without taking a drink, and then twisting back on the red and gold metal cap. "You know, I'm not interested in this whiskey anymore. You want it?"

"Thanks, but no thanks. Anyway, I'm not the new school. Cataresco's the new school."

Drew wasn't really listening. He shifted the bag, scratched his chest, and gently slapped his gut, as if from now on he intended to fill it with food and drink selected at leisure, according to a good plan, excellently carried out, as if he were feeling himself anew. "You know, I thought I'd gone beyond redemption. If you'd said to me, 'There are some people who can't be saved. They're just bad old bears that need to be hit with an iron club once in a while,' I'd've said, 'Yup. That's me. I'm that guy.' I thought I was finished. I thought it was too late, over. And there's the other thing, but I don't want to get into that. The point is, you know what Ellen said to me?"

"What?"

He was shaking his head, smiling, pleased and amazed by the memory. "She said, 'It's never too late. You can make a fresh start with your final breath.' Isn't that something?"

"It sounds like her."

"It does, doesn't it?" He spoke softly, almost with a reverence, and I had to lean toward him a little to make out the words above the hammer of the rain. "I should have told you sooner. I had no right letting you find out that way. I love her. That's what I want to say." He looked about, slightly panicked, remembering he should find some nearby wood to touch. "She's trying to cure me of that. I love her, I really do. Can you beat it?"

With that he pretty much fled, opening the door and springing out, then popping his now tweed-hatted head back in to say, "See ya." Then he was gone, slamming the door with such nervous vigor that the car rocked for a full minute while I reviewed the signs of recent months, all in clear focus now. There was the issue of his recently revived professional aspiration. There was his determination to quit drinking. There were the fancy duds that no longer smelled of cigarette smoke.

I'd no doubt of Ellen's power to effect a pretty miraculous change in anybody, but why Drew, why now? He seemed proud and happy, and I envied him, which was something new, though I wasn't quite sure I liked the idea of his sharing my hard-won two half-millions, only one of which I currently had. Then again, why not? Good luck to them, if that was what Ellen wanted and they were secure.

The rain kept on pounding the roof. I turned the key in the ignition, and the Porsche kicked into high-pitched life. I took off the hand brake, glanced at the passenger seat, and all the air whooshed out of me. The seat was empty. In a panic I leaned over and searched with my hand down in the flooding well: empty also. The bag was gone, with the money in it. "Drew!" I shouted, rubbing at the misted-up windshield to see where he'd gone. "Shit, Drew!"

The door opened and he was there, with the storm again, clamping the porkpie hat to the top of his head with one hand while with the other he nestled the bag back down on the passenger seat. "I'm sorry again, Billy. I don't know what I was thinking. I plain forgot I had this thing in my hand when I got out of the car. The way things are going, it's brain surgery I'll be needing. I'll see you tomorrow at the office, OK? Take care now."

Driving back along Electric, toward Oakwood, I took a deep breath, letting my heart slow down. I passed the old library building, its walls wounded by gunshots, given an unexpected drenched solidity. In the summer I used to sit with Lucy on the lawn there, reading Dr. Seuss.

There was a car behind me, a big four-wheel-drive, black, and when I turned up Palms, its powerful headlights did the same. I took a right on Lincoln; the headlights grew larger and more brilliant in the mirror. I was a little on edge by then, starting to wonder, Am I being followed? I pressed down on the gas to hit a changing light at Venice, and he was left behind. Heading up Washington, I checked several times. He was gone. It had probably been nothing. The money was safe beside me, wombed in its black nylon casing.

At first I thought of stashing the bag in left luggage out at LAX or in one of the lockers at Union Station, but that was too elaborate, and I wanted to have the cash close at hand, because I wasn't planning on holding on to it too long.

In the precinct parking lot two black-and-whites were gassing up, ready for the night shift. I parked near the back door and trotted upstairs past the snack bar, the gym, and shouted, "Hell-o," before going into the men's locker room. There was no reply; it was empty, and I found the locker I was looking for at the end of the second row on the right, number 17c. Its most recent user was a twenty-eight-year-old Korean boot; I can't even remember his name. He'd been having marital problems, he'd been involved in an incident under investigation by the police commissioners, and one afternoon when his Toyota stalled in afternoon traffic, he'd walked over to the median and shot himself in the mouth.

His locker had an unsightly dent on the door, most likely never noticed by all the uniformed guys who walked by each day, as if by ignoring the whole locker itself they could charm themselves away from any similar fate. Most cops are superstitious. It would be a year or more before anyone would think about using this particular locker. Then they'd hand it over to another unknowing boot and make a joke: "Hey, watch out *you* don't eat the gun, cuz. SPOOKY!" Comedy was only a matter of time. Everyone forgets, even some murderers, or if they do remember, they see their actions in terms of pride or vanity, not conscience. I wondered how Charlie Corcoran felt. Maybe he'd convinced himself that Denise had never happened. He was about to be reminded.

The key, difficult at first to turn, came away smoothly in my hand and joined the others on Mae Richards's key ring, alongside the masks of gold.

19

FOR A WHILE I HEARD NOTHING. I WENT TO THE OFFICE, I drove home, I ordered plenty of pizza to go. There was no phone call from Ricky Lee, no summons to a crime scene to discover the body of Charlie Corcoran. At the precinct house the air was so moist, the pages of the Mae Richards murder book curled in my fingers as I collated and cross-referenced the crime reports, the death reports, the property reports, and copied out the witness list, the interview list, and the list of wounds on Mae Richards's body, together with the coroner's assessment of what had caused them. The more thoroughly I did the job, the more information I amassed, and the more time elapsed since the murder, the more confusing the picture would become to anyone else who looked into it, and when the chance came to get Cataresco out of the picture for a few days, I grabbed it. A suspect who'd fled out of state some months before had been picked up by the Denver P.D. I told her I wanted her to go there, conduct the interrogation, and bring the guy back.

"Leave right away. Take your time," I said. "Do a good job with the interrogation."

Cataresco looked at me across the table, neither angry nor suspicious. There was nothing unusual in this, and she liked to travel as much as the next guy. Fifteen minutes later she got off the phone, got to her feet with a snap, ran a hand through her hair, and said, "Remember what Francis told you about his flight to Las Vegas having been canceled because of the storm? Well, I just got through checking with the airlines, every one of them. Of course there were delays that night, but no cancelations."

I was cautious yet full of resolution about getting Cataresco on her way. "That's good," I said. "Though he may have decided not to go because of the delay. For a muckety-muck guy like that it would be as good as a cancelation, an unacceptable hitch in his plans."

After Cataresco left, I got myself a coffee, turned to the *LA Times* funny pages, and sat, hoping that I could find my old routine and unwind. It was no good. There was always the chance that Francis, if he had killed Mae, was in such a sweat and panic by now that he might walk in off the street and confess. For an hour or more the notion loomed so large that each time I looked up from "The Far Side" I almost imagined I saw Francis, standing there beneath the harsh fluorescent lighting, with Ricky Lee saying, "You *fucked* with me."

Alone in the office, I scanned the idea that I should go at once and make the drive again to Palos Verdes. Tell Francis to get the hell out of Los Angeles, shack up somewhere while things cooled off. Easy, easy, I told myself; that was silly, there was no need to let the alarms jangle so. I just needed to gauge the guy's state of mind, that was all, so I punched seven digits on the phone and he picked up. "Dr. Francis? Hi, this is Billy McGrath. Sorry to bother you. Look, I've been meaning to ask.

This is gonna sound crazy It's a long shot. Did you ever meet Denise Corcoran?"

His silence was almost grateful. Then he said, "How extraordinary."

"Why so?"

"You've put me on the spot, morally."

I said nothing, thinking about moral spots.

"I only met Denise on the one occasion."

I'm not sure why I said, "You delivered her baby. The Downs boy."

"How on earth do you know that?"

"I didn't until now."

"She and Mae were friends. I promised them both I'd never say anything about any of this, but I suppose now they're both dead, I'm relieved of my contract."

"Death's useful that way. What do you know about the photographs?"

"Photographs? Of whom?"

"Denise and Mae."

"I never saw any," he said, almost offended. "Mae kept things pretty secret about her. Are there photographs?"

"Yes, sir, there are. In fact, it was your friend or employee Radek Gatti who showed them to me."

"How extraordinary," he said, an Englishman coolly surprised by a discovery in the jungle. "I didn't know that."

I let this go. "Take me back a little. What happened after the boy was born?"

"Denise left the hospital as soon as she could, and I didn't see her again. I understand the boy used to come and see her; they'd meet at Mae's. But that was always a big secret."

"Because of Charlie?"

Now he dropped his bombshell. "He wasn't the father, of course. The father was some other man, not Denise's first husband, either. She was an overwhelming phenomenon." His voice became hopeful. "You think all of this was connected in some way with Mae's death?"

"I really can't say. Maybe. Sit tight. I'll be in touch."

Hanging up, I felt reassured. Francis didn't sound like a guy who was about to panic and mess up my plans. A larger part of me at that moment was just fascinated by this amazing, surprising case, but, not wanting to think too much and slow myself up at that moment, I made another call, to check that Ted was at his gallery, and went upstairs to the locker rooms. The lights were out in the corridor, but a glowing wedge of light and the sound of laughter came from beneath the door of the snack bar, where the TV was tuned to one of the late-afternoon talk shows. The locker room was quiet and quite empty. The mid-P.M. shift had gone out and wouldn't be back for hours.

I looked this way and that to check that there was really no one before putting the key in the lock. It stuck a little, as before, so that I was pulling too hard on the handle when the door opened and the bag came out, hitting me in the chest and falling on the bench and then to the floor with a thump. I stood quite still and counted with my heart. The TV's murmuring babble was the only interruption. I swept up the bag from the floor and on my way out met a uniform coming in, the beefy Cuban with the kicked-dog air I'd encountered on the night of Mae Richards's murder, when Ricky Lee was in the interrogation room.

"Sir," he said, and touched his Smith & Wesson in its quickdraw holster, that twitch he had. Somehow he was the shifty one. "I was helping my boot with her reports in the TV room."

"Is she pretty?"

"Yes, sir, and a promising officer in prospect."

"Way to go." I had to glance at the badge on his chest again. "Good work, Campes. Good night."

I left him there, looking more confused than usual. I trotted back down the stairs, bearing the bag with giddy excitement, and left the office, heading down on Culver and Jefferson before making my way through the thin traffic toward the marina and Venice. The rain had eased up and given way to fog. Buildings rose, having substance for a few seconds only before fleeing the Porsche's headlights and vanishing into the vapor. Holes had opened in the surface of the street where the storms had washed away the foundation soil and the tarmac had sunk like toffee. The entire area of the low-lying Ballona wetlands was a lake, with melancholy palms and clumps of pampas grass for islands. The trees themselves were wet through. A sodden palm frond made no crash as it fell in front of the car at the junction with Washington. A distant gunshot lost its sharpness in the muffling fog. The bridge across the Linnie Canal had been sapped and swept away. Everything had an eerie, swamped beauty, almost unreal.

The lights of the Softly Gallery loomed through the fog on Draker, where I parked behind Ted's white boat and hauled the bag after me as I got out of the car. It was about five-thirty, a still evening. The rumble of the ocean was amplified and carried closer, as if the fog had made the Pacific rear its head and consider the possibility of sweeping the whole of Venice away, like so much temporary and unwanted clutter.

The gallery itself, still open, was deserted, apart from

a few visitors, a couple of grunge trendies, the attendant at the front, who knew me and smiled, and a lone security guard, resting with his legs stretched out across two metal chairs. I bounded up the stairs toward Ted's office, still clutching the bag.

Gray-faced, baggy-eyed, disheveled, and straggly, but alert, sober, Ted threw his pencil aside on the desk in front of him and, leaning back in the chair, slid a pair of Walkman headphones down from his ears over his neck, and smiled a warm welcome. He held up a copy of *Art Monthly.* "Just catching up on my homework. It can wait. But I have to ask you this. Is Los Angeles ready for two buckos like Ted Softly and his old friend Billy McGrath? Is this the night we go out and get wasted, or what?"

"It comes into the latter category."

He noticed the bag. "Planning a vacation?"

"Not exactly," I said, laying the bag down.

"You are looking serious. Well, *mon vieux,* what's up?" The phone rang, and after a moment he grabbed it, leaning his head intimately into the receiver while he rocked to and fro in his chair. "No, no, no, that's my final word," he said, and hung up. To me he gave a smile and a wink, saying, "Final, of course, until the next time. Now what can I do for you, my friend?"

I sat down, then stood up again, pacing the room, excited, trying to propose this right. At that moment I was counting on getting the second half of the money from Ricky Lee. I wanted Ted to go ahead at once with what I had, and if I got the other later, well, I'd say thanks and come back to him again. "Say I had five hundred thousand dollars."

Ted almost exploded with excitement. "I love this so far."

"Could you buy me a picture that would be worth five or more times as much in ten years' time?"

"These things are always a gamble, you know. But, yeah, a guy with my nose in this area, I could do that. Five hundred grand now, two and a half mill in ten years. I can think of a number of artists I'd be prepared to back in that way."

"OK. Now here's a tougher question. Go back twelve, fifteen years, to whenever it was that we first met, would the work of any of these five-hundred-grand artists have been available at that time for, say, ten thousand?"

Ted rocked in his chair, chewing on the wire from the Walkman. "Actually, that's an easier question. It's history already, not McFuture. The answer is several. I even know some of them myself. Where are we going here?"

Picking a book from one of the unpacked boxes, laying it down again, touching the corked neck of a champagne bottle cooling in its bucket, prowling and stalking the room, now with my back to Ted, now turning to face him, I explained what was required. I wanted him to buy two pictures for $250,000 each. One certificate of ownership should be in Lucy's name, the other in Ellen's. Those certificates should say that these works had been bought back then, ten, eleven years ago, for $10,000 apiece, and that they'd been bought, not by me, but by Ted himself.

He flicked a bushy, white eyebrow. "Why would you want to do any of this?"

"Not important. The questions are—can it be done; will you do it?"

He shrugged with a little smile, wary, making a steeple of his fingers. "Yeah, yeah, it can be done. It's a little illegal, but I could bring it off. I'd have to monkey with the lines of provenance, the bills of sale. But stuff like that happens." He slapped his hands together, rocking in his chair again now. "Shit, I just had a better idea. The deal is this, correct me if I'm wrong—I buy a painting for two-hundred-and-fifty-thou now and get a piece of paper saying it was bought for only ten thousand some time back then."

"Say on Lucy's birthday, eleven years ago. Yeah, that's the deal."

"There's an easier way to do this. I could go to a couple of artists I know who have pictures they've never sold that would be worth that kind of money. I hand over the cash, they give me a piece of paper saying I bought it for peanuts eleven years ago. I can see all sort of tax reasons why they'd be deliriously happy about the idea."

"As I say, it has to be clear that the original twenty grand came from you. If Ellen presses you, say you were paying off a debt. I beat you in a poker game. No, she'd never buy that." Walking to the window, looking out into the fog, I thought of the night I'd driven away from here with Lucy, the print of Ted's gun blazoned on my forehead. "Say you owed me, because of some cop shit I'd done, but say you don't want to talk about it. It's too personal."

"I *do* owe you."

"Say that, then. Say you wanted to do something for me, and I said, no, if you must do it for somebody, if you think you're that deeply indebted, do it for those guys. Say the deal was that you bought the pictures on the day Lucy was born, but the plan was to hand them over when they'd really be worth something." I picked up the champagne bottle and smiled, telling Ted he could certainly convince her. He was good at verbal smoke and mirrors, especially with women "Show her the beauty of your soul."

Ted took the bottle from me, eased out the cork with practiced flair and a muted pop, and filled two frothing glasses. "I love this plan. It's amusing, Billy, it really is. It's cool. There's only one snag. I don't have the twenty thousand this would have taken back then, let alone the half a mill we need now." He dropped, and the rings around his eyes grew darker still. "It's a bummer."

Laughing, I threw one arm around his shoulder while with the other I tossed back the champagne. "Did you think I was expecting you to pay for this? It's your friendship I need, your expertise, and your occasionally imaginative tendencies." Setting down the empty glass, taking the bag from where I'd left it on the floor, heaving it onto the desk, I unzipped the zipper with an air of aplomb. "Shit, Ted, I've *got* the money."

He leaned close, smothering an insane nervous giggle. "There's half a million dollars in there?"

"Yeah," I said, a little giddy myself. "Hey, I just had an idea." I reached in to release three hundred-dollar bills from their elastic banded bondage. I thought I'd pick up that swanky pencil set for Lucy. "Almost half a million dollars, very nearly half a million dollars," I said, but my own cranky impulse made me think better of it, and I put the three bills back. "Don't wanna hex this deal." I zipped up the bag again and gave it a friendly goodbye pat.

Ted whistled, stroking his spiky, shaved hair. "I'm impressed."

"Don't be. I'm trusting you with my life. Actually with something far more important. I'm trusting you with my family. Do this right for me. Whatever happens, even if I should die—no, shut up, even if I should die—

Ellen and Lucy get the pictures and they know nothing of this."

Ted shrugged. "You got it, buddy."

We shook hands, and I drove through the fog to Westwood, where I caught the art supply store as they were trying to shut and lock the doors. I wrote a check that would take my account down to zero, watched them wrap the sandalwood box in something silver and snazzy, and, having driven back to Nowita, leaned the gift against the bottom edge of the front door. I rang the bell, sneaked away without a word.

Larry Murakami left the door open this time when he called me into his office, which I took as a good sign. His pink face beamed at me above bow tie and tuxedo. "Billy," he said, "I want to tell you, that was such a smart thing you did with Charlie Corcoran."

"What was that, Larry?"

"The apology, of course. A stroke of genius. I didn't even mention it to you when his people called with the demand. I told Cataresco, 'McGrath's never going to go for that.' I've no idea even how you found out about it. Have you got your own private deep throat somewhere in the mayor's office?" He wagged his finger, still smiling, and opened the button on his tuxedo jacket. "But you did find out, and, boy, am I glad! You incented that guy for sure. He's invited me to Phoenix in two weeks to play in a pro-am."

"Better hurry get your reservation."

"Yes, of course I will," he said, sweeping back the sides of his jacket to model the pants. "Armani. You like?"

"Gee, it's swell."

"I bought it yesterday, in Fred Segal. Do you shop there?"

"I'm a humble homicide dick, Larry; I don't have the wherewithal."

Larry was defiantly unsheepish. "Fund raiser," he said, with an amused shrug, a man who'd got on and to whom getting on had become a necessary and never tiresome habit. Larry had some special instinct that told him whether anyone he met was of influence, in which case out came the suit or, in this case, tuxedo and, along with it, the snazzy patter, the flattery, the cajolery, the discreet but nonetheless implied request for a favor. He managed to do this without causing offense. I'd seen him work the magic on mayors, movie stars, sundry senators, and, on one notable occasion, the wife of a President togged out in bulletproof vest for a staged narcotics bust. "You should look at this."

He handed me a typed letter, which I scanned and then read again, more slowly. It was Drew Diamond's letter of resignation. "Drew's quit?"

"Effective a month from now. You seem distressed. I thought you'd be pleased. It's what you wanted, isn't it?" His face was very serious and frowning, eyes regarding me sharply now. "Out with the dinosaurs. Everything according to plan, or that's the way it looks to me. Please say if you're seeing it differently these days."

I remembered what Drew had said on first meeting Murakami. He'd asked if Larry had a clue. Did he help at crime scenes? Could he sharpen a pencil? Well, maybe. "It's sudden. I'm surprised."

"Evidently he's been offered a job with the Justice Department." Bending down, he tidied papers away into his briefcase. "In Seattle."

"Seattle?"

His look was inquisitive again. "That makes more sense to you?"

"Somewhat."

"Cataresco will become your number two, of course?"

"Of course."

"Then everything's splendid." His teeth gleamed, sharkish, and as he snapped shut the briefcase I tried to picture Drew and Ellen together in Seattle, romancing each other in some coffee house by the water. The funny thing was, it suddenly didn't seem so unimaginable after all. What was it she'd said to him? You can make a fresh start with your final breath.

"Cataresco's back from Denver?"

"Earlier in the day."

"She's a great cop, isn't she?" He couldn't help smiling, like a prince distributing favors. He moved behind his desk, tidying away papers and pencils, lobbing one of his precious Ping-Pong balls into a bucket on the floor. The phone rang on his desk, and he gave it an almost reproachful glance before picking it up, willing away any detrimental career information. "Murakami," he said, receiver cradled under chin, turning to the wall to make a note on his calendar, and then swinging back again. "Yes, he's here."

I took the receiver.

"Yo, McGrath," said Ricky Lee. "How tricks?"

"Up and down."

"Can you talk?"

Larry looked at me with his princely smile, wondering what was going on in his empire.

"Sure."

"I figured this would be safe for you. Even this city's Police Department might think twice 'bout bugging its own phones; hear what I'm sayin'?"

"Fine, fine." I smiled at Larry, who was straightening his bow tie.

"Tonight's the night. After dinner. It's going down."

"Excellent, outstanding," I said, slipping into Larry speak. His Ping-Pong paddle rested on his desk, atop a ball, atop structure.

"On his way home that motherfucker's gonna buy a ticket to a whole other destination."

"Terrific."

"I'm thinking maybe I'll do this guy in public."

I knew I had to be on my guard. "That might be complicated."

"I wanna see it on TV," he said. "Should make *lotsa* headlines."

Larry was gesticulating in the background, pointing at his watch. He had to go in a couple of minutes.

"Tomorrow. Rose Café, same time. We'll discuss the football scores," I said, and hung up.

"Informant?" said Larry.

"Yes," I said, blinking. I couldn't quite believe the waiting was over.

"Excellent, excellent," said Larry. "What these people do to each other. The *violence*. How do they stand it?"

"I don't know, Larry, I really don't know."

He stood with the sides of his Armani tux swept back, hands on hips and eyes narrowed with two vertical creases burrowing up from between his eyes through the waxy, almost albacore smoothness of his forehead, for a moment truly worrying at it, this problem of murder. "Well, if you find that out, *do tell.*" Larry's smile, fixed around his bleached teeth, had nonetheless the provisional quality of something stamped into sponge.

20

AT THE CORNER OF ABBOT KINNEY AND CALIFORNIA, sheltered back from the street behind a thick hedge, Nick's Bar and Grill was a place I knew all about but had never been inside. Handing my keys to the valet, I showed him my badge and asked him to keep the Porsche close by, since I might be needing it in a hurry. A skinny basehead pimp on the other side of the street sized me up with all the attitude he could muster, an expression that was three parts hatred and one part curiosity. Perhaps he'd been placed there, though I doubted that Ricky Lee would use anyone so obvious or so out of it. The guy was standing, swaying, rather, watching the unapproachable other half swish up in their fifty thousand-dollar automobiles. The night air was thick with the smell of jasmine.

On the patio tall lamps wrapped themselves in lit-up bonnets of fog. Inside, the lights were soft and yellow, and glasses chimed gently to the accompaniment of a smoky French voice on the CD player. A wood fire blazed and spat, sending forth gusts of burning pine. The ceiling was low, the tablecloths crisp, and one wall was hung with stark black-and-whites, portraits, not of

celebrities, but of the weathered faces of farmers, peas-
ants, bums. The tail of a mouse was caught between the
lips of one of them. A tall black sculpture in the Russian
constructivist style cut the room in two. The hostess
wore a floppy beret, a suede miniskirt nine inches above
her knees, and, leading me to my table, walked as though
balancing ball bearings between the hidden insides of
her thighs.

There was a party of movie brats in front of the fire,
busy laughing and drinking and sure their lives would
never end. A lone candle flickered bravely on top of a
chocolate birthday cake, while the young woman in
front of it paused, holding back the glossy black hair
that threatened to tumble in front of her eyes, then
ducked down to blow out the light. Raising her head,
she swept back the hair and caught my eye, bothering
me, though I couldn't put my finger on why. Only when
she looked down, slightly to one side, did her features
come almost mechanically into shape, like the sliding
shapes in a jigsaw, making themselves into a face I recognized. I waved and at once felt foolish, having realized why I knew it: she was an actress, a rising star.
Someone pushed a knife into her hand, and she sliced
the cake with a big smile.

Ward Jenssen had on a sleeveless black dress, high at
the neck and low in the back, with no earrings or other
jewelry. Her blond hair was in its usual state of artful tur-
moil, and she'd gone ahead and ordered a bottle of
Chardonnay, the green neck of which leaned against the
side of an ice bucket. I'd called her at the last moment to
insist she break her date and join me instead. She looked
up, smiled, and then, flattered and flustered by my presumption, didn't seem quite sure whether to be angry or
not. "I'm surprised," she said as I sat down, her smile

back again. "I didn't think this was your kind of place."

"The girl over there, the actress, what's her name?"

She didn't have to look. "Shane Dartle."

"I saw her in a movie my daughter rented. She played someone or other. I can't remember what happened in the end."

"It clearly made an impression."

"Yeah, I'm more of a facts kinduvva guy."

She laughed. "How is Lucy?"

"You remember her name?"

"Sure, why wouldn't I?"

"She's great, just great. I don't know what I'd do without her. You want kids?"

"I'm waiting for the right guy."

"There must be a million candidates. All eager for those afternoon kisses."

"Are you on duty, Billy?"

"Never not, I guess."

"Tiring."

"A homicide is like a ticking clock. Most get solved within a week. By then of course another has happened, or several."

"And the earlier one?"

"The path gets pretty much trodden over," I said. All this was nuts. I hadn't been able to resist coming here, though I knew it was the wrong move. I should have been in a movie theater in Santa Monica, watching one film, then another, then going home to sleep and wake and greet, if it came, the news of Charlie Corcoran's death with dazed astonishment. Instead, I was here, at Nick's, with a reporter who could do me harm, watching the drama I'd created play out at close hand.

"Like all logical, lazy men, I love unity. A solved case. A murder book with a yellow dot on the spine so that I can close the cupboard behind me and feel completion."

"You're not lazy."

"Maybe not."

"But you are trying to sell me a line."

"Am I? I wasn't really aware."

"Sure you are. You seem to be cool and smiling and dedicated, boring really . . ."

"Hey, thanks."

"I think you're much more complicated than you let on."

"I think you're way too smart for me. I think we should order."

It was now fifteen after nine. I didn't want to think about the variables, they were so many, so much that could go wrong, not that anything was going to go wrong. It could, but it wouldn't, it *could*. Logic told me. Corcoran might cancel his reservation. God knows, he probably had plenty of social options, even if Thursday night at this place was more than merely routine, a part of his mythology. Ricky Lee might have a change of heart, or decide at the last minute on a different night. His homeboys might mess up or find themselves in another rumble. These guys had dull, un-Corcoran-like calendars nearly all the time—hang out, cruise, catch a video, get laid, smoke some weed, catch another video, hang out some more, cruise, weed, and then suddenly their lives would explode: a drive-by, a robbery, a dope deal in Long Beach, a dis and then a retaliation, blood that had to flow today, at once, or violence that was being visited upon them. Ricky Lee probably had one steady guy, his baddest dog, the one he'd trust to be his partner in something like this.

Ward was looking at me with a different smile, not amused, not quite tender either, leaning forward a little and speaking in a whisper as if about to take the two of us exploring where we'd never been before. "I know your secrets, Billy McGrath."

A waiter in black rushed by.

"Really?"

"I know all your secrets."

"I sincerely hope not."

She said that after what had happened before, when we had our affair, she'd made it her business to find out who, exactly, I was.

"It's a question many people ask themselves."

"Your grandfather was a cop."

"Still is, in his own mind. Eighty-six years old, alive and very kicking."

"He was one of the great ones, wasn't he? Broke heads, kicked butt, and helped Chief Parker clean up the Department back in the 1950s."

"The Department needed it. My grandfather drove the chief to work in the morning, drank whiskey with him in the mid-P.M.s, and poured him into bed at night. Then he'd set about the task of law enforcement. He'd fistfight anyone and worked sixteen hours a day. He never knew when he was licked."

"And your father—he was lazy, a quitter."

"I'm not sure that's right. He was a hard worker, but he never engaged with any one type of work for long. He became a cop because my grandfather wanted him to. He was a real Southern California child, you know, like a seal in the water. He'd rather have been an athlete. That's what he was cut out for. Still, he surfed his way to the rank of detective, and that's not so easy."

"He was murdered, wasn't he?"

I saw the symmetry of Shane Dartle's face fall apart—unrecognizable. I felt as though I'd been slapped.

Maybe that's why we give the other cheek — so we can be hit. Opening my mouth, I found I couldn't speak, I could only clear my throat. I took a sip of water, remembering that I'd been in a Westwood movie theater when my father was killed. Afterward, I'd walked in the velvet Los Angeles summer night with no idea that my life was about to be changed. A Department Chevrolet was waiting outside my apartment, its doors open like wings, and the building manager stood in the courtyard, staring at me with excited and almost malevolent curiosity, an expression I would come to recognize down the years, as if some secret part of each of us longs to rubberneck the wrecked blood-bespattered car on the freeway. Later that night I went to see my grandfather. He said not a word, but went to his living room and turned up the volume, and I was by myself, trying to make sense of the event. It made no sense. I wanted to set things right, but I couldn't. I was in a role I didn't know how to play. I felt myself breaking down.

Ward was staring at me across the table with genuine concern and distress. "I'm so sorry," she said. "I didn't mean to hurt you."

I managed a smile. "Hey, it's OK, it wasn't so bad, really. You took me by surprise, that's all. It's fine. You've assailed my history. I guess I should be flattered. I'm still trying to figure out what his death meant to me."

The waiter helped me out then, coming to take our orders, and afterward I looked around the restaurant, at the photographs, the steel sculptures, and the beautiful people. "Nice place."

Ward leaned close, the air between us drunk with the musky sweetness of her perfume. "No one comes so they can have a good time," she said, her voice a whisper of mock conspiracy, as if she and I were the only ones who knew the truth about this corrupt and fallen world. "It's a bazaar where we all barter for potential advancement. Everyone's afraid. Every look is an appraisal. Behind every word there are the same questions. What can you do for me? What might I have to do to you and will it be worth it? Right now Shane Dartle's talking about this hot young director whose next movie she's hoping to be in. See the way her eyes are closed? That's to signify that neither she nor anyone else can pass judgment on this godlike being. Heaven forbid that anyone in this town might say what they actually think. Everyone's an actor, even if they're not." She took in the room with a moment-long sweep. "Look, talk of the devil—Charlie Corcoran just walked in."

A dark raincoat was slung over his shoulders, and he wore a graceful off-white shirt hanging loose outside the trousers. He held the doors open with the tips of his fingers and had spent a lot of time combing his hair to get that tousled look. He hoped, expected, and maybe even feared that people would stare at him; of course he was even more afraid that they wouldn't. He held the doors for about a half-second more, an almost imperceptible beat, and then came in with impeccable movie timing, smiling, waving, and making I'll-be-there-in-a-moment gestures at the birthday party table before heading over to ours.

"Oh, boy," said Ward in a whisper, watching his imperial approach across the floor of the restaurant, "this is going to be embarrassing."

"It'll be hunky-dory," I said, pushing back my chair, standing up, and offering my hand. "Mr. Corcoran, sir, nice to see you again. Please, join us?"

Charlie puffed up like a blowfish, absurdly pleased with himself, and said, with that familiar boyish hesitation, "Well, thanks, just for a moment, if I'm not intruding." He sat down, reached out for a roll, broke off a piece, and popped it in his mouth. "Ward, I'm surprised, charmed, *delighted* to find you here. May I?" He picked up her glass and sipped, saying, "Mmm, Far Niente. It's sublime. God sent it," and then turned to me with the full grace of his attention. "Detective McGrath. I can really say that it's a pleasure to see you. Ward never told me that the two of you were such good friends."

"Well, she's a mystery."

He grinned, the great shy lady killer. "It's why we love her."

I kept up with his banter. "You love her, too?"

"I did, no, I do. I love them all. I'm the last of the romantics. Ask any of my five wives. Or is it six?"

Ward, watching with bright eyes, now burst into laughter. "Oh, Charlie. You're too preposterous."

"I am, it's true."

She looked from one of us to the other. "When did you guys become such good friends?"

Charlie smiled, lounging in the chair, weighing his effect, aloof and appealing. "May I? Am I awful? Can I tell her?"

"Sure, absolutely, go ahead, Charlie."

"Billy—may I call you Billy?"

"Absolutely."

"Detective McGrath, *Billy,* had the good grace to come to my house and offer an apology."

Ward's eyes were sharp now. "For what?"

"Let's say," said Charlie Corcoran, with his seductive smile, "let's say he apologized for pursuing his case with a little *too* much determination."

"Absolutely," I said to Ward. "I was out of line."

"Isn't that great?" said Charlie. "It's the hardest thing

in the world for a man to admit in public that he was wrong. Especially a man like Billy McGrath. I'm not just saying this. I know you, because my lawyers made it their business to make me know. You're the best there is. And that means you're proud, maybe even a little arrogant. Because you have to be. So, thanks. My *chapeau* is duly doffed."

After that he made a big show of grinning, of standing up and saying with a gleeful expulsion of breath: *"Well."* He scanned the restaurant, then mumbled his goodbyes, and made his way to Shane Dartle's table, where the movie brats greeted him with glances that mixed outright envy and an indifference some forced themselves to feign. Not Shane Dartle, who threw her arms around his neck, shouting, "Charlie!"

Ward watched with amusement. I said, "The two of you were lovers?"

"No," she said, eyes still on Charlie, then sweeping toward me. "I wouldn't be part of a harem. It was funny, the way we got to know each other. I met him at a party a few years back and he asked me this and that, and we got talking, and I said I was mixed up about all sorts of things. He said, 'I know more than any therapist in the city. After all, I've seen most of them. Don't talk to anyone else. Call me.' And I did."

"He helped you?"

"His career advice was impeccable. You've no idea how amazing it is that he's stayed at the top for so long. That doesn't happen by accident. It takes maniacal devotion. And cunning. And ruthlessness." She said the trouble was that Charlie went in search of your flaw so that he could feel secure. "That whole shy thing's such an act. Anyone who comes close to Charlie sheds some feathers. He tends to maul you."

"If you're lucky." I couldn't resist. "Otherwise he shoots you in the head."

"He was acquitted of that."

"I do remember."

"He likes to be around women, especially if they're young and pretty, and he gets on well with every one of them, even if he always has to let you know that he's smarter and cooler, as well as more beautiful. But every man is a competitor," she said. "He enrages you, doesn't he? He goads you. There's something about him that makes you a little nuts."

"You just saw what great buddies we are these days."

"I wondered why you chose this place. You wanted me to see that you'd patched things up with Charlie."

"Oh, not really."

"You don't have a grudge?"

"I never did. I just happened to believe that he killed his wife."

"You've changed your mind?"

"I've realized I'll only damage myself worrying about this anymore."

"You've decided to lay the problem to rest?"

"In a manner of speaking."

While we ate I told her about Ellen and Lucy and the move to Seattle. Did I blame Charlie for my father's death? No. He'd been a part of my father's bad luck, a process that had begun before Charlie's entry into his affairs, and that continued long afterward. Some people have unlucky lives, that was all. Charlie himself, by contrast, seemed never to have been touched by dismay and disappointment. Right now the wedding ring he still wore glinted on his left hand, and he was listening to Shane Dartle as if she were changing the world, giving him the most important news of his life.

"I'll tell you something," she said. "I believe that he's capable of murder. I'm not saying that he killed Denise, only that I'd guess him capable of it."

"You've got a hunch?"

"If you like."

"In the way you had a hunch about me and Charlie and my father?"

"I don't presume to know the truth, Billy. I report honestly the facts as far as I can find them. The case was a joke. You and I both know that. His lawyers ate the Department, gobbled up the district attorney's office, and then looked around, asking, 'Where's the entrée?'"

I realized that I did hate him. I hated the hopeful smile in his eyes and his soft, pulpy, ego-blown mouth. I hated his arrogance and his condescension. I reminded myself of Denise Corcoran, face shattered, head electric with pain, and I was still glad that he was going to die, glad that I knew, and glad that for once I was the one with all the cards, feeling effortlessly superior. I was glad that after tonight there'd be no more sharkish movie deals for Charlie. His rhumba would be over.

Besides, as Charlie knew full well, this was pragmatic Los Angeles. You had to figure out how to get around and ahead. Money itself wasn't a bad thing, and I wasn't a bad guy. Charlie Corcoran was. I was trying to take care of my family. I didn't swallow any of that Marlon Brando Mafia bullshit, but in the end what good was any man unless he could look after his own? I was doing something I absolutely knew was wrong because I believed the guy was a murderer and because his death would enrich the family I loved and had lost.

"Why did you become a cop after your father was murdered?"

"I felt guilty. I never valued his mind or work."

"You liked him, though, right?"

"I don't know. I didn't know him that well. I certainly didn't respect him. I forgave him almost anything because he was proud of me. It's not really enough, is it?"

"I don't know. What did he want for you?"

"I think he always assumed I'd go back to England. Never an establishment figure himself, he hoped I'd join one."

"You did."

"Not in the way he intended. He wanted me to be a lawyer or a banker or something. A classy guy."

"You're not?"

I raised a hand for our waiter, who was at the front, helping his companion, the beret-clad hostess, hook a raincoat from the rack by the fire and then help Charlie Corcoran on with it, the two of them caressing the material snug over his shoulders. I realized now there was another reason why I'd come. This was my last chance to stop the show. I could walk over, take his arm, say, "Listen, I think you'd better let me give you a ride home."

Charlie was hesitating, shifting his weight from one leg to the other, and scuffing at the floor with his toe, keeping up with the whole bashful thing, while he openly appraised the hostess's legs, her face, her eyes. He said, "Where did you get that fabulous beret? Is it Agnes B?" He grinned and without looking waved bashfully at the room in general because he assumed a fair proportion of people were watching, as they were. Now was the final moment when I could call him back, my last chance. I did nothing, and then he was gone, exit every bit as showy as entrance.

I didn't look at my watch. I didn't want Ward to see how interested I'd been in his leaving. Whatever final anxiety or scruple I'd been feeling had vanished, I told myself. It was done now, too late. I felt a thrill, a sense of power, and also a shudder I had to restrain, the fear that it was a part of myself I was killing. I still find myself wishing that I'd rushed out after him into the fog, for I imagine this as the moment when my guilt fished deepest, though in reality everything was unstoppable by then; events had been mixed; the bomb was about to go off.

"Are you jealous of him?"

I was surprised by the question. "Of Charlie? No."

"Whatever you think of these people and the business they're in, in this town it translates into something very real. Money, glamour, power. A joke becomes as solid as a brick wall. A nice set of teeth and a movie smile can bring down a senator or make their owner a member of the power elite in the land where lemons used to grow. Doesn't it make you angry?"

My mind was with Corcoran in the car. Maybe he'd brought one of the Ferraris, which would please Ricky Lee no end. Who could resist the chance to bloody and pepper that pretty red paint? I wondered what weapons he'd have his guys use—shotguns, I guessed, and then Ricky Lee would bring his 9 mm up close for the head shot, the *coup de grâce*. And I wondered what Charlie would feel. Rage, fear, panic? What would pass through his mind? A man can think a lot, when pressed, in just a few seconds, and the brain keeps working even as it dies.

"I've wondered about my dad's last thoughts, what was in his head when he was going down. There's the ego thing, right—was he thinking of *me*? You brought me into the world, Dad, you helped create me, so I damn well should be with you in some form when your own being dissolves." I shrugged. "Did he remember the day he met my mother or a happy day at Dodger Stadium or was he thinking about a glass paperweight lying right there on the carpet that seemed so close and was terribly out of reach?"

The story of my father's death wasn't a secret, exactly, nor was it common knowledge. I didn't trade the information as a bar story. Ellen and I had been through it all, and I told Ward that in the last two years of his life my father had owned a little business, a travel agency on Manchester Avenue, and that by then we were friends, though we never agreed on much of anything and rarely even quarreled. Once I got to know him, I was surprised that he'd ever been a cop. He was a salesman, good at it. He drove a cab sometimes, if he was bored or things were slow, but only because he wanted to. He couldn't bear stillness. In the house he'd always have the TV on, or the radio. He liked bars. They kept him busy. He hustled, he scammed, never on top of himself, but always with money for a beer, a splashy ride.

One night he was in the office, working late, when a guy came in and made him open the safe. The guy didn't take the blank traveler's checks or the airline ticket vouchers. He was only interested in cash. There was $29. He made my father lie on the floor, gagged him, hogtied him with a length of nylon rope, and ran away down Manchester toward his car, which he'd parked in the lot of the 7-Eleven. My father choked to death trying to crawl across the floor to the phone. Even now I wake up in the night, unable to breathe, imagining it's me down there, inching toward a phone I'll never reach.

"That's why I became a cop. From the start it was homicide. Always homicide. I studied the books, the history. What drove people? What was it like in those terrible intense moments? I thought I could help those left behind, the loved ones, the families. I realized how much I'd been helped by the fact that my own father's murderer was caught. I'd bring justice and completion myself. Fix destinies. Noble, worthwhile goals. The job's still fine; I just disappeared out of it."

I was thinking that I'd known grief after my father, and I'd known depression in the time following Ellen's accident, but what I'd been going through these last months was something different. I didn't feel it all the time, yet it was always there, waiting to storm the door. And when it came, it was a tempest both inside and out. I wanted to live, but was ripped and haunted by a voice saying, "Die, die."

Ward reached across the table for my hand. "Come home with me, Billy. Let's go. Now."

My beeper went off, a detonation at the hip.

Ward still held my fingers. "Damn," she said. "Will you have to go?"

"Maybe." I glanced at my watch: eleven-twenty. "I'd better find out."

The pay phone was in back. From there I had a clear view of the restaurant. Ward had her right elbow resting on the table and her forehead cupped in the palm of her upturned right hand. The log fire hissed and crackled. A guy from Shane Dartle's table, another face I knew, a TV actor with a goatee beard and long hair, bumped my shoulder on his way to the men's room.

"Hey, McGrath the ghoul," said the desk sergeant. "Looks like you've got yourself one." He said that Cataresco was at the scene already, and that Diamond had been paged, but Cataresco had suggested I get over there right away, because this was weird.

"Did she say why?"

"Only that it's gonna be big."

I went into the men's room to wash my hands. The

bearded young actor was there, tweaking his dick, slipping it back in and hitching up his pants. He shrugged
and tossed up his head as if to say: *Isn't this all a joke, this
fucking life bullshit?*

"For you, pal, maybe," I said, but he didn't get it. In
the mirror my face was pinched and anxious. I splashed
cold water on my cheeks and neck.

"I'm coming with you," Ward said, and when I told
her I didn't think this was such a good idea, she pointed
out that her station would know about the homicide by
now, so she'd get there anyway, with or without my
cooperation. "I'm a reporter again, not a date," she
warned me.

Two minutes later we were side by side in the
Porsche, and she was holding her little tape recorder at
my mouth. "You're driving carefully," she said.

"I'm cautious," I said. "Besides, the guy I'm going to
see, he isn't going anywhere."

"What are you feeling?"

"Look at it like this. I'm in a forest and it's very deep
and dark, and each tree I walk past—there are a lot of
trees—each one of those trees is a possibility, and all the
leaves I hear rustling above me in all those trees—each
one of those leaves is a fact that might be helpful but
most likely not, even though I have to pay attention to
every one anyway. So many facts, it's bewildering. And
what do I do to find the path? I look at the compass,
right? It's procedure, it's training. I use my tools."

She pushed out her lips, disappointed—no drama in
doing it by the numbers.

"But sometimes."

"Sometimes, right."

"Sometimes."

"Sometimes." She was hooked. "Go on."

"Sometimes I know right from the first fucking moment."

There was a big mechanical clown on the end of the building at the corner of Main. It was nodding, grinning, and kicking its leg as I took a right up Rose and saw red and yellow lights in the fog, searching out from the top of three patrol cars, parked lengthwise across the street to form a barricade up by one of the flophouse motels. A helicopter thundered overhead, dragging its searchlight in a tight circle, and a patrolman stood behind traffic diversion signs, waving his flashlight at cars and letting me through after I'd stopped and showed him my badge. I wondered why they'd shut down the entire street. I wondered why Ricky Lee had done this so close, and on my turf. To keep me on my toes, maybe, or to remind me again who was calling the shots. After all, whatever happened, I couldn't point the finger at him.

I followed my usual procedure and parked some distance away to come up on the scene quietly, in my own way. I walked slowly up to the lines of yellow caution tape with my badge flipped over my pocket so that I wouldn't have to speak, trying very much to behave as normal and finding it easier than I'd expected, for the moment, to deal with and push down the knowledge that this one I'd set in motion myself. At the same time I had a sense of disconnection, as if once again there were two Billys. Here I am, I thought, I'm a cop, playing at being a cop, yet knowing already that I'm starting to behave like a crook.

A patrolman I didn't know in a black slicker but who knew me stepped up, took my arm, and ushered me toward Cataresco. Standing on the curb beneath a big red-and-white umbrella, even though it wasn't raining anymore, she was dressed in a black leather suit, sexy, and cloddish sneakers she'd presumably slipped on to replace something more formal. "You must have known ahead of time. I never knew you were psychic, Cat," I said, "You're dressed all in black."

"Can you believe it? I was on the way with my mom to the Nuart, you know, for the late night of *Rocky Horror Picture Show*. Don't make a face, Billy; she's from the sixties."

"So, whatta we got?"

Cataresco came closer with her smile flashing through the fog and her notebook open. "Rock *and* roll. This one's a honey," she said, but then, on seeing Ward Jenssen, her manner changed. "The bitch from the TV. What's she doing here?"

"She's with me."

Cataresco frowned, not understanding.

"It's OK, OK?"

"If you say," she said, her shrug letting me know that she'd want an explanation later. "Here's the deal. Our victim's right here." She nodded to a spot where six or seven uniforms had gathered in a cordon, maggots on the corpse of the murder. One of them, a big guy with a squared-off crewcut, caught my eye and waited, wondering what I'd do, Billy McGrath the homicide magician. Overhead, the clatter of the helicopter grew loud, deafening, filling my face with its noise, and then faded. Cataresco went on, "And also there, on the other side of the street."

"Double header?"

"Same victim."

A moment went by before I got it. "He's in two pieces."

"Bingo," said Cataresco.

"Holy shit."

"Bank on it." Cataresco unwrapped a stick of gum and folded it into her mouth without once removing her eyes from Ward Jenssen or letting up on her glare of contempt. "This one's too much, even for TV. Someone cut the guy in half, my guess is with a chain saw. Then they put Rose Avenue through him. Marinara sauce all over the sidewalk."

Ward, at the center of attention, wasn't uneasy. She was used to it. "The blood, the death—don't they bother you?"

"You mean because I'm a woman?"

"No. I assume you're one of the guys. I mean because you're a human being."

"Yeah, sometimes," Cataresco said, furious. "At least I pretend it's all in the same category as Walt Disney."

"I try to tell the truth."

It was hard to say whether Cataresco laughed or snorted. "The truth? Man, you people are kind to yourselves. What a crock."

She hadn't said anything yet about the victim's identity. "Enough already," I said. "Let's cut the bullshit. What else?"

Cataresco said, "Male John Doe, no ID. No wits. Guy in the Arco station across the street says he saw a black four-wheel drive come down Rose, stop, then come back up the other way. But he wasn't paying attention. Couldn't say whether anything was dumped out the car or not."

"I'd better check out what this guy looks like."

"Like hell," said Cataresco. "A street guy. African American."

I made my way across the street with my head down. Those words: African American. I think I was swaying.

The air was sharp with the smell of skunk and urine,

trapped in the fog, and added to those, as I wove my way through another gang of patrolmen gathered around the second half of the body, the odor of shit and offal. For once I had no trouble relating a man, a life, to what was in front of me, a sack with its insides hanging out. Sharp chips of shattered bone were sticking up out of the flesh. The arms looked incongruous and long, stretched on either side of the cut-off torso. The eyes were still open.

A small jet passed overhead like a muted dinosaur, even its lights invisible in the fog. Cataresco came up beside me. "Billy, what's the matter? Did you know this guy?"

"Yeah, I did." His staring lifeless eyes had either nothing or too much to say. His mouth was shut with a length of that two-inch silver tape. The tape was jagged at the edge and had lifted away from the stubble on the face beneath the sideburn. I leaned down and touched his eyes closed. "His name was Jack Brewster."

21

THE REST OF THAT NIGHT WAS A FEVER. I RAN TO THE Porsche without a word, desperate to get a handle on what was going on, trying to think, telling myself, *Think, think.* What happened? Why? What went wrong? Everything was fuzzy, mysterious in the fog. The metal of the door handle was warm as blood against my hand. Jack Brewster had died when Corcoran was supposed to. Having known them both, having been the link between these two souls, having involved Jack Brewster in the plot—the little hunch man said this was at my door, but in my dismay I clung to the hope that it was a coincidence, that Corcoran was dead, that he'd been snatched, that Ricky Lee had nothing to do with what I'd seen, that there was no connection between Jack's death and my move. I had to find out.

I drove five short blocks to the blind windows at the front of the Stardust Motel and went in alone and with my gun drawn, a little amazed that it was in my hands for anything but a cleaning or target requalification. My legs ached, my shins felt splintered, and even at midnight the smell in the lobby of the Stardust was thick, stupefying. The beam of my flashlight picked out a pair of fleeing rats and the edges of a heaped-up pile of garbage. Someone shouted "*Cops!*" and I jumped, flicked off the flashlight. They were used to searches here at all hours. Gung-ho sergeants would bring in their boots for tactics training. There was a scuffling above, and not just of rats, living people, before a silence settled back around. Inching out from the lobby into the courtyard's cooler air, I saw a light up on the second story, its beam picking out a section of corridor and a yard or two of twisted railing before melting into the fog.

Another voice: *"Anybody hear the cops? Man, there ain't no fuckin' cops."* I didn't even have a radio. The light went out and I was left in the dark again, exposed as if I were alone in a pitch-dark field. Turning the flashlight back on, telling myself that holding it at arm's length was a smart move in case anyone decided to take a shot at me, I made my way to the corner of the courtyard, up crumbling concrete steps that were still slick and slippery from the rain, then along the corridor, past flaking walls and the doors that were scratched and torched with graffiti.

Jack Brewster's room was a ruin. The paint tubs that had caught the leaks had been kicked over. I sloshed through water inches deep and banged my foot against something hard, his typewriter, lying on its face in a jumble of keys. Beside it the flashlight picked out pieces of torn paper and a Polaroid shot. The muslin drapes had been slashed, the mattress ripped open, and the paraffin heater was on its side, filling the place with an oily reek. I got down on my hands and knees and picked up as many of the fragments of snapshot and paper as I could find. Many crumbled, leaving only pulp between my fingers, but others I was able to store in my pockets, hoping for any clue. "What happened, Jack?" The leaking walls gushed and glimmered.

Perhaps he'd been killed up here and dumped out on the street, but there was no blood. If not here, where? To cut a man in two: this wasn't just murder, it was messy, noisy, the act of someone who enjoyed or was dead to it or was putting out a very big sign. I pushed back the image of him lying there on the sidewalk, a man who earlier tonight had been walking, grumbling, eating. Perhaps he'd tapped away at his typewriter. Then someone had come to him. Had taped his mouth. Had cut him in two.

This was the wake-up call.

Something moved on the far side of the room and I jumped back from this near-human shape, one of Jack's shirts, still hanging on the line, or not even that, I realized, but the shirt's shadow, which I watched for a second or two before spinning on my heel and running down the corridor to hammer on the door outside which I'd spoken with Jack's friend, the whore Ruthie Pump.

A bored male voice said, "Fuck you."

A shout came from far down below in the Stardust, "Fuck *you* too, man. I gotta go work in the morning."

I held myself flat against the wall next to the door and knocked again. "This is the police. Let me in *right now* or I'll shoot the fucking door down."

A light went on—it *was* the same light—and the door opened a crack. The male voice said, "You got a badge, cop?"

Ruthie's pimp was tall and wide, bare-chested, his arms badged with tattoos. He had hair to the shoulder, a beardless face so pitted with acne that it resembled a pizza crust, and he was young, nineteen at most. There was another tattoo on his neck. Ruthie's age was hard to guess. She might only have been twenty-two or -three, but she seemed tired, ancient; I'd seen sixty-year-olds in Brentwood who bought themselves a better look. Bored, based out of her mind, she sat in bed and drew her knees up to her chest, then the covers up to her chin, and rolled over to face the wall.

A storm lamp gave out a yellow, gauzy light from one corner. Shadows went dancing. Three or four joss sticks burned in an empty beer bottle by the bed, their musky odor mingling with, but not quite covering, the Stardust's foundation stink of decay. The boom box sat on a pair of unopened cardboard boxes, brand-new electrical equipment—pimp's theft or bounty. He'd nailed up and painted drywall, and the floors crackled with plastic sheeting. There was even décor of sorts: one poster of Madonna, another of the Mexican soccer team.

"You got a warrant, cop?" This hulking kid spoke with a lisp, misshaped mouthfuls of air, or else it was something he'd copied from Mike Tyson. I assumed the deal between him and the girl was the usual one, slavery. She fucked guys or whatever and gave him the money while in exchange he stopped them from beating her up and kept her supplied with drugs. Maybe he didn't beat her up himself, though I doubted that.

"No, I don't got no warrant. What's your name?"

"Mariquito."

"I'll call you pimp, pimp."

His little boy's voice said, "Fuck you."

My shadow jumped as I flew at the kid, pinned him against the wall, and Ruthie screamed, "Don't hurt him."

I swung myself around with my back flat to the wall and pushed the 9 mm in the kid's ear.

"Please don't hurt him."

"Ruthie, shut the fuck up; this cop ain't gonna do *nuthin'*."

"Bully," she said, drawing the covers up tighter.

I let the gun's barrel flick the tip of his ear. "Ruthie—

it's you I want to talk to," I said, "so let me explain to you how this can go. Your pal here is assaulting a police officer. I know, I know, I'm a bad boy, but who are they gonna believe, Ruthie, you or me? Why, I bet if I search this place even not very hard I'll find a concealed weapon. That makes you involved, too. The two of you in a conspiracy together to kill a police officer in the line of duty."

"Bullshit. We ain't innerested."

"I'm not talking to you, pimp. And then there's the other way. Tell me if you saw Jack today. Tell me when and tell me where. Tell me what Jack was doing and the words you exchanged."

"This is harassment, man. I'm going straight to Internal Affairs."

"Go ahead." I smacked the barrel of the gun against his teeth. "Get down."

He was kneeling with his legs apart while between them from his mouth hung down a thick gooey dribble of blood.

"Maybe you're interested in this. Maybe you're interested in the next part of how it's gonna go, which is me blowing you away right now."

"Shit, man," he said, a telltale tremor of fear.

"Do you both understand now? I blow the scumbag's head off unless you tell me everything I want to know, right now. I'll count to five. One-two-three."

"HEY!"

"Four."

"Shit, tell him, Ruthie, tell the fucking guy."

"Tell him what?"

"Tell the guy, tell him what he wants, *just fucking do it*."

Her knees pumped beneath the covers. "There was a guy."

"What guy?"

"This guy, tonight, I saw him with Jack, I guess, on the street."

"When?"

"'Bout three hours ago."

"Who was he, Ruthie? Did you know him?"

She shook her head, scared; she didn't want to say.

"Who was the guy, Ruthie? I got to know."

"I can't, I can't say his name."

The cocking of the pistol was almost in itself like a shot. "Look! I'd love to do it. I'll shoot him."

There was a final moment of hesitation while she tried to balance the probabilities, to consider how what she was about to say might change her future. She shook her head; it was hard, saying it in a whisper and facing the wall: "Tookie."

"Tookie Cross?"

She nodded.

I think I swayed a little again, wiping my brow with the hand that had the gun in it. I said, "Shit," and pressed my forehead against the musty smell of the dry-wall. Three years before, on trial for armed robbery, Tookie Cross and two other gangsters had escaped from the Santa Monica courthouse, storming the doors together before the bailiffs drew their weapons. He hadn't been seen or heard of since, though the legend of his name had attached itself to robberies and tit-for-tat dope homicides all the way from Mexico to Montana. In bygone years he'd been Ricky Lee's main man, a killer. Had that been Tookie Cross in the Rose Café? Maybe. I was trying to put all this together.

Ruthie was saying, "What's happening? What's happened to Jack?"

"I'm sorry, Ruthie, but he's dead. We'll talk about it later, OK?"

"He's dead. My friend's dead?"

Turning from the wall, I saw her bewildered face and thought of what Jack, with a great grin, had told me the day we went to the coffee shop, about Ruthie Pump knowing someone's soul by the shape of their shadow. A primeval idea: I wondered what shape my shadow was now. I'd been willing to get Jack involved in this very dangerous game, and now he was dead. I'd got him killed. I felt guilty and flattened. I felt sick. I rushed out to vomit. A dark part of this would follow me for the rest of my life; that's if there was to *be* a rest of my life. This might be just the way Ricky Lee would go about it: kill Jack Brewster, *pour encourager les autres,* and scare the shit out of Billy McGrath before dealing with him. I was a dead man unless I took care of him first or got out of town, not an option because he'd only come looking for my family. Ruthie Pump had turned to face the shadows flickering on the wall again, and I had a terrible thought. Perhaps he'd gone looking for them already. He probably knew where they lived or could find out easy enough. I had a vision of Lucy, lying in bed, eyes open, her pillows spattered with blood and bone.

The house on Nowita was all dark. The door was locked, but I knew where Ellen had at one time kept a key, taped under a back crossbar on the locked gate at the side of the house. Reaching over, searching with my fingers, I found the key and tore it free.

The door swung open without a sound and I walked into the darkness, gun drawn and down at my side. My eyes were dazzled and a voice said, "Drop the gun, asshole, and lie down on the floor, *slowly.*"

I almost laughed, washed by a warm ocean of relief. "You're OK. Thank God."

"Billy?" she said, puzzled, and orange fireworks

swam in front of my eyes as she lowered the flashlight. "What are you doing here?"

"Where's Lucy?"

"Asleep."

"Are you sure?"

"Billy, what's wrong?"

"Are you *sure?*"

"Of course. I looked in on her when I heard you crashing around outside. For Christ's sake, Billy, I could've shot you."

She was still holding the gun, a Smith & Wesson that I remembered we'd bought at Pistol Pete's in Redondo Beach; it's funny the details that pop into your mind.

"I'm taking the two of you to a hotel. And then I want you out of here on the first plane to Seattle tomorrow. Don't ask why. There's something going down. I need to know that the two of you are safe."

She showed no surprise. We'd been in trouble like this before, when I was working Internal Affairs and busted a motorcycle cop who'd raped and killed two women after ticketing them for speeding on the freeway. While the investigation was ongoing, he'd threatened to kill me and my family. We'd lived in a hotel in Ventura County for a month until the case was complete, the guy behind bars. "Just bring what you need. We can organize the rest later. Look, this isn't some stunt. Let's go, let's go."

She said, "It's bad, isn't it?"

"I don't know. Maybe. Come on."

While Ellen got a bag together, I knocked gently on Lucy's door and went in to wake her, rubbing her shoulder, whispering, "Luce, it's Dad, c'mon." I folded the wheelchair and stowed it in the Porsche. Carrying Ellen out there into the night was a strange reflection of the past, bringing back memories of happier days. She was in my arms again, starting to get a little resentful and pissed-off, now that the surprise of this sudden intrusion was wearing off, but nonetheless with her cheek pressed against my heart, while Lucy, thrilled at the adventure, scrambled into the ledge seat with her satchel and sketch pads, clutching the new pencil set I'd bought her.

Checking the mirror, I turned south on Lincoln, driving slowly through Venice, then spurting ahead through the Marina and out across the still-flooded wetlands to rise through Westchester toward the airport, making sure that we weren't followed. This calmed me, even if it didn't stop the guilt and pain crisscrossing in my chest. I'd created the potential of this harm from which I was trying to guard them.

Lucy had fallen asleep again. I said, "Where's Drew? Did he get called to the crime scene?"

"He left not long before you came. Who was it who got killed, Billy? What's this all about?"

I said, "I don't know, I don't know all of it," and nothing more. At one A.M. the Hilton lobby was a wilderness where an entire army might have been hiding. Now it was the sleeping Lucy I held, slung over my shoulder, completing the check-in. The scenic elevator offered views of advertisements for cruises in the Caribbean and the *filet mignon* in Chris's Steak House, and then, as we rose to the seventeenth floor, a panorama of the coast in shrouds all the way north to Malibu and Point Dume, the fog pricked and given patches of ghostly glow by lights pushing up through its cushions. At the airport nothing came in to land. No jets rose from the runways. Only the control tower stood above it all, a lofty beacon.

The room had twin beds, huge lamps, hotel art, and a beige carpet whose pile had been scrubbed all to the right by the vacuum cleaner. Having taken off Lucy's scuffed sneakers, swept back the covers, and tucked her into the farthest of the two beds, I was sitting on the other, eyes closed for a moment, when I felt the cool touch of Ellen's fingers. She said softly, "You should rest. Stop it all for a couple of hours."

I leaned my cheek against her hand's comfort. It was what I wanted to do, to stay, to rest, but Jack Brewster was dead, and somehow I didn't think Ricky Lee Richards was sleeping. I whispered: "Remember when we took that cruise and saw a school of whales rolling north, their backs glistening in the sea?"

"I remember."

I shook my head. "Man, that was something." Opening my eyes, I said, "I'd better go. I'll call in the morning and try to get to the airport. But if I'm not, the two of you be on the plane. Promise me."

"I thought you didn't want us to go to Seattle."

"Don't kid around, Ellen. Promise me, OK?" Lucy stirred in her sleep, sighing gently from her throat, as I kissed her cheek and stroked her forehead. "Don't let her out of your sight."

"You know I won't."

"Yeah, I know. You've got your gun, right? And you want me to let Drew know where you are?" My beeper went off again as she nodded. It was the precinct house. "I'd better get that."

She held me back. "There's something I want to tell you, something you should know." She turned to check that Lucy was still safely sleeping. "When I found out, when I saw the look in your eyes . . ." She sighed, briefly halted. "When I knew you were having the affair with Ward, I wanted to see you burn, Billy, I wanted to see you flayed alive. Scorpions and snakes, that's what I wanted, eating up your brain. You betrayed me. You disgraced me. You *humiliated* me. I remember that first night, lying awake, thinking, 'My husband did this?' I punched a hole in the bathroom wall."

I remembered seeing the evidence the next day. It had been a fair punch. She'd sent me out of the house for that and several following nights. I'd slept in the car.

"I walked around daydreaming of the bad things that would happen to you. I'd see you dead in your car. Or bleeding on the street. But instead, something happened to me. I was shot."

A door slammed down the corridor somewhere, and then the hotel returned to its watchful middle-of-the-night stillness.

"I used my anger. It gave me the will to be strong, so I kept it glowing. I told you that I'd forgiven you, and sometimes I thought that I had, but my mind would turn a corner and my rage would jump out at me. 'I'm angry, goddammit, and he *should* feel guilty.' I saw no reason why you should ever be let off the hook. I know I've been the center of your life, even now that we're divorced, and I came to like that. I wanted to punish you at first. Then I realized I was scared of losing what I mean to you."

"You won't, ever."

She shook her head as if I were missing the point. "You've been my safety net, and that's wrong. It was for my sake that I forgave you in the end. It was Drew who showed me that. Now you've got to stop being so tough on yourself."

We were still sitting together on the bed, with Lucy's breath a soft rhythm behind us, while outside a siren whooped, clamoring at the night. Lucy shifted in her sleep. "It was my fault," I said. "None of this would ever have happened if I hadn't slept with Ward."

"You know what? That's true and it isn't. None of

this would have happened if I hadn't been born. And you know what? I'm glad I was. I can't argue philosophy with you, but I'll tell you something. This has been my life, my responsibility. I made my own choices. I chose you, and I let you go. Now you've got to find someone else, Billy. I have. To hell with anger and guilt."

She didn't offer to kiss me, and she didn't wave, but her eyes didn't leave mine as I shut the door. I imagined them still on me as I walked back down the dim, silent corridor, as the elevator doors closed and I was plunged down into the thickness of the fog and then the street, deserted at that late hour except for the cautious passage of a single yellow cab on its way to the airport.

The desk sergeant didn't pick up until the tenth or the eleventh ring, and whether his voice was drugged from boredom or sleep or a surfeit of years on the street, it was hard to tell. I put a face to the attitude. He had a big round head like a balloon. He usually worked the beach, muttering about the dangers and eccentricities of crowd behavior, and at five o'clock on a Sunday night, as the sun was going down, he'd say, "See, the shopping bags are turning into gangsters." He was about to retire, to go into the paint business, which, he said, would allow him time to complete his master's degree in sociology. "Woman's been trying to get in touch with you."

"Who?"

"She's called two or three times already. You have admirers," he said, and yawned. "Like Don Juan."

"Who's he?"

"Here's the thing. The lady left a number, but no name. Said you'd know who she was if I said she was the guitar player. The *guitar player?* I tell you, detective, this world abounds with all manner of crazies and fuck-ups. Perhaps she was abducted by UFOs and took an alien lover."

Renata Richards lived not in Venice, but in a bungalow three blocks back from the ocean, between Manhattan Beach and Hermosa. A cat balanced on top of her garbage can was startled at my approach and vanished into the fog. She opened the door quickly, as if she'd been waiting, and we faced each other for several seconds of puzzled silence, her face hauntingly familiar, like a cherished snapshot I'd forgotten and found again. Fresh from the shower, her short hair slightly damp, she wore a white T-shirt, cut-off gray sweats, and no shoes at the end of those long legs. While she offered me a cup of too-milky coffee, which I accepted, I saw that at some point during her life three parallel inch-long scars had been slashed or burned across her right cheek, the side she tried to make no show about keeping turned away from me. Her nails were bitten to the quick. She came straight to the point, telling me that Ricky Lee had been to see her earlier in the night.

"What time?"

"About seven. He had some story about Charlie Corcoran having killed Mae. He said that he'd heard Mae went to Corcoran's house, the night of Denise's murder, the night he didn't come to the theater."

"What did you say?"

"I told him he was barking up the wrong tree. Where could he have got a cockeyed story like that?"

I waited while my heart settled down. "I've no idea."

"I was with her all that night. She never went anywhere near Charlie Corcoran or his wife. We took in a movie."

I tried to make my voice calm, despite the constriction in my chest. "How did Ricky Lee react?"

"He went quiet."

"Which means?"

"Someone's in a lot of trouble." Her green eyes were like her ex-husband's for a moment, shooting fireworks. She said that she'd been around it all her life. People hurting each other, being killed, killing. Some found the strength to get away, as she had. Others, neutered by fear, held on until their souls withered, dried, crumbled. And there were a few who thrived on the chaos and rage, who drank them in and spat them out redoubled to create a new life for themselves and, perhaps, abolish someone else's. "That's where Ricky Lee goes. You don't want to be around him when he's like that."

"You married the guy. You should know, I guess, better than anyone."

"I married him because I was pregnant. I slept with him because I was sixteen and he was gentle, polite, a guy who seemed so different."

"He's that, all right." From the window I looked across her garden, where there was a lawn and a chain link fence that gave onto a concrete path leading down toward the invisible ocean. The path was empty. There was no traffic, no sound, except the rumble of the waves amplified and borne upward through the thinning fog. Asleep, the population of Los Angeles was one big happy family. In a few hours they'd wake up and get on with the business of confounding and murdering one another. Dismay was banished once more by the stubborn determination to get on top of this. Ricky Lee had come here, heard what Renata had to say, and figured out that my story, the story I'd told Jack Brewster to tell Ricky Lee's boys, was bullshit. So he'd gone looking for Brewster.

She said, "I hope you don't think I'm wasting your time. But believe me, I've seen him when he's like this. He'll burn anything he touches."

"You're not wasting my time."

I wondered where Ricky Lee was now, trying to feel him out with my nerves. He must have a place, I thought, where he'd taken Jack, to question, torture, and finally kill him. It wasn't the kind of thing you did in public. There'd have been noise, mess. "Where's your little girl?"

"Asleep," she said. "Why do you ask?"

"No reason. You knew Mae well?"

"Better than Ricky Lee did."

"You were both keen on music."

"That's right."

"Yeah, my wife, too. What do you know that might help me find who killed her?"

"She was a good person."

"I'm not saying different."

Renata watched me, bristling, wondering if she should trust me. She was nakedly herself, composed, scarred, strong, an artist, young, hurt, shy, tender. "I've got the feeling someone got her involved in something. Don't know how or why, but all those video machines she had. I asked her about them one time. She said, 'Oh, they're nuthin'.' Well, they weren't *nuthin'*."

The house had an airy and happy character, like Ellen's. Books. Toys and other kids' stuff. Everything clean but not too neat. Guitars resting their thin necks against the walls, a saxophone on a stand in one corner, mouth open to the room with a chair behind, as if waiting for the right man to get in there and sit and play it. "How did you get out of the marriage?"

"With difficulty," she said. "Look, you're a cop, I know what you're thinking, 'Here's this lady, she's living in a nice neighborhood, in a nice house, bought with drug money, I bet.' Well, let me tell you something, mister. It's not true. I didn't get one cent from Ricky Lee toward all this. He pays child support, and that's all I'll take."

She talked about Ricky Lee, about his past, his roots, and how his life had taken a sudden turn when his brother was murdered. That hit him hard, and then he was in gangster life forever.

"So I got out. That's all I'm gonna say. The hazards of our relationship are none of your damn business."

Ricky Lee had gone his own way, not chasing success, almost surprised by the discovery that he had a knack, a skill, a talent for organized murder and mayhem. As a result, he'd seen very little of his mother in recent years. He hadn't even known of her love affair with Richard Francis.

Renata said, "He was asking tonight, 'Who was that old white dude?' He wanted to know what he was doing at the funeral."

"Did you tell him?"

"No. He'll find out."

All through this interview I'd pushed down and tried to ignore my feelings about Jack; otherwise I didn't see how I could function. Now I saw ripples, extending out and out.

I got on the phone to Francis at his home in Palos Verdes, where the answering machine gave another number, that of St. Augustine's Hospital in Long Beach, where the operator tried the number of his office, no reply; but yes, she said, he was in the building. Another call, to the Long Beach Police Department, was less successful. Having explained who I was, and asked the night sergeant to send a couple of men to the hospital where they could check on Francis, I waited for several minutes while he checked if anyone was available. In the background I heard the squawk and babble of the precinct radio, bringing news of a mugging, a knifing, a break-in, a gunfight, man down. I leaned against the high back of a steel dining chair. I laid the receiver flat against my chest for a moment, because Renata was looking at me with a strange expression. There was a sparkling space in front of her eyes. I said, "What?"

Then the Long Beach sergeant came back, saying he'd do his best but could offer no guarantee. They were having a crazy night; several homicides and an explosion at the old naval station, arson suspected. I'd have to go down there myself.

Before I left, Renata said she had something she wanted to ask me. She leaned against the wall with one foot crossed over the other and reached for one of the guitars, hugging it to her belly. As a kid she'd been in the hospital, she said, and then a foster home, because she'd been unable to speak. She remembered that a white guy had visited her. She'd never known why. "I had the wildest feeling that first time when I saw you in the theater. It was as if a door in the wall opened and I was hearing music I hadn't listened to in years. It was you, wasn't it? You were the guy."

I didn't know whether to feel crushed or blessed. Her expression was neutral, questioning, though there was a quality in her voice, a wistful wonder and sadness.

"Did you know my parents?"

"No."

"They were murdered, weren't they? They told me at the home. I could never find out anything else."

"You don't remember?"

She shook her head. "No."

It was a blessing, and I'd no intention of stirring up her repressed horror, though my own memories began to rise and burst: the stunned eyes of the little girl tied to the chair, her silence when the gag was removed, the floor with its mess of blood and bone, the pieces of scattered flesh, the suffocating stench, the frail white arm, junkie-thin, thin as a spindle, lying by itself on the floor, the brain matter clogged in my shoe, my failure to hold to the promise I made on that day. "I'm embarrassed," I said. "I've wondered so often. For years I've been all burned up about the fact that I stopped coming to see you."

"I don't remember that. I only remember what you were like. Young and hopeful in a boxy charcoal suit, bringing me stuff, leaning forward with your hands on your knees and telling me a story. I used to daydream about you being my father. You'd take me away and we'd live together in a cabin in the mountains someplace."

I had tears in my eyes.

"Are you OK?"

"It's nothing," I said. "It's crazy, I'm sorry. You thought well of me all this time?" Looking at her, I had the scary idea that destiny was interested in me, had pinned me down, and that something, my fate, was being worked out. A machine I'd started now had me on the inside.

She put aside the guitar, smiling, and I pressed my fingers into my eyes. "I have to go."

"Yeah," she said, "I guess you do."

After this sudden intimacy we didn't know how to say goodbye to each other. There were so many questions I wanted to ask, and no time. The silence was filled with the thunder of the refrigerator and the ocean's distant rumble, pulsing deep in my blood. "Listen, thanks."

"No problem. Drop by sometime. Let's be friends."

We clasped each other in an awkward hug, and I left feeling happy, excited, a little breathless, having glimpsed something thought lost long ago, found now by a sudden beam.

22

I T WAS AFTER THREE, AND THE BRIEFLY CLEAR NIGHT AIR had fallen to a sudden calm. There was no wind. The revealed moon tossed a bridge toward me across the ocean; it swayed and rippled, silver, a lifeline on the ever-changing waves. I gunned the Porsche fast down Coast Highway, sweeping by the cheap motels, the murky cocktail lounges, the spanking new malls, the antique and guns-and-ammo stores. The smoke and twinkling lights of the Redondo Beach refinery seemed less a glowering image from a German Expressionist movie than a forest of pipes and soaring steel.

The drive took me past the Wayfarer's Chapel again, though this time I didn't pause for the detour. A corny thing, really, getting married there, as if the beautiful gesture could carry over into our lives: it had to do with youth, being in our twenties, when each action, each decision, has an irredeemable air and must therefore be perfect. My ambitions themselves had been chiseled, clean: to love my wife, forever, and, after my father's death, to become the best homicide detective in the city.

A halo surrounded the moon's brilliance. Still making quick progress, weaving through the mud and rocks, the sinkholes, the fallen trees that weeks of storms had left littered throughout Rancho Palos Verdes, down past Portuguese Bend and the countless white concrete tract homes that commanded the bluffs, I didn't seem the same man I'd been even twelve hours before. I was more awake, more aware, in shame and agony when I thought of Jack Brewster, but at least feeling, alive to shock and fear and wonder.

That was the gift, it seemed to me then, riding a high as the Porsche swept down toward Long Beach, that Renata had made me. And it still seems true, though I'd wish to add something else. The image in my mind is of a man freeing himself from the ice, momentarily unaware of the shadows outside and within, monsters gliding upward through the warmed water.

St. Augustine's was high as a hotel, a honeycomb of light with a fountain in the forecourt at the end of Magnolia Avenue. I parked up front, smack in the red zone, telling the security guy I was an officer of the law. He didn't even smile. Inside, the dim lobby was empty. St. Augustine's, with no emergency room, goes quiet at night, when all hospitals, even the busiest, tend to change, to shuffle and shift inside the crisp white coat of science. The staff thins out, and the carpeted, noiseless corridors are filled with weak light from those power-saving fluorescent beams. It's then that you feel the magic of these places, neutral ground, waiting rooms, where life comes in and is held in sudden abeyance before death, or life, is fetched away again.

On the seventh floor I got out, turned right past the soft-lit peace of the nursery, and headed down a gray-carpeted corridor that swallowed my footsteps and gave back no echo, though I did see my reflection, comforting if ghostlike, in the windows that were all along one side. Below, fleets of tethered yachts bobbed on the Pacific swell, and the floodlit triple stacks of a moored ocean liner rose into the night sky. Far out, beyond the harbor, the distant lights of Catalina were strung together, pearls.

The bespectacled night nurse was a dragon of efficiency. The pockets of her white smock, pulled tight over Wagnerian breasts, were bandoliered with pencils, thermometers, ballpoints. Her eyes sank deep into her face when I told her I was a policeman, looking for Dr. Francis.

"Really?" she said.

I showed her my badge, and she reached, in no great hurry, for the phone. Whoever she called wasn't there. She asked to see my badge again and sniffed. Reluctantly, she divulged that Dr. Francis was indeed on duty.

"Why do you think I'm here?"

She clicked the ballpoint in her hand several times, as if arming a weapon. "Try delivery room seven."

He wasn't there, so I poked my head around the door of all the other delivery rooms, and then tried the restroom. No luck, so I trekked along another deserted and soundless corridor. This one, sloping down, looked onto an interior courtyard and led at right angles into yet another, dimmer still, where a nurse soaping her hands at a sink said she'd seen Francis in the Natal Intensive Care Unit, first door on the right, and if I wanted to go in I'd better scrub up. This done, my hands smelling sharp and clean, I pushed open the door with my elbows, finding myself in a small space, warm and womblike. Under the dim light, babies snoozed inside respirators with tubes snaking from their tiny nostrils. Francis wasn't here either. A woman sitting in a rocker with her child in her arms, burrito-wrapped, said in a whisper that he'd been beeped a couple of minutes ago. She thought he'd gone to make a call.

The darkened corridor was empty again. Turning the corner, I headed back up the incline, thinking I'd have to try my luck for a second time with the dragon nurse, and Francis appeared, coming toward the elevators from the far end, with the lit window of the nursery behind him. He was with three guys, one on either side, each holding an elbow in a fashion a little too firm to be friendly, while the third came up behind, a small, smooth-faced boy I recognized, rolling from side to side with the laces not even tied in his hightops. It was the kid Nelson, who should have been in bed already. If they were bringing him out on a caper like this, it was probably part of his slamming in. He looked down at his sneakers, avoiding my glance. There was no time for this now. The other two were serious hardcore. The one on the left was tall and spindly-thin, with eyes lit up like Christmas trees, though it was the other, Tookie Cross, who really caught the eye. Tall, built like a fridge, Tookie was nonetheless quick and nimble in movement, an athlete, with sharp black pants and the clip of a beeper outside his right pocket. He wasn't young, though it was hard to tell how old he might be. He was impassive as stone and wore a black T-shirt with BEWARE 187 in Gothic script on the front. I didn't figure he was an orderly; 187 is the California penal code number for murder.

They were taking Francis away, to Ricky Lee, for questions and probably much more. There was no doubt in my mind what I had to do, and I was lucky, for by now they were waiting beneath the light by the elevators and I came up on them out of the dark. "Excuse me, gentlemen," I said. "I need to have a word with Dr. Francis."

I wasn't looking at Francis at all, but smiling at the skinnier of the two gangsters, who gave a cocky glance over at Tookie and said, in a malevolent drawl, "He's busy right now."

"Well, he's going to have to find time for me."

"Yes, I'm sure this will only take a sec," said Francis, glassy green eyes hopeful beneath the lumps on his forehead and a wet lick of silver hair.

"Shut up," said Tookie Cross, giving Francis a look like the one I'd had myself from Ricky Lee when I took the bribe, as at a man whose existence is already starting to gutter. The spindly guy meanwhile made a move with his hand toward the back of his pants, for a knife, most likely, and without thinking I sprang forward and pushed hard in his chest. He fell on his ass; then the Beretta was in my hand and in the face of Tookie Cross.

"Beware one-eight-seven," I said.

"Fuck you," he said, not scared, not bothered, not angry, but honoring me with his full attention, as he might dogshit squeezed between grooves in the soles of his Nikes.

A red circle of light went on above the elevator, a bell went *ping,* and the doors opened at a welcoming glide. Grabbing Francis by the shoulder, throwing him in, I never let my eyes off the stonily impassive face of Tookie Cross, who, as I backed into the elevator myself, leaned forward toward the barrel of the gun, not moving his feet, but as if his eyes alone might burn up the air between us and set me aflame. At last the elevator doors glided shut again, a more effective if not final barrier, and together with Francis I was heading down.

"Did you kill Mae Richards?" I was beyond worrying about protocol or trying to make this stand up in court. I just wanted the truth. "Did you kill her?"

Francis took an angry step from where he'd been leaning, rattled, in the corner. "How *dare* you?"

"This isn't the place to act the offended Englishman. I'm asking what those guys want to know, only they won't be so polite about it. Your life's in danger, which means mine is too, and I need to know the story." I grabbed his wrist and made him look me in the eye. "Tell me."

His eyes didn't flicker. He didn't hesitate. "No," he said, "I did not kill her," and I believed the angry truth erupting from his heart into his eyes. He was sincere. "Who are those men? I don't understand. What did they want with me?"

"You don't know?"

"No."

"You can't guess?"

"Detective, stop playing games."

"Why should I, when you've been dicking with me?"

My belly rose up through my throat as the elevator slowed to a sudden stop at ground level. The lobby, empty, showed itself beyond the opening doors, and I stepped out with my gun down at my side but still in hand. Perhaps Tookie Cross had men down here he'd alerted on a cellular. I'd no doubt he'd be following. Heading past the darkened pharmacy, a shut-up souvenir stand, Francis to my right and a little behind, I saw the security guy, feet up, nose in a fat paperback. "Call nine-one-one," I told him. "Tell them where you're calling from. Tell them an officer's in trouble." It came to me that Francis would most likely have his car parked in one of the basement lots. We could have ridden the elevator straight down there. Too late now: we'd take mine.

Guiding the Porsche up the exit lane, around the fountain gushing its wedding cake of luminous spray, I glanced in the driver's mirror to see the two gangsters coming out of the hospital doors, the kid Nelson running behind. Tookie Cross stopped, swiveled his head, made us, and turned, waving hurry, hurry, to a Toyota Land Cruiser whose lights came on in a sweeping dazzle as it curved down the ramp on the other side of the fountain. I hit the street and headed right, only because it was easiest, on the phone and calling 911 to tell the dispatcher that I was Homicide Detective Billy McGrath, badge number 1458, in need of assistance and being pursued by armed suspects in a Toyota Land Cruiser, black, with smoked windows and shiny mag wheels. I was on Ocean speeding south past the convention center, hitting a light as it blinked from orange to red and making a left onto Long Beach Boulevard.

Francis twisted around, peeping through the rear window. BEWARE 187: I knew this wasn't mere bravado. Hitting the gas, I sent the Porsche up to sixty for three blocks, whipped the wheel around and cut over onto Fourth Street, and sped south another two blocks before making a left on Elm. There, I eased on the brakes, swung into an alley, and killed the lights. We were alone beside an empty parking lot, out in the open, but huddled in the shadow of a two-story brick building.

"I think we lost them," said Francis.

"Maybe."

"The carpet in your car is soggy."

"Sorry about that. You lied to me. The first time we met, in the car. You told me your flight was canceled. It wasn't. Now why would you do that?"

He was eager to be frank. "I shouldn't have. But the news of Mae's murder, coming at me out of the blue like that—it was all too much. I wanted to stay put. I didn't call the airline at all, and I told you a stupid lie. It seemed like the thing to do at the time."

"Who did you call?"

"Radek."

"The Polish guy?"

"My assistant."

The back streets of Long Beach, at four-thirty by the dashboard clock, were silent and empty. From the far distance came music, a jazz club's after-hours babble. I stared at a sign for the Bank of America. Above, up on the second story of the brick building, a Latino guy in a sleeveless shirt sat smoking a cigarette, with his legs dangling over the ledge of his open apartment window. He hadn't seen us. He was gazing at the moon. A clanging bell announced the arrival of the downtown Blue Line trolley car on Long Beach Boulevard and, from the distance, came the now comforting wail of a police siren. I'd known it wouldn't take long. Soon there'd be more. Given the chance, every cop in the city, let alone Long Beach, would respond to the call of an officer in trouble. Tough, if you happened to be a regular civilian simultaneously experiencing difficulties in the neighborhood— but I was family.

Even while I was trying to assess what Francis had told me, I heard the pounding, the approaching rumble of rap, a thunder that grew louder, rattling my chest until my heart hurt. Twisting in my seat, I was dazzled by sudden headlights, full beam, about fifty yards back in the alley. Something went bang, suddenly, *bang* on the car. Francis shouted, clapped a hand to his mouth. The passenger side wing mirror wasn't there anymore. It had exploded. I had an impression of glass flying, of glass tinkling to the ground, of glass reduced to motes of dust so fine they hung and spun, buoyed on the air. I hadn't even heard the gunshot.

I stamped the gas, and the Porsche sprang forward, a

surge that took us to the end of the alley and a screaming right onto Long Beach Boulevard, where instead of hitting the brakes I floored it again through a red light to pass beneath the approach and thunder of the northbound Blue Line trolley. I got a good look at the driver, high in the lit bubble of his cab, wearing a San Diego Chargers baseball cap and an expression of glazed shock or fear. "It's OK, it's OK," I shouted, on Third heading toward Pine.

"Damned close shave," said Francis in a mumble. Suddenly angry, he let out another cry. "Shit, I got *shot* at."

Most cops, especially the patrol guys, live for this: they get to turn on the lights, the sirens, and zoom fifty mph over the speed limit to where the action is. They pump their arms and make fire-engine noises, shouting, *"Let's go kill some bad guys."* It had never been quite my bag before. I made a left onto Ocean again, then a right, glimpsing through the tops of palms the hospital's high honeycomb shimmer.

I thought I'd lost them, but they came up again on Terminal Island among the silos, the scorched railway stockyards, the smells of burning rubber and smoke tangled. "I see them, about three blocks back," said Francis, peering through the back window with an almost professorial interest, or perhaps he was numb. My head felt calm, wildly out of line with the way my heart was beating.

A bus went slowly by on the other side. In the docks, the great angular cranes used to load and unload and rebuild the ships were lit, prehistoric carnivores with night lamps crawling up their legs and bellies, skeletons about to dip their beaks and feed. In the driver's mirror lights burned closer. I heard the angry approaching violence of rap, offstage thunder. We were in for it, a gun-tight, and no way to win. We'd both be killed. Maybe we should make a dive for the shipyards. Perhaps we'd find help there. I told Francis to try 911 again and, hearing sirens, gave the mirror one last hopeful check, to see whirling lights, two patrol cars, veering in behind the Land Cruiser. Those guys, suddenly in trouble themselves, responded by coming even faster, since we had the upper hand now, and to an extent I hadn't guessed. Speeding across the span of the Thomas Bridge, with the waters of the main harbor and the port's dreamy nightscape flashing, sparkling below, I led them to the welcome of a roadblock at the far end. Black-and-white cruisers were stretched three deep across the north-bound lanes. A chopper must have been up above, monitoring the later stages of the chase, for they were ready, those officers on the bridge, crouched with automatics in twin-fisted grips, or leaning up against opened cruiser doors, the easier to sight along the barrels of pump shotguns. I counted twenty, maybe thirty faces, tense and adrenaline-pale.

The Land Cruiser stopped a couple of hundred yards back up the bridge. Its lights went out, but its frame still shook from the sheer blasting clamor of the music, filling the bridge, shocking the air. They were surrounded. They had to give up. There was no other option for them, not that this was so horrible. They'd be taken in, charged, and Ricky Lee's lawyers would have them back on the streets within hours. They'd say nothing. I knew I need have no worries on that account, so the question became how little I could get away with when explaining myself, in my certainly upcoming dialogue with the Long Beach fuzz. I was trying to remember if I knew any of the detectives down here. I was thinking that I'd get that little kid Nelson in an interview room and scare the shit out of him, then take him back to his mother. Francis, meanwhile, was laughing, slapping his thigh and bouncing his legs up and down. "Damn it all, we did it, damn it." He lifted his fingers in a lazy V, the gesture of the English bowmen triumphant at Agincourt. "Fuck off, you fuckers. We're here and you're there." He cackled. "*Now* how do you feel?"

Behind us a cop, a three-striper, a real Marine Corps type whose neck was wider than his head, swaggered in front of the roadblock, arrogantly brave, the butt of a shotgun grazing his hip. Through a bullhorn in his other hand he announced that the occupants of the Land Cruiser should exit their vehicle with their hands in the air and lie face down on the bridge. Somehow he made it clear he wouldn't much mind if they failed to comply. That way he and his troops would get to cap off a few rounds, or a few hundred, most likely. He said he was going to count to five, though the guys in the Cruiser didn't wait for him to start before swinging around and heading back the way we'd all come, the wrong way down the northbound lanes toward the boomeranging lights of the two patrol cars that had picked us up on Terminal Island.

I stared through the windshield in shock for a few moments and set off, but there was no way I could catch them. They must have hit a hundred already when they came up on the patrol cars and swerved right to jump the concrete median. It bounced them back, spinning. The Land Cruiser flashed its white headlights, winked its red rear taillights, glanced white again, and plowed into the high mesh fence at the side of the bridge. Then all the lights were gone.

23

AFTERWARD THERE WAS THE SETTING UP OF A CRIME scene, the usual somehow desultory frenzy with all its paraphernalia: more officers, yellow tape, a couple of choppers whopping and circling overhead. I took Francis aside and briefed him, basically to the effect that I was going to take care of everything. "Whatever you think best," he said, pleased by the idea. "You saved my life."

The Long Beach detective was one I knew from my time with South Bureau, a tall, stooping, balding guy named Humbolt Raffi, who drank like a fish and went through wives like courses at a Chinese banquet. "Hey, Billy. Long time. What's shaking?"

I was trying to figure out what to say, how much of the truth to tell without bringing in Ricky Lee's name, a flag I didn't want to hand Raffi at this stage, when it was quite possible he'd wish to shut the book on what had happened up here, an accident after all, not a homicide. The guys in the Land Cruiser had been gangbangers, I explained, trying to abduct a witness to a homicide that had occurred in my own precinct. I'd got there first, and the chase had ensued.

"After which they went swimming," he said, gazing with no great interest through the wrecked fence. Raffi was several hundred alimony payments past being surprised. Perhaps an alien invasion would wake him up, though that was far from certain. Far below, container ships, thin as matchsticks, were being loaded under the fairy lights of the harbor, and a tiny speck, a police launch, sliced its way through the water from Smith Island to search for survivors. The shock of the impact would most likely have killed them before the deep cold waters of the channel. He said, in the same bored, nasal tones, "Divers'll go down once it gets light. Didn't you once pull back a jumper from up here?"

"Years ago." I was thinking about smooth-faced Nelson. He'd probably pleaded with Tookie Cross with his eyes: take me along, take me along. All his short life he'd watched guys like Tookie, admired them, heard stories about them. He'd dreamed about the gangster life like a stray dog dreaming of a bone. It was, I realized with a sudden quenching of the spirit, all he'd had. "Oh, fuck, *fuck.*"

"Thought so," said Humbolt Raffi, scratching the bald spot at the back of his head, then rubbing it gently. "How's Ellen?"

"We're divorced now."

"No shit," he said, shaking his head. "Think she'll take me? Here come the vultures."

A white TV van had pulled up. The passenger door slid open, and Ward looked out. She'd been home and changed, or got a different set of clothes from somewhere. In jeans, boots, a black leather vest with a black leather jacket over it, she jumped down, planting her feet and taking her bearings, scanning the scene until she found me, pulling me in with all her gaze. At that moment, tired, happy to be alive, I felt myself warmed and gratified by attention I presumed to be other than professional. "Billy," she said, taking my hand. "Are you all right?"

I didn't let go of her hand. I said that I was fine.

"They picked up all this on the radio at the station. Are you gonna tell me exactly what's going on?"

"Who's asking? You or the reporter?"

"Is this where it happened?" At the edge of the bridge, having leaned over, she pulled back and took a sharp breath, as if feeling airless vertigo. "It could have been you."

"Maybe." I realized that because of my confused, driven, burned-deep feelings about Ellen, I'd been hovering around women, fluttering and flirting, drawn to them, not afraid, but not wanting to get close. "Let's go. Let's get out of here."

She frowned. "Oh, Billy, I can't. I've got to do the story. Meet me at home later." She squeezed my hand. "Or stay here and wait." She tried to be bright. "Give me an interview."

"I'll pass on that."

"Then see me at home. OK? Please?"

"You won't come now?"

"I can't. You know that. Come on, Billy, give me a break here. Don't be so goddamned proud. Give a little. It won't kill you."

I stared for a moment down into the harbor, toward the horseshoe arrangement of piers and the steel cranes that grew like scaffolds planted in the deep forest of the port. "Good night," I said, and walked across the bridge to where Francis stood by himself. I told him that it wasn't safe for him to go home, that I was going to arrange for the Long Beach guys to check him into a safe hotel. "Just until this blows over," I said. "I'll be in touch. Don't move without them. And don't talk to anybody." I asked Humbolt Raffi to make sure all this happened, and to keep him out of the hands of the reporters.

"That'll be my pleasure," he said. "By the way, I was talking to one of the patrolmen who was in a black-and-white on the bridge. He says he only saw two bad guys in the Toyota."

"No way," I said. There'd been Tookie Cross, Nelson, the skinny guy, and there must have been a driver. "Had to be at least four."

"You're probably right. We'll drag 'em up and see for ourselves soon enough. Hey, what's a coupla scumbags more or less between friends?"

"I'll see you around, Humbolt."

"Perhaps we'll both have new wives by then. Well, what's life without hope?"

Driving north, not looking back, passing more black-and-whites as they rolled the other way, lights swinging, toward the scene, I felt suddenly sick, thinking of Nelson and the men who'd gone over the side of the bridge. I didn't feel guilty. I hadn't made them chase us. All the same, lives were gone that had been there moments before with such force, with such exuberant energy, violence, and, in Nelson's case, innocence. I'd won this round, I was still alive, and for a moment I didn't much like the idea.

I hadn't made things easy for Ward. To expect her to absorb and respond favorably to my revived romantic longing at the precise sudden moment I expressed it, to drop her work and flee with me to bed because I'd come around to the idea at last, wasn't, I saw, entirely reasonable. Thus I rationalized my disappointment and the perceived rejection. I'd call, but not tonight or, rather, not this morning, for the sky toward the east, above the city, was at last hinting at the dawn. What I wanted most, at that moment, sweeping down the exit ramp onto Front Street, was sleep, to rest for at least a couple of hours before being faced with Ricky Lee's next move. I knew he'd make one, and I'd better be on my guard; otherwise, he'd swat away my one and only life.

The sinking moon was lower in the sky, but its motionless and springlike light shone down on San Pedro, silvering the harbor, the grim, nodding oil derricks, the surface of the streets. Even though I mourned the deaths of Jack Brewster and Nelson and my own involvement in them, I'd escaped the jaws of the machine, at least for tonight. I was exhausted but no longer angry, even with Ward.

A shadow came up on my left, a black four-wheel drive swinging around from the other side of the street. Something nagged at me, an unease or something I'd forgotten. I wasn't sure what. I'd meant to call Charlie Corcoran's house, to hear his voice, to check that Ricky Lee hadn't gone after him after all. That wasn't it. The events and progress of the night had been evidence enough. He was alive, I was sure.

The black car pulled up alongside at the next stoplight, its smoked glass windows impervious to my glance. A Toyota, I thought, as the light changed to green and the black car veered sharply, cutting off my lane, and I hit the brakes to avoid a collision.

There'd been another black Toyota. I'd seen at least two before, during the course of these last days, and there'd obviously been two in Long Beach tonight. The first lay at the bottom of the East Basin Channel, pummeled by the ocean's deep currents. This one must have looped around Harbor Scenic Drive, Coast Highway, and come back into San Pedro on the tail end of the freeway. I pulled the shift into reverse, trying to retreat in a hurry, but there was nowhere to go, the way back cut off now by a Cadillac of 1970s vintage, an impractical boat of an automobile, but useful for this purpose, as roadblock or battering ram, from whose four doors emerged four redwoods, each carrying a pump shotgun. One casually held the butt so that the barrel, pointing groundward, kept pendulum measure with his approaching steps, and two others clutched theirs across the chest, while the fourth aimed his at my head and gave me the mad dog.

I turned away, refusing to meet his stare, and faced the Land Cruiser, not moving or trying to reach for my gun in case one of those tree-sized guys had an itchy trigger, but with a slow tick of fear rocking up and down my spine.

I sat watching while a huge, familiar figure eased himself down from the Land Cruiser's passenger side and came almost dancing toward me across the street, not carrying a weapon, but raising a clublike paw to scratch the chest across which a black T-shirt said BEWARE 187. He was followed by Nelson, clambering toward the ground with the laces still untied on his Nikes.

Nelson was alive, though before the glimmer of this realization had a chance to turn into relief or joy, I was faced with Tookie Cross leaning in through the open driver's door window, for all the world like a highway patrolman. "Would you mind stepping out of the vehicle, please?"

I got out, stepping on eggshells, turning in my mind the chance that I was about to die, a possibility that seemed to worry not at all those surrounding me, gangsters whose blankness of expression suggested they'd shoot on command or at the merest hint of resistance, or maybe even sooner.

Tookie said, "Where's Francis?"

"I can't help you there."

"Can't or won't?"

"Take your pick." I shouted to Nelson, "Hey, Nelson, you're keeping bad company." This time, leaning against the side of the Toyota, having been blooded, having seen some action, he stared right back with a reasonable imitation of the hardcore.

A step closer, and Tookie loomed over me like a mountain, whispering, "I can think of so many reasons to kill you. First, you're a cop. Second, you're a lying pimp. Third, your car's a piece of shit. Fourth, it would make me laugh to see your head burst open like a watermelon. Fifth, I'd like myself a Department-issue Beretta. Sixth, your dress sense disappoints me. When did you last change your shirt, bro? Seventh, I don't like the way you look at me. Eighth, just for the fuck of it. Ninth, so I can take your wallet and jack somebody for dope. Tenth, 'cos I'm buzzed by driving too fast. It's made me all high and bent. It makes my wounds itch, man. Eleventh, you think you're so smart. Twelfth, and most important, you got my homeboys killed tonight. All of these, any one of which in normal circumstances would suffice, all of these are pleading with me to ring the buzzer on you. And on the other side, arguing that you should live? Only one reason. My boss wants to meet with you tomorrow, as arranged. He's a man who takes things like that very seriously. I could lie, of course, say that one of my inexperienced homies got carried away, and that the trigger on one of these twelve-gauges was a little light. But he'd probably kill me. He hates to be disappointed in anybody."

"Ricky Lee," I said. "He's such a people person."

The punch he gave me to the belly I didn't see coming. Delivered with his right hand and a quick shift to the left, his body barely moving, it drove almost through to my spine, and as my legs buckled I was aware of a shotgun arriving in his hands with a slap, thrown by one of the others. With a second economical movement he swept its butt across my exploding head, while another hammer blow punched in the center of my back, forcing me to my knees.

Groggy, I saw the mica-sparkling pavement splashed with blood from the side of my head and heard him say, "So until tomorrow. Fail not our feast." I tried to lift my face, mumbling, but another blow came crushing down. There was no pain in my head this time. A bright glare got brighter, and then there was a brief aching flash, sweeping me off into the dreamless dark.

It seemed that I was back in a car, not the Porsche, sitting on the passenger side. Another light shone in my face, so I closed my eyes again, and squinted out through the windshield. It was daylight. A car burst by, too close, an explosion, and then another. I was on the freeway, but not driving. I moved my head a little, carefully. It hurt, so I went back to not moving it, concentrating instead on trying to figure out what had happened. I remembered the hospital, the bridge; I remembered being angry with Ward. The entire left side of my face was numb. Maybe I'd been to the dentist? It didn't seem likely.

A voice with an accent said, "You are lucky man, detective. They might have killed you. Oh, yes. Very easy. Easy as that." He snapped his fingers too close to my head.

"Don't do that."

Radek Gatti, the doctor's gofer, the guy who'd slipped me those troublesome photographs of Denise Corcoran and Mae Richards, went on in his mangled yet fervent English about Los Angeles. "There is the bus-boy tribe, the day workers tribe. There is the gangster tribe—oh, yes, I know you know about them. Some hunt movie deals or old ladies with their many facelifts in Brentwood and Beverly Hills. It is grotesque, you think? Some fish for souls, others sell the souls they've got for ten percent."

With head back and eyes shut, I nestled in the passenger seat's warm and musty-smelling old leather. I was tired; I wanted to nap. He had a pair of gold rings in his right ear, and his hair was tucked up under a different black cap this time. "What's going on, Radek? You following me?"

"My father, you know, he repair fountain pens for many years. He belonged to the fountain pen tribe. That was his calling. Penmanship, yes! He maintained that the Mont Blanc had never been the same straight arrow since the war; that's the Second *World* War. Why? Beats me. I still believe it's the best, the very best, though the most fine Parker Fifty-one with the hooded nib, that's a winner too! It gets the job done!"

"What about you, Radek? Where do you fit in?"

"I fish for millions. To catch my millions I set my snares." Gatti turned his head from the freeway for a moment, watching me, smiling, but only with his mouth. His magnetic eyes never heard about it.

He drove with reckless disregard, flitting in and out of traffic, with his right hand caressing the wheel while his left trailed out the window in the fresh breeze from the ocean. I'd been wrong before; this wasn't the free-way. We were on Coast Highway, heading north. Nor was the daylight so bright, even though it hurt my eyes. The daylight, in fact, was dim. The weather was overcast, and my vision was a vanished promise of clarity.

"I don't ask myself where I stand. I act. The man who follows a straight line, he is an idiot. There are laws, but there are no such things as—principles? Is that the right word? Yes. Well, no principles. Only wants. Only needs. Only desires. And the most important law anyway is expediency. Don't you agree, detective? We live in an era of lies and deceit. Look at the top. Why should I be more particular than the President?" He took both hands from the wheel and brought them angrily down. "I am only little refugee from Poland."

Slowly I turned my head to the side, the pain a little less jagged this time, though I felt nauseous, as if the rest of the world wasn't moving, while my head was the catherine wheel, spinning, sputtering, firing. An MTA bus flashed by, and a bum negotiating the curb with his trolley, who I thought for one moment must be Jack Brewster until I remembered. Palm trees rose up on either side with their nods and glimmers. Bungalows huddled behind chain link fences and the protective steel that blinded their windows. "Los Angeles," he said. "Wants to be Mozart. Is Bartok. Where you want me to drop you? Your apartment? Your wife's house? I, too, once was married. Within a week she was unhappy. Calling her friends from phone booths. Saying, 'He wants too much sex!'"

Glimmers of consciousness began to move around in me, wary tenants looking over an apartment building of dubious stability. "Why did you give me the photos, Radek?"

"Listen, I screwed this Japanese dancer two nights ago. Fantastic!" We were paused at a stoplight, where a bodybuilder, a guy in baggy sweats, ambled away from a Jeep while his girlfriend, a too-pert blonde with a pout, parked it. "Hey, look at those two," he said. "They fuck, it would be an episode out of Greek mythology. The girl would have to turn into a tree."

I listened hard, head throbbing. "What time is it?"

He took his left hand from the wheel, showing tanned, squared-off, capable-looking fingers, and glanced sideways at his wrist. "It's eight o'clock."

"In the morning?"

His laugh was boisterous. "Yes, in the morning. They really fucked you up good, no?"

"Where are you taking me?"

"Wherever you want to go. I'm the Good Samaritan here. Or didn't you notice?"

His face was lined and gaunt, chiseled, with a mole on the upper lip, a luxuriant lick of too-black hair escaping from beneath the cap, and those extraordinary light blue eyes that suggested the glare of ice, brutal Polish winters he'd presumably come to Southern California to avoid. He certainly didn't look like a Good Samaritan. "I have to get back to my car."

"No can do, buddy boy. They took it away, those nasty men with their shotguns. I think they had plans for it."

A huge black wave came toward me. I wasn't nimble enough in the head to flee, so I slipped down again, mumbling an address before I was dragged back under into unconsciousness.

Ward went about her business, stinging me with cotton wool doused in peroxide that she dabbed gently at the side of my face, my mouth, the broken skin above my eye. "Keep still," she said; "you're such a baby." I was sitting, legs astride a stool, in the cool and talcum-sweet luxury of her Coldwater Canyon bathroom, so much nicer than my entire apartment that it alone might have been making me feel faint. She said, "You must have seen blood before."

"Usually not my own."

When I'd arrived she'd been back home for only thirty minutes or so. She was in bed, and came to the door wearing a gray T-shirt, no shoes or make-up. She was shocked at the sight of me, saying she'd take me to an emergency room for a check-up, X-rays. "You lost a fight with a truck," she said. "You probably have a concussion." I said there was no time for that and asked to use her phone, calling Ellen and Lucy at the airport Hilton, where breakfast was going on and Ellen was skeptical after a night in a strange hotel bed, questioning the need of going to Seattle at all. She'd been a cop, she said; she could look after herself, whatever was going on.

Ward tossed aside a bloodied cotton wool ball, ripping open a fresh pack with her teeth, and spilling out a mountain more on the top of the marble sink. "I'm surprised you make it through the average day, living like this. Ow! I'm sorry," she said, trying to be gentle as she tore away cotton fibers stuck to a section of my cheek where hair had matted with skin and blood and dirt into a mess of dried-up gore. "How are you doing?"

Wincing at myself in the mirror, I heard sirens, the gulp and whoop of a fire truck rushing down the canyon. "I've been better."

"You should sleep."

"I have to be somewhere at noon."

"That leaves a while. Who *did* this to you? Aren't they supposed to stop when you say you're a policeman?"

"Please don't make me smile. It hurts too much. I'll

take you along next time, and *you* can try telling those guys."

"Why would they do this to you, Billy? That's your friend asking, not a reporter. Are you in trouble? I want you to get help."

A pulse fluttered in the corner of my eye. My tongue flopped in my mouth, an explorer that discovered a bloody hole where two teeth had been. Had I swallowed them? I had no memory of spitting them out. Ward's black-and-white bathroom tiles were spinning and moving about, so I shut my eyes until the dizzy spell passed. My lips felt thick as tires.

Ward rubbed Neosporin into my cuts, her face so close to mine, her breath fanned my eyelashes. She brought me a brandy.

"Is this advisable?"

"I'm no doctor, Billy. I'm just doing the best I can."

"Don't think I don't appreciate it."

"Drink."

The liquor warmed my blood into a semblance of life.

"Maybe you should try reducing the dose," she said.

"Of what?"

"Action. It doesn't seem to be good for you."

"Thanks for the vote of confidence."

"You're welcome." We gently kissed. "How was that?"

"Not too bad. Really." The contact with my face had badged her cheek with blood, which she wiped away and touched against her tongue.

"You're a mess, Billy. You taste of bullets."

"Tell me about it."

She took me upstairs. Her bedroom was light and airy. A mirrored door led to another bathroom beyond the king-size bed I'd dragged her out of. An open copy of *Newsweek* lay on the floor, where she'd left it. A pair of reading glasses was on the night table next to a bottle of mineral water. Busily she straightened the sheets and walked around the bed to draw back the curtains. One window was shut, and the other was open a crack so that a breeze capered through, ruffling the pages of the magazine. At the bottom of the garden a row of cypress trees were bending their backs, working hard in the wind.

She said, "Are you sure you want to do this?"

"I want to do it."

Before, we'd made love on the run, checking into hotels with a bottle of wine. There'd been hours of pleasure, but always heightened and tainted by guilt.

She unbuttoned my bloodstained shirt and gently slipped her fingers through the tight curls of hair on my chest. She slid down my pants, and the buckle of my belt banged the floor. Her lips grazed my chest, my neck, and then her mouth was on my mouth again, harder this time, her hands taking my bare shoulders and easing me down onto the bed before she herself slipped out of her T-shirt. Ward's legs were long, her breasts full and round, even though my hands slipped so easily around her slender waist.

Love, they say, is a dangerous thing, whose touch may burn, and on that morning her fingers scalded my flesh. I cooled myself, sucking childhood from her breasts, kissing her long thighs, tasting the juices flowing between them. I couldn't believe I was lucky enough to be allowed to touch her again in this way. Her skin was soft and silky-smooth, smelling still of sleep and linen.

We drank another glass of brandy while our tongues played together. She touched my prick delicately with her fingers. It grew eager under the command of her tongue, the teasing nip of her teeth, the soft weight of her body as she eased herself down, settled her knees wider on the bed, and took me inside. She smiled and moved up, almost letting my prick go, and then sat back down, enclosing me deep within her once more.

I burned and shivered.

"I've wanted this for so long," she said. "I want to fuck you again and again."

"I could live with the idea," I said, and pulled her head down to mine, thirstily kissing the moisture from the firmness of her throat, brushing away the hair that agitation had tossed into her eyes. I licked the sweat from her breasts while she gently fingered my balls. Ward's eyes were swimming, her lips swollen as she urged me on. She was looking at me, not as if seeing me, but as if, approaching climax, she'd found some other self.

She came, her breath crying out in my ear, and I melted inside her a few moments later. She nodded, still breathing hard, not moving, still keeping me inside her. Then she lay on my chest while we both smiled and the fresh air brought my conscious self back from wherever it had been hiding. The cypress trees murmured outside as Ward's head rose and fell on my beating heart.

24

ELLEN WAS PISSED, PISSED THAT I'D GOT HER AS FAR AS the airport, doubly pissed that I'd arrived ten minutes late with one side of my face like minced meat, and triply so that I'd brought tears to Lucy's eyes as she threw herself against my chest crying, "Daddy, you're hurt."

"Shush," I said. "Luce, don't worry about it. I fell and banged my face, that's all. You know how clumsy I am, right?"

Her arms were clasped tight around my waist. "Are you OK? Are you sure? I hate it when you get scars on your face."

"It happens, hon, sometimes. But it doesn't matter."

Ellen fished in her purse, saying to Lucy, "You want some pizza? How about the four cheese? That's your favorite. I'll just take a soda, OK?"

"Let me," I said.

"We got it, Billy. OK? Here, sweetheart, here's a twenty."

We were in Wolfgang Puck's, departure level, Terminal 2, people bustling around, making calls, thumbing magazines, or chewing and drinking, feet poised on suitcases. Life felt as if it was rushing me toward something, but not this, not a pause before my family's departure to another city. It was stupid, but I felt I was saying good-bye forever, and I knew I mustn't let either of them see any of that.

Ellen, having got me seated at a table, wheeled her chair closer and whispered that she wasn't going to let me control her or push her into anything. "This is operatic bullshit, Billy. If it's as bad as you say, why don't you get us surrounded with guys from the Department? Is it a guy from the Department you're afraid of? Or is this something you've done yourself?"

These were tough questions, which I didn't want to have to try to answer. She didn't let me get away with a thing. "I spoke to Drew this morning. He said he didn't know about any of this. He said all he knew was that some street guy, one of the guys you were friendly with, was killed last night."

"It was Jack Brewster," I said, watching Lucy up at the counter, watching her as she stooped and squinted a little, studying the menu. Did she need glasses? I remembered that years ago Jack had brought her a rose he'd picked from a garden in the neighborhood. He'd walked up the path like a knight bringing tribute to his lady.

"The black guy? Didn't he come to the house one time?"

"That's him." Across the other side of the walkway the shoeshine guy was trying to persuade a bored businessman to have his suede shoes shined. "He was cut in two, literally. I'm not kidding."

"Who'd do a thing like that?"

"I know who did it, and that's why you have to leave. I know it's incredibly inconvenient and you're pissed. I know that, and I'm sorry, really I am. But I'm not trying to pull anything here. I need to know that the two of you are safe."

"Isn't there anywhere safe in LA? What about my folks' place?"

"Look at it this way—couldn't you use a couple of days up there?"

"Maybe," she said grudgingly. "Where are we going to stay?"

"You can scope things out, find an apartment. Pick your own hotel. Pick the best. I'll pay. Just call me and let me know where."

"Maybe," she said, turning to check on Lucy. There was more gray in the red of Ellen's hair, I saw, more of age's seasoning, and then she swung back, grabbing my wrist with a hand as strong as guilt. "Who beat you up, Billy?" Her temper was mixed with tenderness now, but she was still angry. "Don't you dare die. Don't do that to us."

"I don't intend to."

"Good," she said, stubborn.

"I've gone past that."

This she let go, not quite believing me.

"Actually, I feel better than I have in a long time." I shrugged. "Call it crazy optimism."

Lucy came back with two pizzas and a basket of French fries, which she duly anointed with ketchup from a packet she tore with her teeth, taking me back for a second to Ward's bathroom.

"So what's funny?" said Ellen, catching my smile.

"I'm looking forward to this pizza," I said, helping myself, watching Lucy repeat the ritual with the ketchup on her own slice, "but wondering how I'm going to eat it." I asked how she'd liked the night at the Hilton. "The *Hilton,* sugs. That's fancy."

She said, "Who paints the pictures in those rooms, Daddy?"

"Weird, aren't they?" A sliver of crust stabbed into the pulped gum at the side of my mouth where a tooth had been. As my mouth filled again with blood, which I had to swallow, I realized that attempting the pizza wasn't so clever. "I think they have a factory in Arizona where they produce all that stuff and then pay people to put their names to it. It's the only conceivable explanation."

Ellen didn't smile. Lucy said, "Mom, how long are we going to be in Seattle?"

Ellen looked to me for an answer.

"A few days. That's all. It'll be fun."

"Won't it be raining up there?"

"There are lots of galleries. Hundreds. Really good ones."

For a moment I wanted to tell them about my gift, considering how best to phrase my story of Ted and the pictures I'd had him buy all those years ago which they didn't even know were theirs yet, but I resisted the idea, knowing it wouldn't be smart for them to know until all this had blown over, which would be soon enough, one way or the other. Ricky Lee was out there, making his moves. En route to LAX I'd rehearsed the reasons for and against going to meet him. There was the matter of my honor, daft but demanding, and the fact that if I didn't go, he'd come looking for me anyway. I couldn't avoid him for long, not without leaving town myself. Besides, I still thought I could get away with this thing; it was a workable situation. Of course the stakes had been raised. Ricky Lee and his guys had merely bisected Jack Brewster. I didn't care to think of how many pieces they'd chop me into; but then if he'd wanted me dead immediately, why not last night, in San Pedro, with Tookie?

"How's the pizza?" I said to Lucy, while I scanned the walkway and adjacent lounge for anything untoward, and Ellen followed my look from the shoeshine guy, to the ticket counter, to the phones, to the security gates and the metal-detecting women with their crackling wands we'd passed through together to get into departures.

"Is anything wrong?"

"No."

"You seem jumpy."

"I'm tired, Ellen. I haven't slept in a couple of days." This was the way we'd been in the bad days, failing to connect, everything a little bit off, as if we'd glanced away from each other and became strangers when we looked back again. I wanted to tell her about Ward, but realized she might not be in quite the mood to appreciate my liberation.

"Is Daddy being followed?" said Lucy, excited and a little scared for me again. "Is that what this is all about?"

"No, sweetheart, it's nothing like that."

A woman walked away from the phone, leaving a soda can on top of it, a man scooped up a squirming toddler, a couple laughed and hugged each other in the obvious bliss of new love; all of them paused here before taking another jump into the mysterious experience of their lives. It struck me that, according to any rational assessment of probability, they were more likely to make it through the next forty-eight hours than I was, but that was up to me. At least the boy Nelson was still alive, not decomposing at the bottom of the harbor. That felt like a blessing; Ward was another. "Something wild happened. Remember the girl who went dumb when she saw her parents die?"

Ellen thought for a moment. "You used to visit her?"

"That's right." Why had I quit? I'd said to myself that

you can't look after everybody. I hadn't realized that loyalty itself can sweeten and strengthen. Now I'd been given another chance. A dark line in the murder map had turned to gold. "I met her."

"When?"

"Last night. She ended up marrying Ricky Lee Richards. Isn't that something? They're divorced now, but she has a little girl." I was fiddling with one of those little packs, pepper segregated into toothpick-sized portions. "She got her voice back, everything. But the greatest thing was that she actually remembered me. I felt as though she'd given me a Christmas present."

Ellen nodded, too agitated to get into this, her right eye a little wider and rounder than the left, as if it had witnessed something awful, shocking, or as if it had simply seen too much, worked too hard, and couldn't relax again. She was bushed, not interested right now in my tales of light and darkness, and I thought of the ways we'd fought over the years, the squabbles that often started over trifles, over nothings, and swept us both through storms, whirlwinds, life-and-death wars of the will that miraculously stopped just short of physical blows. I thought of the months, the years of coping, all that time without a safety net, and still we hadn't made it. None of this was going as I'd intended. Part of me had been hoping for the big farewell, some symbolic closure.

I looked up and saw Drew Diamond, without the tweed hat, waving a rolled-up copy of the *Los Angeles Times* from where he was standing at the departure gate. He was wearing tan slacks, brown loafers, and a blue cashmere blazer, his spiffy attire nothing brand new, but suddenly triumphantly coordinated—another aspect of Ellen's influence, I assumed.

"Hey, look, here's Drew," I said, adding in a whisper,

"He walks like a man who knows how to walk like a man." Cramming pizza crust into my mouth, miming a pain I did in fact feel, I gained the desired response, laughter, from Lucy and another glare and stuck-out tongue from Ellen. "Look, I'm sorry," I said, chewing on the dough. "I didn't mean to bring any needle into this. Really."

Drew came over, offering me his hand and wondering if the change in the weather was an omen. Ellen smiled, looking up at him. "It seems that we're flying to Seattle," she said brightly.

"If Billy says you need to," he said, "then I think you should—no question."

"You think so, really?"

"Absolutely."

I felt in need of a great dose of fresh air, wondering how long it would take me to get used to seeing Ellen regard Drew with the same open and trusting look she'd once bestowed on me. Maybe I'd never get used to it, even if I found myself reluctantly admiring this pit bull of a guy in a way I never had before, for at least making the effort to exorcise his demons. If a man could feel the call to courage and beauty, all was not lost.

Lucy, as we made our way from the restaurant toward the departure gate, had on her excited airplane face already. She liked flying in airplanes. There was a moment after take-off, she said, when the 767 would head out over the ocean, and if she had the window seat, she could look down and see the Venice Pier and imagine where our house was, and maybe even scope it out, knowing that everything would be all right.

They were pre-boarding already, so it was time for them to go. It all happened fast. Ellen kissed me first, and then Drew, and disappeared down the jetway, wheeled by an attendant. Lucy followed after her, but ran back, coming the wrong way through the crowd to throw her arms around me again and say, "I love you, Dad." Then she too was gone, rushing forward with that eager and familiar stoop, clutching her sandalwood pencil box.

Drew and I stood for a minute or so in silence while the other passengers shuffled forward with their yellow boarding numbers. "You come in the Porsche?" he said, rocking on his English shoes.

"I lost the Porsche," I said. I'd borrowed Ward's second car, her toy, a white Alfa Romeo in which even on that sunny morning I felt large and old, absurd, squeezed behind the wheel, a tall man trying for a laugh. "It was stolen."

Drew nodded to himself, sucking his teeth, as if to say: But of course, Billy lost the Porsche. Despite his slick appearance, having dressed for the occasion, he was edgy now, a little ragged himself. He said, "What's going on, Billy? What the fuck is all this about?"

I hesitated, molding my face into—I hoped—a smile, and his fleshy palms came down on my shoulders. "I don't get it. Mae Richards and Jack Brewster. Don't get me wrong; I'm sure they were wonderful people, but from the outside it's just two more ghosts in Oakwood, and yet here you are, you're *evacuating* your family. For why? Because Ricky Lee's involved in this? Is he threatening you, Billy? Has he got something on you? Because if he isn't, if he hasn't, I'm puzzled out of proportion. And if he is, if he has, if something of real magnitude is going down, why don't I know about it? I still work with you, goddammit. If you're in some kind of shit, I need to know."

"Look, Drew, I can't talk about this."

His claws tightened. "Bullshit," he said. "Bull*shit.*"

What could I tell him? I didn't know what Drew was prepared to believe, he was such a blunt instrument, yet not without sensitivities, bells that chimed in unexpected ways. My lie was outrageous. I said that Megan, Ellen's psychic, had told me to get Ellen and Lucy out of Los Angeles for the rest of the week.

He took his hands off my shoulder, spinning away and stamping his foot. "Shit," he said. "That woman drives me crazy."

"Me, too."

He was still for a moment. "Why didn't she tell Ellen herself?"

"Didn't want to freak her out. Wanted me to do it instead. Can you believe that?"

"Only too goddamned well," he said slowly. "Remember when someone called her in on that serial killer case? What was the name of the guy? It was Kaplan, wasn't it?"

"I don't remember."

He stamped his foot again. "Jeez, what a day already."

"Tell me about it."

"I just got through with a meeting with Murakami."

"No shit, what did he want?"

"My blood," said Drew. "I found him the distraught recipient of a phone call from Internal Affairs."

"What?"

"They told him they believed that a senior detective at Ocean was on the take, big time, to the tune of *hundreds* of thousands of dollars. Maybe a mill. Larry was of the opinion that I was the detective in question."

I didn't blink. I didn't look off toward the woman with a smile stapled to her face behind the Southwest counter. Instead, I kept my eyes on Drew, staring as he lifted his hands and pushed them through his hair. I said, "That's ridiculous."

"It's fucking *bullshit,*" he said, almost shouting, and then, turning to apologize, lifted his hat to a woman affronted and astounded on the walkway. "Excuse me, ma'am." He went on, voice hushed, leaning toward me. "Of course it's ridiculous. I was fucking furious myself, even though I appreciate that Larry's such a politician he probably consults the mayor before flossing his teeth in the morning. I'm an easy scapegoat. That's all it is. Larry, fucking Larry! What a monumental fuck-up. Who the *fuck* does he think he is? He seemed to think there was a sinister deep shit voodoo connection between this information and the fact that I was leaving the Department, heading for Seattle. And this on the basis of one friggin' phone call from Internal Affairs." He kneeled down, attacking and furiously tightening the laces on his wingtips, revealing the little .38, his back-up piece, strapped at the ankle. I knew there was also the matter of the throwing knife in his belt, and the four spare clips, two in each jacket pocket, for the .45. Drew carried more hardware than the Seventh Cavalry. He stood up, brushing down his slacks, straightening his tie, and jutting out his jaw, while I tried to absorb this latest twist.

There was the chance that it had nothing to do with me. Civilians were always calling Internal Affairs, alleging that certain cops were abusive or corrupt. Since Internal Affairs was charter-bound to follow through on each and every complaint, crooks and bad guys themselves were wont to get on the horn, just to run interference, for the diversion.

But the way things were going I knew this *had* to do with me. Someone was hanging out a big sign that Larry, dear Larry, had been smug, or devious, enough to read the wrong way. The whole situation was sorry, impassioned, and, as Drew said, a monumental fuck-up.

"There used to be loyalty," said Drew. "You take away loyalty, people are just passing through, piss in the wind. These days the Department's willing to take a complaint from Charlie Manson. I feel like I've been beaten, beaten, beaten, and they still expect me to build a rocket to the moon. It's why I'm getting out."

He talked about the old days, the 1980s. "Remember that guy down in Compton?"

"Deion Connolly?"

"Yeah, the guy with gold faucets in his bathroom." Connolly's parents had run a used-furniture store, through which he'd laundered money from his own business, dealing dope. Eventually he'd bought eight houses on the corner of a block, knocked them down, and built one huge one, a compound that became known as Compton's San Simeon, the Hearst Castle of South-Central. Deion, flaunting more gold than Ivana Trump, had driven a '67 Mustang, a restored green-and-white convertible '57 Chevy, and a Ferrari Testarossa so clean and lovingly burnished that he'd once presented Drew with an In 'n Out burger and invited him to eat off it. "Now there was a guy you could understand, a guy who was saying, 'I'm a crook. Come catch me if you can.' These days guys like Larry seem to think you can't tell cops and crooks apart. Everything's slipping and sliding."

And so was I, I thought, glancing up at the clock; I was shirking and sharking, making my move.

Drew said, "It's just one big messy old world. What happened to ol' Deion anyway? Did we ever bust him?"

"He got shot eight times in the face."

Drew's eyes gave off an angry shine again. "I'm an old

guy, Billy. I don't need this. I want respect. I *deserve* respect. I don't understand this. We're the working dogs, you and me. Politics shouldn't come into it. Money shouldn't come into it. Right and wrong, the law, that's what should come into it. The system used to protect us; now it's throwing us to the wolves." He shook his head, slow, nodding and smiling at another group of flight-bound passengers, streaming past toward their journeys, futures. He looked to me for understanding, for explanation. There was no hint of anything else in his eyes, no seeming suspicion that I might be the one. "A guy that'd take a bribe? Him I got no time for. Him I wouldn't piss on if he was on fire."

I figured I'd stop by the precinct because it would look strange, even suspicious, if I didn't. There'd be excitement and hullabaloo about the news from Internal Affairs, since cops, like all good elders of the tribe, love to gossip, throw aspersions, and contemplate the thrill of a purge from within. I was curious myself about what news, if any, had filtered back from Long Beach and Humbolt Raffi. I needed to show myself, calm and in control.

Before driving over there, while still at the airport, after Drew had put back on his hat and shouldered angrily in the direction of the escalators, I called the Softly Gallery, where an assistant told me that Ted was out of town and unreachable. My first thought was that Ted was either spending the $500,000 or else had gone off someplace with it, never to be heard from again, which was the risk I'd taken. He hadn't left a number. The assistant, with pride in his voice, as if this were an amusing and even laudable aspect of his boss's character, said he had no idea what state Ted was in, geographically speaking, let alone which exact city. Ted had gone fly-about. He might be in New York or Hawaii or Nova Scotia, for all anyone knew. He'd bought his tickets in cash, hadn't called in for messages, and wasn't expected to surface for days.

Cataresco was sitting at my desk in front of the custom-made varnished cabinets, on the phone, *my* phone, an open murder book at her fingers. She looked slick, sexy, confident, unhurriedly restoring the phone to its cradle. Staring at me, her mouth wide open in mock astonishment, she said, "Billy, this is real decent of you to show up. Jeez, what happened to your face?"

"Cat, can I get my chair back, please?"

"Excuse *me,*" she said, standing up and straightening her jeans. "I was under the impression that I actually belonged to this homicide unit. Despite the fact that its chief, my partner, has stopped talking to me."

"I'm not talking to anybody."

"Oh, that's great." She worked her way around to her side of the desk, tugging the murder book after her and reaching back for her decaf. "Where'd you go last night, Billy? Who'd you run after? What is it with you?" She was snotty and sneery, saying, "What's happened to your sense of timing, Billy? A homicide's a ticking clock. Your own words. Remember?"

I said that in this case the clock was thundering.

"What's that supposed to mean?"

I glanced at the wooden gun and smiled, saying, "What's up? Anything new?"

"Two Culver City bangers got all shot up this morning."

"Where?"

"Outside Blockbuster Video. The store on Lincoln."

"Dead?"

"One. The other's in ICU. They don't expect him to make it."

"Shit."

"I've gotten zip on the guy who was chopped in half last night."

"Really?"

"And Internal Affairs seems to think there's someone in our midst who's taken a bribe for a million dollars. Apart from that, it's been an average day."

"What's Larry say about Internal Affairs?"

"He's frantic."

"Most likely he can't figure out why he's not the one who was offered the money."

She didn't smile. Sharpening a pencil, she kept her eyes on the murder book in front of her. "I don't get it, Billy. We were working well together. Then—excuse me—things start getting weird. Little things, but they add up. You send me off to Colorado. You don't want me to push on the Mae Richards case. You don't seem interested in solving it at all. And now this. It's just boys' club bullshit. You don't want to let me in because I'm a woman."

"It isn't that."

She sipped at her coffee. She seemed angry, then thwarted, then angry again. She leaned down, neat and trim, to collect the pencil shavings in her cupped palm. Her eyes and voice pushed at me, not abrasive, not shy either. She wasn't about to give this up. "No, sure. Nothing on your conscience, right, Billy? It's a clean bill of health for Detective McGrath. He's too wise and perfect, after all, to make any mistakes."

She was looking at me now as if she knew something I didn't, and for a crazy moment I thought she'd guessed it all. How? I remembered the interview with Ricky Lee, the recording I'd made of the offered bribe. I'd destroyed that; she couldn't know.

She said, "I think I'm going to have to talk to Larry about this." Her eyes softened, giving me another chance. "I'd rather talk with you. What did happen to your face? That must hurt."

"Go ahead. Take the powwow with Larry."

"I will," she said into her coffee, gathering her wounds and ambition.

25

THE COOL AIR WAS FRESH AND DECEPTIVELY CLEAR, with a salt breeze that slanted from the north across Main Street, rattling the palm trees and fluttering the red-and-black banners for the symphony that hung from streetlights: LOS ANGELES—HEAR THE MUSIC! It was late in the afternoon, a little after five, and light was fading. The sun was slashed by horizontal bars of purple cirrus cloud. The bright red paint of the Fire Engine House Restaurant grew darker, coagulated in the thickening twilight. I sat in the Rose Café, watching out the window as a Santa Monica Blue Bus drew up, expelling two passengers, an old lady, dressed in white, wearing wraparound sunglasses, and a gawky kid with a bicycle slung over his shoulder. On the other side of the street a bodybuilder waited to cross, his body squat and so muscular that the arms hung, baboonlike, away from his torso, as if his ribs sensed that the merest contact with those fists could do terrible damage. I remembered Gatti's crack about Greek mythology. He was a classicist, as well as a joker, that five-foot Pole, and he didn't have a criminal record. I'd checked at the office.

I called Humbolt Raffi at Long Beach to find out

where he had Richard Francis holed up, and then I got in touch with him. Radek was a restless soul, Francis said; he liked to move around. He didn't have his own house or apartment, but tended to stay in Francis's guest house or on his boat, or else with other friends, wherever he could find a bed for a month or two. Francis was OK, not yet bored, the sometimes fatal disease of those in safekeeping, and I told him to stay inside and make no calls. I was a dangerous man to know, such a proportion of my acquaintance having been forced into hiding.

The bodybuilder crossed the street, awkwardly swinging his arms, and Ricky Lee slid in beside me at the table. He wore aviator sunglasses with rims of solid silver, a black denim vest with the sleeves ripped off, several gold herringbone chains twisted together, and a floppy cap, made from a hundred pieces of different-colored suede, that was tilted over his right eye. I didn't see where he'd come from. I'd been watching the street, so it hadn't been from there. I must have blinked and he'd come in through the back, silent on his feet like a predator. He didn't say anything, looking at me with the merest hint of a nod. He ordered a pastry, which he wolfed down, chewing with his mouth open and smearing the cream off his lips with his forefinger. His bony bare arms were scarred, with burns, with many cuts. There was a gunshot wound up by the shoulder, around the pinkened edges of which were tattooed the letters O-U-T-L-A-W. His silence was cold and threatening, a challenge. At last he said, "I got the rest of your money."

My heart took a tumble, a swift somersault. Was this a joke? To be followed by the flourishing of a weapon, a shot to the head? I was all gaze. "Good," I said, "that's good."

Ricky Lee was nodding, kissing cream from his finger, staring around me at the counter. "You like whipped cream? Man, I could eat this shit all day. Bad for the heart, yeah, isn't that what they say. Mmm-*mmm*. Give me that sugar. Bring on that cholesterol shit. I can take it. Yes, please. Bring it home to daddy." Removing his glasses, holding them gently by their delicate silver arms, he laid them gently on the table, stroked his beard, and looked suddenly at me with eyes that flared into ferocious malevolence. "For a while back there I was very angry with you, McGrath. I said to my crew, 'This cop, he's fuckin' with me, he's dickin' me, he's givin' it to me up the ass.' And you were, a little, your dick was *pokin'*. See, I found out that my mother never went to Charlie Corcoran's house the way you said. You lied to me about that. Or maybe you was speculating, trying to fill in the edges of the picture. Either way, it wasn't so, and it was wrong of you to tell me, so I don't feel too bad about the dustin' Tookie and the rest of the crew gave you. How is your face, by the way? Man, that looks sore. That looks evil, man."

"I'll survive."

"Let's not jump to any outrageously premature conclusions," he said, flashing me the diamond in his tooth. "By the end of last night I figured I was gonna have to kill you in some particular way that would have meaning. That would signify, know what I'm sayin'?"

I got the drift.

"Then I found out you was telling the truth after all. Charlie Corcoran *did* kill my mother. So, like I say, I got your money in the car."

"What made you see the light?"

Outside, a Rolls-Royce convertible, yellow and freshly minted, was stopped at the crosswalk. He said, "A guy came to me with this." He reached into his pocket and tossed something that jingled, a key ring. The twin faces of comedy and tragedy regarded me from the table. Turning the masks over, seeing the diamonds embedded in comedy's either cheek, and the engraved message in the back of tragedy's head, those words from Ricky Lee to his mother on the occasion of his brother's death, I had to resist the impulse to reach and grab at my own pocket, where these same keys should have been weighing heavy. I straightened my lapels and drew my jacket closer, as if feeling a slight draft from the door, and confirmed that the keys were indeed gone. I couldn't remember when I'd last checked, when I'd last fingered them—sometime the previous day.

"I gave them to my mother after my brother was killed." His bulging eyes turned on me with a different light, questioning, curious. "Did you ever meet him?"

"I don't think so."

"When he was nineteen he told me he felt like forty. Back then I didn't understand what he meant. They stuck a bayonet through his gizzard and they blew his head off." His voice was quiet, stirred by this memory, this hint, about the course and future of his life. He'd raged, accepted, manipulated; he'd worked, planned, enjoyed; he'd killed, only to have to rage again. He'd lived for years with the discipline and tumult of being a gangster, so close to all that electricity, it was a wonder his eyes hadn't exploded by now; but one day they would, or somebody would put them out.

"Why don't you quit?"

"And go live in fuckin' Tahiti?"

"I'm serious. You've got the money; you could go legit."

"You think I don't know that? You think I ain't tryin'? Fuck you, McGrath. This shit, I tell you, man, it keeps coming back to haunt me. It pulls me in. What can I tell you?"

I reminded myself that the face before me was, if not an illusion, an aspect of Ricky Lee it was dangerous to think too much about. The previous night he'd ordered the torture and death of my friend Jack Brewster. He'd order the same for me, without hesitation.

Somehow his mother's key ring, with those sibling faces of comedy and tragedy, had got out of my pocket, into his hand. I had to improvise, get him to tell me the story.

"So Corcoran's guy took the key ring from your mother's house? Is that it? What a dumb fuck."

"This kid comes to me, he *works* for Corcoran, says my mother came to Charlie's house the night his wife was smoked. My mom left them there. The kid said he thought I should have them back. Said he thought they might mean something important to me."

"Smart little kid with glasses? Looks like he was born asking if anybody wanted a cappuccino?"

"Yeah, that's the kid."

"I know him."

Ricky Lee's eyes brightened. "Hey, I just had a thought! Maybe it's this kid who should get the deal." He laughed, watching my face, his shoulders kicking up and down. "Don't worry, cop. You'll get your money."

"Corcoran's dead already?"

"He's taken care of. You ready to roll?"

I opened the door, glancing left to check the street, and walked out into the twilight. There was no sign of the bodybuilder. The twenty-foot clown perched above the doors of the building at the end of Main was jerking his leg as usual, slow but never somehow easy. Looking the other way, I saw Tookie Cross standing in front of the newspaper-vending machines, a black leather satchel swinging in one hand, listening to Charlie Corcoran, who was making a point with his hands, wagging his finger and touching Tookie on the shoulder. The door slammed behind me and an engine started up at the far end of the block, chugging louder as the now familiar Toyota Land Cruiser rolled toward us, headlights blazing.

Not a muscle in my face moved, though I knew that Ricky Lee must have seen everything, the brief electric current of shock and uncertainty that had shivered through my spine like a tree assailed by lightning, and the almost immediate return of my self-control, my mind working very fast. "Hello, Charlie," I said. "What brings you down to this part of town today?"

Dressed in jeans, scuffed cowboy boots, and a beige jacket of rumpled linen that matched the recently-risen-from-bed tousledness of his hair, Corcoran glanced toward me, tanned face aglow with its customary arrogance and good health. "Mr. Cross and I were discussing the *Oedipus* by Sophocles."

"I didn't know he knew the play."

"Nineteen-ninety drama group. Soledad," said Tookie.

"The hero is his own destroyer," said Charlie. "He is the detective who tracks down and identifies the criminal—who turns out to be himself. He's guilty even though he doesn't know it. A trap has been spread for him, and now it's about to snap shut."

"Ain't that a bitch?" said Tookie.

"It's not a play about fate so much as our terror of the unknown, the future we can't control," said Charlie, who really seemed to be enjoying himself, mouth sparkling, a smile as white as a winter slope. He glanced sideways to catch the dazzled stare of a woman jogging by. I wondered how come he was alone. Guys like Charlie never went anywhere without someone. Or else they took meetings on their home turf.

The driver, one of the redwood crew, had got out of the Cruiser, nodding at Ricky Lee, crossing the street to the other side of Electric. He'd left the engine running. Behind me, Ricky Lee said, "Let's all go together in the one vehicle."

"Charlie Corcoran, meet Ricky Lee Richards," said Tookie.

"Of course," said Charlie, his eyes curious, checking through the files, wondering why Ricky Lee's name should mean something to him. I wondered why he was wondering, just how had they got him down here. "All the way back then," said Charlie, banging on, almost giddy with the sensation of meeting strangers, "the guy who wrote this was asking, 'Is there a design, or does man have complete freedom, in which case it makes no difference what he does, *nothing* makes sense?' Oedipus searched for the truth, about the world, about himself. The truth was that he found the design, and it ate him like the spider ate the fly. But the search made him great."

"Yeah," said Ricky Lee, drawling, letting his mouth relax in a smile. Idling at the curb, allowing a glimpse of blood-red upholstery inside, the Land Cruiser had its passenger-side rear door open. "Shall we?"

The drive in the end took us only a few blocks south on Electric Avenue, though first we turned east on Rose and passed the yellow caution tape fluttering on either side of the street that marked where Jack Brewster had been found. A jet passed overhead with a single gulping roar, as if it had yawned and swallowed the sky. With

Tookie at the wheel, and me beside him up front, with Ricky Lee and Corcoran silent in the back, the Toyota merged into rush hour traffic on Lincoln, kicked a right down a garbage-strewn alley called Flower, and terrified a sniffing mutt boosting down Seventh toward Indiana. Tookie worked the Toyota effortlessly, leaning back with only the one hand on the wheel, while the other was inside his jacket, resting perhaps on the butt of a weapon as he took us to where either Corcoran would be killed, or I'd be, or maybe the both of us together. I wondered if Ricky Lee and Corcoran were somehow in cahoots. Maybe Ricky Lee had gone to him, had said, "Hey, this is going down. What's your side of the story?" It didn't seem likely. Corcoran would have responded in some way other than joining us for the ride. Send Van Duzer. Call a senator. He'd been duped in some way.

Having come around in a big loop, back to Electric, we made a left alongside a mural, a yellow fist brandishing an outsize green water-ice, above which a sign said FUNTIME CARNIVAL SUPPLIES. The next unit was VENICE BEACH AUTOBODY, guarded by a black steel fence with coils of barbed wire, and, as the Toyota passed through a chain link gate on rollers, I saw that the two lots had been knocked through into one. A pair of newish Mercedeses sat up on ramps, original paint jobs scorched down to the bare metal, stolen, most likely, and being stripped down for resale. The eyes of a fairground bumper car stared out from a pile of heaped-up old sinks and yards of twisted pipe. Beyond that a fake stone arch gave on to another steel fence topped by wire and the back of a billboard scratched with gang graffiti. The front end of the lot was dominated by a comedy mask, forty feet high, with a drooping nose, bulging bloodshot eyes, and bushy green hedgelike brows.

"What is this? It was once a studio, right?" said Corcoran, craning his neck to get a better look out the window. "An independent. Maybe it's Roger Corman's old place."

"Yeah, they used to shoot movies here," said Ricky Lee. "Appropriate, since this is the place you're gonna die. Asshole."

In just a few seconds Corcoran's face showed a look of shock, a look of fear, and then a look of embarrassment at his own unmanly terror. If he was acting, he couldn't have been better or quicker, with such subtle and swift shades of feeling; but this wasn't a performance, even though, after that first start and jolt, he assumed and hoped Ricky Lee was joking. He tried a smile, teeth snowy as ever, but the cockiness cracked and crazed. He glanced toward me for hope and encouragement, assurance fatally decayed. "These guys," he said, trying to make light. "Who are they?"

"The two of us?" said Tookie Cross, his colossal frame leaning over the wheel, never taking his eyes off me, willing for me to try a move. "Just a couple of clowns. Now get out of the car."

They took us inside the body shop, an aluminum hangar, trapped air thick with the smells of gas and oil, as well as the encroaching nausea of jet fuel. The 747 that had passed low overhead must have dumped its load in an emergency. The whole of Venice smelled as if it would blow up if you held out a match. They marched us between the sides of a couple of trucks, pushing us at the back in front of empty drums that banged and echoed as Corcoran stumbled into them.

Corcoran coughed, working his mouth.

Ricky Lee's hand flashed behind him toward his belt, then forward again with a revolver. He paced in front of us, turning, turning, while Tookie leaned against the flatbed of one of the trucks and pulled out a sawed-off from his jacket.

"I'm gonna piss in your mouth with the last breath you take, you arrogant scum," said Ricky Lee, never still, frowning, fretting, head down as if he were debating on the floor of a chamber. He wasn't really talking to me or Corcoran. He was avoiding eye contact, working himself up, getting to that place where no one else in the world existed, nothing except his anger and his will. "You'll be begging for the lights to go out. Man, I'm gonna fuck you up, you sack of shit, you white-eyed piece of scum."

Corcoran still didn't realize the shit he was in. "This is all an act, right?" Blue light nagged and fizzed, drowning us from fluorescent strips in the rafters. "What's going on? Help me, McGrath."

The black satchel skittered across the floor to my feet. Tookie Cross said, "There's the rest of your money, detective. Thank you."

Corcoran swept his eyes from me to them and back again, getting it at last. "It's McGrath, isn't it? He wants me dead. He thinks I killed my wife." He paused, consoled, because he understood. He thought he could reason and bargain his way out of this now. Maybe he could. I didn't know. He looked at the floor; then his face returned on the attack. I had to hand it to Charlie; he was trying. "What's he paying you? I'll double it." His glance took in the money satchel, grasped at another connection. "Or is there something he's letting you get away with? I'll fix it. I've got friends. I have power. I can help you guys."

"Too late, Charlie," said Tookie Cross, the sawed-off dangling from his huge fist like a toothpick.

"What have I done? Where's the evidence?" Corcoran's eyes were wide, his legs together. He spread his arms. "Tookie. We were getting along. We were talking, we made a connection. You don't want to do this."

On his own Tookie might have given in, but he wasn't on his own, for there was Ricky Lee, turning again, head lowered, bursting with rage, his black vest like armor, with the gun hanging loose by his side. "Enough," he said.

"How much do you guys want?" said Corcoran, trying for the big charming grin, but Ricky Lee would have none of it.

"Shut the fuck up." Staring, dreadlocks trembling, he said, "You thought you could have my mother killed and get away with it? You think I'm stupid? You must be out of your frigging mind. You're goin' *down,* you're goin' *down,* all the way *down, down,* motherfucker."

Corcoran was trying to protest "Your mother?" when Tookie pulled a sack over his head and Ricky Lee handed me his gun, the butt slapping hard and weighty in my palm.

"This wasn't part of the deal," I said.

"It is now, shithead. Finish it. Shoot the fuck. Do it now."

"Yeah," I said, hefting the gun. "I'll do it now."

Jung said that personality is the supreme realization of the innate idiosyncrasy of each living being. It is an act of high courage flung in the face of life. By which I suppose he meant that, some time or another, you have to find the edge to see where your boundaries are. I don't know, but at that moment, taking the gun from Ricky Lee, I felt filled with electricity, I wanted so desperately to live, to be able to carry on doing the most simple and mundane things—turning the pages of the paper, smelling the newsprint, walking down the street and finding a coffee shop. And what I had to do to continue enjoying those things was to press the barrel into Charlie Corcoran's ear and pull the trigger. One shot, and I'd be home free, with the rest of the money. Yet a voice inside spoke up and said, "No, that's not the real Billy McGrath. Where is he? Here he is. Don't do that; do this, do something crazy."

It wasn't that I believed in God or was afraid of any Last Judgment. My interests would best be served by blowing Corcoran's head off, but even as I moved the barrel closer, nuzzling the trembling edge of the sack, I knew I wasn't going to go through with it. Last night I'd been prepared to let Ricky Lee kill Corcoran for money, for my family, and because I believed he was a murderer. Tonight I wasn't prepared to kill him myself. My conscience had mutinied in the meantime. This was inconvenient.

Ricky Lee's raging eyes were watchful and alert. He didn't know it yet, but he'd pushed me to my sticking point. Another moment or two and he'd realize, give the signal to Tookie, who'd raise the shotgun barrel now tapping against the side of his thigh, and we'd both be dead, Charlie and me; *that* would be the reward for truffling out my human side. I should kill him; otherwise I'd be crushed myself and no help to Ellen, Lucy, Ward, or anybody. But conscience had risen up with its claws and snout, a pioneer that had no idea what it was getting me into. With the gun in my hand I wondered if I had any chance against the two of *them*. Maybe I could hit Tookie before he had a chance to raise the shotgun, but most likely he'd squeeze off a round even if my first shot was clean and the field of fire from that sawed-off would be wide and messy. After that there'd be Ricky Lee. I didn't consider it a great bet that I could take them both;

even so, there was a chance, a chance I was surprised they'd given me. Weighing this, putting myself in Ricky Lee's shoes, I wondered why he'd handed me his gun to do the job, and then it came to me: no round in the first chamber. Even though I knew from the .357's heft that it was loaded, I guessed he'd left vacant the first, to torture Corcoran even further if I pulled the trigger, to give himself more time and me a shock if I tried anything. I *guessed*. This was another area where guessing was nowhere near good enough, but it was all I had. I wasn't going to shoot Charlie. If I didn't, they'd shoot me. There was no way to reach my own weapon. I wasn't exactly Wyatt Earp in this area. My grandfather had always been the gun guy. I had to take the risk. As Heraclitus said, things flow.

"OK," I said. "This is it. Say good night, Charlie."

I took the gun away from his head, glanced at Tookie Cross, pressed it against my own temple, and pulled the trigger. The empty click blistered from ear to ear. I rushed the floor and grabbed Ricky Lee's vest with one fist while the other shoved the gun under his chin, drilling the barrel into the fleshy part of the neck. His hat of many-colored suede flopped to the floor.

"Shit," said Tookie Cross, mouth open, shotgun only at halfmast. "Crazy motherfucker."

"Careful, Tookie," I said. "You pull the trigger, your boss's head paints the roof. Then it's between you and me."

"Don't listen to him, Took," said Ricky Lee. "Smoke that movie asshole." His eyes blazed, mad, but his weakness right then was that I knew Tookie wasn't even going to play with the possibility that I might pull the trigger.

I said, "Go ahead, Tookie. Let's do it."

Outside, to one side, on Electric, everything was

dead and quiet, while from the other direction came the shrill voice of Main, of life and Venice, the swish and hoot of traffic, a bum singing, the rumble and clatter of a bus revving up in the MTA station.

He lowered the shotgun.

"Lay it gently on the ground."

He did so.

"Now push it gently toward me with your foot."

The steel barrel scraped against the floor.

I was trying to be careful, trying to figure out everything smooth and easy. "OK, Charlie, play peekaboo. Pull off the sack."

I shoved Ricky Lee flying across the floor toward Tookie. They collided, or rather Ricky Lee bounced off the other's broad chest, and stood up straight, slowly, deliberately. I frisked both of them for any further weapons: none.

"Why you doing this, McGrath?" said Ricky Lee, puzzled, but scarily calm.

I stood back, gathering up the shotgun and pushing Ricky Lee's Magnum in the back of my pants. "This guy didn't kill your mother."

There was a silence. Ricky Lee's eyes alone might have ignited the air.

"Motherfucker," said Tookie Cross.

"I was lying to you all along, taking you for a ride. Sorry about that."

I got us out of there, leaning down to scoop up the black satchel's tempting weight. Shotgun in one hand, money in the other, I ushered Charlie Corcoran toward the Land Cruiser while he blinked, spluttered, and blew dirt from his mouth.

Beyond the eyes of the bumper car wooden steps led up to a darkened office. There was no one else around. I seemed to have all the available guns and checked the Land Cruiser's ignition—the keys were there. I said to Charlie, "You drive."

He said, "What?"

"Do it, Charlie, I gotta watch these guys."

Ricky Lee and Tookie, hands still held up, but halfheartedly, had trailed after us out of the body shop, waiting by the entrance while Corcoran started up the engine.

"I didn't earn this," I said, tossing the satchel at Ricky Lee, who let it drop at his feet. I hadn't even looked inside. The satchel might have been full of newspaper, for all I knew, though I doubted that. To Ricky Lee's right the comedy mask looked down. "I'm keeping the rest because you killed my friend."

Ricky Lee didn't blink. "You're a dead man," he said, with menacing assurance.

"Not yet, bro," I said, stepping up into the Cruiser and pulling the door shut to face Charlie's peevish stare. "What?"

"The gate's locked."

"Drive through it, Charlie."

The chain link flew at us, bounced and screamed beneath, and was left behind, juddering scrap, as Charlie pulled hard to the right, shoulders leaning almost into mine, and swept the Cruiser back onto Electric.

Behind us the rear window of the Cruiser shivered, fell apart. Turning, registering someone shouting—it was Charlie—I saw the redwood guy who'd left the Cruiser on Rose standing legs apart with a shotgun in the middle of the street. He must have been standing guard outside. I shouted, "Go left, Charlie, here, on Brooks," and we were already leaning that way when the next shot scattered its load like hail against the side of the car; then we were out of sight.

Charlie wasn't hurt bad. There was a bleeding scratch on his neck and a deeper cut on his cheek. Neither one was bad, though his jacket was ruined, right shoulder ripped by glass or a couple of shotgun pellets and sprouting its padding. He'd been lucky. The blast could have taken his eye out.

26

IT WAS DARK NOW, THE SKY A TENT OVER THE LIGHTS OF the city that spread themselves toward the velvety dark of the mountains. As far as I could see, we weren't followed, but I kept turning to check. Through the open window I felt the tang of another cold fog rolling in.

Charlie's cut oozed blood. Staring straight ahead, he concentrated all his energies and attention on the red taillights of a Mercedes in front of us. A sign outside a church said, WHERE WILL YOU SPEND ETERNITY? SUNDAY 2 P.M.

"Maybe we should get you to a hospital."

He looked up quickly in a panic to the mirror. "No, I'm OK. They winged me, that's all." It was a self-announcement, as if he were pleased with the idea: they *winged* me.

"At least we should get you cleaned up."

Ahead of us a small plane was making its approach to Santa Monica airport, wings wobbling, the pilot alone in the illuminated fish tank of his cockpit, guiding himself in. I said, "What were you thinking of, meeting with those guys? You get a brain fever, or what?"

He was a little hysterical, but he had himself in check,

explaining that one of the women at his production office on Montana had fielded a call from a man saying he was from Ocean Precinct and that Detective McGrath needed to meet him later in the afternoon. This had been at about midday. The meeting was set for six. Thirty minutes before that, there was another call, saying Detective McGrath had been called to a homicide meeting on Rose Avenue, and would he mind very much joining him there?

Corcoran said, "I was thinking, 'Gee, maybe somebody gunned down Arnold Schwarzenegger in the Rose Café.' No, really, I'm kidding, but I thought it'd be OK." One of his people had driven him down to Venice, where they'd met Tookie, who'd turned out to be his biggest fan, so Corcoran had sent the woman back to the office. "What the heck. As far as I was concerned, I was coming to help the police. I assumed I'd be safe. Obviously it was a pretty foolish assumption. And if I hadn't come?"

"They'd have snatched you. Where was your guy Van Duzer, the bodyguard?"

"He's with Shimon Peres today. You know Shimon? I guess not." Frowning, he moved his hand on the wheel, saying there was something he still didn't quite get. Ricky Lee Richards had wanted him dead because he thought he'd killed his mother—he understood that part. "But where'd he get the idea? Where do you come in?"

"I set you up, Charlie. I sold you to them."

"I thought so." He was squeezing up his eyes, negotiating rush hour's tail end. "How much did you get?"

"A million."

He nodded, pushing out his lips. "That much?"

"I didn't take the second half."

"I saw. That was reckless. You don't just pick up that

kind of money in the street, even though this is America."

"Thanks, Charlie, I'll bear that in mind."

Ward wasn't home, though we'd agreed to try to meet at seven. I fixed a sandwich in the kitchen while Charlie did his own business in the downstairs bathroom, washing and cleaning his cuts. He came back into the kitchen with a towel draped around his neck and leaned against the door. "You and Ward an item now?"

"You could say that."

"Lucky man. You knew her before?"

"It was a while ago."

"She's good at keeping the business and personal separate, even when they seem to intersect. Not like you."

"You want mustard or mayonnaise, Charlie?"

"I'm not hungry." Rubbing at his chin with the towel, he said, matter-of-factly, "You took a bribe. You were going to have me killed. I could destroy you now."

I widened my eyes, handing him a plate. "I guess that's right. I'm going to eat my sandwich. The question is—what are you going to do, Charlie?"

He was suddenly hit again with what had happened. He threw up his hands, raging at me. "You think you can play God? You arrogant son of a bitch."

I snapped back, "Arrogant? Fuck you, Charlie."

He didn't blink. He sat down, stood up, not even speaking. He'd made a ritual of secrecy all his adult life, and I'd seen him twice now with his defenses down, lost—first on the occasion of Denise's death, and tonight, back there in the body shop with the air itself about to explode. This couldn't be an idea he was comfortable with. He normally presented himself as so mysterious, never a question about who was running the show.

He fiddled with a wooden statue from the coffee

table, turning its plump mahogany belly between his fingers. He wanted to know how I'd turned the tables on Ricky Lee and Tookie, so I told him. He said, "You put the gun against your own head. That was—how shall I put it? Bold."

"Damn right," I said with a shrug.

Charlie was silent, fingering the round belly of the figurine. "I got home that night and Denise was crazy," he said. "I'd canceled the engagement at the theater place and I'd been for early dinner with a friend, a director I know. It was only about seven-thirty when I got back. She was drunk. I couldn't figure out why she was so upset. The house stank of gin. She'd broken a couple of glasses already. There were words. I can't remember what they were. I called Van Duzer to tell him to come over and help me talk her down. I'm trying to be honest now, and I have to admit, I was scared of her when she was like that. She ripped at her clothes. She screamed, said a lot of things I couldn't understand. All the grievances came out, as if she'd stored up every one, and I'd given her plenty, I'm not trying to tell you that I was a saint. She came at me with a knife, and then she started ripping up the chairs, the sofa. She took a vodka bottle by the neck and smashed it through the TV. She was talking about her baby, the little mongoloid boy, the child that wasn't mine, about how she'd planned for him to be at the theater that night, she'd had him brought all the way from Texas so that he could see me. I didn't know a fucking thing about it. I'd no idea this was so important to her. She was crying. She said, 'I want to die.' There was a gun, a little Derringer with a pearl handle I'd given her as a gift. She said, 'Go ahead, you asshole. Put me out of my misery. Or I'll do it myself.' I tried to grab the thing out of her hand. I'd no idea it was going to go off. I'd no intention of that, I swear. The bullet went straight through her eye. She was lying on the floor and the blood was spreading all around from her head."

He stared at the figurine, speaking softly, looking at his feet from time to time, but never at me. He wasn't mumbling or putting on any of his various acts; this was all without guile.

"Then Van Duzer showed up. I told him what happened. She just lay there, still bleeding. It seemed to take forever to stop. Van Duzer didn't blink. He said, 'Charlie, these are your options.' He said I could tell the truth, run the risk of an unlawful killing or maybe even a murder charge, and try to handle the spin as best as I could when everything, the whole mess, came out in court. He said there was no way the cops would accept that she'd committed suicide. The gun had been fired from too far away. 'Or you can stay cool, take a chance, and most likely walk away from it all,' he said. 'And here's what we do.' He made me understand that we didn't have to panic. There was no one else in the house. You know what Mulholland is like. No one would have heard the shot. We had time. 'Time can be our friend.' That's what he said. I got on the phone from Van Duzer's phone to my agent, my PR guy. We came up with a plan."

I blinked, looking at him, hearing this: they'd had a conference call?

"Van Duzer got me into the bathroom and scrubbed my hands. He made me take a shower and took away the clothes I'd been wearing, not that I could see any blood on them. He sent me away and said, 'Don't come back for at least three hours, and when you do, forget that you were here before. Call nine-one-one and tell them something terrible's happened. Your wife's dead. You think she's been shot.' He told me to drive down into Beverly Hills, call someone, go to a movie. And I went along with it. I thought, 'I didn't kill her. It's not my fault.' I was confused, scared. I let him do my thinking for me. Wouldn't you have done the same?"

"Can I get you a glass of water, Charlie?" I was trying not to break the mood, but I had to get out of that room for a moment. In the kitchen, twisting the too-tight faucet, I splashed water on the back of my neck and on my face and filled a couple of glasses. I was leaning over the sink with the tap still running when I heard Charlie come up behind me and the fridge door open.

He said, "What are you thinking, McGrath?"

"I'm not thinking anything, Charlie."

He nodded, biting into a strawberry he'd taken from the fridge. He didn't mean anything by it. He was a little startled now, not quite himself. "You wouldn't have done the same, would you?"

"Look, Charlie, I don't know. After what's gone down between us, I'm in no position to judge you." He accepted the glass of water from my hand. "I just want to hear the rest of the story."

We took ourselves back into the comfort of Ward's living room, filled with low tables, art books, art deco lamps, and polished Western chairs of solid wood giving off the smell of wax. Sitting in front of the figurine again, Charlie sipped at the water and set down his glass. "It was after midnight when I went home for the second time, and I got a helluva shock. Her body had been moved. It was the way you found it. And Van Duzer had fired the other round from the Derringer, into her cheek. He'd done it so I'd sound scared and in shock when I called nine-one-one. I was."

"What was in this for him? Blackmail?"

"You don't understand. You hire guys like Ari Van Duzer, this is what you get. The best. They take care of *everything*. It's what money does."

"What went wrong, Charlie? You should have called nine-one-one, waited for us to arrive, and then not said a word except you'd arrived home to find your wife dead and that was all you knew and you'd rather not make any further statement except in the presence of your lawyer. Wasn't that the way it was supposed to go?"

I remembered now the little things that had nagged at me about the crime scene, the details that worried me, not because they didn't fit, but because they'd fit too well. All along there was the suspicion at the back of my mind that someone had gone doo-doo in this particular forest, but I didn't come up with anything definite; it must have been done by an expert. "Most likely we'd never have come close to charging you. Why did you say you'd killed her? Why did you tell me what you did?"

His fingers nudged at the base of the figurine. "It was you, Billy."

"Me? I don't get it."

"Neither did I when you showed up. I flashed back thirty-five years. You looked like your father. The resemblance was amazing. The way you stood, with your legs apart and your hands in your pockets. For a moment I was so confused I didn't know where I was. It was like seeing a ghost."

I thought about standing, but my legs told me to stay put while my mouth fished for air. Los Angeles was an enormous city, but murder so often ended up existing in a small, chaotic world. Some cases were drawn tight as a knot. It was tough to find out where they began or ended, how far they went back, or how wide the ripples might go. This could infect your thinking. A murder cop gets so used to this sense of everything boiling together that he's surprised if he meets someone who hasn't been involved in a homicide.

"I met him only the one time."

"Tell me about that."

He sipped slowly at the water. He said, "Do you remember the first time you were in love? I don't mean your first girlfriend or your first fuck, but the first time you were with someone and you realized that if this person was taken away, your life would change forever, there'd be a piece of yourself you'd never find again?"

In my life Ellen was the one, though I was starting to dream that Ward might make up my puzzle, give me back my whole self.

"It happened in New York. It was October. I'd dropped out of college and was trying to make a start as an actor. People seem to think I was born famous; I've cultivated that idea, but it isn't so. I came from nowhere. Back then I gave the impression of being self-confident, but I was a loner. She was a couple of years older than me. She brought me out of myself. It took me only an hour to decide that she was what I'd been waiting for all my life."

He said that her directness confused and warmed him. She told him he had heartbreaker's eyes. She slapped his face and then kissed the inside of his palm as if he himself had inflicted the wound. A little unbalanced, she treated him with passion, with malice, but never with indifference. Whatever she wanted she went after with the full pressure of her charm. In this instance what she wanted was him, and she helped Charlie along, introduced him to people, to directors, her friends at the Actors' Studio. Part Svengali, part sister, part sexual demon, she took him in hand and, during the year they were together, guided him to Hollywood and the movies.

"She had a husband, a powerful producer guy. He was in Europe—I think he was with Fellini—and we were staying at his house in Malibu. I wasn't supposed to be there. Obviously. We were both stoned. It was dark and she went into the water. I tried to stop her. I was running up and down the beach, and then I went in after her. I dived again and again. She was gone."

Exhausted, terrified, still dressed in jeans and sodden sweater, he hadn't called the cops. He'd run up onto Coast Highway, had flagged down a car, and, not knowing what he was doing, had hitched a ride to Santa Monica. From a bar he'd called his agent, who drove down from Beverly Hills to collect and protect him. They'd put a story together. He hadn't been in town at all that night, but was staying at his agent's retreat outside Santa Barbara.

Describing these moments, when two women died, the nameless one he'd loved, and the other, Denise, by whom he must have been at least obsessed, two women in whose deaths he himself had taken center stage, his voice lost its usual soft quality, its immediate intimacy. The words themselves sounded shell shocked. They came from scorched earth. At the same time, I had the sense that he'd pushed himself beyond shame and the guilt that nagged at me for my own failures. He was wiser, tougher, less scrupulous, a more complete American—take your pick—and at the same time more ruined inside. I understood now the anxiety, the wariness, the ambivalence about himself that was always part of his image, the sense that being Charlie Corcoran wasn't a role he'd be bothered about giving up to someone else. It took all of Charlie's energies to be amused by himself and not surrender to the dismay he must surely feel. He was a sad, lonely, scary guy, a glass of champagne tainted. In the terrible moments of his life he'd always been able to run away. He'd never been forced to sit back and inspect his worst opinion of himself.

He was saying, "There was a detective who put it together that the woman washed ashore twenty miles south two weeks later, mostly decomposed, had been having an affair with a rising young actor named Charlie Corcoran. He came to see me. I remember this big guy in a too-sharp jacket. He really did look a lot like you, Billy. He drove a Porsche, an orange Speedster, that I was surprised he could afford. He asked a few embarrassing questions. He threatened to become a nuisance. My manager took care of it. They were managers back then. The PR guy. My people. I don't know how. I never knew that your father lost his job. I only found out about that a few months ago from my lawyers during the trial. Once I saw a guy I thought looked like him in a used-car lot. On Santa Monica Boulevard, I think it was. Our looks swiped by each other."

He shrugged, sighed, put his hands on his knees. "That's it." A car went by outside, lights heading up the canyon, while Charlie picked up the fat-bellied figurine again, turning the piece in his fingers, sniffing the wood. He looked up with a puzzled frown. "Is this Turkish? I think it must be where Botero got the idea." He was almost dizzy with the telling of these stories. Finished now, he was floating down, an astronaut with the ground rising fast to meet him. "Are you wondering how I live with myself?"

"No, Charlie, I'm not."

Once, I'd believed in the solidity of events. Given enough time, armed with a clear head, patience, and sufficient resources, you could get the facts straight, penetrate to the core of a past experience; but for a while now I'd realized that solving a murder was a matter of work, of luck, of most especially what you could *prove*. As Bishop Berkeley said, you had to keep looking at the tree in the quad to satisfy yourself that it was still there. Reality was a slippery business. Facts told lies. Virtue was relative; everybody had a reason; there were always extenuating circumstances. Put this way, it could be argued that no one was ever really to blame. I was too familiar with the workings of my own guilt to believe that; but guilt was like a poison—it didn't take all vermin the same way.

"I've got other things to worry about."

There was still the case, the work, not to mention figuring out how to stop Ricky Lee from blowing my brains out. At least if something was going to go down, it would involve only me. Only my neck was on the line now. That was the plus side, the thesis.

I said I needed to ask him a few questions. "What's the name of your assistant, the kid I met at the house, the one with glasses?"

"Robert?"

"Do you trust him?"

"To do what?"

"Could he have set you up?"

"Not knowingly. I'm richer and more powerful than those guys. I've got more to offer. Besides, *you're* the one who set me up."

"Not this afternoon. I had no idea you were going to be there until I walked out of the Rose and saw you hobnobbing with Tookie Cross. But Robert had been to see Ricky Lee."

"Really?"

Telling the story of how I'd tricked Ricky Lee into thinking that Charlie had killed his mother wasn't as difficult as I'd thought, not after what Charlie had told me, and certainly a lot easier than coming up with the plan in the first place. Charlie himself was unfazed, pacing around, picking up Ward's books, glancing at the pictures on the walls. He had the knack of occupying any room as though he owned it. I didn't tell him about the art Ted was buying for Ellen and Lucy. I kept very quiet about that, explaining how Ricky Lee had found out a lie in my story, the part about Mae Richards having been at Charlie's house on the night of Denise's murder, and that Robert, sometime earlier today, had papered over the cracks, for some reason telling Ricky Lee the lie was true.

"Why would he do that?"

I shrugged. "You tell me."

"Where does Ward have her phone?"

"In the den."

He was gone only a minute when the phone rang. Charlie must have paged the guy with his special code, a number he'd add at the end. He came back, saying, "He was at dinner. His food had just arrived. I told him not to bother starting. He should be here in twenty minutes."

I was thinking about Charlie's stories, sure that he'd told me the truth as far as he could remember, none of which was going to help my father—he was dead and long buried. Vindication has no value if you're dust.

In the end I knew that I couldn't blame him for my father's death. There was a chain of causation that he'd begun, but there'd been too many events in between. My father had carried with him his litany of bad luck, in which Charlie Corcoran had comprised a single, if important, verse.

"I'm sorry your father was murdered," said Charlie softly, right there with my thoughts. "He got caught in the mechanism. It happens."

There was truth in what he said. My father knew about the machine, but not enough to escape it. Life had crushed him. I'd set in motion my own plan, which had thrown the workings of the great machine off for a while, but it was back on course now, coming down, and though I was still a bare step ahead, I couldn't pretend to myself, the way Charlie did, the way Charlie had to if he was going to make it through an average day with his wheels still on the cart, that all this was fine. It wasn't.

Charlie went to the kitchen, returning with another strawberry, which he bit into, smiling, shrugging, the shy swagger back now. "They really expected you to kill me?"

I nodded.

"And they'd have killed you?"

"In the blink of an eye."

"You saved my life."

"Don't sweat it, Charlie."

"Goddamn," he said, pleased, preening himself. "I was in a gunfight."

27

THERE WAS A KNOCK AT THE DOOR, A SHARP, CONFIDENT rap-rap-rap, and Robert came in, his tight curly hair damp from the fog, his eyes bright behind round-framed glasses. "Where's Charlie?" he said. "What's up?" I'd been planning to offer him a drink and sit him down before we got into things, but Charlie took over.

"Robert," he said, pointing to the cut on his cheek. It would be an exaggeration to describe it as a wound. "I took a bullet for you today."

Robert's ambitious eyes were puzzled, looking to me for the answer—what was going on?

"I almost died because of you today. Can you think what that would have meant? For the news services, for the entire nation?"

Robert's stunned mouth was wide open, revealing a strand of spinach trapped between two stubby front teeth. "Charlie, I . . ."

"Shut up. You remember Detective McGrath, obviously?"

He contrived the nod.

"You're going to answer all his questions. If you hesitate, I'll make sure you never work in the industry again.

If your answers prove to be unsatisfactory, I'll make sure you never work again. Hell, I just might make sure of it anyway. So, please, please me."

Less cocky, even a little scared now, Robert ducked his head. "I don't understand."

"Robert," I said, "why don't you take a seat?"

He perched on the edge of Ward's white sofa, legs apart, hands clasped between his knees. "Whose house is this?" he said, his right leg dancing up and down. "Nice place."

"Where are you from, Robert?"

He glanced at me, almost astonished, as if he had forgotten himself. "Victorville. It's out in the desert."

"I know. I went once." I remembered a dust-bowl town, and a temperature of 110 at ten in the morning. It was a Western nowhere, unless you were Roy Rogers with the local museum in your honor, or happened to own one of the big ranches; somehow I didn't think Robert's folks were the successful cowboy types. "What's your dad do?"

"He owns a shoe store."

"You went to college?"

"UCLA."

"You got out and you're doing well for yourself. They must be proud."

"I guess," he said, with a shrug and a modest smile; he was a good-looking kid when his eyes shed their tough polish.

Charlie was leaning against a bookcase, one foot crossed over the other. He'd found himself some Pellegrino, which he was swigging from the bottle.

I said, "Robert. Don't say you didn't because I know you did. You saw Ricky Lee Richards today. Why?"

His eyes moved around the room. "I had to take him something."

"It was a key ring, right? With two golden masks on it."

He screwed up his eyes. "How did you know?"

If I'd been in a funnier, more playful mood, I'd have told him because it was my business to know such things. "Why did you take it to him?"

"His mother left it at Charlie's house one time. I never told you about it, Charlie, because it was the night Denise died. Really, I forgot all about it."

Then, he said, when I'd gone there asking about Mae and the Powerhouse, he'd remembered.

"I put it together from the newspapers that she'd been the mother of Ricky Lee Richards."

Smiling, I said, "You thought he'd like it back."

"One of the masks was studded with diamonds. I figured it could be valuable."

"And maybe you thought, 'Hey, this guy's a notorious gangster. I'll get to meet him, hang out for a while, maybe there'll be some stuff I could use in a screenplay.'"

"Something like that." His eyes panicked a little again. "I'd have shown the material to you first, Charlie, really."

"Now let me get this straight," I said. "The key ring was at Charlie's house all this time, ever since the night of Denise's death. Mae never got in touch with you in the meanwhile, before she was killed, wondering if she could get it back?"

Frowning, he put a lot of thought into this. "Nossir," he said. "I don't believe she did."

"Bullshit."

His voice rose, endangered. "It's the truth."

"Oh, Robert, Robert, you disappoint me. It's bullshit. It just can't be so. And I'll tell you why. It was in my pocket until yesterday."

His eyes flickered from me to Charlie, silently rippling from the green Pellegrino bottle.

"Tell me the truth."

He stared down at his feet, where electric-blue silk socks were tucked into black suede Hush Puppies.

"Robert, do you know what Jung and William James had to say about human personality? No? Well, essentially, it was some pretty deep-dish stuff that boils down to this. You're in the shit."

He wanted to smile, but my look told him no way.

"Either you tell me the truth immediately, or Charlie will ensure your career ruin and I'll send you to jail for being an accessory to homicide. Have you ever been in jail, Robert? It isn't nice."

There was silence, save for the fridge gurgling in the kitchen. He was shaking his head, still staring at his feet, saying in a broken voice, "He'll hurt me."

I didn't want to ask yet who would hurt him. Instead, I was reassuring. I said, "He won't hurt you, Robert. You know why? Because I won't let him, and I'm the king of the jungle. Who gave you the key ring and told you to give it to Ricky Lee? Who are you afraid of?"

He glanced up at Charlie, shot me a fearful look, and then favored the Hush Puppies again. "Radek," he said softly.

"Radek Gatti?"

"Yessir."

"How do you know him?"

He sighed.

"Come on. No going back now."

He explained that Radek had helped him get the job with Charlie in the first place.

"How did he do that?"

"He knew Denise."

"More. I need more. I need it all."

"Look, this was a while ago. There was nothing weird about it."

"Tell him," said Charlie in a calm voice, neither soft nor loud. "Tell him everything."

"Nothing to tell. Really. He was one of a circle of guys in her life, all good friends, devoted to her. You were away a lot of the time, on shoots, or at the ranch, or in New York."

"Talk to McGrath."

"How did you meet him?" I said.

It was at a gym where Robert had been hanging out shortly after leaving college. He'd been hoping to make contacts. He'd found himself talking to this funny little Polish guy who said he might be able to help and had come through.

"You owed him a favor?"

"He put in a word for me with Denise."

"When was this?"

"Three, four years ago."

"And you've had much to do with Gatti since?"

"Hardly anything. I can't remember when I last saw him, until he showed up this morning."

"You went to a dangerous gangster whose mother was recently murdered and told a lie about your powerful boss because this Polak called in a favor? I don't think so, Robert, I really don't."

He took off his glasses and wiped damp hands up and down his face.

"What else did he have on you? Come on. Cough."

"Tell him, Robert," said Charlie.

"I can't."

Another frying silence.

Charlie sighed, his head on one side. "What Robert

doesn't want to say is that he slept with my wife."

"Christ, you knew?" Robert's hands were trembling.

"Not until now." Charlie turned away, reaching a book down from the shelf, a big art book that he opened and thumbed through.

Robert didn't know how to proceed. He was sweating. "It was three years ago. Gatti showed up today. He was going to tell you. He's a scary guy. It's like he has no emotions. I did what he said. I went to Ricky Lee Richards. I was trying to protect you, Charlie."

"I appreciate all your efforts," said Charlie with an aloof smile, as if to say, Look, I don't care about any of this. His face hadn't registered any anger or surprise. It was impossible to guess his emotion or intent as he turned another page of the book.

Robert, meanwhile, relieved of his guilt, had his head in his hands and was sobbing. I was reminded of a story Drew Diamond had told me, about how in the Department's golden days they'd invite a murder suspect to take off his clothes before an interview, theory being that it was hard not to make a clean breast of it while sitting naked in front of two or three toughened homicide dicks puffing cigarette and cheap cigar smoke at your genitalia. Robert's shoulders were heaving. I'd stripped the kid in front of his god, a god he worshiped and probably despised as well.

I wondered how Gatti found out that he and Denise had slept together. Maybe Robert had bragged, "Hey, I fucked Charlie's wife and I've got the carpet burns on my knees to prove it." That was maybe unfair, but this was a flaky kid.

It was nearly ten o'clock, and there was another knock at the door, this time announcing Ari Van Duzer, who Charlie must also have called from Ward's den, and who breezed past me without a word, dressed in bow tie, black tuxedo, and shiny black patent leather shoes, on which he moved his bulky frame with a gymnast's nimble swiftness, or an assassin's. "McGrath," he said, without seeming to move his lips, checking the room and all its corners. A half-smoked cigar leaked smoke from between his fleshy lips. He had a degree in psychology from USC, property in Manhattan and Manhattan Beach, and most likely a million per. I wondered what extra little sweeteners might have come his way since Charlie's acquittal. I was finding it hard to reconcile this cultured and smart guy, now reaching in his pocket to don a pair of golden half-moon spectacles, with the operator who'd heaved about Denise Corcoran's body and shot her after she was already dead. I knew I couldn't even think about trying to bust him, but all the same I wondered how he'd disposed of the weapon. Call it the completist in me.

Charlie said, "How was Mr. Peres?"

Van Duzer said, "Fine. How are you, Charlie?"

Charlie knew that for a while back there he'd brushed unknown territory, real life, ordinary life, with all its vivid danger and risk. Now, with Van Duzer's arrival, he was about to enter again his more familiar world, secret and safe. He said, "You know, I'm not sure."

"What's Robert doing here?"

Charlie shrugged, and Van Duzer didn't push the point.

I said, "I wanted to ask you something. About a guy named Radek Gatti."

Corcoran was gazing out the window, saying, "It's OK, Ari. Go ahead."

Van Duzer couldn't quite decide whether to look amused or curious or ill. "Radek Gatti?" he said. "Wow. There's a blast from the past. This goes no further?"

"I can't promise that."

"Tell him anyway," said Corcoran. "Be as brief and blunt as you like."

Van Duzer's eyes lightened up, and, even a little interested now, he said, "Yeah, Radek, he was one of Denise's loyal puppies for a while. Then I discovered he was maybe a little dangerous, so I got him out of her life in a hurry."

"How did that happen?"

He didn't bother to look at Charlie. Now that he'd been given the nod, he went ahead. "She came home one night and she'd been roughed up. Arms and legs bruised, lip cut. Charlie was out of town. She wouldn't tell me who'd done it. I guessed it was Gatti. So I went and saw him, scared him off."

"Was he angry?"

"Cool as you like. He said, 'I bet you kill me with your bare hands.' He never showed his face again."

"You check him out?"

Van Duzer grinned, though the set folds of his face budged not a muscle. The effect was scary. His head was shaped like a fruit, a pockmarked melon that had been working weights every day for the last twenty years. "Born in Warsaw; late 1950s. Father a doctor, died from cancer when Radek was a little kid. Studied film at one of the universities in Warsaw, packed that in when his mother died. Came to Los Angeles in 1981, studied medicine this time, at UCLA. Don't know why he didn't complete that. The guy had trouble finishing anything. Met Denise at a UCLA extension course for photography, 1992. Conveyed qualities of energy and violence. Knew French and German, as well as Polish and English. Intelligent, volatile, vain. Dangerous? Potentially. Kind of a guy who has an evil nose for opportunity."

"You ever see him again?"

"Never."

"You know he recommended Robert to Denise for his job?"

"That was a while before, and since Robert had checked out OK, and was working well, it seemed unfair to hold that against him."

"Denise and Robert?"

Van Duzer shrugged his huge shoulders, letting me know that he knew everything, while Corcoran off-handedly watched Robert, who was listening, stroking his chin, fingering his side burn, a vague smile on his lips, hoping to woo his way back into this situation, his job, his life, as if to affirm that his ambition and eagerness to please would in the end be as useful a quality to Charlie as Charlie's charm. It was a little painful to watch Robert treading this thin line.

"Thanks," I said to Van Duzer. He knew more about Charlie's life than Charlie did himself. It was his job to acquaint himself with every nutcase, harmless or otherwise, who crossed Charlie's path. There were a lot of nutcases, most of them not nearly so impressive or inventive or scary as Gatti. "Let's hope our paths don't cross again," I said, and his quick, sunken eyes went across to Charlie, wondering what had been divulged here.

Charlie, composed, was looking around Ward's living room with an almost startled expression, as if it were a strange laboratory or theater he'd found his way into. When he asked whether I was finished, I said, "I guess so," and he nodded, not smiling, already starting up again on the job of keeping himself busy. He told Robert they'd talk in the morning, and Robert smiled, anxious and avid to please.

When Robert had gone, Charlie asked Van Duzer for

a ride and, before stepping to the door, turned to me. "My father was a schoolteacher, here, in the San Fernando Valley."

I'd made a note of the fact in Denise's murder book.

"He drove himself out of his mind, he worried so much about his work. Even when I was a kid he seemed old. He was so reckless with himself. Always giving his time to other people, dumb little projects and trips. When I became an adult I thought, 'Brother, that's not for me.' There are so many pitfalls out there, so many greasy spots to trip you up, that I'd thought, 'Treat the world lightly, on the surface, make it work for *me*.' I've done pretty good, a lot of the time." He smiled, showing teeth of perfection. "But you think you're gliding over the surface, and then life opens up. It swallows you. We're none of us safe."

I appreciated the sentiment, rising, as I was sure it did, from the sense of connection between us. All the same I knew we were different. Come the morning, he'd be back at it, surfing. "I take your point, Charlie. But some of us are safer than others."

Outside, the fog had thickened, bringing with it a smell like kidneys tainted with urine. Van Duzer and Robert had gone ahead, down into the street, and sounds of car doors opening, being slammed, engines starting up, came thickly, hovering in the air. Charlie took short and ginger steps on the moist flags, afraid of falling, and for a moment I thought of my father, seeing this suddenly vulnerable guy whose arm I reached out to touch and steady. Of course, Charlie wasn't my father, or me, but another sort of man, intrepid and not ill intentioned, who'd nonetheless stepped over the corpses of others on the staircase of his own fame.

Charlie paused, smiling, quick and youthful again.

He started to say something and stopped. He had the head and face of a dreamer. He was in love with and puzzled by the extraordinary idea of what he'd become. He said, in his intimate way, "You know, I think you're wrong about Tookie. He wouldn't have let anything serious happen to me. He truly admires my work." And then Charlie was gone, moving down carefully into the mist.

28

BACK INSIDE, I LET GO A BIG SIGH, SHIVERED A LITTLE in the warmth of the house, and helped myself to a beer. Popping the cap, I strolled through into the den to call my apartment and check the messages. I was hungry, not having had the chance to eat the sandwich I'd fixed earlier. I went back into the kitchen to grab it, together with a few strawberries from the near-full tray in the fridge. I ate slowly, enjoying the food, sipping the beer, and then I called Ellen, who'd left the number of a hotel in Seattle.

"Billy, I've been so worried," she said. "Thank God you called. I just spoke to Drew, and he said he hadn't seen you since the airport. How are you?"

"I'm here."

"That good, huh?"

"It's been a little hairy. But it's OK."

"You wanna talk about it? Lucy's sleeping."

"How is she? How does she look right now? Describe her to me."

"She's in bed. She's lying on her side, facing me, with her hair a little mussed up from the shower. She's snoring, that little charmer of ours."

I laughed, and it felt as if a weight were lifting. It did feel better, somehow, knowing about Denise Corcoran and my father.

"She's still holding that damned pencil box."

"When she wakes up, tell her that I love her."

"I'll do that."

"I'd better go now."

Ellen drew a breath. "Billy, I want you to know that I know you're trying to do the right thing. I'm sorry I made such a fuss about coming up here."

"Don't be. It was an outrageous thing to ask you to do."

"But necessary."

"Thanks." There was a pause: warm feelings down the line. "Listen, I'll call again in the morning."

"Get some sleep. Take good care."

I walked into the empty living room, seeing my reflection prowl across the darkened panes of the bay window. The wooden figurine was on the table. The book about Robert Longo that Charlie had flicked through was where he'd left it, propped with its cover facing the room against some other books in the middle shelf of the case. Above it was a picture of Ward, in shorts and a plaid shirt, grinning and squinting against the sun in the high desert somewhere, maybe Joshua Tree; below, the crushed green star of a strawberry stalk. A slight pressure came back, tickling my gut.

I called the TV station and was put on hold. A production assistant came on, saying that as far as he knew Ward had gone home, though it was also very possible she was somewhere with Zed, working a story. They did that.

In the den I paged her.

I remembered what Charlie had said about the way

she treated her career. In the past she and I had handled pretty well the potential of any conflict between the cop's often secretive duty on the one hand and the reporter's investigative needs on the other. That's to say, we'd pretended we didn't know each other, going about our respective businesses with neither one expecting any favors. It was interesting to speculate how we'd work this out in the future, given the chance.

I knew I should be addressing the issues of Radek Gatti, and what he was up to, and Ricky Lee Richards. Maybe the way to stop *him,* I thought, was to nail him for the murder of Jack Brewster, and then face the embarrassing, and true, story he'd tell. With the food and beer kicking in, I was too woozy for the minute to think straight. I needed to freshen up.

While in the shower I heard the bedroom phone ring and slithered and stumbled toward it, naked and soapy-assed. I expected and hoped it would be Ward. It was Radek Gatti.

"Detective McGrath," he said. "Where you have the money hidden? In your apartment? Oh, no, I don't think so. Too obvious. You are much more bold and— *subtle?* Is that my line? You have it in the station house, yes? In*cred*ible!"

"I don't have a clue what you're talking about," I said. I felt sick in my stomach. He must have been the one who called Internal Affairs.

"You're thinking, 'Ah, yes, nasty Radek, he's the one who told that horrible story to Internal Affairs.' And it's true, I did, and the next time I'll be much more specific. I'll give them many more chapters. I'll give them your name and all the pretty details of your deal with Mr. Richards. Listen—I'm eating." His lips smacked. "I fix myself a good little portion. With ice cream."

I was wondering how he'd found me here. How did he know Ward's number? The bad feeling in my stomach knotted and tightened. "Listen, Radek, this is fascinating, no doubt. But to me it's a fairy story in another language. It doesn't mean anything." Standing in Ward's bedroom, facing a framed photograph on the wall, this one of Ward in a long gown picking up an award, I had an intuition. "Those pictures you gave me of Denise and Mae. You said you found them in the trash?"

"It's true."

"But you took them yourself, right?"

There was a silence. He carried on chewing for a while before breaking out again in his rusty staccato voice, English remembered in the hectic excitement of a fever. "You pretty scary guy, you know that? Very frightening detective. Oh, yes. Yours is a true adventure. But you're in a lost balloon, comrade. You see, I know you let Ricky Lee Richards kill that arrogant son of a bitch Charlie Corcoran for one million."

Seeing myself in the long mirror that Ward had opposite her bed, I was reminded that I was naked. Gatti thought Corcoran was dead. Why? Because he'd sent Robert to confirm my story and Corcoran should be.

He went on, "In fact, I have assisted you in this endeavor to some very considerable extent. To the merry tune, I should say, of that entire one million."

I didn't say that I'd only taken $500,000, funds that were no longer available. "I don't have any money, Radek. It's as simple as that."

"You want me to tell this saga? Gangster offers bribe. Detective takes it. Innocent man dies. Movie star is murdered. Oh, no, I don't think so."

"Go ahead, Radek. You can try. I'll enjoy hearing everybody laugh."

"You very stubborn and cynical guy, you know that? But you just don't understand the situation."

I was still wondering how he'd tracked me down to Ward's. Then I remembered that I'd paged her from the den, and the shoe dropped.

He said, "I am holding a deck entirely full of aces. Listen."

After a brief empty silence another voice came on the line, saying, "Billy, who is this creep?"

"Ward? Are you OK? Where are you?"

"Billy . . ."

She was frightened, hiding it. Below my throat something sucked at my heart and liver. I wanted to speak, to tell her not to worry, that I'd take care of everything, but for a moment, now that I realized the reality—he had her—no words would form in my mouth.

Gatti was back. "See?" he said. "Now everything is clear. Everything is simple. No more forked paths. The cobwebs are all blown away. We may proceed."

"You'll get the money."

"Of course I will. I'll get it now."

I reminded myself: he thought I had the full one million. I said, "It's in a safe deposit box."

"The banks were closed by the time you met Ricky Lee this afternoon."

"He only gave me the second half today. That's hidden. It'll be noon before I can get it all together."

He obviously didn't care for the idea. "I'll call you here at twelve-thirty tomorrow. No tricks. Be swift. Your friend is very beautiful."

"I want to talk to her again."

The line was dead.

In the corner of the room was a scrubbed pine table on which sat a laptop, a pile of green notebooks, a jar of sharpened pencils. Next to it was a fire, with paper and logs ready. This was Ward's haven. Shivering, the water cool on my skin, I saw myself again in the mirror. The pride I'd taken in keeping in shape seemed vain and hopeless. I drew people close to me, and they ended up getting hurt. As a man I failed even in protecting those I loved. I was nothing.

From the bathroom came the sound of water still running. Scrambling out, I'd left the shower on. Already that moment seemed like days, rather than minutes, ago. The requirement that I go turn it off started to neutralize the real anguish, dismay, and self-pity I felt. There was no other way than to go forward, go on, with blind hope if need be, if that was the only available opiate. I toweled myself dry, pulled on my shorts, pants, and shirt. Dressed, I went downstairs.

I understood now something that had been bothering me.

Opening the fridge, I saw that a tray of strawberries stood lengthwise on the top rack, covered loosely with plastic wrap that was dewed and misted with moisture. There'd been strawberries at the Mae Richards murder scene. A fruit fly, having corrupted a berry with its eggs, rattled under the plastic wrap and lazily came out to greet me in the kitchen's warmth.

I called Humbolt Raffi. I was in Ward's den again, a warm pool of light spilling across the desk in an otherwise darkened room. "How's our baby?"

Raffi mumbled, mouth full. Everyone was hungry.

"What are you eating, Humbolt?"

"Thai. It's terrible. We had pizza for lunch. I don't think this is a diet the good doctor is used to."

"How is everything?"

"Quiet."

"I need to talk to him."

"Say, Billy," he said. "This is all OK, isn't it?"

"What do you mean?"

"I had Drew Diamond on the phone, asking if I knew what was going on with you."

"Just the usual shit, Humbolt. Trying to burn them before they burn me."

"A rule which each of my ex-wives somehow understands much better than I do," said Raffi with a world-weary sigh. "Here he is."

Francis came on.

"You made a phone call last night." I didn't have time or feel inclined for the formalities. "It was to Gatti, right? What was discussed?"

He said he'd briefly told Gatti what had happened and that he expected to be out of circulation for a couple of days. "I told him I was on the Vincent Thomas Bridge with you, surveying the sunken remains of my would-be destroyers."

"Where was he?"

"In his car. In one of *my* cars. He said he was close by. He said he could come and pick me up himself if I wanted. I told him it wasn't necessary."

"Why would he be close by?"

He hesitated a little, and then said he really didn't know.

A paperweight restrained an unruly heap of papers on Ward's desk. Leaning across, flipping the thing over, I saw that set inside it was a paycheck from the *LA Times* and a little plaque reading, FIRST STEP TO A PULITZER? I understood now how Gatti had found what was left of me after Tookie had finished down in San Pedro. I understood how he must have gone through my pockets and found Mae's keys, and I understood the use he'd made of them. What I didn't understand was how he'd figured there might be money in this for him, an angle. How had he found out about my deal with Ricky Lee?

I said to Francis, "Have you spoken to him today?"

"No."

"Who did you talk to?"

"To my office. There were various appointments and consultations to be canceled or rearranged."

I turned the paperweight flat. I wanted Ward to have the chance to win that Pulitzer. I was beginning to see that everything that had happened since Mae Richards's death wasn't just the accident of another case. It was my destiny. Beforehand, until only a couple of days ago, I'd felt that my ability to endure was finite in the face of my loss of faith in myself. A single event, a straw, might have been enough to trigger my suicide. Then, by initiating a drama, as well as trying to solve a mystery, I'd provided myself with reasons to act and survive. Now I realized that unless I penetrated right to the heart of this, unless I got Ward back, I'd be in a far darker place than before. After that bad moment in the bathroom, as soon as I'd got off the phone from Radek, I felt no inclination to give in. No one in my life apart from Ellen knew how stubborn and unbending I could be. At the same time I knew I'd caused this and was to blame. I had to suppress the urge to panic.

I remembered that Francis had told me Gatti had no place of his own, and was always sponging off others. You didn't snatch a well-known TV reporter and shack up in a motel in the Valley. Ward was too conspicuous for that. I said, "Do you know where Gatti is now? At your house?"

"In the guest cottage, perhaps. I have the number."

Even though Gatti believed he had me cold, he must

have anticipated my thinking about this. Francis's guest cottage was too obvious. "What about your boat?"

"Yes, sometimes he stays there. Is this urgent? Why are you so anxious to get in touch with him?"

"What's your boat's name again?"

"Little Knell."

Francis had tried to see Mae the day she died. Gatti had driven him. Then he'd put on a frog suit and checked the bottom of the boat. Why did that bother me? Then he'd taken Francis home, that slow journey in the rain down to Palos Verdes.

Wittgenstein, as if terrified of his own ideas, never developed an embracing philosophy, a scheme with which to explain the world in the manner of, say, Kant. He didn't trust his own mind. As a detective he was always his own first suspect. Yet his mind was bold. His statements were like arrows, shots at the truth.

Swinging in the chair in Ward's den, reaching for a scratch pad on the desk, taking a sharpened pencil from another jar she had here, I said, "Mae. Remind me. On the day she died, in the storm, when you went to see her, did you actually go inside her house?"

"No."

I was wondering if the body might have been there already. I was wondering about Ward and trying not to wonder about Ricky Lee and why Drew Diamond had called Humbolt Raffi and what exactly might have been going on at the precinct house after I left. I couldn't imagine that Larry Murakami regarded me as his star pupil right now. I doubted very much whether the Department in general was happy with me at the moment. I didn't think I could go to them for help, not in the middle of the night, not with all the explaining such a move would entail.

"On that afternoon, where did Gatti pick you up?"
On the scratch pad I noted: "Radek—quick, impulsive,
smart." I began to surround the words with doodled
zigzags and tightening circles. He was the kind of a guy
who, if he stumbled, got up quickly without the perilous
stuff of conscience. He was like an animal in that way,
different from Ricky Lee.

Francis said, "I'd been at the Daniel Freeman Hospital. He picked me up, and we went right over to Mae's."

Radek could easily have been there before.

Einstein believed that theories and stories were suits
on a rack. You try them on until you find the one that
fits. As circumstances change, so must the theory, the
story. Some suits might stare you in the face for years
without catching your eye.

"Whose idea was it to go check on the boat?"

"You know, I really can't remember. Radek's, I think."

Maybe that was where he'd hidden the murder
weapon. He hadn't dumped the thing right away, in
some nearby trash can, because he was thorough as well
as quick; he made plans. Later, he'd have dropped the
.22 in the ocean, way out in Santa Monica Bay. Perhaps
he'd killed her on the boat, in the storm, maybe even out
at sea. But why go back to check the hull? He wouldn't
have needed to hide the gun in that case. It would
already have been at the bottom of the ocean.

"How big's the boat?"

"I don't know. Big enough."

"Sailboat."

"No."

"It could handle the storms we've been having?"

"Certainly. I once took her across the Atlantic. But
who'd want to?"

"Radek." I decided now was the time to hit the nail.

"He murdered Mae Richards." The line crackled in the silence while I swung in the chair and made another doodle on the pad. "Dr. Francis?"

"That's ridiculous. Why would you think that?"

"Strawberries."

Gatti had been here and there, too.

"I don't understand."

"What's it with Radek and strawberries?"

"He loves them. He says they remind him of his mother. What on earth's that got to do with Mae?"

"He killed her, believe me."

"Oh, it's absurd." His first angry impulse was turning to surprise and puzzlement. "Why would he? What was his motive?"

"You tell me."

"They always got along. They didn't know each other that well."

"I think better than you think."

"Radek?" he said, his voice stunned now.

My mind reached for another detail. Why were there those five or six VCRs in her house? "I assumed it was something to do with the theater," he said. "I can't believe this. He's not a murderer. He's honest, he reads books, he knows about people. I always thought he should be a poet or a film-maker. I trust him. He's a good boy."

I didn't want to say from how many mothers, fathers, sisters, brothers, sons, daughters, husbands, wives, friends, and even enemies I'd heard that statement or something similar. The wife of the Pakistani guy who cut his own son into more than six hundred pieces refused to believe her ideal husband capable of telling a lie, let alone such a horror. Pity the man whom no eyes find innocent.

Gatti was energized by a world for which he also burned with contempt. He was fascinating, alarming, adroit. Part of him must hate Francis, I thought, because he, Radek, was smarter, quicker, and yet the servant of the more distinguished man. Twenty years ago he might have been printing pamphlets, marching in the streets, trying to get the Soviets out of Cracow. But now he was in Los Angeles, dreaming up plots with steady nerves, and then acting out his inventions on real characters. "A few minutes ago, when I asked why it would have been natural for Radek to be close by in San Pedro, you didn't want to say. Why?"

"Look, this is difficult." He hesitated again. "You really think he killed her?"

I let that go.

He paused, sniffing, sighing, embarrassed, before in a low voice he explained that two years ago Radek had come to him with a business venture, something on top of their usual arrangement. He'd promised to take care of all the details. "Import-export," said Francis. "Medical supplies."

They were shipping in second-rate antibiotics from Poland and selling them to clinics around California for just slightly less than top-grade price, while at this end Francis used his contacts to bulk-buy prescription drugs that could turn a nice profit in the former Eastern bloc— a story that, if it were to leak out, would leave a nasty stain on Francis's reputation.

He said, "We have a warehouse down in San Pedro. A huge space, much bigger than we needed, but the Harbor Authority was more or less begging for us to take it off their hands. Radek spends some time there. He says he likes the quiet. I don't even know how he's used all that square footage. I only saw the place once."

He said that Radek had brought various other gear that was stored down there. "He says he's going to set up another business. Rent it all out to the movies. He's always full of ideas. You can't really be serious about his having killed Mae? She said he was a harmless joker."

I was thinking about San Pedro. With its maze like topography, its truck parks the size of football fields, its spaghetti networks of railroad tracks, its refineries stinking and belching smoke, its warehouses, piers, and huge ships that might appear as if out of nowhere, gliding in the gaps between factory buildings, San Pedro seemed somehow desolate and scary, despite the constant traffic of commerce; it was a whole other continent, monstrous and indifferent, an industrial forest teeming beneath the Vincent Thomas Bridge, whose dizzy span I already knew too well. It was a perfect hideout, a dark place unfriendly to man. I was always a little afraid down there. I had been last night during the chase. I had been when I pulled back the jumper. It was a place where I saw myself dying.

"Which pier?"

"Pier Fifty," said Francis.

"Sit tight," I said. "I'll call you tomorrow."

When I got off the phone from Francis I called Danny Wejahn, the accountant, my friend with the boat in the marina, and asked if he could get on the radio to the San Pedro harbor master and find out whether a boat named *Little Knell* had come into port that night. Waiting for Danny to call back, I heaved myself out of the chair and stretched, turning away from the desk and the pool of warm yellow light that brimmed on its surface, to stand in the darkness in a corner of the book-lined den. I was equally conscious of how much I could do and how little, of the work that lay before me and the effort required. Even if I kept myself going, I wasn't sure I could pull this off.

If Danny came back with the word that *Little Knell* had come through into San Pedro, I'd know where Ward was. Getting her was another issue. Once before during all this I'd rushed in too quickly. Maybe there'd be no other way, maybe something else would have gone wrong, but I'd made that one fateful lie—Mae Richards went to Denise Corcoran's house on the night of Denise's murder—and everything had bubbled and boiled from there. There was no room for another hasty error. On the other hand, time would crush me if I didn't move now. Ricky Lee was pressing in, as were Cataresco, Diamond, and Internal Affairs, not to mention Gatti himself and Charlie Corcoran, who might have a whimsical change of heart and blow the story wide open. Like my father, I was learning that what you do matters, that actions, right or wrong, have consequences. Come morning, I'd either be dead, or alive and in all sorts of trouble.

The phone rang and it was Danny, saying, "She's down there, all right. Came in through Angel's Gate at about nine o'clock." I spoke to Danny for a while, telling him about the favor I needed, and then I made one more call before pushing out from the safety of Ward's den into the night and the fog, whose kidney-smelling thickness muffled up the sky and shocked the senses.

29

M Y GRANDFATHER WOULD NEVER ADMIT THAT HE WAS afraid to go to sleep, and maybe he wasn't. He'd stay awake through the dark hours and doze when the dawn light broke. He opened the door wearing slippers, slacks, and a faded yellow-and-black rugby shirt. His voice was deep, moving with the same slow, rattling deliberation as the covered wagon that had brought his grandparents to California in the 1840s. Or it may have been just the whiskey. "How are you, Billy?"

"I feel good. I don't have much time."

"When did you ever? Come in and take a libation."

My grandfather was a gnarled old guy with huge hands that never stopped shaking and a ruined nodding face. After fifteen years of Parkinson's disease, there wasn't much left of him, but he'd been built to last. A graying mustache and startling blue eyes maintained order over his wasted face.

In his living room, with the TV on and the sound turned low, he pressed a glass of Johnnie Walker in my hand and then pressed my hand. Stumbling, because of loss of muscular control, not the drink—he could still drink like a longshoreman—he aimed himself at the pillowed refuge of his chair.

His nurse had found him on the floor with his wrist broken three months ago. She came every day, cleaned, organized his medication, and pleaded with him to admit himself back into the hospital. He'd have none of that, and, in truth, he wasn't so far gone that he'd ceased to cope. The thing scaring him was that his mind had started to drift.

I told him I was in bad trouble.

"Fuck 'em."

"Believe me, Grandpa, that's my intention. But in case I'm unsuccessful, there's something I'd like you to do for me."

I said I wanted him to let Ellen and Lucy know I'd taken care of them as best I could. This brought a sharp, watchful look.

"There's something else. I don't know if this matters, or why it should, because it can't make any difference now, but I want you to know anyway. I was with Charlie Corcoran tonight and he told me my father had been right all those years ago. Charlie was there when that woman drowned up in Malibu."

I watched him while saying this, not knowing whether I was handing him poison.

He clawed at the chair arms with his huge, bony fists, knuckles turning white with the effort of heaving his disobedient body toward the liquor cabinet. He hated to be helped, but I took his arm anyway, holding him steady, saying, "Let me, Grandpa. I'll pour you this one."

"Thanks, son," he said, bringing the glass to his trembling lips and emptying it with one turbulent swig. It was hard for him to drink, but this was one of his few remaining pleasures. He didn't eat much anymore. "Are you really gonna buy that car?"

"What's that, Grandpa? I didn't quite catch that."

"I said—are you gonna go ahead and buy that car?"

He stared at me, his frown petulant and angry, while I tried to pinpoint his thoughts. "Which car? I'm not sure I know what you're talking about?"

"That stupid Italian car."

Now I understood.

It was the year of my father's death when my father had come to him wanting to borrow money for a Lancia two-seater, a speedy and pretty silver toy for which my grandfather had had nothing much good to say. You'll never find the parts, he'd told my father; it'll fall apart in six months or less; it's a rusted heap of shit. Young, then, and still confident and full of my own dreams, I'd been egging my dad on: go for it, it'll be great, make the gesture. My grandfather had shaken his head, written the check, and was still shaking his head a week later, when the Italian job, as my father had named the Lancia, scattered its gearbox all over Manchester Avenue. The car was up on bricks when he was killed.

Hand shaking, eyes brimming with sorrow and anger, my grandfather was saying, "Go right ahead; buy the thing if you have to. You never did listen to a goddamned word I say."

Gently, taking his shoulders, I waited until his darting eyes came around into mine. "It's Billy, Grandpa. I'm not my father. It's Billy."

Whatever his memory had been looking at—my father's grinning mischievous face, that wretched car still awaiting repair—faded from view. He snapped back to the here and now. "Billy? Is that you, Billy?"

"That's right, it's me, Billy."

His slippered foot pawed at the carpet. He looked down, ashamed of himself, like a little boy. "I hate this shit when it happens. God*damn.*"

"I know, Grandpa. It's fine." Shifting my grip to his elbows, I guided him back to the chair, settling him among his cushions and rustling papers. A helicopter passed not too far away while I fixed him another drink. On the TV an old Bogart movie flickered silently in black and white. I didn't see enough to figure out whether in this one he was the good or the bad guy.

My grandfather said, "He was right all this time. Well, I'll be darned." He shook his head, chuckling. "But you're in trouble, Billy. Isn't that what you said? It happens to us all, kiddo. We've all been there. Don't pay it any mind. You need money. You need me to call the chief?"

"No, Grandpa," I said, handing him the glass. This wasn't merely a sentimental visit. "I need guns."

I went back out into the streets again. Having loaded up the back of the Land Cruiser, I climbed into the driver's seat and, glancing at myself in the mirror, slightly altered the disordered arrangement of my shirt, the overcoat my grandfather had insisted I take, which smelled of mothballs, and my wild hair. I felt refreshed and, heading down to Venice, spoke aloud: "OK, OK, it's coming up on one o'clock in the morning. Renata Richards is waiting. Take care, take care, take care. Think it out."

I parked a couple of blocks away so that no one would see the car and walked through foggy Oakwood. Renata came down the steps from Mae Richards's front door to meet me. She was wearing a black leather trench coat over sweat pants and sneakers, and a red woolen beret was pulled down snug over her cropped hair. She said, "You got peculiar ideas about how to amuse a lady." She glanced at her wrist. "And you're late."

I settled my shoulders inside the overcoat. "I had to see an old friend; I'm sorry," I said. "Did you find someone to look after your little girl?"

"Oh, sure. You know what a cinch it is to find a babysitter after midnight." She softened a little, not smiling, but easing up. "Actually, it wasn't a problem. My girlfriend came around from next door. You said your daughter's name was Lucy, right? How's she?"

"Safe. Sleeping, I hope, dreaming sweet things."

Her key worked the lock, but the door was swollen from the rain and not being used, and I had to heave against it with my shoulder before it budged a crack and then swept across the carpet.

The air that hit my face was damp, musty, actually foul-smelling, bored with being contained all these days and eager to get out and attack throat and bone. Renata was coughing already, covering her mouth. I'd picked up a flashlight at my grandfather's, but the electricity was still working. I flicked on a light and heard her voice behind me: "Oh, my."

Mae's house was in decay. There was a huge pool in the center of the carpet, with cigarette butts and a crack pipe floating in it. A base head must have broken in to take a hit. There was a taint of urine. Pats of brown plaster had fallen from the ceiling and stood up in hills over the floor, as if moles had been pushing up to escape the other life scurrying there beneath the boards. A fat black widow had draped her web between the family portraits on the coffee table. Jesus was looking at me a little askew from above the fireplace. The CDs and all the VCRs were still there, which surprised me. Maybe the base head had found out whose house this was and decided against coming back.

When Odysseus journeyed to the underworld, the souls he met raged at where they found themselves, ripped out of the bodies they'd inhabited with such glory. Unhappy, still shocked, they talked at him in an empty babble. Even the bravest whined for the joy that had been life, saying he'd come back as a slave rather than remain as king over all the perished dead.

It's always terrible to go back to an untended home after a death. You're assaulted in a different way with the brutal finality of life's loss. If the house was Mae's soul, it was screaming.

Renata was shocked into silence, moving sadly about the place with her memories, picking up a picture that had fallen to the floor, straightening the one of Christ above the fireplace. At last she said, "Why hasn't Ricky Lee taken care of this?"

I was checking the VCRs to see if there were tapes still inside, a long shot, because almost certainly Diamond or Cataresco would have done this when they came to the scene. There was nothing. I said, "I think maybe he wants to remind himself. He'll clean up after."

"After what?"

I didn't answer that.

In the kitchen all trace of the strawberries had vanished. The fruit would have rotted long since, or would have been carried away by ants, but I'd expected to see the tray. It wasn't there on the counter. It wasn't in the trash.

There are moments that are too vivid, made up of too much stuff, to be lived as they actually occur. Murder is certainly one. Afterward, when the mind re-creates the picture, anxiety and guilt can make strange details intrude. I knew a guy once who'd lost a shoe and became convinced that he'd left it somehow at the crime scene.

On going back, he was amazed not to find it. He didn't get caught, but he became obsessed with the lost shoe. Eventually he turned himself over to me and asked if I had it. Then he confessed.

Gatti wasn't the possessor of those sorts of nerves. His imagination was snappish and sprightly but on a leash, barking to his own command. If he'd come back, it wasn't for fear of having left a clue but because he was looking for something he hadn't found. Maybe he'd been the one to drop the butts and the pipe, take a leak on the carpet.

He'd given me the photographs of Denise and Mae to throw me off the scent. He most likely hadn't been aiming for any more than that. My involvement with and disappointment over the Corcoran case was public knowledge, but he couldn't have guessed how far I'd go. Or had my face been such an open book, the print of my hatred embossed all over it?

Francis had said that Mae thought Radek was harmless, a little Polish joker. I wondered if she'd ever expressed that opinion to his face. Radek would have smiled, grinning, "Yes, yes," while his gut curdled. He was a clown, true, but a clown on the make, a dangerous clown, a clown in revolt. He'd have hated driving her around. Had he ever made a pass? He might have murdered her to show what he could do, to prove that he had the power, like a child cutting the legs off a frog. He must have known that his plot, like my own, was dangerous to the point of madness. No doubt that was a part of it.

There had to be something else, some deeper connection between him and Mae and Denise.

I remembered when I was in this kitchen for the first time, hearing the exhausted clang of that distant church bell. I thought of Mae Richards lying here on the floor, her eye shattered and sightless. I thought of Denise Corcoran, face shot away. I thought of Ward, and another image rose unbidden: Gatti slicing off Mae's finger ends. The hatred expressed in that, the anger. I shivered.

I was about to join Renata again in the living room when I heard the gate and footsteps outside, the tread of one pair of feet coming up the path. They stopped. He's suspicious, I thought as I moved swiftly back into the kitchen; he hasn't lived this long by coming into someone else's house, alone, and late at night. Then the door opened, the masks of comedy and tragedy were hanging from the lock, and I realized he must have been patting himself down, looking for the keys so recently returned to him.

"This had better be good, Renata," said Ricky Lee, his tone suggestive of both anger and the ex-husband's weary acknowledgement that she had the right to call the shot. The two of them had been married, had drifted apart, but were still joined in mind, if not heart, by the child who was between them. He didn't know what this was about. I'd told her to tell him just to get here. I'd made her play him the way Ellen played me.

He was wearing a black suit and a white silk shirt clenched at the collar by a golden knot the size of a walnut. Evidently he'd responded to the disappointment of my not spilling Charlie's brains over the body shop floor by dressing up and going out to dinner. Maybe he'd had a prior. I didn't imagine he dressed this way at home, scheming the next big score.

I waited in the kitchen for a moment longer and then stepped out. "Hello, again," I said. "This must be our night."

For a moment he cracked. He looked at Renata, imagining for a second that she'd set him up, brought him here to be arrested, or worse. The idea worried at his face and then, with no uniforms bursting out of cupboards or from behind the bedroom door, and with me neither having a gun in my hand nor reaching for the one in my shoulder holster, he just as quickly put it together that he was safe; something else was going on. His face became a wall that you could beat yourself against forever. "What the fuck's he doing here?"

"Just hear him out."

"Say what?"

"Listen to what the man has to say."

"I understood the words, Renata. What the fuck is it with you and him?"

"He's an old friend."

"First I ever heard about it."

"I gotta tell you every detail of my social life? Don't see nothing in my divorce papers about that."

"What's behind this shit?"

"Like I said, hear him out."

I told Ricky Lee I knew who'd killed his mother.

He laughed, saying with real venom, "Fuck you, McGrath." He shook his dreadlocks, a nervous rather than a conscious gesture, a function of his rage. "You're a fucked-up situation."

"Listen, I'm not going to make any great pitch. I'm on my way to get this guy. I don't necessarily expect you to believe me."

"I don't give a fuck what you expect. I'm done listenin' to you."

"I need your help."

"My help? You took my goddamn money, motherfucker. Now you're trying to fuck me up with somethin' else. You're goin' down. That's all I know. That's the *end* of the story."

"You'll never find him. You'll be walking down the street. You'll be driving in your car. You'll always be wondering. Is that the guy? Or him? He cut off my mother's fingers. He raped her."

He hesitated, glancing around the ruined house; then his eyes hit mine again.

I said, "What do you want? What do you really want, Ricky Lee? You want me? Well, here I am. You want your mother's murderer? Then come with me. I'll give you the guy and I'll still be with you. Me you get as a gift. Look, I'm not playing any tricks here. If I'd wanted *you* dead, you would be. You were mine when you walked in the door."

His eyes checked the sofa, the fireplace, the spattered plaster, and the stinking mess in the center of the floor. He looked at the portraits on the table, the CDs, the VCRs. He looked at the curtains and the window, where a fly made its frantic late-night patrol. He looked at three of his old tennis trophies given pride of place in the corner cabinet. I wondered how it had been between him and Renata. No wonder the marriage hadn't worked out, the most he knew of family life being revenge. The thought was unfair, I realized; there was a time when he and his brother had lived here as boys with Mae. They must have been happy.

He'd survived and risen by stepping in the face of what he witnessed, by using violence first when he needed to, and more brutally, by courage, by luck, by deceit and guile, by saying, in effect, that no one in the world existed except him.

"Shit," said Ricky Lee, shaking his head, touching his hand against the glass front of the corner cabinet. "How are you, Renata? Who's lookin' after our little angel?"

Renata was leaning against the kitchen doorway.

She'd been gazing at me, touching the scars on her cheek, clearly asking herself what sort of man I'd become. I'd told her I needed this meeting. I'd told her someone I cared about was in danger. Both statements were true, and yet here I was, jousting with Ricky Lee. She'd already had enough for a lifetime. Tall and determined, extraordinarily beautiful, no longer his woman, she turned to him and replied coolly. "My girlfriend, Elizabeth, she lives next door. You remember? She teaches at the mid-school on Manhattan Beach Boulevard."

He nodded, thinking, inattentive. He went over to the window and looked out into the fog. I wondered if he'd really come alone. I'd used his grief against him the way Radek had piggybacked on my numb despair, but Ricky Lee was not to be underestimated. I didn't make that mistake. As well as what I'd involved him with, he had his own workings, his own war with the world. Who knew what was really going on with him? He had an appetite for control and action too eager ever entirely to be overcome by sorrow, only made scarier and more unpredictable.

He said, "So where's this sucker at?"

"San Pedro."

"Let's go," he said. "And I'll tell you this, McGrath. If I want you dead, you will be."

30

I HEARD A FOG HORN HOOTING. I HEARD THE STEADY PUT-
ter of the two Cummins diesel engines that vibrated
beneath my feet and an explosion of static and voices
from the fly bridge as Danny went back and forth on the
radio. I heard a wave slap against the bow, tossing spray
against the cabin portholes. I heard the snap and rattle
of a gun being stripped as Tookie Cross checked out the
hardware. My grandfather's arsenal had included some
old guns, but a lot of surprisingly new stuff as well. He
liked to keep abreast of the times, in this one regard at
least, and I'd taken a Glock 9 mm with seventeen rounds
in the magazine, an AK-47 assault rifle, and an Uzi
machine gun, which Tookie was now fondling and
stroking like a puppy.

Tookie didn't care for the ocean. "Niggers don't do
boats," he'd muttered when he'd heard where we were
going. "Niggers don't tan and niggers don't ski and niggers especially don't do boats." He'd been waiting outside Mae Richards's house all along, and came up, scaring
off a considerable area of fog, while I was walking Renata
to her car.

In the Land Cruiser, heading down from Venice to

the marina, I'd explained the situation. "He's yours," I said, "but first we make sure my friend's safe." Ricky Lee had said nothing. He hadn't even nodded or moved his head, no longer in the dealing vein. I got the impression that his strategy was for Tookie to handle me while he served violent revenge on Radek. Ward, I hoped, he didn't care about one way or the other.

Ricky Lee prowled around and around the cabin. For him the boat, a Grand Banks fiberglass trawler that Danny had bought from a bankrupt rock star, was a chugging prison surrounded by vapor. He couldn't wait to get this over. Tookie's mood had lightened once he saw the guns. All his energy had flowed out toward them. They affected him like Quaaludes. He seemed a little dazed.

Still with my eyes closed, I said, "What was the story with Jack Brewster? Why did you have to kill him?"

The engine kept up its steady beat. Another wave heaved against the bow and scattered its dwindling strength down the side of the boat. I'd been asking myself if perhaps Gatti had killed Jack Brewster after all, if he'd got to Jack after Ricky Lee, and that was how he'd put it together about me and the money. Ricky Lee scotched that theory. He said, "He went down. What can I tell you? But he was tough, that old man. He stuck to his story. He wouldn't blow the whistle on you."

Opening my eyes at last, I saw Ricky Lee stooped in the companionway that led down to Danny's crib, while Tookie was sliding the magazine into the butt of the Glock, slapping it home with the fleshy part of his palm. Hunched forward, peering along the barrel, head down like a bloodhound, Tookie didn't merely dislike me anymore. He was starting to hate me as a threat to his boss's equilibrium.

"Were you there when he died?"

I gathered from Ricky Lee's shrug that the answer was no.

"I was," said Tookie. "He was shrill, man. He begged not to die. He kept cryin' out, 'I'm tellin' the truth, I'm tellin' the truth.' You fucked with us, cop, and now he's rubbed out into nothing."

"His death's down to me," said Ricky Lee. "You got a problem with that?"

I did, I certainly did, though I was chary of letting it show. In the end, in certain situations, it didn't matter whether you were right or wrong. Morality, the law, and punishment, these might come later, but for now you had to win. "I'm as much responsible for his death as you are."

"You're letting it go?" said Tookie.

"I have to."

"Damn fucking right," he said.

"Tell me about this guy," said Ricky Lee. "Did I ever see him? What's he like?"

"He's a little Polish guy. He works for Francis but he knew your mother through Denise Corcoran. This is a guy with fingers in altogether too many pies."

Ricky Lee gathered his coat around him. "What's he look like?"

"Short, dark, a lot of lines on his face and eyes as if they remembered feeling something about a hundred years ago."

Frowning, nodding, fingering his beard, Ricky Lee said, "Yeah, I think I saw the dude one time."

"Around the neighborhood?"

"Maybe. Not sure. Is he a cop?"

"No, he's not a cop. Why would you think that?"

Ricky Lee shrugged, while Tookie, wiping off another barrel, said, "'Cos cops are crooks and gangsters just like us."

"You'd know if you ever spoke with this guy. Talks a mile a minute. Thick accent. Puts his sentences through the wringer."

Ricky Lee said, "What's he want from you?"

"Your money."

His eyes shot out. "You want your friend back, just give it to the motherfucker."

"He thinks I have the other half. He thinks Charlie's dead."

For a minute or more nothing was said while Ricky Lee contemplated the devious knot tying us together. Maybe even he didn't know at this stage quite how he wanted it to unravel. He said, "How'd you figure out I left that first chamber empty? You good with weight?"

"I guessed. I figured you were too smart to give me a .357 Colt fully loaded. There'd have been time to take a shot at one of you at least."

"Crazy-ass motherfucker," said Tookie Cross, babying the AK-47 now, his enormous hands scattering shells onto the table in the center of the cabin.

"You had some personal beef with Charlie Corcoran?" said Ricky Lee.

"It's a long story."

"Yeah? Don't bore us," said Tookie.

I shrugged, saying that I was going up top, and headed forward to the five steps leading to the fly bridge. In thick-soled shoes, dark woolen pants, and a knee-length padded ski jacket with a fur hood, Danny stood at the wheel, eyes fixed on the green glow of a radar screen whose sweeping arm disclosed a shadow, land, to our left. He gestured with his chin toward the screen. "That's Point Fermin. We're making pretty good time with the currents from the north. Shouldn't be too much longer."

He knew Pier 50. It was at the northern end of the

turning basin, he said, a wide open area of water in the middle of the port for the big ships to maneuver. "In the old days cruise ships would fetch up at Pier 50. It's a huge place. The crews slept there. Nobody's used it for years now."

I told him that after he'd got the three of us off the boat, he should turn right around and head north.

"You don't want me to stay?"

"This could go down any number of ways. Get yourself out of there."

"How about this? I'll wait for you in the west basin, on the other side of the railroad tracks." He showed me a chart beneath a plastic cover that he had on this side of the wheel. "Pier 146. That's where I'll be."

"Are you sure?" I smiled and lightly laid a hand on his shoulder. "Thanks, Danny."

"Hey, no problem. You and your family should come out one night that's not dreadful."

I tried to imagine. On a clear night in Santa Monica Bay you'd probably see all the way to Pasadena. You'd see the golden ribbon of Sunset Boulevard winding twenty miles inland. You'd see the city turned inside out, golden again and restored. "I'd like that," I said.

I went to the front of the boat, where all ahead was fog. I could see only about fifteen feet in front of my face. Waves broke against the bows, tossing spray in my face, and the hooting horns seemed closer now. A loud blast was followed almost immediately by another and then silence after the fog dragged the life out of it.

I saw, or I imagined I saw, dark specks moving across the ocean's surface, pelicans heading home. It must have been near here that Ellen, Lucy, and I had been out in the boat. The sun was shining that day. It was so fine. We'd seen porpoises, dolphins, flying fish, and, at last, cruising again toward San Pedro, a school of whales.

Los Angeles was such a strange place to raise a child. Seattle would most likely be better, safer. At that moment it seemed more pleasure and happiness than I could expect from life to be able to visit them up there, maybe with Ward. I'd come a long way since Mae Richards was murdered. I'd driven myself backward and forward. I thought of Charlie Corcoran, and even in my exhausted state I still couldn't condone what he'd done, though I understood it now; but who was I to judge? I thought of Jack Brewster, and pondered painfully on friendship and loyalty. I thought of Radek and Ricky Lee and Ward and what the next hour would hold. I had a calm sense of approaching climax. I badly wanted this over, done, while the fog thankfully cooled my impatience, warning me to tread soft, make no more false moves, telling me to live.

A light loomed out of the fog and then disappeared again. Two blasts from a horn, so close they seemed to have been blown directly into my resounding ear, and then the light was back, swinging as I felt the boat begin to sweep to port. I realized we were coming up on Angel's Gate, the entrance to San Pedro from the sea, which meant that off to my near side, invisible in the mist, was the sea wall that guarded the harbor.

As we rounded the light, suddenly the waves were less steep. A few moments later we were chugging calmly beyond the breakwater, and the sea's only movement was a long, flat, sluggish swell. Ricky Lee and Tookie, sensing that we must be about to arrive, had come up to the fly bridge. Tookie was for once visibly happy, bouncing on his feet, sniffing land.

We passed shimmering lights and belching stacks, a power plant to the port side. We passed the red star of the radio tower atop San Pedro Hill and oil tanks that bulged briefly slick and shiny gray before the fog consumed them again. A warning blast came out of the mist, loud, and the bows of a huge ship steepled above us, carving the channel the other way, lights swimming, engines for a moment throbbing and near, before we were left, shaken, rocking in its wake.

Tookie, smile gone now, disappeared down below, while Ricky Lee laughed at his back. "Hey, Took-man, you cowardly motherfucker. What is it with you and water anyway? You afraid to take a bath or what?"

A string of lights, suspended high above in the fog, told me we must be sailing beneath the Vincent Thomas Bridge. It would have been in these waters that launches searched this morning for wreckage from the Land Cruiser that went over. Wondering whether Ricky Lee knew where we were, I said nothing. Danny peered forward, easing his bulk against the wheel, and said we were coming up on Pier 50. I asked him to take the boat on a while, down the East Channel basin, so that I could look at the building. The near end of it was dark, with a jetty running up to a broken wall, and doors beyond. We slid past a fine old wood eighty-footer, well appointed and with a radio mast swaying gently on the tide, and Danny said, "Yeah, that's *Little Knell.* She's one of the most beautiful boats in the county." Then there was the pitted unlit hulk of a dredger, above which towered the warehouse, two stories high and a couple of hundred yards long; the windows were dark; as we went on I saw that most of the wooden doors had been replaced by rolling steel shutters. There were no graffiti, and here the brick walls were solid, but still the place gave off a powerful sense of destitution and desolation. Only at the very far end was there any sign of life—lights beckoning from three or four of the windows, shadows moving within.

31

THE FLASHLIGHT LIT UP A VAST EMPTY SPACE, LITTERED with rubble, the one-time entrance hall, with a tile floor and a stairway at its heart, broad and white, leading up into the ominous dark. I heard the scuffle of rats and, from outside, the faint double hoot of the horn on the Los Angeles light. There was the smell of ozone and crushed brick, but no damp. The walls were sound, though the paint was flaking. A couple of the windows were cracked, but unbroken. Twenty or thirty years ago, when the big cruise ships had docked here, this must have been a splendid place. Even in desolation it retained a vestigial sturdiness, a dismaying glamour. No one had used this particular entrance for years. My feet left tracks in the dust.

Ricky Lee was at my back, assault rifle in hand, pistol tucked in the front of his pants. Danny had dropped us at the front of the building, on the wrecked jetty, after we'd let Tookie off by the dredger and he'd suggested that he and I would have business when this was all over. "Always supposing you survive the more pressing problems at hand," he'd said. And to Ricky Lee: "Take care."

At the top of the stairs we found a darkened doorless

doorway, so narrow in the width of the encompassing wall that it seemed like the entrance to a grave. Passing through, moving as softly as we could on the crunching debris, we came into a long straight corridor with more sightless doorways, empty space I felt at first only through some tiny disturbance in the currents of the air, and then searched out with the flashlight to reveal an empty dormitory, a men's toilet (urinal trough still intact), and a bathroom stripped of brass fittings that glinted in a heap. The corridor itself was cramped and narrow, but much warmer than the entrance hall. Behind me I heard Ricky Lee's feet, the excited rhythm of his breath. From ahead the hollow air brought a pulse that grew louder. "Generator," said Ricky Lee in a whisper. "Someone's at home."

The corridor gave onto another staircase, taking us down this time, again to ground level and into another wide-open space, overwhelmingly, massively huge, though clean, swept, and far from empty. The flashlight picked out a covered wagon of the type that my great-grandfather must have once sat in, the wings and nose of a dismembered airplane, an old Chevrolet, lovingly restored, an old Buick, a Ford Thunderbird up on bricks, another covered wagon, a second airplane, a biplane—this one complete— a third covered wagon, then a fourth and a fifth.

It took us probably ten minutes to weave our way through to the far end. Ricky Lee was muttering and shaking his head. "I can't believe this shit." We were in the dark, out in the open, waiting for the sledgehammer attack of bullet against flesh. There were tools and tarps on sections of the floor. There were more cars and covered wagons. There was a three-lane bowling alley, complete, with the balls stacked up in pyramids. As I said, the place was huge, the size of an aircraft hangar. Perhaps it had been a ballroom, or maybe Radek had cleared away what was once here. The darkness pressed in from sky-lights thirty, forty feet above. A steel gallery ran down the left side, with steel steps at the far end. There were boxes stacked up in one corner with script on them in Polish. The medical supplies, I assumed. All the rest was fodder for Radek's movie-set business. The stuff must have been worth a couple of hundred thousand dollars. My throat tried to jump out of the prison of my neck when I suddenly saw lights moving, a black wall sliding by the windows. Thinking for a moment that my eyes must be playing me tricks, I stood quite still with my heart bursting; but the black wall kept on, moving like a curtain. It was a ship, I realized, heading out to sea from the channel that ran along the building's entire right side.

At last we stood at the far end, faced with a closed door. From beyond I thought I heard movement, the distant echo of voices. Ricky Lee edged around one side of the door while I took the other, reached out for the handle, and eased it open, stepping through onto the other side, drawn Beretta in hand.

There was light on the other side, a flickering fluorescent strip suspended from the ceiling with picture wire, and there was a room to our left, a dormitory, smelling of fresh paint and carpeted with tough gray material that made my feet bounce, stuff that was most likely wear-resistant, fire-resistant, rot-resistant; it would be around a lot longer than I would.

The dormitory was empty. Heart pounding, sweating, mouth dry and my insides all liquid, I remembered how much I hated weapon-drawn searches. Your nerves are wires. Each deserted room brings anticlimax and a tight reassurance that might be rudely shot away at any moment. The air seems corpulent. You have to wade and carve through it, sweeping your weapon the way they teach you in tactics, the way you see in the movies. Each time, you think, Today might be the day.

I thought of Ellen, the time she was shot. So many times I'd punished myself for not having been there, fantasizing that I would have stopped time, invented a different kind of clock, another history. I'd imagined as well all the various scenarios that might have sprung to life if I hadn't slept with Ward, or even if Ellen hadn't found out. There were so many, but only one was written, only one had become reality: Ellen, bleeding on the floor with a shard of glass in her spine, and a new life beginning for the both of us, she as a cripple, while I marched to guilt's despotic gait. However viewed, with the benefit of hindsight, with gained experience and knowledge, with wiser perspectives, I was always to blame. However many times I scratched away the scab of subsequent events—her conquest of adversity, my own fall—the wound was always raw and leaking. Bertrand Russell said that everyone is doomed to grow fierce sooner or later. Maybe it's not doom, but a useful thing. Either way, that had been Ellen's moment. She'd been forced to act and I'd let myself grow stale.

I was back in the corridor where, above me, the fluorescent strip buzzed and crackled, flickering off, then lighting up Ricky Lee's face with an inhuman blue glow. He was tense and armed and angry but holding the AK-47 across his chest with an almost delicate grasp. The other gun was stuck in his belt like a jewel. I was frightened in my very bones. There was another light, some twenty yards down the corridor, this one glowing steady. The corridor itself continued for perhaps another twenty beyond that before giving onto darkness.

I counted eight doorways on each side, some seemingly lit from within, some not. The next room on the left was empty. The one opposite had a shower rigged in one corner—no one there either. Water dripped from the shower, drumming the hollow bottom of the cubicle.

We covered three more rooms and suddenly I heard voices burst out, close, somewhere within the warren. I had to guess at the conversation, though there was no doubting the mood. Two men were arguing, shouting at the same time. Ricky Lee positioned himself silently on the far side of the doorway while I took the other. Quickly their voices fell away into a choppy murmur, silence, as if sensing some brief electric disturbance in the air, but then they started up again.

Richard Francis was nervous, agitated, saying, "You assured me there was no problem. You would just use my name. I wouldn't be involved. Now I am."

Radek Gatti's voice was a little too loud to be soothing. "Richard, my friend, my *patron,* you are fretting over trivia. *Pfuft!* Where's the problem?"

"McGrath knows what's going on here."

The laugh seemed disembodied, almost hysterical. "McGrath? Oh, yes. I will worry about him I think, OK. Don't you worry. Listen, Richard, everything is smooth, everything is OK. We do nothing illegal here. We are honest businessmen, a little immoral maybe, a little *dubious,* that's all. Look on it as a Polish campaign contribution. Do these supplies conform to a standard? Yes, they certainly do."

Ricky Lee's eyes were puzzled, asking me what this was about. I raised my finger to my lips, cautioning silence, while Francis went on, not calmed or soothed or smoothed over, the way he was supposed to be. "There's something else," he said, wary and even frightened.

"Nothing else," said Gatti in a definite voice. "No more questions. What else could there be?"

Silence fretted at the air. At last Francis cleared his throat and said, "McGrath said you killed Mae." He sounded close to tears. "He says you murdered her."

"McGrath says that? Bull*shit*. McGrath says that? When you talk to him? That fucking prick cocksucker. It's bullshit. You believe him? You take his word over mine?"

I sensed Francis backing off, surprised by the outburst. "You're loyal, you're my friend, I trust you."

"So why you trying to fuck me with this bullshit? It isn't right, Richard."

"I wanted to ask something, that's all."

"You wanted to ask something. *You* wanted to ask *me*. Shit."

Francis started talking about that day when Mae was killed, when Gatti had picked him up from the hospital and taken him over to her house. "You were in a strange mood. I said so at the time. You were excited, thrilled. You kept snapping your fingers and slapping the wheel. You wouldn't stop talking. About Wall Street, about politics, about the football game, about black holes in space. I can't even remember what else. Then you wanted to go to the boat."

"You think this is funny? You think this is a big joke? I was in a weird mood. Maybe it was something I ate. Maybe I had indigestion." Gatti's voice was shaky, wobbling at the edge of violence. "It was those fucking clams I had for lunch at that place, you know, on Abbot Kinney. Was it shrimp? No, clams."

"Did you see her that day?"

Radek was almost pleading with him now. "Why you ask that? It's an insult. Everyone insult me. Poor little Radek. No one gives him respect. He is so small and from a foreign country. Everyone think they can spit on him. Go ahead. You, my friend, turn against me."

"Did you see her?"

There was a strange lull, a poised and dangerous calm. "I saw her, yeah," he said in a quiet voice, sighing, letting a different energy rush crackling in. The unease Gatti had always inspired in me was a weak and transient feeling to what I now experienced. The guy was about to send flames running up the walls. "Yes, indeed, I saw her. And you know what? I fucking killed that bitch. But not before I put my cock in her mouth. Not before I fucked her up the ass."

Having been worn down, nudged into the confession, Gatti was now primed to prod and poke and goad, to let Francis know in whose hands the power truly lay; he was reveling in this upset of the assumed order of things. "I came in her hole. You like that? Huh? You like that, you fucking arrogant medical prick? What you gonna do now, Mr. Millionaire? All your degrees gonna march in here to help you? All those nurses and little baby boy doctors who think you're so smart and dignified? I fucked your girlfriend. I killed her. I cut off her fingers."

Francis, stunned, said nothing, while I saw Ricky Lee's eyes become inflamed. His grip tightened around the rifle and his head was motionless, while his shoulders trembled with the effort of keeping still. This was going down any second now.

"I hated that dumb pretentious bitch. Almost as much as my own mother. And you should have seen what happened to my mother. Little Radek stuffed her in the garbage, where she belong. Little Radek cut off her head. Now maybe I kill you. What you say to that, my friend. You're very successful, no? Will it help you now to shun the danger? I don't think so, buddy boy. I won't need a gun. I kill you with my teeth."

I swept in first, Ricky Lee at my heels, expecting to

face Gatti and Francis but finding instead yet one more empty room, another of those steely carpets. Swinging left, I saw an archway. Two of these areas had been knocked into one, and there I did see Francis, on his knees, nearly blinded from the blood that rained down from the gash above his eye where Gatti had bitten him. Gatti himself I glimpsed disappearing around the arch, heading for the door on the other side and the escape route of the corridor beyond.

Ricky Lee was out first, chasing with a pattering burst from the AK-47, but Gatti was gone, vanished probably into a room on the other side, or maybe he'd even reached the darkness at the end of the corridor. "Motherfucker," said Ricky Lee, and set off in pursuit, dodging left out of the corridor into the next lit area, while I went the other way to check on Francis, who was shaking, dazed, holding a bloody handkerchief to his head.

I didn't have time to ask how he was feeling. He was alive; he'd make it. I took his shoulders. "Radek's holding a friend of mine. A woman. Have you seen her?"

He was still too stunned.

"How long have you been here?"

He shook his head, blood flying in a spray. "Not long. Fifteen minutes."

"Have you seen anyone else since you've been here? Apart from Radek. Come on, Richard. I need an answer."

"No one, no one, only Radek." His eyes were bright, oddly hopeful for a moment, while the blood continued to trickle down his face, and then he jumped in alarm, shocked again by the nearby stutter of the assault rifle and a dreamy hissing silence before three shots from a different weapon, one after the other, hard flat cracks.

Running, in the corridor, I passed beneath the fluorescent strips beckoning me into the darkness at the end.

I slowed down, edging close to the wall, pushing it with my shoulder while I held the Glock outstretched in two hands. All my gut was jammed up against the back of my throat as my feet felt for two concrete steps I didn't dare glance toward and inched down.

Ricky Lee was only a few yards beyond the door. He lay as if dumped, or blown against the wheel of another car in Gatti's motor museum. It was a rusted Chevy pickup. He lay with one leg twisted beneath him at an impossible angle. There'd been three shots but only two wounds that I could see, one in the right side of his chest, the other a neat hole through the center of his throat, where the protesting flesh had puckered up around the entry wound. His right hand lay stretched out on the running board of the truck. Feeling for his pulse, weakly there, my fingers brushed the nick that had been taken from the tender area of his palm, the third wound, only a scratch. He coughed, choking, and I fetched something out from the back of the throat; Radek had paused to wrench away the walnut-sized hunk of gold from Ricky Lee's collar and stuff it in his mouth.

I remember the first time I watched a man die in front of my eyes. It was at night, in MacArthur Park, where he'd lain beneath a eucalyptus tree that stank as though a hundred horses had urinated against it. He'd been a John Doe, a homeless street guy. His eyes swam with moisture, staring somewhere beyond the sky, and the moisture hardened into a glaze while whatever he was observing went away or changed into some other vision. This is the reality, I'd realized; this is what will happen. There'll be those few final moments when memories, thoughts, dreams, impulses, when all life's radiant stuff seeks a final flowering before consciousness is snuffed out. People make the mistake of being frivolous about death; they think it happens to everybody, it's natural, it's no big deal, they'll be fine. That's a fine theory, until you're dying.

Ricky Lee's prominent eyes had that faraway look. I squeezed his hand and felt the slightest of returning pressures. His hushed, rattling breath and weak voice came from another animal trying to escape inside.

"Tookie?" he said. "Hey, Took, man, you get that cold shit for my little girl? She's gotta cold, man. You gotta get that shit to Renata."

"It's not Tookie," I said. "It's McGrath. Listen, listen to me." I tried to make his eyes turn into mine. "You're young, you're strong. You can make it."

I went back along the corridor to find Francis in the bright light of the empty room. He hadn't moved, but startled when I took his arm. "Come and do your job," I said.

I'll never forget the look on Ricky Lee's face. He frowned, puzzled, and then turned weakly to me, still frowning, as if he wished to share the affront he felt while this old white guy ripped open his shirt and fingered his chest.

I said, "Hold on. We'll get you to intensive care."

"I'm blind, man," said Ricky Lee, mumbling as blood frothed at his lips. "I can't see."

Francis shook his head: it was no good.

My grip tightened on Ricky Lee's hand. "Bullshit. I've seen guys shot up worse than this still make it," I said. "Breathe. Take a breath. Look into my eyes. Look at me."

"I must, I must," said Ricky Lee, the words barely traveling beyond his tongue. "I must find . . . McGrath, is that you?" His eyes dimmed. "Oh, shit, I'm dying. You fucked with me, man. Where is she? Who's looking . . ." Death cut him short.

32

THIS TIME THE FLASHLIGHT PICKED OUT AN EMPTY stretch of concrete floor and was bounced back at me from darkened windows that ran down the other side of the building. Its light brought into being a neatly stacked mountain of brown cardboard boxes, two more cars, and another of those covered wagons. There was a doleful hoot of a distant horn. Above the first level of windows was a dirty second story, with an iron gantry running around it. We were in another open empty space similar to the one Ricky Lee and I had passed through before, with objects lying here and there, some large, some small, scattered like dice of various sizes across a giant's negligently kept table. There were shouts and more gunshots from beyond the window, and the sense of a shadow creeping across everything as another big ship went by. The damp cold air was searching, pricking the heat of my skin. I heard my breath and the slowing murmur of my heart. It was a fine night to give my friend Randy at the county coroner's office some extra business.

I swung the flashlight into the far left corner, where, beyond a sparkling workbench and a bottle lying on its belly, it found a squared-off concrete angle and an entrance within that, giving onto dark stairs. Having crossed the space, I began to climb, perhaps twenty steps and three turns to the right, the flashlight glancing at distempered walls and rusted iron railings, until I was faced with a heavy wooden door and light slivering through a crack at the bottom. The door was locked.

My first kick thanked me with a shock of pain surging from my ankle through the shin and knee. With the second and third the door creaked and cracked, beginning to yield, and then burst open, wood splinters heaving from the jamb. The lock crashed to the floor and I was faced with a little boy, a toddler, perhaps four years old, staring at me with hard eyes of wonder. He stood only five or so yards away, not scared, but starting to giggle and moan at what I'd done to the door, his round head flopping from side to side. There were folds of skin above his eyes that made the lids seem heavy. His forehead bulged out at me from beneath thick tufts of dark hair. There was nothing of Denise Corcoran in his face, nor would I have expected there to be, though I recognized him from the photograph Louise Szell had shown me. He was Denise's little boy, the Downs baby. I could barely speak or gather my thoughts. "Hello, youngster," I said at last in a soft voice that sounded unreal and astonished.

The room was in the shape of a pentagon, sparse but not uncomfortable. There was a rug on the floor, a sofa, a pinball machine, a refrigerator. There were lamps, chairs, and an electric furnace that fanned the air with warmth. There were windows on each side, looking out into the fog, thicker now that beginning daylight had arrived to give it substance. The boy didn't move. His eyes stared at the gun hanging by my side while his head still rocked to and fro.

A voice behind me said, "Hello, Billy. I'm very glad you decided to drop by."

Ward stood to one side of the door I'd burst through only seconds before. In her hand, swinging down at her side as my automatic was at mine, she held a chair leg, with which I presumed she'd been ready to knock unconscious the intruder. She was leaning against the wall, blowing air from her lips, and running her hands through her hair so that parts of it stood up almost fiercely straight. Her black cashmere blazer was scuffed and dirty, with a rip where the sleeve met the shoulder. Her nose was a little pink and her eyes, which had been crying, were toughening up from relief into anger.

"Are you OK?"

"Oh, sure. I was bound and gagged and thrown in the trunk of a car. I was kidnaped, goddammit. Why? What's going on, Billy?"

"I can't talk about it now."

"Fuck you."

"I've got to get you out of here."

"I'm not moving an inch without the little boy. Andy, come to me, sweetheart."

The boy, unsure, didn't move. He was still smiling and opening his lips, though no sound came forth. Ward threw aside the chair leg, which bounced across the rug, and walked over, gathering him in her arms and stroking his thick, unruly hair. "It's OK, sweetheart. We're gonna go somewhere now with this man. He's a friend, so it will be OK."

"You know the kid?"

"Not until tonight. Not until I was thrown in this room."

"What's he doing here?"

She seemed surprised I didn't know. She took me to

one side, whispering, "What's his name? The one who brought me here?"

"Radek Gatti."

"Radek. Right. Andy's his son."

"What?"

"Worse luck for Andy."

"Radek's the father?"

The boy was singing softly to himself, bouncing on his feet, wagging that great head, flapping his hands. He seemed old beyond his years, grave with trapped thought and sweet emotions that couldn't help bubbling out. Louise Szell had thought that Charlie Corcoran was the father of Denise's child. Francis had said not, offering no alternative. I'd never suspected it might be Gatti.

Ward said, "You've come with an army of uniforms, right? They're taking care of everything. They're cleaning up down there so we can get the hell out of here. I'm hungry. Is it breakfast time already? I could eat a horse. Well, pancakes would be better." The fingers of her left hand were curling in her hair. "All that noise I've been hearing? It's the cops, isn't it? It's your guys?"

"Not exactly."

"Well, what, exactly?"

I told her that I'd come by sea with Ricky Lee Richards, who'd been shot, and another gangster, whose real ambition was to kill me. Our only ally in this was a doctor, shocked and with a nasty cut to the head, and a friend waiting on the boat we had to get to.

"You're telling me you're by yourself?"

"Pretty much."

"It's true, then, what the guy said. You took a bribe."

"You were there when Gatti called?"

"You telling me you didn't take the bribe?"

"Yeah, I took it."

"And Charlie Corcoran's dead?"

"Gatti thinks so. Charlie's OK."

The boy was huddling against her leg. Outside, it was growing lighter, though I still couldn't see the distant refineries or the ships that gave out warning blasts on the invisible waters. "You took money from Ricky Lee Richards, so how can I believe you about the other? How do I know Corcoran's not in a ditch someplace or at the bottom of the ocean or in an airplane about to be dumped in pieces over the desert? How can I believe you about anything? It turns out you're one of the bad guys." Her wide-open blue eyes were sharp and watchful. "Yet you're here. Why?"

I stood there shuffling for a moment, wanting to say "I came to get you." As a story to be told later, to our grandchildren, if we were lucky and survived to have grandchildren, all this would be terrific. As moments to experience, they were something else altogether: fast, scary, so heightened that the mind only fumbled at their nature. In these circumstances I couldn't speak the words. I couldn't tell her the truth. At least I didn't. I reached out to brush her cheek with my fingers.

"I see," she said, her eyes never leaving mine.

The next things happened quickly. I left the five-sided room, went quickly and carefully down the stairs, and stood for a moment at the bottom, alert, listening. There were no shots. There was no rustle of human activity. I saw no one, so I went back upstairs and came down again with Ward and the boy, opening the door on one of Radek's cars that was up on bricks and wasn't going anywhere, and having them hide in the back seat.

Just then Francis came over, his forehead badged and disfigured by the wound, which was no longer bleeding. His shirt was torn, stained with blood, and he was still wobbly. I thought of how, during that night, when I'd put Ricky Lee's weapon to my head and pulled the trigger, my body had shrunk from annihilation, or, rather, it had backed off and risen in protest as if it too, as well as my mind, were capable of making a decision, demanding a better and more radiant geography for my faculties than the violent landscape I was living in. This was all very different from the night in the art gallery with Ted Softly, when in essence I'd been quite ready to die. I was afraid of death now. This wasn't only a good thing. In some cases reckless disregard instilled a physical clarity and grace, became a useful means of self-preservation. It wasn't always so, though being tentative was as likely as anything to get you killed.

Francis had seen Gatti while I'd been upstairs. "He was holding a gun. He looked crazy, grabbing my shirt and threatening me. He said something about a boy. He told me I was to look after the boy and he'd be in touch. Does that make any sense to you?"

"Some. Where's Gatti now?"

"I don't know," he said, shaking his head. "I assume outside."

I knew I couldn't allow him just to walk away. I had to bust him, to bring him to book for Mae's murder, and risk the consequences. If he were to sit in an interview room, telling all he knew, then so be it.

Ricky Lee's face was covered with a white cloth. "The least I could do," said Francis in a murmur. "Poor Mae. He was born such a little runt. I told her she'd never rear him. They both proved me wrong. He was always a fighter."

I took the silver-barreled Magnum still at his waist, the butt hot from his ebbing warmth, and gave my own, the Beretta, to Ward, showing her how to slide off the safety, telling her she most likely wouldn't have to use it.

I walked with the three of them to the left of the building, to the far end, where I opened a window, slid out, and, having checked that all was clear, helped them through. Within minutes we'd crossed between railway cars, negotiated a truck park, and passed the boarded-up windows of a ruined café to find Danny's boat in the West Basin. I got them safely on deck and turned to go.

Ward said, "You're not coming?"

I wanted to say so much, to apologize for getting her into this, to ask forgiveness.

"Look, I really have to take care of this."

There were distant gunshots, hard flat sounds, and she met my apologetic shrug with a smile whose wistful neutrality gave no clue to her feelings, gathering the head of the boy into her arms.

I said, "Can I see you later?"

"You'd better," she said, and then I was alone, running back toward the action, hearing only the sound of my breath and my footsteps.

Night had given way to a gloomy and cold morning. The sun was invisible. Through shifting vapors of low-lying fog, I saw the looming hulk of the dredger, solid and black, white letters on its side announcing the port of registration: St. Louis. The dock was paved, and my footsteps made an echoing sound on the flags while the ocean slapped gray and sullen against the dredger's side. Gazing up, I made out the span of the Vincent Thomas Bridge, early-morning workers creeping across, the headlights of their cars gauzy and weeping in the mist. In the distance one of the big ships gave out its twin warning blasts. From close at hand came the sudden chug and putter of engines from a much smaller vessel. Breaking into a run, Ricky

Lee's weapon held away from my body, I saw the white shape of Francis's boat, the words *Little Knell* forming a careful crescent on her stern, turning away from the dock. I was about to try to make the leap, thinking I could still make it to the deck, but reared back, my body telling me that the distance was already too far.

I stared at the waters churning and frothing beneath the boat's propellers, knowing that he was gone, he'd escaped, I was too late, though I made out the dark bulky figure on the bridge, spinning toward me. He's waving, I thought; the bastard's gloating—until three cracks punctured the chill morning air and I threw myself forward by instinct, even though I'd already heard the rounds ricochet to safety across the stones behind me. He shot twice more, and I capped one off myself, taking careful aim with my elbows resting up on the cobbles, before the fog enclosed *Little Knell.* I saw the tall radio mast wave goodbye and heard only the retreating engines, oddly loud for a second, then absent.

I stood up, angry rather than rattled and tasting blood, my teeth having taken a bite at my tongue when I threw myself on the ground. I wiped my hands on the back of my grandfather's coat and a hectic voice spoke unexpectedly out of the fog. "You going in? You going *swimming?* Be careful. There are dangerous currents. They could sweep you anywhere. I see that nice weapon you're holding, my friend. Very pretty piece. Now toss it in the ocean. Let it join the many other treasures rotting and rusting down there."

Down the gun went, splashed, and disappeared into the sluggish waters.

"Good. Very nice. Now turn around."

Radek Gatti stood some five yards away, booted feet apart on the stones, the AK-47 that I'd last seen in Ricky

Lee's hands draped negligently across his crooked elbow. "That big black guy? You needn't have worried; he can't shoot for shit, you know, not at that range. Up close. Boom! He'll blow your head off. No problem. Not even thinking about it. What's his name, anyway?"

"Tookie Cross."

"He's tough. I think he was angry because I killed his boss, you know, and he try to shoot me, like I'm a rabbit or something, so I shoot him back. Twice. And still he makes it to the boat." He gazed regretfully out into the turning basin behind me. "It's a beautiful boat. Maybe I get it back. What do you think?"

Still acting the clown, the persecuted Pole, he waved the rifle's barrel in my direction. "What's going on with you, anyway? You bring my money with you already? Of course not. You try to cheat Radek. You very nasty fellow. You bring those guys and come looking for your girlfriend." He began to rant, taking a step forward, then back, then rubbing at his forehead with the hand not holding the rifle. "You determined to fuck yourself, no?" His face was flushed and spotted with blood. "It was going to be easy. Ricky Lee kills Charlie. You take the cash, I take the girl. You give me the money and get the girl back. Nobody has any worries. Why you fuck up so bad? Now maybe I have to kill you and her, too. It's a fucking shame. She's nice. You think she marry me? Maybe I woo her." He looked up in wonder. "Of course! You didn't kill Charlie. What was the matter? You have an attack? You feel funny or something?"

I asked him how he'd found out about my deal with Ricky Lee.

Nothing changed in his face. He shook his head, eyes filled with that wild humor. "No, no, no," he said. "I'm not giving away any secrets."

I told him in that case I was arresting him for the murder of Mae Richards.

"Sure, sure. Any minute now you gonna read me my rights. Fuck you, buddy. *Fok* you."

"Why did you kill her? What did she do that made you so mad, Radek? Or was it just for fun?"

"You think I'm a psycho?" His voice was soft and quiet, deliberate. "You think I'm nuts? I'm smart. I'm clever. I beat you all."

"Maybe, maybe that's true," I said. "But what's it going to get you? You kill me, you don't get the money, you get nothing."

"I get away with murder," he said, voice rising again. "I get away with that sexual feeling. It has an exhilaration in it. It is a state to entertain. Sometimes it is good to hold in your rage, like squeezing your body around a sack full of adders. Sometimes I let the snakes go. They hiss. They snap. I am so far into myself as if I had never been, while my snakes go about their business. Look! There's a big banana boat out there. Why they paint a ship white? What do you think about that? It must get dirty real quick."

From behind me I heard the beat and throb of huge diesels while Radek peered over my shoulder and I wondered if this was the moment to make a grab for my spare piece, a little .38 my grandfather had made me strap to my ankle. There was a sliding in my gut as my mind, willing my hand to action, warned that Radek was too alert, too aware, ready to snap. I said, "Did Mae know about you and your son?"

"Why you say that?"

"I met your son inside. He's a beautiful little boy. What happened, Radek, after Denise died? Did Mae try to make you face up to your responsibilities? Were you so angry with Corcoran that you thought you could make me have him killed? You were nearly right."

His eyes were busy, realizing he needed to figure out what I'd been doing while he was killing Ricky Lee and trying to deal with Tookie Cross. He said, "You very clever guy, I always said so. Where's my son?"

"He's safe. They all are. Nowhere you can find them. There's no one left to kill, Radek. What you gonna do?"

He roused himself into a new frenzy, stepping forward, hollering. His spit sprayed in my face while the rifle barrel jabbed at my chest. "Give him to me. Tell me where he is or I kill you, you fucking asshole." His eyes fizzed with impatience, with crazy and murderous rage. "Tell me now."

"Shoot me and you'll never know. Maybe you'll never find him. Why did you kill Mae?"

"Because she wouldn't stop. Because she was looking at me with those eyes, asking what kind of a father did I think I was? Because she thought I was nothing. Because she found out I had my son and was working with Denise's parents to take him away." He stepped back, away across the stones, stretching out his left arm and carefully aiming the rifle. "Now I blow your ass into the ocean."

"I don't think so," another voice said. "Throw down the weapon."

Gatti turned, firing a blind burst into the fog. I drew the .38 from my ankle holster and hit him twice in the chest, while a shot from the right spun him around. He fell face down with the rifle still clutched in his hands, and Drew Diamond strolled out of the fog, that cannon of a Colt in hand, a wing-tipped toe prodding at the already motionless body. Drew's eyes were pinkish and swollen with fatigue. "Hello, Billy," he said. "Long night. You wanna get a cup of coffee?"

33

I T WAS THREE DAYS LATER.
Before leaving, I made minute preparations and
had a thousand hesitations about how to dress. I put on
one suit. "No," I said, "they'll think I'm going to a
funeral." I put on another and said to myself, "Jeez, now
I look like John Travolta." In the end I settled for jeans,
a shirt, and a black blazer, and hopped from one foot to
the other waiting for the elevator, which announced
itself with a flashing red light and the ping of a bell
before plummeting me to the basement.

It was dismal down there in the garage. Rain water,
pooled and puddled from the storm, was filthy with oil,
soda cans, and cigarette butts. A damp cold atmosphere
attacked the bone, while fizzing fluorescent lights flickered off and on, as if about to give up the ghost overhead. Looping around one of the bigger pools, anxious
to keep my shoes dry and out of it, I was making my way
to the Porsche at the far end when Drew Diamond
stepped from behind a concrete pillar. He'd obviously
been waiting. Drew himself was dressed to the nines,
and as usual armed to the teeth, the Colt bulging
beneath the arm of a spiffy dogtooth tweed.

He said, "I figured we'd take this ride together."

"Should we even be talking?"

"Fuck the regs," he said with a hungry grin, all shark's teeth.

He'd found me in San Pedro that night through Humbolt Raffi, who'd tracked down Francis after he went on the run from the safe hotel. Drew had arrived first, followed by hordes of Long Beach uniforms, the cavalry. We'd both known the drill. We hadn't said anything, either to each other, or to anyone else, nor had we been expected to.

I'd smudged the edges of the story when the Officer Involved Shooting guy came around the following day, telling him only what I'd thought necessary. I left out the parts that involved Ricky Lee. I said I didn't know how he came to be down there. I imagined, I'd said, that he'd also been on the tracks of his mother's killer. I didn't pretend to myself that this was the end of it, even though Tookie Cross was also dead, having finally run into something bigger than himself only a few minutes after he pulled away from me on the jetty—a banana boat bound for South America. *Little Knell* had exploded and sunk in seconds, Tookie inside.

Drew opened the passenger door of the Jag for me before scampering around to the driver's side. He grinned, facing me across the top of the car, and I wondered what had transpired during *his* interview with OIS. I hadn't bothered going back to the office yet. Cataresco was the acting head of homicide, a temporary position she'd pressed for and was no doubt handling with frisky aplomb. Murakami, I gathered, was incenting ever more furiously with his Ping-Pong paddle, unsure whether this was all over now, or whether the shit was just about to start raining down.

Drew drove smoothly, working the Jag's manual shift with a practiced hand and easing us into the late-afternoon traffic on Admiralty Way. The sun had been shining all day, making a thousand shimmering pools of silver in the dark ocean. Scores of small boats were coming home to the marina, darting and bobbing on the waves, a still strong breeze filling their festive sails. To the north, beyond the dozing dinosaur headland of the bay, a pile of dark clouds hung over the mountains.

"You'll get a kick out of this," he said, straightening his neck as we swept past a wobbling bicyclist outside Killer Shrimp. "I've been working Internal Affairs. It's true, just temporary, ever since I got passed over for the homicide promotion and applied for my thing up in Seattle. And the guy they originally asked me to watch out for? That slippery dog Larry Murakami. Seems like he bought one Rolex too many. So the word went out: 'Where is Mr. Murakami getting the greens?' Of course I was devastated to discover that old Lar was cleaner than the inside of one of his fucking Ping-Pong balls. He's a shameless but unfortunately completely spotless asshole. And I was also a little surprised when I found out that maybe the guy I should really have been after was you. What have you got to say?"

I said nothing.

"At a loss for words?" Drew flashed his smile. "I don't know about you, Billy, but I'm out to *get* corrupt cops."

Drew eased the Jag to the curb outside a 7-Eleven at the junction with Pacific. Directly ahead, I saw the ocean's sparkle, tunneled and squared off by the buildings.

He pulled his next surprise from his pocket, a cassette tape, which he pushed into the player on the dash.

There was a flutter, a hiss, a crackle, a great symphony of distortion, but I could still make out the two voices—my own and Ricky Lee's—as the terms of the offered bribe floated on either side of us through the speakers set in the Jaguar's doors. "Five hundred thousand? Hell, Billy, that's a shitload of money. Did you take it?"

I made no answer. I was thinking that I'd ripped out the guts of that tape and had watched the storm whip them away. A piece had fluttered, clinging to the window of my apartment. "Where did you get this?"

"It was lying around in that guy's warehouse down in San Pedro."

A street guy passed in front of the car, his torn coat flapping at his ankles, and he turned toward me, staring, almost fiercely, while a jet passed low overhead, making the air shudder, and I threw my mind back to the first night of the case. I'd been in the interview room with Ricky Lee. I'd chased him out to the front of the precinct house, where I'd been confronted by Ward and the gonzo with the lens in the T-shirt, Zed. I'd rushed back to pocket the tape, which then hadn't left my person until I got back to my apartment. Therefore, I had to conclude, the tape I'd destroyed hadn't been the one on which I'd recorded the conversation with Ricky Lee. Someone had made a switch.

The street guy's hand waved at the sky, making a point, or maybe protesting the racket of the passing 747, and I thought of the Cuban patrolman, the ex-ballplayer with the six-shooter. Maybe he'd taken the tape and had given it to Gatti in turn. Then, picturing the Cuban's hangdog demeanor, I dismissed the idea. There had to be another explanation.

The street guy shivered, drawing his coat around him, and it was then that I netted the detail. I'd bumped into someone in the corridor coming back from the men's room, a dark ferrety figure. I'd assumed it must be one of the guys working early-morning vice, but it was Gatti, I realized. The guy had actually been snooping around in the precinct house; he must have seen Ricky Lee leave, slipped into the interview room, and pocketed the tape. He had some gall, that Gatti. Los Angeles must have seemed boundless to him, virgin territory across which he could play and romp. He'd been playing me all along.

The street guy shivered again and shuffled off, while Drew was asking, "C'mon, Billy, did you or did you not take the fucking money?"

The world had never been clear-cut for me. I didn't see things in sharp black and white; I wasn't a zealot, like Drew. I didn't believe that a man is only either good or bad, but that a man is more like a journey, meandering here and there, certain to come to an end, perhaps an end that is abrupt and unforeseen, random, and all the while proceeding in the fog, trying to find a way. I thought too much. I poked around things, and tried to view them from all the angles, a habit that had made me a great murder cop. Yet Drew had saved me. He deserved a straight answer.

"Yes, Drew, I took the money."

He banged a fist against the top of the steering wheel. "I knew it. Shit. Why, Billy? That was so fucking *dumb.*"

"It was wrong, Drew. I don't know that it was dumb."

He did the thing with his fist again. "Damn it, Billy. Haven't you learned anything? Get outta the car."

"Look, Drew. I was on fire, and you pissed on me, and you put the fire out. I'm grateful, and I realize that I smell. I'm going to have to learn to live with that, whatever happens."

"Go on, get outta the fucking car. I'm not riding with you." Looking up, Drew saw that we were in front of the gallery already. "Oh, shit," he said, his square powerful face suddenly deflated.

Ted Softly stood inside the door, his trim hair washed and perfumed, his dark suit clean and freshly pressed. He wore a silk tie with horizontal stripes, and his pale, startling eyes loomed even larger out of his face, as if he'd lost a couple of pounds in some campaign for health, and he had a glass of Evian in one hand while the other hugged the bare shoulder of Holly—I remembered her name, the exotic beauty from Japan, who stood with the same teetering skill on a different pair of heels. "I owe you an apology for the last time," she said. "The whole thing with Ted and the gun. He and I were both so out of it."

"No big deal," I said, aware of Drew pushing his way through the crowd, searching for Ellen and Lucy.

"You were amazing," she said. "You saved my life."

"That's a little dramatic. Ted wasn't going to pull the trigger."

"Hey!" said Ted, spluttering in his Evian. "I might have. I'm a dangerous guy."

"Sure," I said. "Have it your way."

"My dangerous guy," said Holly, pressing in close to him. "Who's going to marry me."

"Really?" I said, surprising myself, I was so genuinely delighted. Why not? Give it a shot, I thought. "Happiness to you both."

"Yeah, well, what can you do?" said Ted brightly. "C'mon. I'll lead you to your investment."

My mouth opened and a bird flew out, my heart, when I saw Lucy with her back to me in front of the two

canvases. I stood watching her as she turned from one to
the other, leaning forward a little with her characteristic stoop, her head pushed shyly tortoiselike into her
shoulders as her eyes gazed up, admiring, wondering.
The first picture showed figures in a boat, a helmsman
and a little girl, who were moving through a forest as
crowded, colorful, and menacing as Los Angeles itself.
The canoe-shaped boat was patched together from red-
dish material the color of crumbled brick. It looked neither sturdy nor seaworthy, ploughing through the wild
river current, and its passage was espied on all sides by
tigers, wolves, lions, and jackals, not to mention sinister
citizens in their urban glitter and jazz. The helmsman, a
warrior in a helmet, offered a fragment of hope, the perhaps foolish offer of a way forward. Strong, bold, he
aimed his arm at the horizon, blocking out the threats
and panic.

This canvas was small, surreal, and untitled, yet clearly
about the acceptance of a titanic challenge, while the second, *Venice Beach,* was simple and abstract, a huge canvas
about fifteen feet by nine, a scheme of squares and
oblongs and parallelograms in an almost infinite variety of
shades of blue, all threatening to fly away and burst from
the canvas, but held contentedly at bay by the bar of
golden yellow that stretched across the top like sand. The
piece tempted you with its somehow peaceful mingling of
order and chaos. It said, "Jump in! Swim!" I walked up
behind Lucy, softly laying my hands on the stooped curve
of her shoulders, and felt for a moment an ecstasy, a total
forgetting of any worry, of anything concerning the past
and the future, as if I were inside a warm beachhouse and
would live there forever, looking out a big window at the
sea. Something better that was within me suddenly
awoke, full of joy and youth.

"Hi, Dad," she said, leaning back into my arms while I closed my eyes, driving this moment deep into memory.

I heard Ellen's careful voice. "Hello, Billy."

I had to regain my poise before turning to face those clear green eyes that, as always, took my measure. "You're looking great," I said, true. "Tell me about Seattle."

"First you tell me about the pictures."

Lucy said brightly, "Don't ask Dad. He knows nothing about art."

Ellen asked Lucy if she'd mind popping upstairs to fetch her purse. She watched Lucy dodge through the crowd, ducking first left, then right, and looked at me with a question. "Did you say anything?"

The previous day I'd had Ted call Ellen. He'd told her the story, that ten years ago I'd laid out twenty grand for a couple of pictures that were now worth a lot of money, and she'd believed him; but she'd told me, when I got on the phone, that she didn't want the pictures, not at any price. "You're still trying to control me, Billy," she'd said. "I don't want to go to Seattle with the security of your nest egg. It's sweet of you, but I'm making this fresh start for myself. No ties, no obligations." I said that maybe she should let Lucy take the pictures. I said I didn't see how she could have any objection to that, not if they were just for Lucy. She thought hard before saying, "I guess not. But do you think that's the way you can help her best?"

I'd gone to and fro a thousand times before concluding that it wouldn't be right. These paintings had blood all over them, and the blood wasn't mine. True, they were also coin for what I'd been through to get them; they spoke of my preparedness to die for my family; but that was another consideration spun only around me. I understood now that my relationship with Lucy wasn't about money or things, and certainly not about dramatic gestures on my part; it was about being there for her, whenever, and for whatever was required, through everything, even though Ellen was gone from me and would be with Drew, building another life.

Ellen asked me now, "Did you decide what you're going to do?"

I said, "Yeah, I had Ted make all the arrangements. He's keeping me out of it."

"That doesn't quite answer my question, does it?"

"I guess not."

Drew had come over. He repositioned himself inside all that hairy tweed, straightening his neck, then clearing his throat. "That guy over there. What's his name?"

"Ted?"

"Yeah, the guy who looks like he's been amused for the last twenty years of his life. He says these pictures, these two you've been looking at, he says they're worth in the neighborhood of five hundred thousand."

"That much?" said Ellen.

I said, "You having second thoughts?"

"No way, Billy. I'm just wondering about you."

Looking over toward the door, I saw that Renata Richards had arrived, dressed in black, with her daughter, wearing a red dress with a black bow in her hair. I held up my hand to wave, and Renata raised a diffident black glove in return. They were never going to see any of Ricky Lee's money; DEA and IRS, not to mention Ricky Lee's own crew, would see to that. They were going to get the pictures. I'd told Ted to fix the paperwork to make sure that they were secure in Renata's name, and she'd never know that I'd been involved. The story would be that they were Ricky Lee's secret legacy for *his* daughter. I didn't know if this was right, but it was an idea I felt comfortable with; after all, they'd been bought with Ricky Lee's money.

"Who's that?" said Ellen.

"Her name's Renata Richards."

Drew said, "She's the wife of a big-time gangster just got killed down in San Pedro."

Lucy was back in the gallery, walking with that familiar slope-shouldered stoop, pausing in front of every picture with Ellen's purse clutched tight in her hand. I went over and whispered to her, "You see that little girl over there? She looks cool, don't you think? But, you know what, I think she could use a friend. Why don't you go talk to her?"

Then I waved at Ted, who waved at me, and I went back to Ellen and Drew. She said, "Is there something I should know?"

I said, "Definitely not."

She said, "Drew?"

Drew heaved his jacket straight on his shoulders.

I said, "You look uncomfortable, Drew. What's the matter? A little warm in here?"

He glanced at Ellen, taking her hand. "He's quite a guy, your ex-husband. Quite the surprise package."

Ellen looked at me with her eyes narrowed. "Billy, did you just put something over on me?"

"Absolutely not."

"Really?"

"Really."

A bead of awareness formed between us. She smiled then, pressing her cheek briefly into the curve of my palm, and my mind flew back to the first time we met, at Marty McFly's sports bar, when she made the crack about Wittgenstein and German beer. I understood that this was about to be final. We'd meet again, of course, and often, but never in the same way. She said, "Bye, Billy."

Drew had the last word, slipping the cassette tape, the recording of my interview with Ricky Lee, into my blazer's breast pocket.

"What's that?" said Ellen.

"Rap music," he said. "Crap music, *dangerous* music, in my opinion. But I'm known as a boring guy. So long, Billy."

"So long, Drew. I *like* rap."

34

I'M IN THE OFFICE, WITH THE HANGING GUN ABOVE MY head, the murder book cabinets at my back. I've been here ever since leaving the gallery, where Lucy walked me to the door, kissed me, and we promised to see each other tomorrow. I feel a little dizzy, because it's tomorrow already. I've been talking into this tape recorder all night.

It didn't occur to me until after the Charlie Corcoran trial that I might be interested in vengeance. Duty and ethics had faded away. I saw that I could get some money for the two people I cared about. All this worked toward the conclusion: in a world where justice isn't working, vengeance is good. Since no moral order presented itself to my imagination as real anymore, I made up my own, and as a result men died, my family was endangered, I risked the life of a woman I'd come to love and who might love me, and in the end I didn't even feel comfortable with the money. The experiment, in other words, wasn't an unqualified success.

Ward and I have been in touch, talking on the phone until late at night, but we haven't seen each other since San Pedro. She says that she believes and hopes there's something serious going on between us, and I hope so, too. She's a wonderful, smart, and ambitious woman, and she also deserves to know the truth. Hence the tapes, which I'll take to her as soon as I'm done.

I don't know whether she'll do the story or what her angle will be.

Don't ask if this is smart. It could be that I have no future as a cop.

When I first came back from England, Los Angeles had seemed a heaven—dazzling, fast, so free and filled with energy. I imagined my friends talking of me as though I'd died and gone to a more agreeable place. It was through the eyes of its murdered that I came to understand the city better, until at last, driving about, I no longer saw buildings or billboards or freeways. I saw cobwebs, what went down. I became a ghost, and I know now that for years I lost sight of life's air and lightness. Following the deaths of my father and mother, in the wake of Ellen's crippling injury and all those homicides, I felt smothered, numb from a despair that was often my first sensation on waking. No wonder I wanted to die.

Then, last night, standing in front of those pictures with my daughter, I'd felt a sun on my face, a sensation of being released, let loose. It had been a glowing moment, as if I were suddenly a giddy balloon, floating high, reminded of a different way life could be. I've been humbled, I've lost Ellen for good, and I may end up going to jail. Handing Ward all this is putting another gun to my head; confession is like suicide, an obliteration of the old self, except that this way I will get the chance to start over, with the earned certainty that my life is no longer meaningless; maybe that certainty will be provisional, maybe not. I realize that Montaigne is right.

A man doesn't require philosophy to learn how to die. Life itself contains all the necessary information.

It's seven A.M. I can smell coffee. Outside, the air is cool and clear, a pretty day, with no haze or smog in the foothills. At last I can close the Mae Richards murder book and return it to the shelf behind me, with a yellow dot saying "solved." There'll be another homicide today, and one tomorrow, and I'll work them all, if they let me, not through any greater belief in justice, but because this is what I do.

Cataresco came in a moment ago, with a leather jacket slung over her shoulder and a Starbucks cappuccino balanced in a tray. She said, "Hey, Billy, good morning," in a surprised voice, and with a look as though I shouldn't be sitting in her chair, as though I should be somewhere else or someone better.

I know who I am; I'm the murder guy.